OXFORD WORLD'S CLASSICS

SHERLOCK HOLMES

SELECTED STORIES

SIR ARTHUR CONAN DOYLE was born in Edinburgh in 1859 to Irish Catholic parents. He was educated at Stonyhurst, the Jesuit college, and studied medicine at Edinburgh University, graduating in 1881. He practised medicine at Southsea in the 1880s as well as in a Greenland whaler, a West African trader, and (after twenty years' retirement) a Boer War hospital. His literary career began in 1879 with the publication of a short story in *Chambers's Journal*, and the first Sherlock Holmes adventure, *A Study in Scarlet*, was published in 1887. After moving to London Doyle began to publish Holmes short stories in the *Strand Magazine*: fifty-six stories featuring the detective appeared between 1892 and 1927. A master of short fiction, Doyle's other great series revolved around Brigadier Gerard and Napoleon, and he also wrote historical novels and supernatural and Gothic tales. He ran unsuccessfully for Parliament and became a leading public figure, as an enthusiastic cricketer, an activist against miscarriages of justice, and the foremost English publicist of spiritualism. He was knighted in 1902 and died at Crowborough, Sussex, in 1930.

BARRY MCCREA is Professor of English and Comparative Literature and Keough Family Chair of Irish Studies at the University of Notre Dame. He is the author of *In the Company of Strangers: Family and Narrative in Dickens, Conan Doyle, Joyce, and Proust* (2011), and a novel, *The First Verse* (2005).

OXFORD WORLD'S CLASSICS

For over 100 years Oxford World's Classics have brought readers closer to the world's great literature. Now with over 700 titles—from the 4,000-year-old myths of Mesopotamia to the twentieth century's greatest novels—the series makes available lesser-known as well as celebrated writing.

The pocket-sized hardbacks of the early years contained introductions by Virginia Woolf, T. S. Eliot, Graham Greene, and other literary figures which enriched the experience of reading. Today the series is recognized for its fine scholarship and reliability in texts that span world literature, drama and poetry, religion, philosophy, and politics. Each edition includes perceptive commentary and essential background information to meet the changing needs of readers.

OXFORD WORLD'S CLASSICS

===

ARTHUR CONAN DOYLE

Sherlock Holmes
Selected Stories

===

Edited with an Introduction and Notes by
BARRY McCREA

UNIVERSITY PRESS

OXFORD
UNIVERSITY PRESS

Great Clarendon Street, Oxford, OX2 6DP
United Kingdom

Oxford University Press is a department of the University of Oxford.
It furthers the University's objective of excellence in research, scholarship,
and education by publishing worldwide. Oxford is a registered trade mark of
Oxford University Press in the UK and in certain other countries.

Published in the United States of America by Oxford University Press
198 Madison Avenue, New York, NY 10016, United States of America

British Library Cataloguing in Publication Data
Data available

Library of Congress Control Number: 2013948405

ISBN 978–0–19–967206–6

Printed and bound in Great Britain by Clays Ltd, Elcograf S.p.A.

Links to third party websites are provided by Oxford in good faith and
for information only. Oxford disclaims any responsibility for the materials
contained in any third party website referenced in this work.

CONTENTS

INTRODUCTION

AMONG the members of the Baker Street Irregulars, the most famous society of dedicated Holmes fans, a convention known as 'the game' requires one to treat Holmes as a real historical personage, Watson as his biographer, and Arthur Conan Doyle as the unimportant, even unreliable publisher of Watson's writings. The Irregulars' practice, playful as it is, points to a real truth about the Holmes stories: the huge gulf that separates Holmes and his creator. The stories are proof, if it was ever needed, that the writer and the work are wholly distinct entities. Doyle thought of the stories as a trivial and frivolous distraction from his real literary ambitions, and his several attempts to kill off his creation were all foiled. Holmes is a bohemian bachelor who abhors family life, whereas Doyle was a middle-class professional and devoted family man. The Holmes adventures are, along with the novels of Charles Dickens, the quintessential London stories, even though Doyle was a Scot who did not even know London that well (he had to use a Post Office map while writing them to help with street names and directions). Most of all, Holmes's unrelenting devotion to reason and hard facts, and his disdain for superstition, are at odds with the character of a man who devoted his greatest efforts to spiritualism and the paranormal; Doyle was a peculiar mixture of scientific rigour and a *naïveté* that at times bordered on philistinism (his conviction as to the authenticity of the infamous Cottingley fairy photos, for example—in which children had added paper cut-outs of dancing fairies to photographs of themselves in the garden—made him an object of some ridicule).

Doyle's first stories, written while he was studying medicine at the University of Edinburgh, were more in keeping with his idiosyncratic mix of the scientific and the supernatural. He had some modest success with them, but his breakthrough came with a short novel, *A Study in Scarlet*, stripped of his usual paranormal or Gothic flights of fancy, a highly rational crime-story narrated by one John Watson, a doctor just back from military duty in Afghanistan, who is wandering London in search of a flatmate. He ends up sharing with an eccentric private detective called Sherlock Holmes, a character partly modelled on Joseph Bell, who had been one of Doyle's teachers

at Edinburgh. Holmes asks Watson to accompany him in his investigation (the device of having the story narrated by the detective's
live-in companion was borrowed from Edgar Allan Poe's creation C.
Auguste Dupin). Doyle had no luck in getting his novella published
until it was finally fished from the slush pile of a downmarket publishing house, Ward, Lock and Company, who specialized in cheap,
sensationalist fiction. It was published in 1887 in *Beeton's Christmas
Annual*. Doyle received a modest fee for the text and was forced to
relinquish all copyright to the publishers.

A Study in Scarlet was well received, and although Doyle was more
interested in promoting his long historical novel *Micah Clarke*, he
accepted a commission from an American publisher to write another
Holmes narrative, the short novel that became *The Sign of the Four*.
Following this novel's success, Doyle hit upon a new genre for his
detective: a series of short stories, each complete in itself, but involv-
ing the same principal characters of Holmes and his companion
Watson. The first of these was 'A Scandal in Bohemia', and the stories were published serially in the *Strand Magazine* to immediate and
enormous success. The first twelve stories were collected in 1892 in
the volume *The Adventures of Sherlock Holmes*. Despite several efforts
to give Holmes up—including asking for an extortionate fee, which
he claimed he was sure no publisher would agree to, for the second
dozen tales—Doyle continued to publish Holmes stories in the
Strand, which were syndicated in American newspapers. Altogether
the Holmes corpus consists of fifty-six short stories and four novels.
In addition to *The Adventures*, four other collections of the stories
were published: *The Memoirs of Sherlock Holmes* (1893), *The Return
of Sherlock Holmes* (1905), *His Last Bow* (1917), and *The Case-Book
of Sherlock Holmes* (1927).

The success of the Holmes stories allowed or forced Doyle to dis-
continue his ophthalmic practice and devote himself entirely to writing; they also made him, it goes without saying, a very wealthy man.
But Holmes was a constant source of irritation and self-recrimination
for Doyle, who longed to spend his energies on and garner his fame
from historical novels, scientific and spiritualist research, and political writings. In 'The Final Problem', published in 1893, he sent
Holmes tumbling over a ravine in Switzerland. He recorded the writing of it in his diary with the two words 'Killed Holmes', but left
just enough ambiguity in the ending of the story to keep the door

open a sliver. In response to popular demand—and pressure from his mother—he wrote a further novel, set retrospectively, before Holmes meets Watson (*The Hound of the Baskervilles*, 1901). In 1903 he finally reversed Holmes's death, concocting a complicated story of Holmes's survival and intervening travels through Italy, Persia, Sudan, and France, a period known among Sherlockians as 'the great hiatus' and the subject of much conjecture. This allowed a final run of new stories.

However much his passions may have lain elsewhere, and however much his own sensibilities and world view were at odds with those of the detective, posterity, of course, remembers Doyle for Holmes. There is no need to rehearse the unrivalled mass appeal of Sherlock Holmes which has now spanned three different centuries and which, far from showing signs of diminishing, seems, if anything, to be blossoming. At the time of writing, three major filmed adaptations are running in parallel on television and in cinemas. Holmes's influence is palpable in all detective and crime fiction whether written or on screen. There is simply no other fictional character who comes close to having the cultural influence of Holmes. How can we account for the bewildering success of Doyle's creation? What is it about the stories that has caused them to exercise such an unparalleled and enduring hold on the popular imagination?

Part of it has to do with the distinctive socio-historical backdrop to the stories. Holmes is not an obvious product of Arthur Conan Doyle, but he is clearly a product of his times. The Holmes stories are in part the result of a confluence of nineteenth- and twentieth-century currents: faith in progress but also scepticism and fears of regression; the age of empire but also of the crime and disorder of huge industrial cities; neo-Gothic flights of romantic fantasy alongside new literary commitments to unsparing social realism; sensational crime fiction and decadent aestheticism. Many of the concerns that run through the stories are peculiarly relevant to our own age. Among them we might include rapid and widespread social change; perplexity about the economic system, how it works and how it affects the individual; newly emergent networks of information and power; the consequences of European colonial adventures coming home to roost; and, the defining word of our own times but a concept absolutely central to the Holmes stories, globalization. None of these concerns is ever addressed directly, and we are given no lectures, facts, or analysis. There are many long digressions in the stories but none of them is

political in nature (although Doyle himself was a passionately political man who stood for election to Parliament). The mechanism of the
stories is to focus our attention entirely on the mystery while imperceptibly exposing us to social, economic, psychological, and historical
realities.

At the same time, the fascination of the past is only part of the
stories' draw. Many filmed adaptations recognize no limitations of
historical period. The BBC television adaptation *Sherlock*, whose
first series was broadcast in 2010, moves Holmes, Watson, and the
plots themselves seamlessly to a world of mobile phones, iPads, and
Google. There is something in the stories' form, as opposed to content, that has nothing to do with historical context but which draws us
in wholly and inexplicably. The stories deal with the most primordial
dynamics of storytelling: how information is withheld and revealed.
Watson, supposedly the mere biographer and assistant of the great
detective, is quietly central to the stories' appeal and to their underlying meaning. He is our way into the stories because we learn the facts
more or less as he does (or at least as he chooses to reveal them to us;
we cannot know something that Watson does not know), and because
his blindness and puzzlement in the face of these facts mirror our
own experience of reading the story. The sense that Watson incar-
nates of missing the big picture, of not 'getting' how everything *really*
fits together, is part of our experience of life itself.

What everyone seems to be agreed upon—casual readers, diehard
fans, and literary scholars alike—is that the whole of the stories adds
up somehow to more than the sum of their parts. Even as they grab
and hold our attention with the solving of crimes and enigmas, they
expose us to other things entirely, and leave us with other, unsolved
mysteries.

The 'Science of Deduction'

What we and Watson are missing, of course, is mastery of the fantastical method employed by Holmes, which he calls the 'science of
deduction'. Like much else in the Holmes stories, the term and many
of its characteristics are borrowed directly from Poe's Dupin who
outlines its principles in the story 'The Murders in the Rue Morgue'
(Doyle playfully acknowledges this source by having Holmes speak
disparagingly of Dupin's methods). Holmes sees almost everything

and he understands everything he sees, often immediately. Watson sees the same things but he does not understand how they fit together. It is one of the sources of fellowship between ourselves and Watson that we never master Holmes's skill, and it is part of the stories' compulsive hold on our attention that we keep feeling we might.

The science of deduction has a literary genealogy but also a scientific one. The practice of reasoning back to a bigger picture, especially from small details or fragments, shows affinities with many strains of scientific thought in the late nineteenth century. As a medical student at Edinburgh, Doyle was exposed to forensic science, which was increasingly being used in the courtroom. In British India, fingerprinting as a means of identifying individuals was being pioneered for use among illiterate Indians. Alphonse Bertillon, a police investigator in Paris (and the son of a statistician), was a proponent of anthropometrics, the use of precise bodily measurements to describe criminals (and even supposedly to predict their behaviour). A parallel development in art history was pioneered by Giovanni Morelli, who proposed ascertaining the authenticity of Old Masters by looking for the artist's 'signature' in small details such as fingernails.

The Victorian enthusiasm for economic and industrial expansion was also dogged by darker fears of regression and degeneration, an unsettling anxiety about the origins and future of the human species, the worry that savage traits might return and reassert themselves once more. This interest in the use of science for detecting crime also took some troubling forms at the close of the century, notoriously in the eugenicist theories of the Italian criminologist Cesare Lombroso, who argued that criminals were born, not made, a 'type' which could be identified through certain hereditary physical features. For Lombroso, criminality and deviance were atavistic propensities that reasserted themselves through the generations. Holmes has sometimes been linked with Lombroso because of his supposed use of eugenicist theories to solve crimes, but when we look at the plots of the stories, we find that heredity plays no role at all in Holmes's investigations (and an attachment to genealogical inheritance is even considered to be vaguely suspect in itself). Rather than inherited traits (such as the swollen lips or enlarged jaws of Lombroso's deviants), Holmes's science of deduction is interested chiefly in how the body is shaped, not by genes, but by experience: how a typist's wrist is marked by her work ('A Case of Identity'), the particular way an artillery officer's face is sunburnt ('The Greek Interpreter'), how a carpenter's hand is swollen ('The Red-Headed League'). When Holmes shows off his powers by 'reading' Henry Baker's hat in 'The Blue Carbuncle', he does draw one inference from phrenology (that Mr Baker must be intelligent because his head is so large), but the rest of what he deduces is based on the dents or accretions of lived experience—tallow-stains, accumulations of dust, snapped elastic. Clues come from the bumps and scratches of acting in the world rather than from the dark pool of inherited features.

In his actions, if not in his words, Holmes almost ignores heredity altogether. The anxieties of his age about origins and regression manifest themselves not in Holmes's methods but in the plots of the stories. The desire to read causes back from signs, the conviction that the circumstances of the present are symptoms of something in the distant past, were part of the general emphasis of Victorian thought and Watson's melancholy, lyrical flights (notably in *The Sign of the Four*) are an expression of it.

Psychoanalysis

The desire to understand the present by knowing the past, and the idea that the past is always liable to return, were key impulses in another new frontier of human knowledge which was emerging in the late nineteenth century along with criminology, forensic science, and biological evolution: psychoanalysis. Although his notebooks reveal an interest in the work of Jean-Martin Charcot, the French neurologist whose studies on mesmerism are credited with founding the field, Doyle was largely ignorant of the theories of Freud and certainly had more truck with spirits and mediums than with the unconscious. The stories similarly offer scant psychological insight, Holmes's own psychological speculations are generally flippant and superficial ('When a woman has been seriously wronged by a man she no longer oscillates, and the usual symptom is a broken bell wire', p. 126), and the 'science of deduction' takes no account of underlying mental states or suffering.

On other levels, however, the stories show powerful resonances with the Freudian age in which they were written. The nervous wrecks who ring the bell of 221B Baker Street and are ushered by Mrs Hudson into the consulting rooms, have something to tell and something they are hiding. Holmes reveals what his 'patients' do not wish to reveal. He employs a special kind of listening in which minor details are of revelatory significance. Like a psychoanalyst, he asks questions that seem to have no relevance; he focuses on seemingly trivial details rather than the major facts of the story. Often, his clients do not understand their own story and they need Holmes to tell them what it means.

But it is in their structure most of all that the Holmes mysteries show affinities with psychoanalytic ideas. The mysteries are frequently structured around a surface disturbance in the present, which is ultimately explained by a forgotten or repressed traumatic backstory, one which only Holmes can reconstruct. In 'The Dancing Men', indecipherable scribbles suddenly appear scrawled around the family home, and they provoke a hysterical, traumatic response in Elsie Cubitt, the woman of the house. As with many of Freud's patients in Vienna, the husband comes in desperate hope of a cure for his wife's inexplicable mental distress. Like the mysterious symptoms investigated and treated by Freud and Jung, Holmes traces this graffiti, and Elsie Cubitt's response to it, back to a series of events in her early life. Elsie, it turns out, had grown up with her father's criminal gang in Chicago, and was engaged to one of its leaders, Abe Slaney; she fled to England, put America, her father, and the gang behind her, and became Mrs Hilton Cubitt with a quiet, genteel life in rural Norfolk. The crazed drawings that suddenly materialize in the Cubitts' property mean that Abe Slaney has returned, and with him, her suppressed past.

Empire

The psychoanalytic principle that what is repressed will return in an unfamiliar form structures the stories in many other ways too, most notably in the treatment of colonialism, empire, and wealth. They are not outwardly political stories, and at the outset we see only occasional signs of Britain's colonies, former colonies, and foreign wars. London's role as the centre of a network of current and former foreign possessions manifests itself in unremarked background details, such as the wounded or down-and-out veterans who crop up throughout the stories, from Watson himself, wounded in Afghanistan, to the clinical but heartbreaking description in 'The Greek Interpreter' of the widowed Royal Artillery officer, recently returned from India and observed, without sentiment, by Holmes and Mycroft as he buys a toy for his motherless child (p. 248). Here, the effects of Britain's adventures overseas appear at home in reshaped bodies, as limps, comportment, or 'sun-baked skin', part of an unexplained backdrop. But as the investigations themselves go on, it is remarkable just how often they stumble upon the empire, just how often it is the consequences of Britain's colonial adventures that provide the answer to the mystery—indeed often turn out to *be* the mystery.

This is clearest in a single plotline that is repeated several times throughout the Holmes corpus. It is represented in this collection most clearly by 'The Dancing Men', but there are elements of it to be found in *The Sign of the Four*, 'The Speckled Band', and even in 'The Musgrave Ritual': Holmes is called in to deal with a disturbance within a noble English family, usually in their ancestral home. In the course of his investigations he uncovers a hidden story in the past, often linking the family's wealth to a violent secret society in the colonies or in the New World. The secret society is hunting down one of the family members (usually the head of the household or his wife) for transgressions committed or debts incurred during these colonial adventures (often the source of much-needed capital reinjected into the family back in England).

The details of the stories vary, of course. But what is consistent and notable is that the stories are often set in the most emblematically English of locations: aristocratic country houses, icons of an ageless connection between families and the soil of England, of the continuity of territory, race, and family. Hilton Cubitt in 'The Dancing Men' makes a point of explaining to Holmes that his people 'have been at Ridling Thorpe for a matter of five centuries' (p. 264). Sir Grimesby Roylott in 'The Speckled Band' is also a country aristocrat, 'the last survivor of one of the oldest Saxon families in England' (p. 205). But Sir Grimesby's military experience in India cannot be erased by a return to his ancestral manse: his stepdaughter tells Holmes that his violent temper had been 'intensified by his long residence in the tropics' (p. 206) and that he keeps deadly Indian animals on his ancestral estate; the traces of India are indelible even here in the deepest, oldest English countryside manors. In *The Sign of the Four*, the mark of India on England is signalled by the name of the house, Pondicherry Lodge. In this novel, the source of both the wealth and the mysteries Holmes is called in to solve is in the bloody Indian Mutiny of 1857 and the notorious penal colony on the Andaman Islands. In both *The Sign of the Four* and 'The Dancing Men' the backstory is not only to be found in the colonies or New World, but in an earlier crime. What seems to be an alien intrusion into feudal English continuity turns out to emanate from within the family.

The insistent tracing of crimes committed in England back to the colonies has provoked a great deal of postcolonial interpretation of the Holmes stories. Holmes and his investigations are frequently understood as encoding a Victorian fear of contamination from all the trafficking with the colonies. According to this mode of interpretation, Holmes would function both as an embodiment of this anxiety and a comforting salve for it: he identifies the source of contamination, and expunges it, purifying the nation and upholding the existing imperial social order. And if we take the personality and values of Holmes himself as our interpreter of the stories, such a case can easily be made. Holmes is certainly not an anti-imperialist or a class revolutionary. In 'His Last Bow', he infiltrates the Irish anti-colonial rebels as a British government informer. He shares no thoughts with us on the subject of British imperialism, and seems, like Doyle, to be a supporter of the regime.

But Holmes's work achieves quite different results. Its effect is to reveal the connections that remain otherwise hidden, or unspeakable. He shows that the origins of 'English' wealth, especially the cleanest, most apparently legitimate, and longest-standing, inherited money, is in fact generated far away from England, in sweat, labour, and violence. The stories, time and again, demonstrate that the sources and location of wealth are surprising and require investigation: jewels are hidden by manual labourers inside their cheap, mass-produced trinkets ('The Six Napoleons'), or in the gullet of geese destined to be eaten by the poor ('The Blue Carbuncle'). For all their apparently blind acceptance of capitalism and the social order, in the end the stories point to the idea that money is tainted and cannot be laundered. There is no such thing, the stories show us, as old or clean money.

The Metropolis and Social Class

Much of the wealth of late nineteenth-century London was produced abroad or far away, in mines and factories and plantations, but showed no signs of its origins. Holmes is an appealing figure in an overcrowded

world and a bewildering global economic system because he reveals
unseen or disavowed connections. This is true of the relationships
between Britain and its colonies and between labour and wealth, but
also within the vast and still rapidly swelling London crowd. At the
beginning of 'The Blue Carbuncle' Holmes tells Watson that he is
investigating 'one of those whimsical little incidents which will happen when you have four million human beings all jostling each other
within the space of a few square miles' (p. 184). London was not
simply a huge city in the 1890s, but one that had mushroomed as
a result of sudden in-migration, largely from the British provinces.
Most of its inhabitants had previously lived in small towns, villages,
or rural hamlets, and carried with them the expectations of that different model of life and community. Before the rise of big cities, the
life experience of most people was, as Raymond Williams puts it,
a 'knowable community',[1] a small world in which, even if an individual's family connections are not directly known, then they are likely
to be quickly discoverable. The average migrant to late nineteenth-
century London had left that kind of community to find himself
cheek by jowl with millions of newly uprooted individuals from all
over the country, with people whose family connections, history, and
background were unknown.

   This is part of the background impulse to the rise of the figure of the
detective in nineteenth-century fiction. The London Metropolitan
Police was founded in 1829, but did not have a detective branch until
1842, at the same time that Poe's Dupin first entered popular fiction. The introduction of a detective by Dickens, Inspector Bucket
in *Bleak House* (1853), to help with the revelation of secrets necessary to the movement of the plot, and the runaway success of Émile
Gaboriau's fictional policeman Lecoq (*Monsieur Lecoq*, 1868), are
signs not only of a rise in urban crime, or of fear of it, but also of
a society which feels its relationships are so hidden or unclear that
they need a professional to investigate and uncover them. Holmes
reveals new, unexpected connections and conjunctions generated
from the new circumstances of metropolitan living. Part of his work
is to show how the different social classes of the city, now at uncom-
fortably close quarters, are inextricably bound to one another, even if
they imagine themselves to be worlds apart.

   [1] The phrase is from Raymond Williams's book *The Country and the City* (Oxford:
Oxford University Press, 1973).

Even those stories set in ancient feudal manors deep in the countryside, stories which on the surface have little or nothing to do with new urban classes and new ways of living, are on some level about this 'problem' of London. In 'The Musgrave Ritual', for example, we see not a single sight or sound of London: we are among long stone passages, ancient elms, suits of armour, family portraits. But the story is for all that a reflection on the new life of the metropolis, on social mobility and rapid social change. In it we see old models and systems of continuity, knowledge, property, and power starting to creak and fall apart in the face of new social cohabitations. Sir Reginald Musgrave, a 'scion of one of the very oldest families in the kingdom', calls upon his old college friend Holmes to help defend himself against his once-trusted butler, Brunton, whom he has surprised at night studying private Musgrave family papers. Musgrave's downfall is that, unlike his butler, and unlike Holmes, he is blind to the possibilities unleashed by accidents of adjacency. Brunton's physical intimacy with the Hurlstone estate allows him to unscramble an ancient aristocratic code and expropriate a lost family treasure. The sharing of the physical space of the metropolis at such close quarters means that social strata cannot be so easily kept apart from one another—or rather, their once-hidden interconnection is rendered more easily visible.

'The Musgrave Ritual' seems far from the alleyways and pawnshops of 'The Red-Headed League', in which the physical density of London's diverse buildings and their inhabitants is the setting and focus of the plot, but beneath the surface the two stories have a shared set of concerns. In 'The Red-Headed League', a classic 'city' tale, Holmes sees something invisible to the police, to the characters who are victims of the scam, and, of course, to the eternally astonished Watson—namely, that 'the line of fine shops and stately business premises . . . really abutted on the other side upon the faded and stagnant square' (p. 153). The fact that two neighbourhoods are physically next to each other is invisible to Watson because socially and imaginatively they are so far apart.

The effect of the stories is to show how people, places, spheres of life are connected, and this includes social classes. Holmes seems to have little personal sympathy or interest in the plight of Brunton the butler or Wilson the pawnbroker. We never hear Holmes railing for revolution or reflecting on his own privileged position in the late Victorian hierarchy. He boasts about offering services to all the crowned heads of Europe, and we do meet at least one of these in 'A Scandal in Bohemia', but his clients come from a range of social classes, including the insecure Victorian lower middle class.

During the industrial nineteenth century, the middle classes expanded hugely and split into a variety of subdivisions, from the professionals at the top—doctors and lawyers—, through shopkeepers, clerks, and typists down to those barely out of the workhouse. Their fears and ambitions are in the background and unremarked upon by Holmes, Watson, or Doyle, yet they imperceptibly define the stories' context. Feudal manors or fretful baronets may provide settings or atmosphere for the Holmes mysteries, but the heart of their world is in this anxious, emergent class of clerical workers and small-time tradesmen. We feel the precise scale of their hopes and fears, and the sort of dangers and reversals of fortune to which they felt exposed. Told in a straightforward, almost simple way, without complex stylistic or formal devices, the stories operate on a principle which will be taken up in a different literary key just a few decades later by modernists such as James Joyce: that unremarkable lives and repetitive routines are worthy of scrutiny. It seems more logical to imagine that detective fiction attracts us with the escapist possibility of encountering fantastical characters and situations, and both Holmes and Watson encourage us to think this way. Holmes himself is so bored by regular life that he turns to cocaine. What Holmes is always waiting for, and what the stories are built around, are exceptional events: a murder ('The Speckled Band'), a theft ('The Blue Carbuncle'), unexplained or threatening behaviour ('The Musgrave Ritual'), a disappearance ('A Case of Identity'), the arrival of a mysterious letter (*The Sign of the Four*). While the stories offer on the face of it exceptions to the daily round, enigmas or threats that must be explained or righted, the sources of the mystery are always invisible. The strangeness is hidden somewhere within ordinary life. For the mystery to be solved or the criminal identified, commonplace doings and commonplace people, not usually worthy of enquiry, must be scrutinized.

Such characters are not chosen for the interest of their own lives or stories, but because they have an incidental role in the plot, they do not carry symbolic weight, sentimental associations, or individual psychological depth. They are mostly not centre stage, at least not for long. The story forgets about them as soon as they are of no more service to the plot. But the result, paradoxically, is that they impress themselves on our consciousness in an unusual, affecting way. We get vivid, unfiltered snapshots of their quotidian reality, frozen, unsuspecting, at a single moment in their lives. This is not something that the reader notices consciously, but the inadvertent depiction of middle-class life through suspenseful mysteries is absolutely funda-mental to the Holmes stories, to their strange grip on the imagin-ation, to their meaning and their success.

Holmes himself has no interest in these personal stories for themselves, only insofar as they advance his investigation or provide opportunities to show off his powers of deduction. But as we read the stories collected in this volume, there passes before us a parade of the unexceptional denizens of late Victorian London—the typists, grooms, clerks, and pawnbroker's assistants, the details of whose day-to-day lives would otherwise have no reason to be narrated. One of the most moving examples must be Mr Henry Baker, the loss of whose goose in an altercation as he returns tipsily home from a Christmas party in the pub with his friends is the first event in 'The Blue Carbuncle'. Henry Baker never sees the jewel in question; he never even learns of its disappearance or of the fact that he was holding it under his arm. But the story begins with him, and more particularly with his hat, which has been found with the goose and brought to Holmes's attention. Holmes hands Watson the tattered hat, stained with tallow and ink, greasy with hair cream, battered around the edges, and asks him to deduce what he can about its owner. 'I can see nothing,' Watson says, handing the hat back. Holmes, however, gives a brutally compact and comprehensive mental sketch: the owner is a middle-aged, well-educated man, who was once well-off, but now, due to alcoholism, is in reduced circumstances, with the result that 'his wife has ceased to love him' (p. 186).

Watson, like ourselves, is astounded, until Holmes walks him through the steps of his deduction. Shortly afterwards, there is a ring at the door and in walks Henry Baker, whose demeanour and account of himself confirm—naturally—Holmes's conjectures in all their particulars: a red-nosed 'man of learning and letters who had had ill-usage at the hands of fortune' (p. 192). Holmes is interested in only one thing about the man, namely whether or not he is involved in the theft of Countess of Morcar's prize gem. Once cleared of guilt, unaware of the treasure he had been carrying, Mr Baker walks with a fresh goose out of 221B Baker Street and out of the story. We never see him again and his name is not mentioned further.

'The Man with the Twisted Lip' begins with a similarly devastating miniature portrait of a Victorian middle-class couple blighted by addiction and misfortune, whose troubles start the adventure off but quickly fall out of the story's sphere of interest. Kate Whitney, a friend of Watson's wife, wakes the Watsons up in great distress in the middle of the night, as her husband, an opium addict, has been missing for days. Watson finds him, but is quickly distracted by Holmes into a more exciting adventure. On Holmes's instructions, Watson bundles the remorseful Mr Whitney in a taxi and he is driven off out of the East End and out of narrative existence.

The sense of the individual being subject to economic vicissitudes, either frightening or dazzling, is something we get, of course, throughout the work of Doyle's great predecessor, Dickens, in a fully elaborated narrative form. In Dickens we see characters ruined, or 'made', or rescued from misery or ruined again. In some ways the lack of a longer-term perspective or of psychological depth for the enormous supporting cast of the Holmes stories gives us a more superficial account of human character than we get in the great social novels of the nineteenth century. In detective fiction, complexity of character is sacrificed to plot. But precisely because they are cast out of the story as soon as they are of no more use to the plot, we are confronted in a short, sharp way with the consequences so feared by the Victorian middle classes, their dread of becoming superfluous, their terror of being forgotten by society.

A family somewhat higher on the social ladder, though still economically precarious, is at the centre of 'A Case of Identity', and in this case they are also central to the plot. Holmes's client, Mary Sutherland, whose fiancé has disappeared, is a member of a very new sector of turn-of-the-century society, professional women typists. We are given exact details of her economic situation, between remuneration for her work ('twopence a sheet, and I can often do from fifteen to twenty sheets in a day' (p. 128)) and her income from a capital settled on her by an uncle in New Zealand. Holmes's interest is in the puzzle—which he solves immediately—not in sociology or psychology. How typing affects Miss Sutherland's body is instantly clear to the detective and explicitly described ('The double line a little above [her] wrist, where the typewritist presses against

the table, was beautifully defined' (p. 133)), but how being a woman
with an independent income influences her sense of who she is in the
world is left for us to infer from the background details of the story.
Ostensibly, the stepfather is trying to prevent Miss Sutherland from
marrying and leaving home because he enjoys the use of her income
while she is living with them, but even a not especially psychoanalyt-
ically inclined reader will sense that what is at issue is also her sexual
freedom and her stepfather's jealousy of it. We know in the abstract
that the nineteenth century was a moment of radical social upheaval
in Britain; in this story, even with its rather outlandish and scarcely
credible plot, we are made to feel the effects of social change in the
individual as the protagonist hovers between complete patriarchal
submission and a fragile economic independence. Miss Sutherland's
income leaves uncertainty of many kinds about what exactly her role
is: in this secondary sense, too, the story is, indeed, a vexed 'case of
identity'.

Holmes resembles the criminals he chases, by his ability to perceive
and understand adjacency: noticing that a pawnshop is connected to
a bank, or understanding (in 'The Musgrave Ritual' for example)
that the neighbour or servant derives special knowledge from being
close by, or that a precious stone is concealed in the body of a poor
man's Christmas goose. There is a combination of sociological and
psychological ideas at work here. The pawnbroker and the banker, the
servant and the aristocrat, the colony and the colonizer, may inhabit
the same physical space or economic system, but these roles may
also share the same psychological space: the pawnbroker dreams of
being a gentleman, while the small-time merchant is tormented by
visions of himself reduced to begging on the street. Changeability of
economic circumstances means that the same body can have different social meanings at different times. But we are also shown that we
harbour different people within ourselves, and in our unconscious
minds we are kings, criminals, beggars, murderers, all at once.

Holmes at Home

This portrait of a struggling social class which Holmes's investigations reveal to the reader almost by accident suggests that the
literary realism of Doyle's immediate predecessors, Dickens, Zola,
and Flaubert, are part of the peculiar admixture of these apparently

lowbrow mysteries. But the stories themselves were written at the time of Wilde and Huysmans, and *fin-de-siècle* aestheticism is another vital ingredient in making the stories what they are. *The Sign of the Four* and *The Picture of Dorian Gray* were commissioned on the same evening, when Doyle and Oscar Wilde dined with the American editor John Marshall Stoddart at the Langham Hotel. The connection is more than a curious accident of publishing history. Holmes himself is instantly recognizable in his demeanour, outlook, and habits as a distinct Wildean type, the bachelor aesthete. He suffers from chronic ennui relieved only by cocaine or crime. His fascination is not for the well-being of his clients but for the elegance and beauty of his solutions—art for art's sake. He spurns social convention and rhythms; he sleeps all day, smokes all night, and declares (in 'The Red-Headed League'): 'My life is spent in one long effort to escape from the commonplaces of existence' (p. 161).

Holmes is most often called in to help where the family is failing or under threat, whether from scheming servants ('The Musgrave Ritual'), criminal gangs ('The Dancing Men', *The Sign of the Four*), or ruthless stepfathers ('A Case of Identity' and 'The Speckled Band'). Yet Holmes himself is a confirmed bachelor who lives, on and off, with a male companion. Watson, just as he intermediates between Holmes and the reader, is never fully part of either realm, the bohemian bachelor life he shares with Holmes or the heterosexual family world which he ostensibly joins when he marries Mary Morstan from *The Sign of the Four*. Over the course of the stories, Watson shuttles anxiously back and forth between them, supposedly living at home with Mary, but moving back to Baker Street whenever there is a crime to solve. We see little of Watson's married life; from the point of view of the reader, he is married to Holmes.

Is Holmes gay? The question is hard to avoid. Graham Robb marshals a surprisingly comprehensive array of evidence in favour of the idea that Doyle deliberately set out to portray him as such, though other readers passionately disagree.[2] What we can say for sure is that Holmes stands emblematically outside of the economy of marriage and reproduction. He is not *of* the world he investigates. The only ones who see the world the way Holmes does are the criminals and

[2] Graham Robb, *Strangers: Homosexual Love in the Nineteenth Century* (New York: Norton, 2005), 260–6.

family outsiders (in 'The Musgrave Ritual' Holmes literally walks in Brunton's footsteps).

Holmes's home life is far from a mere eccentric backdrop to the mysteries but part of their meaning. Despite the frequent shifting of the action to rural castles or far-flung colonies, what seems to engrave itself more than anything else on our reading memories is the domestic life of 221B Baker Street: Holmes and Watson sitting in their rooms, reading the newspapers, discussing Mrs Hudson's cooking, or waiting for the doorbell to ring and a stranger to arrive with a new mystery to solve.

221B Baker Street is inhabited by a 'couple' whose partnership cannot bear biological fruit, a household which will not leave a genetic legacy. By the same token, Holmes's professional eye is resolutely turned away from thoughts of the future. We never know what will become of Jabez Wilson or Mary Sutherland or Reginald Musgrave. The gaze of the stories is fixed firmly on the past, on how things turned out as they did, not on what they will or might become. Characters flash before us and vanish without leaving a clue as to their destiny. The mysteries, even when solved, leave us with a sense that underneath ordinary daily life there might always lie something old and dark and violent that will return in an unpredictable form. Where we find clarity and solace is not in the comfort of family life, the marriage and fertility that offers comfort in so many other kinds of narrative, but in the unconventional homestead of 221B Baker Street, a queer source of order from which the strangeness of the world, and how it came to be as it is, is visible with a unique kind of clarity.

NOTE ON THE TEXT

MOST of the Sherlock Holmes stories were first published in the *Strand Magazine*, and subsequently collected in book editions. The publishing history of the individual stories can be found in the Explanatory Notes at the back of the book. The texts reprinted here are taken from the Oxford Sherlock Holmes (9 vols., 1993, general editor Owen Dudley Edwards), where further details of textual history can be found.

SELECT BIBLIOGRAPHY

THE editor wishes to acknowledge the invaluable help of James Martell in the compilation of the Chronology and Select Bibliography.

Biographies of Arthur Conan Doyle

Booth, Martin, *The Doctor and the Detective: A Biography of Arthur Conan Doyle* (New York: Thomas Dunne Books, 2000).

Coren, Michael, *The Life of Sir Arthur Conan Doyle* (London: Bloomsbury Publishing, 1995).

Doyle, Adrian Conan, *The True Conan Doyle* (New York: Coward-McCann Inc., 1946).

Doyle, Arthur Conan, *Memories and Adventures* (London: Hodder and Stoughton Ltd., 1924).

Edwards, Owen Dudley, *The Quest for Sherlock Holmes: A Biographical Study of Arthur Conan Doyle* (New York: Barnes & Noble, 1983).

Hardwick, Michael and Mollie, *The Man Who Was Sherlock Holmes* (London: John Murray, 1964).

Jaffe, Jacqueline A., *Arthur Conan Doyle* (Boston: Twayne Publishers, 1987).

Jones, Kelvin I., *Conan Doyle and the Spirits: The Spiritualist Career of Sir Arthur Conan Doyle* (Wellingborough, Northamptonshire: Aquarian Press, 1989).

Lamond, John, *Arthur Conan Doyle: A Memoir* (London: John Murray, 1931).

Lellenberg, Jon, Stashower, Daniel, and Foley, Charles (eds.), *Arthur Conan Doyle: A Life in Letters* (New York: Penguin Press, 2007).

Lycett, Andrew, *Conan Doyle: The Man Who Created Sherlock Holmes* (London: Free Press, 2008).

Miller, Russell, *The Adventures of Arthur Conan Doyle* (New York: Thomas Dunne Books, 2008).

Nordon, Pierre, *Conan Doyle: A Biography* (New York: Holt, Rinehart and Winston, 1967).

Norman, Andrew, *Arthur Conan Doyle: Beyond Sherlock Holmes* (Gloucestershire: History Press Ltd., 2007).

Pascal, Janet B., *Arthur Conan Doyle: Beyond Baker Street* (Oxford: Oxford University Press, 2000).

Payne, Malcolm, and Weller, Philip (eds.), *Recollections of Sir Arthur Conan Doyle by Residents of Crowborough* (Crowborough: The Conan Doyle Establishment, 1993).

Pearsall, Ronald, *Conan Doyle: A Biographical Solution* (London: Weidenfeld & Nicolson, 1977).

Pearson, Hesketh, *Conan Doyle: His Life and Art* (London: Methuen, 1943).

Pugh, Brian W., *A Chronology of the Life of Arthur Conan Doyle* (London: MX Publishing Ltd., 2011).

Redmond, Christopher, *Welcome to America, Mr. Sherlock Holmes: Victorian America Meets Arthur Conan Doyle* (Toronto: Simon & Pierre, 1987).

Rodin, Alvin E., and Key, Jack D., *Medical Casebook of Doctor Arthur Conan Doyle: From Practitioner to Sherlock Holmes and Beyond* (Malabar: Robert E. Krieger, 1984).

Stashower, Daniel, *Teller of Tales: The Life of Arthur Conan Doyle* (New York: Henry Holt and Company, 1999).

Stavert, Geoffrey, *A Study in Southsea: The Unrevealed Life of Doctor Arthur Conan Doyle* (Portsmouth: Milestone Publications, 1987).

Symons, Julian, *Conan Doyle: Portrait of an Artist* (New York: Mysterious Press, 1987).

Wood, James Playstead, *The Man Who Hated Sherlock Holmes: A Life of Sir Arthur Conan Doyle* (New York: Pantheon Books, 1965).

Major Critical Works on Detective Fiction

Allen, Richard Stanley, *Detective Fiction: Crime and Compromise* (Fort Worth, Tex.: Harcourt College Publishers, 1974).

Bloom, Clive, *Nineteenth Century Suspense: From Poe to Conan Doyle* (Basingstoke: Palgrave MacMillan, 2000).

Bloom, Harold, *Classic Crime and Suspense Writers* (New York: Chelsea House, 1995).

Brooks, Peter, *Reading for the Plot: Design and Intention in Narrative* (New York: Knopf, 1984).

Delamater, Jerome H., and Prigozy, Ruth, *Theory and Practice of Classic Detective Fiction* (Westport, Conn.: Greenwood Press, 1997).

Earnes, Hugh, *Sleuths Inc: Studies of Problem Solvers, Doyle, Simenon, Hammett, Ambler, Chandler* (Philadelphia: Lippincott, 1978).

Eco, Umberto (ed.), *The Sign of Three: Dupin, Holmes, Peirce* (Bloomington, Ind.: Indiana University Press, 1984).

Frank, Lawrence, *Victorian Detective Fiction and the Nature of Evidence: The Scientific Investigations of Poe, Dickens, and Doyle* (Basingstoke: Palgrave Macmillan, 2009).

Ginzburg, Carlo, *Clues, Myths and the Historical Method* (Baltimore: Johns Hopkins University Press, 1989).

Hühn, Peter, 'The Detective as Reader: Narrativity and Reading Concepts in Detective Fiction', *MFS Modern Fiction Studies*, 3/3 (1987), 451–66.

Hutter, Albert D., 'Dreams, Transformations, and Literature: The Implications of Detective Fiction', *Victorian Studies*, 19/2 (1975), 181–209.

James, P. D., *Talking About Detective Fiction* (New York: Vintage, 2011).

Knight, Stephen, *Crime Fiction Since 1800: Detection, Death, Diversity* (Basingstoke: Palgrave MacMillan, 2010).

Malmgren, Carl D., *Anatomy of Murder: Mystery, Detective, and Crime Fiction* (Bowling Green, OH: Bowling Green Popular Press, 2001).

Most, Glenn W., and Stowe, William W. (eds.), *The Poetics of Murder: Detective Fiction and Literary Theory* (San Diego, Calif.: Harcourt, 1983).

Murch, Alma E., *The Development of the Detective Novel* (London: Peter Owen, 1958).

Ousby, Ian, *Bloodhounds of Heaven: The Detective in English Fiction from Goldwin to Doyle* (Cambridge, Mass.: Harvard University Press, 1976).

Porter, Dennis, *The Pursuit of Crime: Art and Ideology in Detective Fiction* (New Haven: Yale University Press, 1981).

Priestman, Martin, *Detective Fiction and Literature: The Figure on the Carpet* (Basingstoke: Palgrave MacMillan, 1991).

Priestman, Martin (ed.), *The Cambridge Companion to Crime Fiction* (Cambridge: Cambridge University Press, 2003).

Pyrhönen, Heta, *Murder from an Academic Angle: An Introduction to the Study of the Detective Narrative* (Columbia: Camden House, 1994).

Roth, Mary, *Foul and Fair Play: Reading Genre in Classic Detective Fiction* (Athens, Ga.: University of Georgia Press, 1995).

Rzepka, Charles J., *Detective Fiction* (Cambridge: Polity, 2005).

Scaggs, John, *Crime Fiction* (New York: Routledge, 2005).

Thomas, Ronald R., *Detective Fiction and the Rise of Forensic Science* (Cambridge: Cambridge University Press, 2004).

Thoms, Peter, *Detection and Its Designs: Narrative and Power in 19th Century Detective Fiction* (Athens, OH: Ohio University Press, 1998).

Todorov, Tzvetan, 'The Typology of Detective Fiction', in *The Poetics of Prose* (Ithaca, NY: Cornell University Press, 1978), 42–52.

Trotter, D., 'Theory and Detective Fiction', *Critical Quarterly*, 33/2 (1991), 66–77.

Walker, Ronald G., *The Cunning Craft: Original Essays on Detective Fiction and Contemporary Literary Theory* (Macomb, Ill.: Western Illinois University Press, 1990).

Winks, Robin W. (ed.), *Detective Fiction: A Collection of Critical Essays* (Woodstock: Countryman Press, 1988).

Winks, Robin W., and Corrigan, Maureen, *Mystery and Suspense Writers: The Literature of Crime, Detection, and Espionage* (New York: Holiday House, 1998).

Critical Work on Arthur Conan Doyle and the Holmes Stories

Atkinson, Michael, *The Secret Marriage of Sherlock Holmes and Other Eccentric Readings* (Ann Arbor: University of Michigan Press, 1996).

Baring-Gould, William S., *Sherlock Holmes of Baker Street: A Life of the World's First Consulting Detective* (New York: Bramhall House, 1962).

Barsham, Diana, *Arthur Conan Doyle and the Meaning of Masculinity* (Aldershot: Ashgate, 2000).

Bradley, Alan C., and Sarjeant, William A. S., *Ms. Holmes of Baker Street: The Truth About Sherlock* (Edmonton: University of Alberta, 2004).

Brooks, Peter, *Reading for the Plot: Design and Intention in Narrative* (New York: Knopf, 1984).

Bunson, Matthew E., *Encyclopedia Sherlockiana: An A-To-Z Guide to the World of the Great Detective* (London: Macmillan General Reference, 1997).

Dirda, Michael, *On Conan Doyle: Or, The Whole Art of Storytelling* (Princeton: Princeton University Press, 2011).

Frank, Lawrence, 'Dreaming the Medusa: Imperialism, Primitivism, and Sexuality in Arthur Conan Doyle's *The Sign of Four*', *Signs*, 22/1 (1996), 52–85.

Ginzburg, C., and Davin, Anna, 'Morelli, Freud and Sherlock Holmes: Clues and Scientific Method', *History Workshop*, 9 (1980), 5–36.

Green, Richard L., and Gibson, John M., *A Bibliography of A. Conan Doyle* (New York: Oxford University Press, 1983).

Harrison, Michael (ed.), *Beyond Baker Street* (Indianapolis: Bobbs-Merrill, 1976).

Jann, Rosemary, *The Adventures of Sherlock Holmes: Detecting Social Order* (New York: Twayne, 1995).

Kerr, Douglas, *Conan Doyle: Writing, Profession, and Practice* (Oxford: Oxford University Press, 2013).

Kestner, Joseph A., *Sherlock's Men: Masculinity, Conan Doyle, and Cultural History* (Brookfield: Ashgate, 1997).

McCrea, Barry, *In the Company of Strangers: Narrative and Family in Dickens, Conan Doyle, Joyce, and Proust* (New York: Columbia University Press, 2011).

Park, Orlando, *The Sherlock Holmes Encyclopedia* (New York: Carol Publishing, 1994).

Pasquale, Accardo, *Diagnosis and Detection: The Medical Iconography of Sherlock Holmes* (Rutherford, NJ: Fairleigh Dickinson University Press, 1987).

Porter, Lynnette, *Sherlock Holmes for the 21st Century: Essays on New Adaptations* (Jefferson, NC: McFarland, 2012).

Redmond, Donald A., *Sherlock Holmes: A Study in Sources* (Kingston and Montreal: McGill-Queen's University Press, 1982).

Robb, Graham, *Strangers: Homosexual Love in the Nineteenth Century* (New York: Norton, 2005), 260–7.

Shklovsky, Viktor, 'Sherlock Holmes and the Mystery Story', in *Theory of Prose*, trans. Benjamin Sher, introd. Gerald L. Bruns (Normal, Ill.: Dalkey Archive Press, 1990), 101–16.

Skovmand, Michael, 'The Mystique of the Bachelor Gentleman in Late Victorian Masculine Romance', in Michael Green (ed.), *English and Cultural Studies: Broadening the Context* (London: John Murray, 1987), 45–59.

Steiff, Josef, *Sherlock Holmes and Philosophy: The Footprints of a Gigantic Mind* (Chicago: Open Court, 2011).

Tallon, Philip, and Baggett, David, *The Philosophy of Sherlock Holmes* (Lexington, Ky.: University of Kentucky Press, 2012).

Wynne, Catherine, *The Colonial Conan Doyle: British Imperialism, Irish Nationalism, and the Gothic* (Westport, Conn.: Greenwood, 2002).

Studies of Nineteenth-Century London

Arata, Stephen, *Fictions of Loss in the Victorian Fin de Siècle: Identity and Empire* (Cambridge: Cambridge University Press, 1996).

Flanders, Judith, *The Invention of Murder: How the Victorians Revelled in Death and Detection and Created Modern Crime* (New York: Thomas Dunne Books, 2013).

Fox, Paul, and Melikoglu, Koray, *Formal Investigations: Aesthetic Style in Late-Victorian and Edwardian Detective Fiction* (Stuttgart: ibidem-Verlag, 2007).

Freeman, Nicholas, *Conceiving the City: London, Literature, and Art, 1870–1914* (Oxford: Oxford University Press, 2007).

Gray, Drew D., *London's Shadows: The Dark Side of the Victorian City* (London: Continuum, 2010).

Mayhew, Henry, *The London Underworld in the Victorian Period: Authentic First-Person Accounts by Beggars, Thieves and Prostitutes* (Mineola, NY: Dover Publications, 2005).

Mitchell, Sally, *Daily Life in Victorian England* (Westport, Conn.: Greenwood, 2008).

Picard, Liza, *Victorian London: The Tale of a City 1840–1870* (New York: St Martin's Griffin, 2007).

Shpayer-Makov, Haia, *The Ascent of the Detective: Police Sleuths in Victorian and Edwardian England* (Oxford: Oxford University Press, 2011).

Further Reading in Oxford World's Classics

Doyle, Arthur Conan, *The Adventures of Sherlock Holmes*, ed. Richard Lancelyn Green.

Doyle, Arthur Conan, *The Case-Book of Sherlock Holmes*, ed. W. W. Robson.

Doyle, Arthur Conan, *The Hound of the Baskervilles*, ed. W. W. Robson.

Doyle, Arthur Conan, *The Memoirs of Sherlock Holmes*, ed. Christopher Roden.

A CHRONOLOGY OF ARTHUR CONAN DOYLE

Life	*Historical and Cultural Background*
1859 Born Arthur Ignatius Conan Doyle on 22 May, son of Charles Altamont Doyle, painter, and Mary Foley, at 11 Picardy Place, Edinburgh.	Charles Darwin, *On the Origin of Species* Dickens, *A Tale of Two Cities*
1861–5	American Civil War.
1867 Leaves Edinburgh for England to start a Jesuit education at Hodder House.	Karl Marx, *Das Kapital*
1870 Enters Stonyhurst College, a Catholic school where he will remain for five years.	Jules Verne, *Twenty Thousand Leagues Under the Sea*
1870–1	Franco-Prussian War.
1871	Birth of Marcel Proust.
1874	First Impressionist exhibition in Paris.
1876 Enrols at Edinburgh University to study medicine. There he meets Dr Joseph Bell, on whom Sherlock Holmes was partly based. His father is sent to Blairerno, a nursing facility, to receive treatment for alcoholism and epilepsy.	Wagner's *Der Ring des Nibelungen* performed for the first time in its entirety.
1879 First publication, 'The Mystery of Sasassa Valley', appears in *Chambers's Journal*. Experiments on himself with gelseminum, and publishes the results in the *British Medical Journal*.	In Ireland, Michael Davitt founds the Land League. Henrik Ibsen, *A Doll's House*
1880 Serves as a ship's surgeon on the Greenland whaler *Hope* from February to September. In December publishes 'The American's Tale' in *London Society*.	Fyodor Dostoyevsky, *The Brothers Karamazov* Émile Zola, *Nana*

Life	*Historical and Cultural Background*
1880–1	First Boer War.
1881 Stays with Irish relatives in Lismore, Co. Waterford.	
1881–2 Serves as a ship's doctor on the cargo steamer SS *Mayumba*.	
1882 Renounces the Catholic faith. Opens his own practice at 1 Bush Villas, Elm Grove, Southsea. Publishes short stories in *London Society*, including 'My Friend the Murderer' in its Christmas issue.	British invasion of Egypt. Sigmund Freud begins his medical career in a psychiatric clinic at Vienna General Hospital. Births of James Joyce and Virginia Woolf.
1884 'J. Habakuk Jephson's Statement' published in the *Cornhill Magazine*.	Mark Twain, *The Adventures of Huckleberry Finn*
1885 Death of John Hawkins, a former patient of ACD and the brother of his future wife, Louise Hawkins. In August ACD receives his MD with the thesis 'On Vasomotor Influences in Tabes Dorsalis', and marries Louise.	
1887 *A Study in Scarlet* published in *Beeton's Christmas Annual*.	
1888 *The Mystery of Cloomber* published in *The Pall Mall Budget*.	Jack the Ripper murders in Whitechapel, London. Rudyard Kipling, *The Man Who Would Be King*
1889 Birth of Mary Louise Conan Doyle, daughter of ACD and Louise. *Micah Clarke* is published by Longmans, Green & Co. ACD attends a dinner with Marshall Stoddart, editor of *Lippincott's Monthly Magazine*, Oscar Wilde, and Thomas Patrick Gill at the Langham Hotel, Portland Place, London, at which ACD is commissioned to write *The Sign of the Four*, and	Inauguration of Eiffel Tower. Nietzsche, *Thus Spoke Zarathustra*

Life	*Historical and Cultural Background*

Oscar Wilde *The Picture of Dorian Gray. The Firm of Girdlestone* published in the *People*.

1890 Death of ACD's sister, Annette Mary Frances Conan Doyle, of influenza, aged 33, in Lisbon. *The Sign of the Four* published in *Lippincott's Monthly Magazine*. ACD leaves his practice in Southsea, Hampshire. First issue of the *Strand Magazine*.

1891 Gives up medicine to dedicate himself to writing full time. *The White Company* is published in the *Cornhill Magazine. The Doings of Raffles Haw* is published in the *Pittsburgh Commercial Gazette.* The Sherlock Holmes stories begin to appear in the *Strand Magazine* with 'A Scandal in Bohemia'.

Death of Charles Stewart Parnell.
Oscar Wilde, *The Picture of Dorian Gray*

1892 Birth of son, Arthur Alleyne Kingsley Conan Doyle, known as Kingsley. The *Strand Magazine* publishes the adventures of 'The Blue Carbuncle', 'The Speckled Band', 'The Engineer's Thumb', 'The Noble Bachelor', 'The Beryl Coronet', 'The Copper Beeches', and 'Silver Blaze'. *The Adventures of Sherlock Holmes* published in October by George Newnes, Ltd. *Harper's New Monthly Magazine* publishes 'Lot No. 249'.

Tchaikovsky's *Nutcracker Suite* premieres in St Petersburg.
Rudyard Kipling, *Gunga Din*

1893 Louise Conan Doyle diagnosed with tuberculosis and given just a few months to live. ACD takes her to Davos, Switzerland. *The Refugees* published in *Harper's New Monthly Magazine*. Death of Charles Altamont

Life	*Historical and Cultural Background*
Doyle at The Crighton Royal Institution, Dumfries. The *Strand Magazine* publishes the adventures of 'The Cardboard Box', 'The Yellow Face', 'The Stockbroker's Clerk', 'The *Gloria Scott*', 'The Musgrave Ritual', 'The Reigate Squire', 'The Crooked Man', 'The Resident Patient', 'The Greek Interpreter', 'The Naval Treaty', and 'The Final Problem'. *The Memoirs of Sherlock Holmes* published by George Newnes Ltd.	
1894 Travels to America and visits Chicago, Indianapolis, Cincinnati, Toledo, Detroit, and Milwaukee. *The Stark Munro Letters* published in the *Idler Magazine*. *The Parasite* published by Acme Library, Constable, London.	Rudyard Kipling, *The Jungle Book*
1894–1900	Dreyfus Affair.
1895	Trial and imprisonment of Oscar Wilde.
1896 Acts briefly as a war correspondent for the *Westminster Gazette*. *Rodney Stone* published in the *Strand Magazine*. *The Exploits of Brigadier Gerard* published by George Newnes Ltd.	Olympic Games revived in Athens. H. G. Wells, *The Island of Doctor Moreau*
1897 Meets Jean Leckie, who will become his second wife. *The Tragedy of Korosko* published in the *Strand Magazine*.	Bram Stoker, *Dracula* H. G. Wells, *The Invisible Man*
1898 Visits Rome with H. G. Wells, E. W. Hornung, and George Gissing. In December ACD and family celebrate moving into Undershaw with a fancy-dress ball at the Brecon Hill Hotel, with some of the guests dressed as characters from his works.	Henry James, *The Turn of the Screw* H. G. Wells, *The War of the Worlds*

Life	*Historical and Cultural Background*
'The Man with the Watches' and 'The Story of the Black Doctor' published by the *Strand Magazine*.	

1899 In January gives a speech, together with George Bernard Shaw, on 'Disarmament and Arbitration' at the Tsar's Peace Proposition held at Hindhead. On 12 June, *Sherlock Holmes*, a play written by both ACD and William Gillette, is performed at the Duke of York's Theatre, London. In December ACD applies to enlist in the army to fight against the Boers, but he is rejected because of his age. 'The Brown Hand' and 'The Croxley Master' published in the *Strand Magazine*.

Joseph Conrad, *Heart of Darkness*
Sigmund Freud, *The Interpretation of Dreams*

1899–1902

Second Boer War

1900 From 21 March to 11 July, ACD serves with the Langman Hospital in South Africa. *The Great Boer War* published by Smith, Elder & Co. *Tit-Bits* publishes 'A Gaudy Death: Conan Doyle tells the True Story of Sherlock Holmes's End'. First film adaptation, *Sherlock Holmes Baffled*, with a running time of less than one minute.

Death of Oscar Wilde.

1901 Writes to Greenhough Smith asking for £100 per 1,000 words if Sherlock Holmes is the principal character in *The Hound of the Baskervilles*. The play *Sherlock Holmes* is performed at the Lyceum Theatre, London, Charles Chaplin appeared as the page. *The Hound of the Baskervilles* published in the *Strand Magazine*.

Death of Queen Victoria and accession of King Edward VII.
Thomas Mann, *Buddenbrooks*

Life	Historical and Cultural Background

1902 Knighted by King Edward VII for his pamphlet *The War in South Africa: Its Cause and Conduct*, which justified the UK's role in the Boer War.

André Gide, *The Immoralist*
Henry James, *The Wings of the Dove*

1903–4 *Collier's Weekly* and the *Strand Magazine* publish the adventures of 'The Empty House', 'The Norwood Builder', 'The Dancing Men', 'The Solitary Cyclist', 'The Priory School', 'Black Peter', 'Charles Augustus Milverton', 'The Six Napoleons'. The *Strand Magazine* alone publishes the adventures of 'The Three Students', 'The Golden Pince-Nez', 'The Missing Quarter', 'The Abbey Grange', and 'The Second Stain'.

First flight of the Wright Brothers.
Trans-Siberian Railway is completed.
Henry James, *The Golden Bowl*

1904–5

Russo-Japanese War.

1905 Receives an honorary doctorate from Edinburgh University. *The Return of Sherlock Holmes* published by George Newnes Ltd., London. *Sir Nigel* published in the *Strand Magazine*.

Albert Einstein formulates his theory of relativity.
Jack London, *White Fang*

1906 Louise Conan Doyle dies, aged 49, at Undershaw.

Earthquakes in San Francisco, California, and Valparaíso, Chile.

1907 Death of Bertram Fletcher Robinson. Bram Stoker visits Undershaw. ACD marries his second wife, Jean Leckie. He receives the Order of the Second Class of the Medjideh and his wife Jean receives the Order of the Chevekat from Sultan Abdul-Hamid in Constantinople.

Life	*Historical and Cultural Background*
1908 'The Adventure of Wisteria Lodge', Part 1 and Part 2, as well as 'The Adventure of the Bruce-Partington Plans', published in the *Strand Magazine*.	First commercial radio transmissions. Invention of the Ford Model T. E. M. Forster, *A Room with a View*
1909 Becomes seriously ill with an intestinal blockage, which requires an operation in January. Makes a speech in memory of Edgar Allan Poe at the Whitehall Rooms, Hotel Metropole, London. Birth of Denis Percy Stewart Conan Doyle, son of ACD and Jean.	
1910 Has lunch with President T. Roosevelt. Birth of Adrian Malcolm Conan Doyle, second son of ACD and Jean. 'The Terror of Blue John Gap' and 'The Adventure of the Devil's Foot' published in the *Strand Magazine*.	Accession of King George V. E. M. Forster, *Howards End*
1911 Together with Jean, participates in the Prince Henry of Prussia Motor Tour from Hamburg to London. Death of Dr Joseph Bell, inspiration for Sherlock Holmes. 'The Adventure of the Red Circle' and 'The Disappearance of Lady Frances Carfax' published in the *Strand Magazine*.	Gaston Leroux, *The Phantom of the Opera*
1912 Birth of daughter Lena Annette Jean Conan Doyle. *The Lost World* published in *Associated Sunday Magazines* and the *Strand Magazine*. *The Case of Oscar Slater*, a plea for a victim of a miscarriage of justice in Scotland, published by Hodder and Stoughton, London.	The Republic of China is established. Thomas Mann, *Death in Venice*
1912–13	Balkan Wars.

Life	*Historical and Cultural Background*
1913 'The Adventure of the Dying Detective', 'The Poison Belt', 'How it Happened', and 'The Horror of the Heights' published in the *Strand Magazine*. In November, the film *The House of Temperley*, based on his novel *Rodney Stone*, opens at the West End Cinema, Coventry Street, London.	Guillaume Apollinaire, *Alcools* D. H. Lawrence, *Sons and Lovers* Proust, *Swann's Way* George Bernard Shaw, *Pygmalion* Igor Stravinsky, *Rite of Spring*
1914 Visits America and Canada from 20 May to 3 July. 'Danger!' published in the *Strand Magazine* in July. At the outbreak of the war on 4 August, ACD forms a local volunteer force, the Civilian National Reserve. *The Valley of Fear* published in the *Strand Magazine*. ' "The War" As Seen By Sir Arthur Conan Doyle' published in the *New York Tribune*.	Assassination of Archduke Franz Ferdinand of Austria by Gavrilo Princip, in Sarajevo, precipitates the First World War. James Joyce, *Dubliners*
1916 In May and June ACD visits the western front, and meets with his brother, Innes Doyle, and his son, Kingsley. In July Kingsley is wounded at the battle of the Somme and sent home. ACD announces his full conversion to spiritualism in the psychic magazine *Light*.	Easter Rising in Ireland. Assassination of Rasputin. James Joyce, *A Portrait of the Artist as a Young Man*
1917 'His Last Bow' and 'Some Personalia about Mr Sherlock Holmes' published in the *Strand Magazine*. *His Last Bow* (collected stories) published by John Murray, London.	Bolshevik Revolution in Russia. T. S. Eliot, 'The Lovesong of J. Alfred Prufrock'
1918 Visits the western front in September. His son Kingsley dies in October. *Danger! and Other Stories* published by John Murray, London.	End of the First World War. Murder of Tsar Nicholas II and his family.

Life	*Historical and Cultural Background*
1919 Death of his brother, Innes Doyle, at Halle, Belgium, from the Spanish Flu.	Treaty of Versailles. Establishment of the Weimar Republic.
1919–21	Irish War of Independence.
1920 Meets Houdini after watching his act at Portsmouth. Tours Australia and New Zealand with his family. In December, death of his mother, Mary Doyle (née Foley).	Sigmund Freud, 'Beyond the Pleasure Principle'
1921 In September makes a speech at the Stoll Convention Dinner to celebrate the Stoll films series of Sherlock Holmes. 'The Adventure of the Mazarin Stone' published in the *Strand Magazine*.	
1922	Death of Marcel Proust. Establishment of the Irish Free State. Benito Mussolini comes to power in Italy. Establishment of the USSR. James Joyce, *Ulysses* T. S. Eliot, *The Waste Land* Virginia Woolf, *Jacob's Room*
1922–3 Tours America from April to June, with lectures at Carnegie Hall, New York. Holds a seance in Atlantic City, with his wife Jean as the medium and Houdini attending. 'The Problem of the Thor Bridge', 'The Adventure of the Creeping Man', and *Memories and Adventures* published in the *Strand Magazine*.	
1924 'The Adventure of the Sussex Vampire' published in the *Strand Magazine*. The adventures of 'The Three Garridebs' and 'The Illustrious Client' published in *Collier's Weekly*. 'How Watson Learned the Trick' published in *The Book of the Queen's Dolls' House* by Methuen.	Deaths of Franz Kafka, Joseph Conrad, and Vladimir Lenin. Thomas Mann, *The Magic Mountain* E. M. Forster, *A Passage to India*

Life	Historical and Cultural Background
1925	Virginia Woolf, *Mrs Dalloway*
1926 *The History of Spiritualism*, volumes 1 and 2, published by Cassell and Company Ltd., London. The adventures of 'The Three Gables', 'The Blanched Soldier', 'The Lion's Mane', and 'The Retired Colourman' published in *Liberty*.	Hirohito becomes emperor of Japan. Franz Kafka, *The Castle*
1927 Death of his sister, Bryan Mary Doyle (Dodo). *The Maracot Deep* and the adventures of 'The Veiled Lodger' and 'The Shoscombe Old Place' published in the *Strand Magazine*. *The Case-Book of Sherlock Holmes* published by John Murray, London.	Stalin becomes leader of the Soviet Union. Martin Heidegger, *Being and Time* Herman Hesse, *Steppenwolf* Marcel Proust, *Time Regained* Virginia Woolf, *To the Lighthouse*
1928–9 Tours South Africa, Rhodesia, and Kenya from November 1928 to March 1929, and the Netherlands, Denmark, Sweden, and Norway in October–November 1929. Has his first heart attack on his return. The next day speaks for Armistice Day at the Albert Hall, London, and later in the evening at the Queen's Hall. 'When the World Screamed' published in *Liberty*. 'The Disintegration Machine' published in the *Strand Magazine*. *The Complete Sherlock Holmes Short Stories*, *The Conan Doyle Stories*, *The Maracot Deep and Other Stories*, and *The Complete Sherlock Holmes Stories* published by John Murray, London.	Wall Street Crash and beginning of the Great Depression. Bertolt Brecht, *The Threepenny Opera* William Faulkner, *The Sound and the Fury* Ernest Hemingway, *A Farewell to Arms* D. H. Lawrence, *Lady Chatterley's Lover*
1930 On the morning of 7 July ACD dies at Windlesham, spiritualist funeral on 11 July. In September the *Strand Magazine* republishes *A Scandal in Bohemia*.	William Faulkner, *As I Lay Dying* Dashiell Hammett, *The Maltese Falcon*

SHERLOCK HOLMES

Selected Stories

THE SIGN OF THE FOUR

CHAPTER 1

THE SCIENCE OF DEDUCTION

SHERLOCK HOLMES took his bottle from the corner of the mantel-piece, and his hypodermic syringe from its neat morocco case. With his long, white, nervous fingers he adjusted the delicate needle, and rolled back his left shirt-cuff. For some little time his eyes rested thoughtfully upon the sinewy forearm and wrist, all dotted and scarred with innumerable puncture-marks. Finally, he thrust the sharp point home, pressed down the tiny piston, and sank back into the velvet-lined arm-chair with a long sigh of satisfaction.

Three times a day for many months I had witnessed this perform-ance, but custom had not reconciled my mind to it. On the contrary, from day to day I had become more irritable at the sight, and my conscience swelled nightly within me at the thought that I had lacked the courage to protest. Again and again I had registered a vow that I should deliver my soul upon the subject; but there was that in the cool, nonchalant air of my companion which made him the last man with whom one would care to take anything approaching to a liberty. His great powers, his masterly manner, and the experience which I had had of his many extraordinary qualities, all made me diffident and backward in crossing him.

Yet upon that afternoon, whether it was the Beaune* which I had taken with my lunch, or the additional exasperation produced by the extreme deliberation of his manner, I suddenly felt that I could hold out no longer.

'Which is it to-day,' I asked, 'morphine or cocaine?'

He raised his eyes languidly from the old black-letter volume* which he had opened.

'It is cocaine,' he said; 'a seven-per-cent solution. Would you care to try it?'

'No, indeed,' I answered brusquely. 'My constitution has not got over the Afghan campaign* yet. I cannot afford to throw any extra strain upon it.'

He smiled at my vehemence. 'Perhaps you are right, Watson,' he said. 'I suppose that its influence is physically a bad one. I find it, however, so transcendently stimulating and clarifying to the mind that its secondary action is a matter of small moment.'

'But consider!' I said earnestly. 'Count the cost! Your brain may, as you say, be roused and excited, but it is a pathological and morbid process, which involves increased tissue-change and may at least leave a permanent weakness. You know, too, what a black reaction comes upon you. Surely the game is hardly worth the candle. Why should you, for a mere passing pleasure, risk the loss of those great powers with which you have been endowed? Remember that I speak not only as one comrade to another, but as a medical man to one for whose constitution he is to some extent answerable.'

He did not seem offended. On the contrary, he put his finger-tips together, and leaned his elbows on the arms of his chair, like one who has a relish for conversation.

'My mind', he said, 'rebels at stagnation. Give me problems, give me work, give me the most abstruse cryptogram or the most intricate analysis, and I am in my own proper atmosphere. I can dispense then with artificial stimulants. But I abhor the dull routine of existence. I crave for mental exaltation. That is why I have chosen my own particular profession, or rather created it, for I am the only one in the world.'

'The only unofficial detective?' I said, raising my eyebrows.

'The only unofficial consulting detective,' he answered. 'I am the last and highest court of appeal in detection. When Gregson or Lestrade or Athelney Jones are out of their depths—which, by the way, is their normal state—the matter is laid before me. I examine the data, as an expert, and pronounce a specialist's opinion. I claim no credit in such cases. My name figures in no newspaper. The work itself, the pleasure of finding a field for my peculiar powers, is my highest reward. But you have yourself had some experience of my methods of work in the Jefferson Hope case.'

'Yes, indeed,' said I cordially. 'I was never so struck by anything in my life. I even embodied it in a small brochure, with the somewhat fantastic title of "A Study in Scarlet".'*

He shook his head sadly.

'I glanced over it,' said he. 'Honestly, I cannot congratulate you upon it. Detection is, or ought to be, an exact science, and should be treated in the same cold and unemotional manner. You have attempted to tinge it with romanticism, which produces much the same effect as if you worked a love-story or an elopement into the fifth proposition of Euclid.'*

'But the romance was there,' I remonstrated. 'I could not tamper with the facts.'

'Some facts should be suppressed, or, at least, a just sense of proportion should be observed in treating them. The only point in the case which deserved mention was the curious analytical reasoning from effects to causes, by which I succeeded in unravelling it.'

I was annoyed at this criticism of a work which had been specially designed to please him. I confess, too, that I was irritated by the egotism which seemed to demand that every line of my pamphlet should be devoted to his own special doings. More than once during the years that I had lived with him in Baker Street I had observed that a small vanity underlay my companion's quiet and didactic manner. I made no remark, however, but sat nursing my wounded leg. I had had a Jezail bullet* through it some time before, and though it did not prevent me from walking, it ached wearily at every change of the weather.

'My practice has extended recently to the Continent,' said Holmes after a while, filling up his old briar-root pipe. 'I was consulted last week by François le Villard, who, as you probably know, has come rather to the front lately in the French detective service. He has all the Celtic power of quick intuition, but he is deficient in the wide range of exact knowledge which is essential to the higher developments of his art. The case was concerned with a will and possessed some features of interest. I was able to refer him to two parallel cases, the one at Riga in 1857, and the other at St Louis in 1871, which have suggested to him the true solution. Here is the letter which I had this morning acknowledging my assistance.'

He tossed over, as he spoke, a crumpled sheet of foreign notepaper. I glanced my eyes down it, catching a profusion of notes of admiration, with stray *magnifiques*, *coup-de-maîtres*, and *tours-de-force** all testifying to the ardent admiration of the Frenchman.

'He speaks as a pupil to his master,' said I.

'Oh, he rates my assistance too highly,' said Sherlock Holmes lightly. 'He has considerable gifts himself. He possesses two out of the three qualities necessary for the ideal detective. He has the power of observation and that of deduction. He is only wanting in knowledge, and that may come in time. He is now translating my small works into French.'

'Your works?'

'Oh, didn't you know?' he cried, laughing. 'Yes, I have been guilty of several monographs. They are all upon technical subjects. Here, for example, is one "Upon the Distinction between the Ashes of the Various Tobaccos". In it I enumerate a hundred and forty forms of cigar, cigarette, and pipe tobacco, with coloured plates illustrating the difference in the ash. It is a point which is continually turning up in criminal trials, and which is sometimes of supreme importance as a clue. If you can say definitely, for example, that some murder had been done by a man who was smoking an Indian lunkah,* it obviously narrows your field of search. To the trained eye there is as much difference between the black ash of a Trichinopoly* and the white fluff of bird's-eye* as there is between a cabbage and a potato.'

'You have an extraordinary genius for minutiae,' I remarked.

'I appreciate their importance. Here is my monograph upon the tracing of footsteps, with some remarks upon the uses of plaster of Paris as a preserver of impresses. Here, too, is a curious little work upon the influence of a trade upon the form of the hand, with litho-types* of the hands of slaters, sailors, cork-cutters, compositors, weavers, and diamond-polishers. That is a matter of great practical interest to the scientific detective—especially in cases of unclaimed bodies, or in discovering the antecedents of criminals. But I weary you with my hobby.'

'Not at all,' I answered earnestly. 'It is of the greatest interest to me, especially since I have had the opportunity of observing your practical application of it. But you spoke just now of observation and deduction. Surely the one to some extent implies the other.'

'Why, hardly,' he answered, leaning back luxuriously in his arm-chair and sending up thick blue wreaths from his pipe. 'For example, observation shows me that you have been to the Wigmore Street Post-Office this morning, but deduction lets me know that when there you despatched a telegram.'

'Right!' said I. 'Right on both points! But I confess that I don't see how you arrived at it. It was a sudden impulse upon my part, and I have mentioned it to no one.'

'It is simplicity itself,' he remarked, chuckling at my surprise—
'so absurdly simple that an explanation is superfluous; and yet
it may serve to define the limits of observation and of deduction.
Observation tells me that you have a little reddish mould adhering
to your instep. Just opposite the Wigmore Street Office they have
taken up the pavement and thrown up some earth, which lies in
such a way that it is difficult to avoid treading in it in entering. The
earth is of this peculiar reddish tint which is found, as far as I know,
nowhere else in the neighbourhood. So much is observation. The
rest is deduction.'

'How, then, did you deduce the telegram?'

'Why, of course I knew that you had not written a letter, since I sat
opposite to you all morning. I see also in your open desk there that you
have a sheet of stamps and a thick bundle of postcards. What could
you go into the post-office for, then, but to send a wire? Eliminate all
other factors, and the one which remains must be the truth.'

'In this case it certainly is so,' I replied, after a little thought. 'The
thing, however, is, as you say, of the simplest. Would you think me
impertinent if I were to put your theories to a more severe test?'

'On the contrary,' he answered, 'it would prevent me from taking a second dose of cocaine. I should be delighted to look into any
problem which you might submit to me.'

'I have heard you say that it is difficult for a man to have any object
in daily use without leaving the impress of his individuality upon it
in such a way that a trained observer might read it. Now, I have here
a watch which has recently come into my possession. Would you have
the kindness to let me have an opinion upon the character or habits
of the late owner?'

I handed him over the watch with some slight feeling of amusement in my heart, for the test was, as I thought, an impossible one, and
I intended it as a lesson against the somewhat dogmatic tone which he
occasionally assumed. He balanced the watch in his hand, gazed hard
at the dial, opened the back, and examined the works, first with his
naked eyes and then with a powerful convex lens. I could hardly keep
from smiling at his crestfallen face when he finally snapped the case
to and handed it back.

'There are hardly any data,' he remarked. 'The watch has been
recently cleaned, which robs me of my most suggestive facts.'

'You are right,' I answered. 'It was cleaned before being sent to me.'

In my heart I accused my companion of putting forward a most lame and impotent excuse to cover his failure. What data could he expect from an uncleaned watch?

'Though unsatisfactory, my research has not been entirely barren,' he observed, staring up at the ceiling with dreamy, lack-lustre eyes. 'Subject to your correction, I should judge that the watch belonged to your elder brother, who inherited it from your father.'

'That you gather, no doubt, from the H.W. upon the back?'

'Quite so. The W. suggests your own name. The date of the watch is nearly fifty years back, and the initials are as old as the watch: so it was made for the last generation. Jewellery usually descends to the eldest son, and he is most likely to have the same name as the father. Your father has, if I remember right, been dead many years. It has, therefore, been in the hands of your eldest brother.'

'Right, so far,' said I. 'Anything else?'

'He was a man of untidy habits—very untidy and careless. He was left with good prospects, but he threw away his chances, lived for some time in poverty with occasional short intervals of prosperity, and finally, taking to drink, he died. That is all I can gather.'

I sprang from my chair and limped impatiently about the room with considerable bitterness in my heart.

'This is unworthy of you, Holmes,' I said. 'I could not have believed that you would have descended to this. You have made inquiries into the history of my unhappy brother, and you now pretend to deduce this knowledge in some fanciful way. You cannot expect me to believe that you have read all this from his old watch! It is unkind and, to speak plainly, has a touch of charlatanism in it.'

'My dear doctor,' said he kindly, 'pray accept my apologies. Viewing the matter as an abstract problem, I had forgotten how personal and painful a thing it might be to you. I assure you, however, that I never even knew that you had a brother until you handed me the watch.'

'Then how in the name of all that is wonderful did you get these facts? They are absolutely correct in every particular.'

'Ah, that is good luck. I could only say what was the balance of probability. I did not at all expect to be so accurate.'

'But it was not mere guess-work?'

'No, no: I never guess. It is a shocking habit—destructive to the logical faculty. What seems strange to you is only so because you do not follow my train of thought or observe the small facts upon which large inferences may depend. For example, I began by stating that your brother was careless. When you observe the lower part of that watch-case you notice that it is not only dinted in two places, but it is cut and marked all over from the habit of keeping other hard objects, such as coins or keys, in the same pocket. Surely it is no great feat to assume that a man who treats a fifty-guinea watch so cavalierly must be a careless man. Neither is it a very far-fetched inference that a man who inherits one article of such value is pretty well provided for in other respects.'

I nodded, to show that I followed his reasoning.

'It is very customary for pawnbrokers in England, when they take a watch, to scratch the numbers of the ticket with a pin-point upon the inside of the case. It is more handy than a label, as there is no risk of the number being lost or transposed. There are no less than four such numbers visible to my lens on the inside of this case. Inference—that your brother was often at low water. Secondary inference—that he had occasional bursts of prosperity, or he could not have redeemed the pledge. Finally, I ask you to look at the inner plate, which contains the keyhole. Look at the thousands of scratches all round the hole—marks where the key has slipped. What sober man's key could have scored those grooves? But you will never see a drunkard's watch without them. He winds it at night, and he leaves these traces of his unsteady hand. Where is the mystery in all this?'

'It is as clear as daylight,' I answered. 'I regret the injustice which I did you. I should have had more faith in your marvellous faculty. May I ask whether you have any professional inquiry on foot at present?'

'None. Hence the cocaine. I cannot live without brain-work. What else is there to live for? Stand at the window here. Was ever such a dreary, dismal, unprofitable world? See how the yellow fog swirls down the street and drifts across the dun-coloured houses. What could be more hopelessly prosaic and material? What is the use of having powers, doctor, when one has no field upon which to exert them? Crime is commonplace, existence is commonplace, and no qualities save those which are commonplace have any function upon earth.'

I had opened my mouth to reply to this tirade, when, with a crisp knock, our landlady entered, bearing a card upon the brass salver.

'A young lady for you, sir,' she said, addressing my companion.

'Miss Mary Morstan,' he read. 'Hum! I have no recollection of the name. Ask the young lady to step up, Mrs Hudson. Don't go, doctor. I should prefer that you remain.'

CHAPTER 2

THE STATEMENT OF THE CASE

MISS MORSTAN entered the room with a firm step and an outward composure of manner. She was a blonde young lady, small, dainty, well gloved, and dressed in the most perfect taste. There was, however, a plainness and simplicity about her costume which bore with it a suggestion of limited means. The dress was a sombre grayish beige, untrimmed and unbraided, and she wore a small turban of the same dull hue, relieved only by a suspicion of white feather in the side. Her face had neither regularity of feature nor beauty of complexion, but her expression was sweet and amiable, and her large blue eyes were singularly spiritual and sympathetic. In an experience of women which extends over many nations and three separate continents, I have never looked upon a face which gave a clearer promise of a refined and sensitive nature. I could not but observe that as she took the seat which Sherlock Holmes placed for her, her lip trembled, her hand quivered, and she showed every sign of intense inward agitation.

'I have come to you, Mr Holmes,' she said, 'because you once enabled my employer, Mrs Cecil Forrester, to unravel a little domestic complication. She was much impressed by your kindness and skill.'

'Mrs Cecil Forrester,' he repeated thoughtfully. 'I believe that I was of some slight service to her. The case, however, as I remember it, was a very simple one.'

'She did not think so. But at least you cannot say the same of mine. I can hardly imagine anything more strange, more utterly inexplicable, than the situation in which I find myself.'

Holmes rubbed his hands, and his eyes glistened. He leaned forward in his chair with an expression of extraordinary concentration upon his clear-cut, hawk-like features.

'State your case,' said he, in brisk business tones.

I felt that my position was an embarrassing one.

'You will, I am sure, excuse me,' I said, rising from my chair.

To my surprise, the young lady held up her gloved hand to detain me.

'If your friend', she said, 'would be good enough to stop, he might be of inestimable service to me.'

I relapsed into my chair.

'Briefly,' she continued, 'the facts are these. My father was an officer in an Indian regiment, who sent me home when I was quite a child. My mother was dead, and I had no relative in England. I was placed, however, in a comfortable boarding establishment at Edinburgh, and there I remained until I was seventeen years of age. In the year 1878 my father, who was senior captain of his regiment, obtained twelve months' leave and came home. He telegraphed to me from London that he had arrived all safe, and directed me to come down at once, giving the Langham Hotel* as his address. His message, as I remember, was full of kindness and love. On reaching London I drove to the Langham, and was informed that Captain Morstan was staying there, but that he had gone out the night before and had not returned. I waited all day without news of him. That night, on the advice of the manager of the hotel, I communicated with the police, and next morning we advertised in all the papers. Our inquiries led to no result; and from that day to this no word has ever been heard of my unfortunate father. He came home with his heart full of hope to find some peace, some comfort, and instead—'

She put her hand to her throat, and a choking sob cut short the sentence.

'The date?' asked Holmes, opening his note-book.

'He disappeared upon the 3rd of December, 1878—nearly ten years ago.'

'His luggage?'

'Remained at the hotel. There was nothing in it to suggest a clue— some clothes, some books, and a considerable number of curiosities from the Andaman Islands.* He had been one of the officers in charge of the convict-guard there.'

'Had he any friends in town?'

'Only one that we know of—Major Sholto, of his own regiment, the 34th Bombay Infantry. The major had retired some little time before, and lived at Upper Norwood. We communicated with him, of course, but he did not even know that his brother officer was in England.'

'A singular case,' remarked Holmes.

'I have not yet described to you the most singular part. About six years ago—to be exact, upon the 4th of May, 1882—an advertisement appeared in *The Times* asking for the address of Miss Mary Morstan, and stating that it would be to her advantage to come forward. There was no name or address appended. I had at that time just entered the family of Mrs Cecil Forrester in the capacity of governess. By her advice I published my address in the advertisement column. The same day there arrived through the post a small cardboard box addressed to me, which I found to contain a very large lustrous pearl. No word of writing was enclosed. Since then every year upon the same date there has always appeared a similar box, containing a similar pearl, without any clue as to the sender. They have been pronounced by an expert to be of a rare variety and of considerable value. You can see for yourself that they are very handsome.'

She opened a flat box as she spoke and showed me six of the finest pearls that I had ever seen.

'Your statement is most interesting,' said Sherlock Holmes. 'Has anything else occurred to you?'

'Yes, and no later than to-day. That is why I have come to you. This morning I received this letter, which you will perhaps read for yourself.'

'Thank you,' said Holmes. 'The envelope, too, please. Post-mark, London, SW. Date, September 7. Hum! Man's thumb-mark on corner—probably postman. Best quality paper. Envelopes at sixpence a packet. Particular man in his stationery. No address. "Be at the third pillar from the left outside the Lyceum Theatre* to-night at seven o'clock. If you are distrustful bring two friends. You are a wronged woman, and shall have justice. Do not bring police. If you do, all will be in vain. Your unknown friend." Well, really, this is a very pretty little mystery! What do you intend to do, Miss Morstan?'

'That is exactly what I want to ask you.'

'Then we shall most certainly go—you and I and—yes, why Dr Watson is the very man. Your correspondent says two friends. He and I have worked together before.'

'But would he come?' she asked with something appealing in her voice and expression.

'I shall be proud and happy,' said I, fervently, 'if I can be of any service.'

'You are both very kind,' she answered. 'I have led a retired life, and have no friends whom I could appeal to. If I am here at six it will do, I suppose?'

'You must not be later,' said Holmes. 'There is one other point, however. Is this handwriting the same as that upon the pearl-box addresses?'

'I have them here,' she answered, producing half a dozen pieces of paper.

'You are certainly a model client. You have the correct intuition. Let us see, now.' He spread out the papers upon the table and gave little darting glances from one to the other. 'They are disguised hands, except the letter,' he said presently; 'but there can be no question as to the authorship. See how the irrepressible Greek *e* will break out, and see the twirl of the final *s*. They are undoubtedly by the same person. I should not like to suggest false hopes, Miss Morstan, but is there any resemblance between this hand and that of your father?'

'Nothing could be more unlike.'

'I expected to hear you say so. We shall look out for you, then, at six. Pray allow me to keep the papers. I may look into the matter before then. It is only half-past three. *Au revoir*, then.'

'*Au revoir*,' said our visitor; and with a bright, kindly glance from one to the other of us, she replaced her pearl-box in her bosom and hurried away.

Standing at the window, I watched her walking briskly down the street until the gray turban and white feather were but a speck in the sombre crowd.

'What a very attractive woman!' I exclaimed, turning to my companion.

He had lit his pipe again, and was leaning back with drooping eyelids. 'Is she?' he said languidly; 'I did not observe.'

'You really are an automaton—a calculating machine,' I cried. 'There is something positively inhuman in you at times.'

He smiled gently.

'It is of the first importance', he said, 'not to allow your judgement to be biased by personal qualities. A client is to me a mere unit, a factor in a problem. The emotional qualities are antagonistic to clear reasoning. I assure you that the most winning woman I ever knew was hanged for poisoning three little children for their insurance-money, and the most repellent man of my acquaintance is a philanthropist who has spent nearly a quarter of a million upon the London poor.'

'In this case, however—'

'I never make exceptions. An exception disproves the rule. Have you ever had occasion to study character in handwriting? What do you make of this fellow's scribble?'

'It is legible and regular,' I answered. 'A man of business habits and some force of character.'

Holmes shook his head.

'Look at his long letters,' he said. 'They hardly rise above the common herd. That *d* might be an *a*, and that *l* an *e*. Men of character always differentiate their long letters, however illegibly they may write. There is vacillation in his *k*'s and self-esteem in his capitals. I am going out now. I have some few references to make. Let me recommend this book—one of the most remarkable ever penned. It is Winwood Reade's *Martyrdom of Man*.* I shall be back in an hour.'

I sat in the window with the volume in my hand, but my thoughts were far from the daring speculations of the writer. My mind ran upon our late visitor—her smiles, the deep rich tones of her voice, the strange mystery which overhung her life. If she were seventeen at the time of her father's disappearance she must be seven-and-twenty now—a sweet age, when youth has lost its self-consciousness and become a little sobered by experience. So I sat and mused until such dangerous thoughts came into my head that I hurried away to my desk and plunged furiously into the latest treatise upon pathology. What was I, an army surgeon with a weak leg and a weaker banking account, that I should dare to think of such things? She was a unit, a factor—nothing more. If my future were black, it was better surely to face it like a man than to attempt to brighten it by mere will-o'-the-wisps of the imagination.

CHAPTER 3

IN QUEST OF A SOLUTION

IT was half-past five before Holmes returned. He was bright, eager, and in excellent spirits, a mood which in his case alternated with fits of the blackest depression.

'There is no great mystery in this matter,' he said, taking the cup of tea which I had poured out for him; 'the facts appear to admit of only one explanation.'

'What! you have solved it already?'

'Well, that would be too much to say. I have discovered a suggestive fact, that is all. It is, however, *very* suggestive. The details are still to be added. I have just found, on consulting the back files of *The Times*,* that Major Sholto, of Upper Norwood, late of the 34th Bombay Infantry, died upon the 28th of April, 1882.'

'I may be very obtuse, Holmes, but I fail to see what this suggests.'

'No? You surprise me. Look at it in this way, then. Captain Morstan disappears. The only person in London whom he could have visited is Major Sholto. Major Sholto denies having heard that he was in London. Four years later Sholto dies. *Within a week of his death* Captain Morstan's daughter receives a valuable present, which is repeated from year to year, and now culminates in a letter which describes her as a wronged woman. What wrong can it refer to except this deprivation of her father? And why should the presents begin immediately after Sholto's death, unless it is that Sholto's heir knows something of the mystery and desires to make compensation? Have you any alternative theory which will meet the facts?'

'But what a strange compensation! And how strangely made! Why, too, should he write a letter now, rather than six years ago? Again, the letter speaks of giving her justice. What justice can she have? It is too much to suppose that her father is still alive. There is no other injustice in her case that you know of.'

'There are difficulties; there are certainly difficulties,' said Sherlock Holmes pensively; 'but our expedition of to-night will solve them all. Ah, here is a four-wheeler,* and Miss Morstan is inside. Are you all ready? Then we had better go down, for it is a little past the hour.'

I picked up my hat and my heaviest stick, but I observed that Holmes took his revolver from his drawer and slipped it into his pocket. It was clear that he thought that our night's work might be a serious one.

Miss Morstan was muffled in a dark cloak, and her sensitive face was composed, but pale. She must have been more than woman if she did not feel some uneasiness at the strange enterprise upon which we were embarking, yet her self-control was perfect, and she readily answered the few additional questions which Sherlock Holmes put to her.

'Major Sholto was a very particular friend of papa's,' she said. 'His letters were full of allusions to the major. He and papa were in command of the troops at the Andaman Islands, so they were thrown a great deal together. By the way, a curious paper was found in papa's desk which no one could understand. I don't suppose that it is of the slightest importance, but I thought you might care to see it, so I brought it with me. It is here.'

Holmes unfolded the paper carefully and smoothed it out upon his knee. He then very methodically examined it all over with his double lens.

'It is paper of native Indian manufacture,' he remarked. 'It has at some time been pinned to a board. The diagram upon it appears to be a plan of part of a large building with numerous halls, corridors, and passages. At one point is a small cross done in red ink, and above it is "3.37 from left," in faded pencil-writing. In the left-hand corner is a curious hieroglyphic like four crosses in a line with their arms touching. Beside it is written, in very rough and coarse characters, "The sign of the four—Jonathan Small, Mahomet Singh, Abdullah Khan, Dost Akbar." No, I confess that I do not see how this bears upon the matter. Yet it is evidently a document of importance. It has been kept carefully in a pocket-book; for the one side is as clean as the other.'

'It was in his pocket-book that we found it.'

'Preserve it carefully, then, Miss Morstan, for it may prove to be of use to us. I begin to suspect that this matter may turn out to be much deeper and more subtle than I at first supposed. I must reconsider my ideas.'

He leaned back in the cab, and I could see by his drawn brow and his vacant eye that he was thinking intently. Miss Morstan and I chatted in an undertone about our present expedition and its possible outcome, but our companion maintained his impenetrable reserve until the end of our journey.

It was a September evening and not yet seven o'clock, but the day had been a dreary one, and a dense drizzly fog lay low upon the great city. Mud-coloured clouds drooped sadly over the muddy streets. Down the Strand the lamps were but misty splotches of diffused light which threw a feeble circular glimmer upon the slimy pavement. The yellow glare from the shop-windows streamed out into the steamy, vaporous air, and threw a murky, shifting radiance across the crowded thoroughfare. There was, to my mind, something eerie and ghost-like in the endless procession of faces which flitted across these narrow bars of light—sad faces and glad, haggard and merry. Like all human kind, they flitted from the gloom into the light, and so back into the gloom once more. I am not subject to impressions, but the dull, heavy evening, with the strange business upon which we were engaged, combined to make me nervous and depressed. I could see from Miss Morstan's manner that she was suffering from the same feeling. Holmes alone could rise superior to petty influences. He held his open notebook upon his knee, and from time to time he jotted down figures and memoranda in the light of his pocket-lantern.

At the Lyceum Theatre the crowds were already thick at the side-entrances. In front a continuous stream of hansoms* and four-wheelers were rattling up, discharging their cargoes of shirt-fronted men and be-shawled, be-diamonded women. We had hardly reached the third pillar, which was our rendezvous, before a small, dark, brisk man in the dress of a coachman accosted us.

'Are you the parties who come with Miss Morstan?' he asked.

'I am Miss Morstan, and these two gentlemen are my friends,' said she.

He bent a pair of wonderfully penetrating and questioning eyes upon us.

'You will excuse me, miss,' he said, with a certain dogged manner, 'but I was to ask you to give me your word that neither of your companions is a police-officer.'

'I give you my word on that,' she answered.

He gave a shrill whistle, on which a street arab* led across a four-wheeler and opened the door. The man who had addressed us mounted to the box, while we took our places inside. We had hardly done so before the driver whipped up his horse, and we plunged away at a furious pace through the foggy streets.

The situation was a curious one. We were driving to an unknown place, on an unknown errand. Yet our invitation was either a complete hoax—which was an inconceivable hypothesis—or else we had good reason to think that important issues might hang upon our journey. Miss Morstan's demeanour was as resolute and collected as ever. I endeavoured to cheer and amuse her by reminiscences of my adventures in Afghanistan; but, to tell the truth, I was myself so excited at our situation, and so curious as to our destination, that my stories were slightly involved. To this day she declares that I told her one moving anecdote as to how a musket looked into my tent at the dead of night, and how I fired a double-barrelled tiger cub at it. At first I had some idea as to the direction in which we were driving; but soon, what with our pace, the fog, and my own limited knowledge of London, I lost my bearings, and knew nothing, save that we seemed to be going a very long way. Sherlock Holmes was never at fault, however, and he muttered the names as the cab rattled through squares and in and out by tortuous by-streets.

'Rochester Row,' said he. 'Now Vincent Square. Now we come out on the Vauxhall Bridge Road. We are making for the Surrey side,* apparently. Yes, I thought so. Now we are on the bridge. You can catch glimpses of the river.'

We did indeed get a fleeting view of a stretch of the Thames, with the lamps shining upon the broad, silent water; but our cab dashed on, and was soon involved in a labyrinth of streets upon the other side.

'Wordsworth Road,' said my companion. 'Priory Road. Lark Hall Lane. Stockwell Place. Robert Street. Cold Harbour Lane. Our quest does not appear to take us to very fashionable regions.'

We had indeed reached a questionable and forbidding neighbour-hood. Long lines of dull brick houses were only relieved by the coarse glare and tawdry brilliancy of public-houses at the corner. Then came rows of two-storeyed villas, each with a fronting of miniature garden, and then again interminable lines of new, staring brick buildings— the monster tentacles which the giant city was throwing out into the country. At last the cab drew up at the third house in a new terrace. None of the other houses were inhabited, and that at which we stopped was as dark as its neighbours, save for a single glimmer in the kitchen-window. On our knocking, however, the door was instantly thrown open by a Hindoo servant, clad in a yellow turban, white loose-fitting clothes, and a yellow sash. There was something strangely incongru-ous in this Oriental figure framed in the commonplace doorway of a third-rate suburban dwelling-house.

'The Sahib* awaits you,' said he, and even as he spoke, there came a high, piping voice from some inner room.

'Show them in to me, *khitmutgar*,'* it said. 'Show them straight in to me.'

CHAPTER 4

THE STORY OF THE BALD-HEADED MAN

WE followed the Indian down a sordid and common passage, ill-lit and worse furnished, until he came to a door upon the right, which he threw open. A blaze of yellow light streamed out upon us, and in the centre of the glare there stood a small man with a very high head, a bristle of red hair all round the fringe of it, and a bald, shining scalp which shot out from among it like a mountain-peak from fir-trees. He writhed his hands together as he stood, and his features were in a perpetual jerk—now smiling, now scowling, but never for an instant in repose. Nature had given him a pendulous lip, and a too visible line of yellow and irregular teeth, which he strove feebly to conceal by constantly passing his hand over the lower part of his face. In spite of his obtrusive baldness, he gave the impression of youth. In point of fact, he had just turned his thirtieth year.

'Your servant, Miss Morstan,' he kept repeating, in a thin, high voice. 'Your servant, gentlemen. Pray step into my little sanctum. A small place, miss, but furnished to my own liking. An oasis of art in the howling desert of South London.'

We were all astonished by the appearance of the apartment into which he invited us. In that sorry house it looked as out of place as a diamond of the first water* in a setting of brass. The richest and glossiest of curtains and tapestries draped the walls, looped back here and there to expose some richly-mounted painting or Oriental vase. The carpet was of amber and black, so soft and so thick that the foot sank pleasantly into it, as into a bed of moss. Two great tiger-skins thrown athwart it increased the suggestion of Eastern luxury, as did a huge hookah* which stood upon a mat in the corner. A lamp in the fashion of a silver dove was hung from an almost invisible golden wire in the centre of the room. As it burned it filled the air with a subtle and aromatic odour.

'Mr Thaddeus Sholto,' said the little man, still jerking and smiling. 'That is my name. You are Miss Morstan, of course. And these gentlemen—'

'This is Mr Sherlock Holmes, and this Dr Watson.'

'A doctor, eh?' cried he, much excited. 'Have you your stethoscope? Might I ask you—would you have the kindness? I have grave doubts as to my mitral valve, if you would be so very good. The aortic I may rely upon, but I should value your opinion upon the mitral.'

I listened to his heart, as requested, but was unable to find anything amiss, save, indeed, that he was in an ecstasy of fear, for he shivered from head to foot.

'It appears to be normal,' I said. 'You have no cause for uneasiness.'

'You will excuse my anxiety, Miss Morstan,' he remarked airily. 'I am a great sufferer, and I have long had suspicions as to that valve. I am delighted to hear that they are unwarranted. Had your father, Miss Morstan, refrained from throwing a strain upon his heart, he might have been alive now.'

I could have struck the man across the face, so hot was I at this callous and offhand reference to so delicate a matter. Miss Morstan sat down, and her face grew white to the lips.

'I knew in my heart that he was dead,' said she.

'I can give you every information,' said he; 'and, what is more, I can do you justice; and I will, too, whatever Brother Bartholomew may say. I am so glad to have your friends here not only as an escort to you but also as witnesses to what I am about to do and say. The three of us can show a bold front to Brother Bartholomew. But let us have no outsiders—no police or officials. We can settle everything satisfactorily among ourselves without any interference. Nothing would annoy Brother Bartholomew more than any publicity.'

He sat down upon a low settee, and blinked at us enquiringly with his weak, watery blue eyes.

'For my part,' said Holmes, 'whatever you may choose to say will go no further.'

I nodded to show my agreement.

'That is well! That is well!' said he. 'May I offer you a glass of Chianti,* Miss Morstan? Or of Tokay?* I keep no other wines. Shall I open a flask? No? Well, then, I trust that you have no objection to tobacco-smoke, to the balsamic odour of the Eastern tobacco. I am a little nervous, and I find my hookah an invaluable sedative.'

He applied a taper to the great bowl, and the smoke bubbled merrily through the rose-water. We sat all three in a semicircle, with our heads advanced and our chins upon our hands, while the strange, jerky little fellow, with his high, shining head, puffed uneasily in the centre.

'When I first determined to make this communication to you,' said he, 'I might have given you my address; but I feared that you might disregard my request and bring unpleasant people with you. I took the liberty, therefore, of making an appointment in such a way that my man Williams might be able to see you first. I have complete confidence in his discretion, and he had orders, if he were dissatisfied, to proceed no further in the matter. You will excuse these precautions, but I am a man of somewhat retiring, and I might even say refined, tastes, and there is nothing more unaesthetic than a policeman. I have a natural shrinking from all forms of rough materialism. I seldom come in contact with the rough crowd. I live, as you see, with some little atmosphere of elegance around me. I may call myself a patron of the arts. It is my weakness. The landscape is a genuine Corot,* and, though a connoisseur might perhaps throw a doubt upon that Salvator Rosa,* there cannot be the least question about the Bouguereau.* I am partial to the modern French school.'*

'You will excuse me, Mr Sholto,' said Miss Morstan, 'but I am here at your request to learn something which you desire to tell me. It is very late, and I should desire the interview to be as short as possible.'

'At the best it must take some time,' he answered; 'for we shall certainly have to go to Norwood and see Brother Bartholomew. We shall all go and try if we can get the better of Brother Bartholomew. He is very angry with me for taking the course which has seemed right to me. I had quite high words with him last night. You cannot imagine what a terrible fellow he is when he is angry.'

'If we are to go to Norwood, it would perhaps be as well to start at once,' I ventured to remark.

He laughed until his ears were quite red.

'That would hardly do,' he cried. 'I don't know what he would say if I brought you in that sudden way. No, I must prepare you by showing you how we all stand to each other. In the first place, I must tell you that there are several points in the story of which I am myself ignorant. I can only lay the facts before you as far as I know them myself.

'My father was, as you may have guessed, Major John Sholto, once of the Indian Army. He retired some eleven years ago and came to live at Pondicherry Lodge* in Upper Norwood. He had prospered in India and brought back with him a considerable sum of money, a large collection of valuable curiosities, and a staff of native servants.

With these advantages he bought himself a house, and lived in great luxury. My twin-brother Bartholomew and I were the only children.

'I very well remember the sensation which was caused by the disappearance of Captain Morstan. We read the details in the papers, and knowing that he had been a friend of our father's, we discussed the case freely in his presence. He used to join in our speculations as to what could have happened. Never for an instant did we suspect that he had the whole secret hidden in his own breast, that of all men he alone knew the fate of Arthur Morstan.

'We did know, however, that some mystery, some positive danger, overhung our father. He was very fearful of going out alone, and he always employed two prize-fighters to act as porters at Pondicherry Lodge. Williams, who drove you to-night, was one of them. He was once light-weight champion of England. Our father would never tell us what it was he feared, but he had a most marked aversion to men with wooden legs. On one occasion he actually fired his revolver at a wooden-legged man, who proved to be a harmless tradesman canvassing for orders. We had to pay a large sum to hush the matter up. My brother and I used to think this a mere whim of my father's; but events have since led us to change our opinion.

'Early in 1882 my father received a letter from India which was a great shock to him. He nearly fainted at the breakfast-table when he opened it, and from that day he sickened to his death. What was in the letter we could never discover, but I could see as he held it that it was short and written in a scrawling hand. He had suffered for years from an enlarged spleen, but he now became rapidly worse, and towards the end of April we were informed that he was beyond all hope, and that he wished to make a last communication to us.

'When we entered his room he was propped up with pillows and breathing heavily. He besought us to lock the door and to come upon either side of the bed. Then, grasping our hands, he made a remarkable statement to us in a voice which was broken as much by emotion as by pain. I shall try and give it to you in his own very words.

'"I have only one thing", he said, "which weighs upon my mind at this supreme moment. It is my treatment of poor Morstan's orphan. The cursed greed which has been my besetting sin through life has withheld from her the treasure, half at least of which should have been hers. And yet I have made no use of it myself, so blind and foolish a thing is avarice. The mere feeling of possession has been so dear to me that I could not bear to share it with another. See that chaplet* tipped with pearls beside the quinine* bottle. Even that I could not bear to part with, although I had got it out with the design of sending it to her. You, my sons, will give her a fair share of the Agra* treasure. But send her nothing—not even the chaplet—until I am gone. After all, men have been as bad as this and have recovered.

' "I will tell you how Morstan died," he continued. "He had suffered for years from a weak heart, but he concealed it from everyone. I alone knew it. When in India, he and I, through a remarkable chain of circumstances, came into possession of a considerable treasure. I brought it over to England, and on the night of Morstan's arrival he came straight over here to claim his share. He walked over from the station, and was admitted by my faithful old Lal Chowdar, who is now dead. Morstan and I had a difference of opinion as to the division of the treasure, and we came to heated words. Morstan had sprung out of his chair in a paroxysm of anger, when he suddenly pressed his hand to his side, his face turned a dusky hue, and he fell backwards, cutting his head against the corner of the treasure-chest. When I stooped over him I found, to my horror, that he was dead.

' "For a long time I sat half distracted, wondering what I should do. My first impulse was, of course, to call for assistance; but I could not but recognize that there was every chance that I would be accused of his murder. His death at the moment of a quarrel, and the gash in his head, would be black against me. Again, an official inquiry could not be made without bringing out some facts about the treasure, which I was particularly anxious to keep secret. He had told me that no soul upon earth knew where he had gone. There seemed to be no necessity why any soul ever should know.

' "I was still pondering over the matter, when, looking up, I saw my servant, Lal Chowdar, in the doorway. He stole in and bolted the door behind him. 'Do not fear, Sahib,' he said; 'no one need know that you have killed him. Let us hide him away, and who is the wiser?' 'I did not kill him,' said I. Lal Chowdar shook his head and smiled. 'I heard it all, Sahib,' said he; 'I heard you quarrel, and I heard the blow. But my lips are sealed. All are asleep in the house. Let us put him away together.' That was enough to decide me. If my own servant could not believe my innocence, how could I hope to make it good before twelve foolish tradesmen in a jury-box? Lal Chowdar and I disposed of the body that night, and within a few days the London papers were full of the mysterious disappearance of Captain Morstan. You will see from what I say that I can hardly be blamed in the matter. My fault lies in the fact that we concealed not only the body, but also the treasure, and that I have clung to Morstan's share as well as to my own. I wish you, therefore, to make restitution. Put your ears down to my mouth. The treasure is hidden in—"

'At this instant a horrible change came over his expression; his eyes stared wildly, his jaw dropped, and he yelled, in a voice which I can never forget, "Keep him out! For Christ's sake keep him out!" We both stared round at the window behind us upon which his gaze was fixed. A face was looking in at us out of the darkness. We could see the whitening of the nose where it was pressed against the glass. It was a bearded, hairy face, with wild cruel eyes and an expression of concentrated malevolence. My brother and I rushed towards the window, but the man was gone. When we returned to my father his head had dropped and his pulse had ceased to beat.

'We searched the garden that night, but found no sign of the intruder save that just under the window a single footmark was visible in the flower-bed. But for that one trace, we might have thought that our imaginations had conjured up that wild, fierce face. We soon, however, had another and a more striking proof that there were secret agencies at work all round us. The window of my father's room was found open in the morning, his cupboards and boxes had been rifled, and upon his chest was fixed a torn piece of paper, with the words "The sign of the four" scrawled across it. What the phrase meant or who our secret visitor may have been, we never knew. As far as we can judge, none of my father's property had been actually stolen, though everything had been turned out. My brother and I naturally associated this peculiar incident with the fear which haunted my father during his life; but it is still a complete mystery to us.'

The little man stopped to relight his hookah and puffed thoughtfully for a few moments. We had all sat absorbed, listening to his extraordinary narrative. At the short account of her father's death Miss Morstan had turned deadly white, and for a moment I feared that she was about to faint. She rallied, however, on drinking a glass of water which I quietly poured out for her from a Venetian carafe* upon the side-table. Sherlock Holmes leaned back in his chair with an abstracted expression and the lids drawn low over his glittering eyes.

As I glanced at him I could not but think how on that very day he had complained bitterly of the commonplaceness of life. Here at least was a problem which would tax his sagacity to the utmost. Mr Thaddeus Sholto looked from one to the other of us with an obvious pride at the effect which his story had produced, and then continued between the puffs of his overgrown pipe.

'My brother and I', said he, 'were, as you may imagine, much excited as to the treasure which my father had spoken of. For weeks and for months we dug and delved in every part of the garden without discovering its whereabouts. It was maddening to think that the hiding-place was on his very lips at the moment that he died. We could judge the splendour of the missing riches by the chaplet which he had taken out. Over this chaplet my brother Bartholomew and I had some little discussion. The pearls were evidently of great value, and he was averse to part with them, for, between friends, my brother was himself a little inclined to my father's fault. He thought, too, that if we parted with the chaplet it might give rise to gossip and finally bring us into trouble. It was all that I could do to persuade him to let me find out Miss Morstan's address and send her a detached pearl at fixed intervals, so that at least she might never feel destitute.'

'It was a kindly thought,' said our companion earnestly; 'it was extremely good of you.'

The little man waved his hand deprecatingly.

'We were your trustees,' he said; 'that was the view which I took of it, though Brother Bartholomew could not altogether see it in that light. We had plenty of money ourselves. I desired no more. Besides, it would have been such bad taste to have treated a young lady in so scurvy a fashion. "*Le mauvais goût mène au crime.*"* The French have a very neat way of putting these things. Our difference of opinion on this subject went so far that I thought it best to set up rooms for myself; so I left Pondicherry Lodge, taking the old *khitmutgar* and Williams with me. Yesterday, however, I learn that an event of extreme importance has occurred. The treasure has been discovered. I instantly communicated with Miss Morstan, and it only remains for us to drive out to Norwood and demand our share. I explained my views last night to Brother Bartholomew, so we shall be expected, if not welcome, visitors.'

Mr Thaddeus Sholto ceased, and sat twitching on his luxurious settee. We all remained silent, with our thoughts upon the new development which the mysterious business had taken. Holmes was the first to spring to his feet.

'You have done well, sir, from first to last,' said he. 'It is possible that we may be able to make you some small return by throwing some light upon that which is still dark to you. But, as Miss Morstan remarked just now, it is late, and we had best put the matter through without delay.'

Our new acquaintance very deliberately coiled up the tube of his hookah and produced from behind a curtain a very long befrogged* topcoat with Astrakhan* collar and cuffs. This he buttoned tightly up in spite of the extreme closeness of the night and finished his attire by putting on a rabbit-skin cap with hanging lappets* which covered the ears, so that no part of him was visible save his mobile and peaky face.

'My health is somewhat fragile,' he remarked as he led the way down the passage. 'I am compelled to be a valetudinarian.'*

Our cab was awaiting us outside, and our programme was evidently prearranged, for the driver started off at once at a rapid pace. Thaddeus Sholto talked incessantly in a voice which rose high above the rattle of the wheels.

'Bartholomew is a clever fellow,' said he. 'How do you think he found out where the treasure was? He had come to the conclusion that it was somewhere indoors: so he worked out all the cubic space of the house, and made measurements everywhere so that not one inch should be unaccounted for. Among other things, he found that the height of the building was seventy-four feet, but on adding together the heights of all the separate rooms and making every allowance for the space between, which he ascertained by borings, he could not bring the total to more than seventy feet. There were four feet unaccounted for. These could only be at the top of the building. He knocked a hole, therefore, in the lath and plaster ceiling of the highest room, and there, sure enough, he came upon another little garret above it, which had been sealed up and was known to no one. In the centre stood the treasure-chest, resting upon two rafters. He lowered it through the hole, and there it lies. He computes the value of the jewels at not less than half a million sterling.'

At the mention of this gigantic sum we all stared at one another open-eyed. Miss Morstan, could we secure her rights, would change from a needy governess to the richest heiress in England. Surely it was the place of a loyal friend to rejoice at such news; yet I am ashamed to say that selfishness took me by the soul, and that my heart turned as heavy as lead within me. I stammered out some few halting words of congratulation, and then sat downcast, with my head drooped, deaf to the babble of our new acquaintance. He was clearly a confirmed hypochondriac, and I was dreamily conscious that he was pouring forth interminable trains of symptoms, and imploring information as to the composition and action of innumerable quack nostrums,* some of which he bore about in a leather case in his pocket. I trust that he may not remember any of the answers which I gave him that night. Holmes declares that he overheard me caution him against the great danger of taking more than two drops of castor-oil, while I recommended strychnine* in large doses as a sedative. However that may be, I was certainly relieved when our cab pulled up with a jerk and the coachman sprang down to open the door.

'This, Miss Morstan, is Pondicherry Lodge,' said Mr Thaddeus Sholto, as he handed her out.

CHAPTER 5

THE TRAGEDY OF PONDICHERRY LODGE

IT was nearly eleven o'clock when we reached this final stage of our night's adventures. We had left the damp fog of the great city behind us, and the night was fairly fine. A warm wind blew from the westward, and heavy clouds moved slowly across the sky, with half a moon peeping occasionally through the rifts. It was clear enough to see for some distance, but Thaddeus Sholto took down one of the side-lamps from the carriage to give us a better light upon our way.

Pondicherry Lodge stood in its own grounds, and was girt round with a very high stone wall topped with broken glass. A single narrow iron-clamped door formed the only means of entrance. On this our guide knocked with a peculiar postman-like rat-tat.

'Who is there?' cried a gruff voice from within.

'It is I, McMurdo. You surely know my knock by this time.'

There was a grumbling sound and a clanking and jarring of keys. The door swung heavily back, and a short, deep-chested man stood in the opening, with the yellow light of the lantern shining upon his protruded face and twinkling, distrustful eyes.

'That you, Mr Thaddeus? But who are the others? I had no orders about them from the master.'

'No, McMurdo? You surprise me! I told my brother last night that I should bring some friends.'

'He hain't been out o' his room to-day, Mr Thaddeus, and I have no orders. You know very well that I must stick to regulations. I can let you in, but your friends they must just stop where they are.'

This was an unexpected obstacle. Thaddeus Sholto looked about him in a perplexed and helpless manner.

'This is too bad of you, McMurdo!' he said. 'If I guarantee them, that is enough for you. There is the young lady, too. She cannot wait on the public road at this hour.'

'Very sorry, Mr Thaddeus,' said the porter inexorably. 'Folk may be friends o' yours, and yet no friends o' the master's. He pays me well to do my duty, and my duty I'll do. I don't know none o' your friends.'

'Oh, yes, you do, McMurdo,' cried Sherlock Holmes genially. 'I don't think you can have forgotten me. Don't you remember that amateur who fought three rounds with you at Alison's rooms on the night of your benefit* four years back?'

'Not Mr Sherlock Holmes!' roared the prize-fighter. 'God's truth! how could I have mistook you? If instead o' standin' there so quiet you had just stepped up and given me that cross-hit of yours under the jaw, I'd ha' known you without a question. Ah, you're one that has wasted your gifts, you have! You might have aimed high, if you had joined the fancy.'*

'You see, Watson, if all else fails me, I have still one of the scientific professions open to me,' said Holmes, laughing, 'Our friend won't keep us out in the cold now, I am sure.'

'In you come, sir, in you come—you and your friends,' he answered. 'Very sorry, Mr Thaddeus, but orders are very strict. Had to be certain of your friends before I let them in.'

Inside, a gravel path wound through desolate grounds to a huge clump of a house, square and prosaic, all plunged in shadow save where a moonbeam struck one corner and glimmered in a garret window. The vast size of the building, with its gloom and its deathly silence, struck a chill to the heart. Even Thaddeus Sholto seemed ill at ease, and the lantern quivered and rattled in his hand.

'I cannot understand it,' he said. 'There must be some mistake.

I distinctly told Bartholomew that we should be here, and yet there is no light in his window. I do not know what to make of it.'

'Does he always guard the premises in this way?' asked Holmes.

'Yes; he has followed my father's custom. He was the favourite son, you know, and I sometimes think that my father may have told him more than he ever told me. That is Bartholomew's window up there where the moonshine strikes. It is quite bright, but there is no light from within, I think.'

'None,' said Holmes. 'But I see the glint of a light in that little window beside the door.'

'Ah, that is the housekeeper's room. That is where old Mrs Bernstone sits. She can tell us all about it. But perhaps you would not mind waiting here for a minute or two, for if we all go in together, and she has had no word of our coming, she may be alarmed. But, hush! what is that?'

He held up the lantern, and his hand shook until the circles of light flickered and wavered all round us. Miss Morstan seized my wrist, and we all stood, with thumping hearts, straining our ears. From the great black house there sounded through the silent night the saddest and most pitiful of sounds—the shrill, broken whimpering of a frightened woman.

'It is Mrs Bernstone,' said Sholto. 'She is the only woman in the house. Wait here. I shall be back in a moment.'

He hurried for the door, and knocked in his peculiar way. We could see a tall old woman admit him, and sway with pleasure at the very sight of him.

'Oh, Mr Thaddeus, sir, I am so glad you have come! I am so glad you have come, Mr Thaddeus, sir!'

We heard her reiterated rejoicings until the door was closed and her voice died away into a muffled monotone.

Our guide had left us the lantern. Holmes swung it slowly round and peered keenly at the house, and at the great rubbish-heaps which cumbered the grounds. Miss Morstan and I stood together, and her hand was in mine. A wondrous subtle thing is love, for here were we two, who had never seen each other before that day, between whom no word or even look of affection had ever passed, and yet now in an hour of trouble our hands instinctively sought for each other. I have marvelled at it since, but at the time it seemed the most natural thing that I should go out to her so, and, as she has often told me, there was in her also the instinct to turn to me for comfort and protection. So we stood hand-in-hand, like two children, and there was peace in our hearts for all the dark things that surrounded us.

'What a strange place!' she said, looking round.

'It looks as though all the moles in England had been let loose in it. I have seen something of the sort on the side of a hill near Ballarat,* where the prospectors had been at work.'

'And from the same cause,' said Holmes. 'These are the traces of the treasure-seekers. You must remember that they were six years looking for it. No wonder that the grounds look like a gravel-pit.'

At that moment the door of the house burst open, and Thaddeus Sholto came running out, with his hands thrown forward and terror in his eyes.

'There is something amiss with Bartholomew!' he cried. 'I am frightened! My nerves cannot stand it.'

He was, indeed, half blubbering with fear, and his twitching, feeble face peeping out from the great Astrakhan collar had the helpless, appealing expression of a terrified child.

'Come into the house,' said Holmes in his crisp, firm way.

'Yes, do!' pleaded Thaddeus Sholto. 'I really do not feel equal to giving directions.'

We all followed him into the housekeeper's room, which stood upon the left-hand side of the passage. The old woman was pacing up and down with a scared look and restless, picking fingers, but the sight of Miss Morstan appeared to have a soothing effect upon her.

'God bless your sweet, calm face!' she cried, with an hysterical sob. 'It does me good to see you. Oh, but I have been sorely tried this day!'

Our companion patted her thin, work-worn hand, and murmured some few words of kindly, womanly comfort which brought the colour back into the other's bloodless cheeks.

'Master has locked himself in, and will not answer me,' she explained. 'All day I have waited to hear from him, for he often likes to be alone; but an hour ago I feared that something was amiss, so I went up and peeped through the keyhole. You must go up, Mr Thaddeus— you must go up and look for yourself. I have seen Mr Bartholomew Sholto in joy and in sorrow for ten long years, but I never saw him with such a face on him as that.'

Sherlock Holmes took the lamp and led the way, for Thaddeus Sholto's teeth were chattering in his head. So shaken was he that

I had to pass my hand under his arm as we went up the stairs, for his knees were trembling under him. Twice as we ascended, Holmes whipped his lens out of his pocket and carefully examined marks which appeared to me to be mere shapeless smudges of dust upon the coconut matting which served as a stair-carpet. He walked slowly from step to step, holding the lamp low, and shooting keen glances to right and left. Miss Morstan had remained behind with the frightened housekeeper.

The third flight of stairs ended in a straight passage of some length, with a great picture in Indian tapestry upon the right of it and three doors upon the left. Holmes advanced along it in the same slow and methodical way, while we kept close at his heels, with our long black shadows streaming backwards down the corridor. The third door was that which we were seeking. Holmes knocked without receiving any answer, and then tried to turn the handle and force it open. It was locked on the inside, however, and by a broad and powerful bolt, as we could see when we set our lamp up against it. The key being turned, however, the hole was not entirely closed. Sherlock Holmes bent down to it, and instantly rose again with a sharp intaking of the breath.

'There is something devilish in this, Watson,' said he, more moved than I had ever before seen him. 'What do you make of it?'

I stooped to the hole, and recoiled in horror. Moonlight was streaming into the room, and it was bright with a vague and shifty radiance. Looking straight at me, and suspended, as it were, in the air, for all beneath was in shadow, there hung a face—the very face of our companion Thaddeus. There was the same high, shining head, the same circular bristle of red hair, the same bloodless countenance. The features were set, however, in a horrible smile, a fixed and unnatural grin, which in that still and moonlit room was more jarring to the nerves than any scowl or contortion. So like was the face to that of our little friend that I looked round at him to make sure that he was indeed with us. Then I recalled to mind that he had mentioned to us that his brother and he were twins.

'This is terrible!' I said to Holmes. 'What is to be done?'

'The door must come down,' he answered, and, springing against it, he put all his weight upon the lock.

It creaked and groaned, but did not yield. Together we flung ourselves upon it once more, and this time it gave way with a sudden snap, and we found ourselves within Bartholomew Sholto's chamber.

It appeared to have been fitted up as a chemical laboratory. A double line of glass-stoppered bottles was drawn up upon the wall opposite the door, and the table was littered over with Bunsen burners, test-tubes, and retorts. In the corners stood carboys* of acid in wicker baskets. One of these appeared to leak or to have been broken, for a stream of dark-coloured liquid had trickled out from it, and the air was heavy with a peculiarly pungent, tar-like odour. A set of steps stood at one side of the room, in the midst of a litter of lath* and plaster, and above them there was an opening in the ceiling large enough for a man to pass through. At the foot of the steps a long coil of rope was thrown carelessly together.

By the table, in a wooden armchair, the master of the house was seated all in a heap, with his head sunk upon his left shoulder, and that ghastly, inscrutable smile upon his face. He was stiff and cold, and had clearly been dead many hours. It seemed to me that not only his features, but all his limbs, were twisted and turned in the most fantastic fashion. By his hand upon the table there lay a peculiar instrument—a brown, close-grained stick, with a stone head like a hammer, rudely lashed on with coarse twine. Beside it was a torn sheet of note-paper with some words scrawled upon it. Holmes glanced at it, and then handed it to me.

'You see,' he said, with a significant raising of the eyebrows.

In the light of the lantern I read, with a thrill of horror, 'The sign of the four.'

'In God's name, what does it all mean?' I asked.

'It means murder,' said he, stooping over the dead man. 'Ah! I expected it. Look here!'

He pointed to what looked like a long dark thorn stuck in the skin just above the ear.

'It looks like a thorn,' said I.

'It is a thorn. You may pick it out. But be careful, for it is poisoned.'

I took it up between my finger and thumb. It came away from the skin so readily that hardly any mark was left behind. One tiny speck of blood showed where the puncture had been.

'This is all an insoluble mystery to me,' said I. 'It grows darker instead of clearer.'

'On the contrary,' he answered, 'it clears every instant. I only require a few missing links to have an entirely connected case.'

We had almost forgotten our companion's presence since we

entered the chamber. He was still standing in the doorway, the very picture of terror, wringing his hands and moaning to himself. Suddenly, however, he broke out into a sharp, querulous cry.

'The treasure is gone!' he said. 'They have robbed him of the treasure! There is the hole through which we lowered it. I helped him to do it! I was the last person who saw him! I left him here last night, and I heard him lock the door as I came downstairs.'

'What time was that?'

'It was ten o'clock. And now he is dead, and the police will be called in, and I shall be suspected of having had a hand in it. Oh yes, I am sure I shall. But you don't think so, gentlemen? Surely you don't think that it was I? Is it likely that I would have brought you here if it were I? Oh dear! oh dear! I know that I shall go mad!'

He jerked his arms and stamped his feet in a kind of convulsive frenzy.

'You have no reason for fear, Mr Sholto,' said Holmes kindly, putting his hand upon his shoulder; 'take my advice, and drive down to the station to report the matter to the police. Offer to assist them in every way. We shall wait here until your return.'

The little man obeyed in a half-stupefied fashion, and we heard him stumbling down the stairs in the dark.

CHAPTER 6

SHERLOCK HOLMES GIVES A DEMONSTRATION

'Now, Watson,' said Holmes, rubbing his hands, 'we have half an hour to ourselves. Let us make good use of it. My case is, as I have told you, almost complete; but we must not err on the side of overconfidence. Simple as the case seems now, there may be something deeper underlying it.'

'Simple!' I ejaculated.

'Surely,' said he, with something of the air of a clinical professor expounding to his class. 'Just sit in the corner there, that your footprints may not complicate matters. Now to work! In the first place, how did these folk come, and how did they go? The door has not been opened since last night. How of the window?' He carried the lamp across to it, muttering his observations aloud the while but addressing them to himself rather than to me. 'Window is snibbed* on the inner

side. Frame-work is solid. No hinges at the side. Let us open it. No
water-pipe near. Roof quite out of reach. Yet a man has mounted by
the window. It rained a little last night. Here is the print of a foot in
mould upon the sill. And here is a circular muddy mark, and here
again upon the floor, and here again by the table. See here, Watson!
This is really a very pretty demonstration.'

I looked at the round, well-defined muddy discs.

'That is not a foot-mark,' said I.

'It is something much more valuable to us. It is the impression of
a wooden stump. You see here on the sill is the boot-mark, a heavy boot
with a broad metal heel, and beside it is the mark of the timber-toe.'

'It is the wooden-legged man.'

'Quite so. But there has been someone else—a very able and efficient ally. Could you scale that wall, doctor?'

I looked out of the open window. The moon still shone brightly on
that angle of the house. We were a good sixty feet from the ground,
and, look where I could, I could see no foothold, nor as much as
a crevice in the brickwork.

'It is absolutely impossible,' I answered.

'Without aid it is so. But suppose you had a friend up here who
lowered you this good stout rope which I see in the corner, securing
one end of it to this great hook in the wall. Then, I think, if you were
an active man, you might swarm up, wooden leg and all. You would
depart, of course, in the same fashion, and your ally would draw up the
rope, untie it from the hook, shut the window, snib it on the inside, and
get away in the way that he originally came. As a minor point, it may
be noted,' he continued, fingering the rope, 'that our wooden-legged
friend, though a fair climber, was not a professional sailor. His hands
were far from horny. My lens discloses more than one blood-mark,
especially towards the end of the rope, from which I gather that he
slipped down with such velocity that he took the skin off his hand.'

'This is all very well,' said I; 'but the thing becomes more unintel-
ligible than ever. How about this mysterious ally? How came he into
the room?'

'Yes, the ally!' repeated Holmes pensively. 'There are features of
interest about this ally. He lifts the case from the regions of the commonplace. I fancy that this ally breaks fresh ground in the annals of
crime in this country—though parallel cases suggest themselves from
India and, if my memory serves me, from Senegambia.'*

'How came he, then?' I reiterated. 'The door is locked; the window is inaccessible. Was it through the chimney?'

'The grate is much too small,' he answered. 'I had already considered that possibility.'

'How, then?' I persisted.

'You will not apply my precept,' he said, shaking his head. 'How often have I said to you that when you have eliminated the impossible, whatever remains, *however improbable*, must be the truth? We know that he did not come through the door, the window, or the chimney. We also know that he could not have been concealed in the room, as there is no concealment possible. Whence, then, did he come?'

'He came through the hole in the roof!' I cried.

'Of course he did. He must have done so. If you will have the kindness to hold the lamp for me, we shall now extend our researches to the room above—the secret room in which the treasure was found.'

He mounted the steps, and, seizing a rafter with either hand, he swung himself up into the garret. Then, lying on his face, he reached down for the lamp, and held it while I followed him.

The chamber in which we found ourselves was about ten feet one way and six the other. The floor was formed by the rafters, with thin lath-and-plaster between, so that in walking one had to step from beam to beam. The roof ran up to an apex, and was evidently the inner shell of the true roof of the house. There was no furniture of any sort, and the accumulated dust of years lay thick upon the floor.

'Here you are, you see,' said Sherlock Holmes, putting his hand against the sloping wall. 'This is a trapdoor which leads out on to the roof. I can press it back, and here is the roof itself, sloping at a gentle angle. This, then, is the way by which Number One entered. Let us see if we can find some other traces of his individuality?'

He held down the lamp to the floor, and as he did so I saw for the second time that night a startled, surprised look come over his face. For myself, as I followed his gaze, my skin was cold under my clothes. The floor was covered thickly with the prints of a naked foot—clear, well-defined, perfectly formed, but scarce half the size of those of an ordinary man.

'Holmes,' I said, in a whisper, 'a child has done this horrid thing.'

He had recovered his self-possession in an instant.

'I was staggered for the moment,' he said, 'but the thing is quite natural. My memory failed me, or I should have been able to foretell it. There is nothing more to be learned here. Let us go down.'

'What is your theory, then, as to those foot-marks?' I asked eagerly, when we had regained the lower room once more.

'My dear Watson, try a little analysis yourself,' said he, with a touch of impatience. 'You know my methods. Apply them, and it will be instructive to compare results.'

'I cannot conceive anything which will cover the facts,' I answered.

'It will be clear enough to you soon,' he said, in an off-hand way. 'I think that there is nothing else of importance here, but I will look.'

He whipped out his lens and a tape measure, and hurried about the room on his knees, measuring, comparing, examining, with his long thin nose only a few inches from the planks and his beady eyes gleaming and deep-set like those of a bird. So swift, silent, and furtive were his movements, like those of a trained bloodhound picking out a scent, that I could not but think what a terrible criminal he would have made had he turned his energy and sagacity against the law, instead of exerting them in its defence. As he hunted about, he kept muttering to himself, and finally he broke out into a loud crow of delight.

'We are certainly in luck,' said he. 'We ought to have very little trouble now. Number One has had the misfortune to tread in the creosote.* You can see the outline of the edge of his small foot here at the side of this evil-smelling mess. The carboy has been cracked, you see, and the stuff has leaked out.'

'What then?' I asked.

'Why, we have got him, that's all,' said he. 'I know a dog that would follow that scent to the world's end. If a pack can track a trailed herring across a shire, how far can a specially trained hound follow so pungent a smell as this? It sounds like a sum in the rule of three.* The answer should give us the—But hallo! here are the accredited representatives of the law.'

Heavy steps and the clamour of loud voices were audible from below, and the hall door shut with a loud crash.

'Before they come,' said Holmes, 'just put your hand here on this poor fellow's arm, and here on his leg. What do you feel?'

'The muscles are as hard as a board,' I answered.

'Quite so. They are in a state of extreme contraction, far exceeding the usual *rigor mortis*.* Coupled with this distortion of the face, this

Hippocratic smile, or "*risus sardonicus*",* as the old writers called it, what conclusion would it suggest to your mind?'

'Death from some powerful vegetable alkaloid,' I answered, 'some strychnine-like substance which would produce tetanus.'

'That was the idea which occurred to me the instant I saw the drawn muscles of the face. On getting into the room I at once looked for the means by which the poison had entered the system. As you saw, I discovered a thorn which had been driven or shot with no great force into the scalp. You observe that the part struck was that which would be turned towards the hole in the ceiling if the man were erect in his chair. Now examine this thorn.'

I took it up gingerly and held it in the light of the lantern. It was long, sharp, and black, with a glazed look near the point as though some gummy substance had dried upon it. The blunt end had been trimmed and rounded off with a knife.

'Is that an English thorn?' he asked.

'No, it certainly is not.'

'With all these data you should be able to draw some just inference. But here are the regulars: so the auxiliary forces may beat a retreat.'

As he spoke, the steps which had been coming nearer sounded loudly on the passage, and a very stout, portly man in a grey suit strode heavily into the room. He was red-faced, burly, and plethoric, with a pair of very small twinkling eyes which looked keenly out from between swollen and puffy pouches. He was closely followed by an inspector in uniform and by the still palpitating Thaddeus Sholto.

'Here's a business!' he cried in a muffled, husky voice. 'Here's a pretty business! But who are all these? Why, the house seems to be as full as a rabbit-warren!'

'I think you must recollect me, Mr Athelney Jones,' said Holmes quietly.

'Why, of course I do!' he wheezed. 'It's Mr Sherlock Holmes, the theorist. Remember you! I'll never forget how you lectured us all on causes and inferences and effects in the Bishopgate jewel case. It's true you set us on the right track; but you'll own now that it was more by good luck than good guidance.'

'It was a piece of very simple reasoning.'

'Oh, come, now, come! Never be ashamed to own up. But what is all this? Bad business! Bad business! Stern facts here—no room for theories. How lucky that I happened to be out at Norwood over another case! I was at the station when the message arrived. What d'you think the man died of?'

'Oh, this is hardly a case for me to theorize over,' said Holmes dryly.

'No, no. Still, we can't deny that you hit the nail on the head sometimes. Dear me! Door locked, I understand. Jewels worth half a million missing. How was the window?'

'Fastened; but there are steps on the sill.'

'Well, well, if it was fastened the steps could have nothing to do with the matter. That's common-sense. Man might have died in a fit; but then the jewels are missing. Ha! I have a theory. These flashes come upon me at times.—Just step outside, Sergeant, and you, Mr Sholto. Your friend can remain.—What do you think of this, Holmes? Sholto was, on his own confession, with his brother last night. The brother died in a fit, on which Sholto walked off with the treasure? How's that?'

'On which the dead man very considerately got up and locked the door on the inside.'

'Hum! There's a flaw there. Let us apply common-sense to the matter. This Thaddeus Sholto *was* with his brother; there *was* a quarrel: so much we know. The brother is dead and the jewels are gone. So much also we know. No one saw the brother from the time Thaddeus left him. His bed had not been slept in. Thaddeus is evidently in a most disturbed state of mind. His appearance is—well, not attractive. You see that I am weaving my web round Thaddeus. The net begins to close upon him.'

'You are not quite in possession of the facts yet,' said Holmes. 'This splinter of wood, which I have every reason to believe to be poisoned, was in the man's scalp where you still see the mark; this card, inscribed as you see it, was on the table, and beside it lay this rather curious stone-headed instrument. How does all that fit into your theory?'

'Confirms it in every respect,' said the fat detective, pompously. 'House is full of Indian curiosities. Thaddeus brought this up, and if this splinter be poisonous, Thaddeus may as well have made murderous use of it as any other man. The card is some hocus-pocus—a blind, as like as not. The only question is, how did he depart? Ah, of course, here is a hole in the roof.'

With great activity, considering his bulk, he sprang up the steps and squeezed through into the garret, and immediately afterwards we heard his exulting voice proclaiming that he had found the trapdoor.

'He can find something,' remarked Holmes, shrugging his shoulders; 'he has occasional glimmerings of reason. *Il n'y a pas des sots si incommodes que ceux qui ont de l'esprit!**

'You see!' said Athelney Jones, reappearing down the steps again; 'facts are better than theories, after all. My view of the case is confirmed. There is a trapdoor communicating with the roof, and it is partly open.'

'It was I who opened it.'

'Oh, indeed! You did notice it, then?' He seemed a little crestfallen at the discovery. 'Well, whoever noticed it, it shows how our gentleman got away. Inspector!'

'Yes, sir,' from the passage.

'Ask Mr Sholto to step this way.—Mr Sholto, it is my duty to inform you that anything which you may say will be used against you. I arrest you in the Queen's name as being concerned in the death of your brother.'

'There, now! Didn't I tell you!' cried the poor little man, throwing out his hands, and looking from one to the other of us.

'Don't trouble yourself about it, Mr Sholto,' said Holmes; 'I think that I can engage to clear you of the charge.'

'Don't promise too much, Mr Theorist, don't promise too much!' snapped the detective. 'You may find it a harder matter than you think.'

'Not only will I clear him, Mr Jones, but I will make you a free present of the name and description of one of the two people who were in this room last night. His name, I have every reason to believe, is Jonathan Small. He is a poorly-educated man, small, active, with his right leg off, and wearing a wooden stump which is worn away upon the inner side. His left boot has a coarse, square-toed sole, with an iron band round the heel. He is a middle-aged man, much sunburned, and has been a convict. These few indications may be of some assistance to you, coupled with the fact that there is a good deal of skin missing from the palm of his hand. The other man—'

'Ah! the other man?' asked Athelney Jones in a sneering voice, but impressed none the less, as I could easily see, by the precision of the other's manner.

'Is a rather curious person,' said Sherlock Holmes, turning upon his heel. 'I hope before very long to be able to introduce you to the pair of them. A word with you, Watson.'

He led me out to the head of the stair.

'This unexpected occurrence', he said, 'has caused us rather to lose sight of the original purpose of our journey.'

'I have just been thinking so,' I answered; 'it is not right that Miss Morstan should remain in this stricken house.'

'No. You must escort her home. She lives with Mrs Cecil Forrester in Lower Camberwell, so it is not very far. I will wait for you here if you will drive out again. Or perhaps you are too tired?'

'By no means. I don't think I could rest until I know more of this fantastic business. I have seen something of the rough side of life, but I give you my word that this quick succession of strange surprises to-night has shaken my nerve completely. I should like, however, to see the matter through with you, now that I have got so far.'

'Your presence will be of great service to me,' he answered. 'We shall work the case out independently and leave this fellow Jones to exult over any mare's-nest* which he may choose to construct. When you have dropped Miss Morstan, I wish you to go on to No. 3, Pinchin Lane, down near the water's edge at Lambeth. The third house on the right-hand side is a bird-stuffer's; Sherman is the name. You will see a weasel holding a young rabbit in the window. Knock old Sherman up, and tell him, with my compliments, that I want Toby* at once. You will bring Toby back in the cab with you.'

'A dog, I suppose.'

'Yes, a queer mongrel, with a most amazing power of scent. I would rather have Toby's help than that of the whole detective force of London.'

'I shall bring him then,' said I. 'It is one now. I ought to be back before three, if I can get a fresh horse.'

'And I', said Holmes, 'shall see what I can learn from Mrs Bernstone and from the Indian servant, who, Mr Thaddeus tells me, sleeps in the next garret. Then I shall study the great Jones's methods and listen to his not too delicate sarcasms. *"Wir sind gewohnt dass die Menschen verhöhnen was sie nicht verstehen."** Goethe is always pithy.'

CHAPTER 7

THE EPISODE OF THE BARREL

THE police had brought a cab with them, and in this I escorted Miss Morstan back to her home. After the angelic fashion of women, she had borne trouble with a calm face as long as there was someone weaker than herself to support, and I had found her bright and placid by the side of the frightened housekeeper. In the cab, however, she first turned faint, and then burst into a passion of weeping—so sorely had she been tried by the adventures of the night. She has told me since that she thought me cold and distant upon that journey. She little guessed the struggle within my breast, or the effort of self-restraint which held me back. My sympathies and my love went out to her, even as my hand had in the garden. I felt that years of the conventionalities of life could not teach me to know her sweet, brave nature as had this one day of strange experiences. Yet there were two thoughts which sealed the words of affection upon my lips. She was weak and helpless, shaken in mind and nerve. It was to take her at a disadvantage to obtrude love upon her at such a time. Worse still, she was rich. If Holmes's researches were successful, she would be an heiress. Was it fair, was it honourable, that a half-pay surgeon* should take such advantage of an intimacy which chance had brought about? Might she not look upon me as a mere vulgar fortune-seeker? I could not bear to risk that such a thought should cross her mind. This Agra treasure intervened like an impassable barrier between us.

It was nearly two o'clock when we reached Mrs Cecil Forrester's. The servants had retired hours ago, but Mrs Forrester had been so interested by the strange message which Miss Morstan had received that she had sat up in the hope of her return. She opened the door herself, a middle-aged, graceful woman, and it gave me joy to see how tenderly her arm stole round the other's waist, and how motherly was the voice in which she greeted her. She was clearly no mere paid dependant, but an honoured friend. I was introduced, and Mrs Forrester earnestly begged me to step in and tell her our adventures. I explained, however, the importance of my errand, and promised faithfully to call and report any progress which we might make with the case. As we drove away I stole a glance back, and I still seem to see that little group on the step—the two graceful, clinging figures, the half-opened door, the hall-light shining through stained glass, the barometer, and the bright stair-rods.* It was soothing to catch even that passing glimpse of a tranquil English home in the midst of the wild, dark business which had absorbed us.

And the more I thought of what had happened, the wilder and darker it grew. I reviewed the whole extraordinary sequence of events as I rattled on through the silent, gas-lit streets. There was the original problem: that at least was pretty clear now. The death of Captain Morstan, the sending of the pearls, the advertisement, the letter—we had had light upon all those events. They had only led us, however, to a deeper and far more tragic mystery. The Indian treasure, the curious plan found among Morstan's baggage, the strange scene at Major Sholto's death, the rediscovery of the treasure immediately followed by the murder of the discoverer, the very singular accompaniments to the crime, the footsteps, the remarkable weapons, the words upon the card, corresponding with those upon Captain Morstan's chart—here was indeed a labyrinth in which a man less singularly endowed than my fellow-lodger might well despair of ever finding the clue.

Pinchin Lane was a row of shabby, two-storied brick houses in the lower quarter of Lambeth. I had to knock for some time at No. 3 before I could make any impression. At last, however, there was the glint of a candle behind the blind, and a face looked out at the upper window.

'Go on, you drunken vagabone,'* said the face. 'If you kick up any more row, I'll open the kennels and let out forty-three dogs upon you.'

'If you'll let one out, it's just what I have come for,' said I.

'Go on!' yelled the voice. 'So help me gracious, I have a wiper* in this bag, an' I'll drop it on your 'ead if you don't hook it!'*

'But I want a dog,' I cried.

'I won't be argued with!' shouted Mr Sherman. 'Now stand clear; for when I say "three", down goes the wiper.'

'Mr Sherlock Holmes—' I began; but the words had a most magical effect, for the window instantly slammed down, and within a minute the door was unbarred and open. Mr Sherman was a lanky, lean old man, with stooping shoulders, a stringy neck, and blue-tinted glasses.

'A friend of Mr Sherlock is always welcome,' said he. 'Step in, sir. Keep clear of the badger, for he bites. Ah, naughty, naughty! would you take a nip at the gentleman?' This to a stoat which thrust its wicked head and red eyes between the bars of its cage. 'Don't mind that, sir; it's only a slowworm.* It hain't got no fangs, so I gives it the run o' the room, for it keeps the beetles down. You must not mind my bein' just a little short wi' you at first, for I'm guyed at* by the children, and there's many a one just comes down this lane to knock me up. What was it that Mr Sherlock Holmes wanted, sir?'

'He wanted a dog of yours.'

'Ah! that would be Toby.'

'Yes, Toby was the name.'

'Toby lives at No. 7 on the left here.'

He moved slowly forward with his candle among the queer animal family which he had gathered round him. In the uncertain, shadowy light I could see dimly that there were glancing, glimmering eyes peeping down at us from every cranny and corner. Even the rafters above our heads were lined by solemn fowls, who lazily shifted their weight from one leg to the other as our voices disturbed their slumbers.

Toby proved to be an ugly, long-haired, lop-eared creature, half spaniel and half lurcher,* brown and white in colour, with a very clumsy, waddling gait. It accepted, after some hesitation, a lump of sugar which the old naturalist handed to me, and, having thus sealed an alliance, it followed me to the cab, and made no difficulties about accompanying me. It had just struck three on the Palace clock when I found myself back once more at Pondicherry Lodge. The ex-prize-fighter McMurdo had, I found, been arrested as an accessory, and both he and Mr Sholto had been marched off to the station. Two constables guarded the narrow gate, but they allowed me to pass with the dog on my mentioning the detective's name.

Holmes was standing on the doorstep with his hands in his pockets, smoking his pipe.

'Ah, you have him there!' said he. 'Good dog, then! Athelney Jones has gone. We have had an immense display of energy since you left. He has arrested not only friend Thaddeus but the gatekeeper, the housekeeper, and the Indian servant. We have the place to ourselves but for a sergeant upstairs. Leave the dog here, and come up.'

We tied Toby to the hall table, and reascended the stairs. The room was as we had left it, save that a sheet had been draped over the central figure. A weary-looking police-sergeant reclined in the corner.

'Lend me your bull's-eye,* sergeant,' said my companion. 'Now tie this bit of cord round my neck, so as to hang it in front of me. Thank you. Now I must kick off my boots and stockings. Just you carry them down with you, Watson. I am going to do a little climbing. And dip my handkerchief into the creosote. That will do. Now come up into the garret with me for a moment.'

We clambered up through the hole. Holmes turned his light once more upon the footsteps in the dust.

'I wish you particularly to notice these foot-marks,' he said. 'Do you observe anything noteworthy about them?'

'They belong,' I said, 'to a child or a small woman.'

'Apart from their size, though. Is there nothing else?'

'They appear to be much as other foot-marks.'

'Not at all. Look here! This is the print of a right foot in the dust. Now I make one with my naked foot beside it. What is the chief difference?'

'Your toes are all cramped together. The other print has each toe distinctly divided.'

'Quite so. That is the point. Bear that in mind. Now, would you kindly step over to that flap-window and smell the edge of the wood-work? I shall stay over here, as I have this handkerchief in my hand.'

I did as he directed, and was instantly conscious of a strong tarry smell.

'That is where he put his foot in getting out. If *you* can trace him, I should think that Toby will have no difficulty. Now run downstairs, loose the dog, and look out for Blondin.'*

By the time that I got out into the grounds Sherlock Holmes was on the roof, and I could see him like an enormous glow-worm crawling very slowly along the ridge. I lost sight of him behind a stack of chimneys, but he presently reappeared and then vanished once more upon the opposite side. When I made my way round there I found him seated at one of the corner eaves.

'That you, Watson?' he cried.

'Yes.'

'This is the place. What is that black thing down there?'

'A water-barrel.'

'Top on it?'

'Yes.'

'No sign of a ladder?'

'No.'

'Confound the fellow! It's a most breakneck place. I ought to be able to come down where he could climb up. The water-pipe feels pretty firm. Here goes, anyhow.'

There was a scuffling of feet, and the lantern began to come steadily down the side of the wall. Then with a light spring he came on to the barrel, and from there to the earth.

'It was easy to follow him,' he said, drawing on his stockings and boots. 'Tiles were loosened the whole way along, and in his hurry he had dropped this. It confirms my diagnosis, as you doctors express it.'

The object which he held up to me was a small pocket* or pouch woven out of coloured grasses and with a few tawdry beads strung round it. In shape and size it was not unlike a cigarette-case. Inside were half a dozen spines of dark wood, sharp at one end and rounded at the other, like that which had struck Bartholomew Sholto.

'They are hellish things,' said he. 'Look out that you don't prick yourself. I'm delighted to have them, for the chances are that they are all he has. There is the less fear of you or me finding one in our skin before long. I would sooner face a Martini bullet,* myself. Are you game for a six-mile trudge, Watson?'

'Certainly,' I answered.

'Your leg will stand it?'

'Oh, yes.'

'Here you are, doggy! Good old Toby! Smell it, Toby, smell it!' He pushed the creosote handkerchief under the dog's nose, while the creature stood with its fluffy legs separated, and with a most comical cock to its head, like a connoisseur sniffing the *bouquet* of a famous vintage. Holmes then threw the handkerchief to a distance, fastened a stout cord to the mongrel's collar, and led him to the foot of the water-barrel. The creature instantly broke into a succession of high, tremulous yelps, and, with his nose on the ground, and his tail in the air, pattered off upon the trail at a pace which strained his leash and kept us at the top of our speed.

The east had been gradually whitening, and we could now see some distance in the cold gray light. The square, massive house, with its black, empty windows and high, bare walls, towered up, sad and forlorn, behind us. Our course led right across the grounds, in and out among the trenches and pits with which they were scarred and intersected. The whole place, with its scattered dirt-heaps and ill-grown shrubs, had a blighted, ill-omened look which harmonized with the black tragedy which hung over it.

On reaching the boundary wall Toby ran along, whining eagerly, underneath its shadow, and stopped finally in a corner screened by a young beech. Where the two walls joined, several bricks had been loosened, and the crevices left were worn down and rounded upon the lower side, as though they had frequently been used as a ladder. Holmes clambered up, and, taking the dog from me, he dropped it over upon the other side.

'There's the print of wooden-leg's hand,' he remarked, as I mounted up beside him. 'You see the slight smudge of blood upon the white plaster. What a lucky thing it is that we have had no very heavy rain since yesterday! The scent will lie upon the road in spite of their eight-and-twenty hours' start.'

I confess that I had my doubts myself when I reflected upon the great traffic which had passed along the London road in the interval. My fears were soon appeased, however. Toby never hesitated or swerved, but waddled on in his peculiar rolling fashion. Clearly, the pungent smell of the creosote rose high above all other contending scents.

'Do not imagine,' said Holmes, 'that I depend for my success in this case upon the mere chance of one of these fellows having put his foot in the chemical. I have knowledge now which would enable me to trace them in many different ways. This, however, is the readiest, and, since fortune has put it into our hands, I should be culpable if I neglected it. It has, however, prevented the case from becoming the pretty little intellectual problem which it at one time promised to be. There might have been some credit to be gained out of it, but for this too palpable clue.'

'There is credit, and to spare,' said I. 'I assure you, Holmes, that I marvel at the means by which you obtain your results in this case even more than I did in the Jefferson Hope murder. The thing seems to me to be deeper and more inexplicable. How, for example, could you describe with such confidence the wooden-legged man?'

'Pshaw, my dear boy! it was simplicity itself. I don't wish to be theatrical. It is all patent and above-board. Two officers who are in command of a convict-guard learn an important secret as to buried treasure. A map is drawn for them by an Englishman named Jonathan Small. You remember that we saw the name upon the chart in Captain

Morstan's possession. He had signed it in behalf of himself and his associates—the sign of the four, as he somewhat dramatically called it. Aided by this chart, the officers—or one of them—gets the treasure and brings it to England, leaving, we will suppose, some condition under which he received it unfulfilled. Now, then, why did not Jonathan Small get the treasure himself? The answer is obvious. The chart is dated at a time when Morstan was brought into close association with convicts. Jonathan Small did not get the treasure because he and his associates were themselves convicts and could not get away.'

'But this is mere speculation,' said I.

'It is more than that. It is the only hypothesis which covers the facts. Let us see how it fits in with the sequel. Major Sholto remains at peace for some years, happy in the possession of his treasure. Then he receives a letter from India which gives him a great fright. What was that?'

'A letter to say that the men whom he had wronged had been set free.'

'Or had escaped. That is much more likely, for he would have known what their term of imprisonment was. It would not have been a surprise to him. What does he do then? He guards himself against a wooden-legged man—a white man, mark you, for he mistakes a white tradesman for him, and actually fires a pistol at him. Now, only one white man's name is on the chart. The others are Hindoos or Mohammedans. There is no other white man. Therefore we may say with confidence that the wooden-legged man is identical with Jonathan Small. Does the reasoning strike you as being faulty?'

'No: it is clear and concise.'

'Well, now, let us put ourselves in the place of Jonathan Small. Let us look at it from his point of view. He comes to England with the double idea of regaining what he would consider to be his rights and of having his revenge upon the man who had wronged him. He found out where Sholto lived, and very possibly he established communications with someone inside the house. There is this butler, Lal Rao, whom we have not seen. Mrs Bernstone gives him far from a good character. Small could not find out, however, where the treasure was hid, for no one ever knew, save the major and one faithful servant who had died. Suddenly Small learns that the major is on his death-bed. In a frenzy lest the secret of the treasure die with him, he runs the gauntlet of the guards, makes his way to the dying man's window, and is only deterred from entering by the presence of his two sons. Mad with hate, however, against the dead man, he enters the room that night, searches his private papers in the hope of discovering some memorandum relating to the treasure, and finally leaves a memento of his visit in the short inscription upon the card. He had doubtless planned beforehand that, should he slay the major, he would leave some such record upon the body as a sign that it was not a common murder, but, from the point of view of the four associates, something in the nature of an act of justice. Whimsical and bizarre conceits of this kind are common enough in the annals of crime, and usually afford valuable indications as to the criminal. Do you follow all this?'

'Very clearly.'

'Now, what could Jonathan Small do? He could only continue to keep a secret watch upon the efforts made to find the treasure. Possibly he leaves England and only comes back at intervals. Then comes the discovery of the garret, and he is instantly informed of it. We again trace the presence of some confederate in the household. Jonathan, with his wooden leg, is utterly unable to reach the lofty room of Bartholomew Sholto. He takes with him, however, a rather curious associate, who gets over this difficulty, but dips his naked foot into creosote, whence come Toby, and a six-mile limp for a half-pay officer with a damaged *tendo Achillis*.'*

'But it was the associate, and not Jonathan, who committed the crime.'

'Quite so. And rather to Jonathan's disgust, to judge by the way he stamped about when he got into the room. He bore no grudge against Bartholomew Sholto, and would have preferred if he could have been simply bound and gagged. He did not wish to put his head in a halter. There was no help for it, however: the savage instincts of his companion had broken out, and the poison had done its work: so Jonathan Small left his record, lowered the treasure-box to the ground, and followed it himself. That was the train of events as far as I can decipher them. Of course, as to his personal appearance, he must be middle-aged and must be sunburned after serving his time in such an oven as the Andamans. His height is readily calculated from the length of his stride, and we know that he was bearded. His hairiness was the one point which impressed itself upon Thaddeus Sholto when he saw him at the window, I don't know that there is anything else.'

'The associate?'

'Ah, well, there is no great mystery in that. But you will know all about it soon enough. How sweet the morning air is! See how that one little cloud floats like a pink feather from some gigantic flamingo. Now the red rim of the sun pushes itself over the London cloud-bank. It shines on a good many folk, but on none, I dare bet, who are on a stranger errand than you and I. How small we feel with our petty ambitions and strivings in the presence of the great elemental forces of Nature! Are you well up in your Jean Paul?'*

'Fairly so. I worked back to him through Carlyle.'*

'That was like following the brook to the parent lake. He makes one curious but profound remark. It is that the chief proof of man's real greatness lies in his perception of his own smallness. It argues, you see, a power of comparison and of appreciation which is in itself a proof of nobility. There is much food for thought in Richter. You have not a pistol, have you?'

'I have my stick.'

'It is just possible that we may need something of the sort if we get to their lair. Jonathan I shall leave to you, but if the other turns nasty I shall shoot him dead.'

He took out his revolver as he spoke, and, having loaded two of the chambers, he put it back into the right-hand pocket of his jacket.

We had during this time been following the guidance of Toby down the half-rural villa-lined roads which lead to the metropolis. Now, however, we were beginning to come among continuous streets, where labourers and dockmen were already astir, and slatternly women were taking down shutters and brushing door-steps. At the square-topped corner public-houses business was just beginning, and rough-looking men were emerging, rubbing their sleeves across their beards after their morning wet. Strange dogs sauntered up and stared wonderingly at us as we passed, but our inimitable Toby looked neither to the right nor to the left, but trotted onward with his nose to the ground and an occasional eager whine which spoke of a hot scent.

We had traversed Streatham, Brixton, Camberwell, and now found ourselves in Kennington Lane, having borne away through the side streets to the east of the Oval. The men whom we pursued seemed to have taken a curiously zigzag road, with the idea probably of escaping observation. They had never kept to the main road if a parallel side-street would serve their turn. At the foot of Kennington Lane they had edged away to the left through Bond Street and Miles Street.

Where the latter street turns into Knight's Place, Toby ceased to
advance but began to run backward and forward with one ear cocked
and the other drooping, the very picture of canine indecision. Then
he waddled round in circles, looking up to us from time to time, as if
to ask for sympathy in his embarrassment.

'What the deuce is the matter with the dog?' growled Holmes.
'They surely would not take a cab, or go off in a balloon.'

'Perhaps they stood here for some time,' I suggested.

'Ah! it's all right. He's off again,' said my companion, in a tone of
relief.

He was indeed off, for after sniffing round again he suddenly made
up his mind, and darted away with an energy and determination
such as he had not yet shown. The scent appeared to be much hotter
than before, for he had not even to put his nose on the ground, but
tugged at his leash and tried to break into a run. I could see by the
gleam in Holmes's eyes that he thought we were nearing the end of
our journey.

Our course now ran down Nine Elms until we came to Broderick
and Nelson's large timber-yard, just past the White Eagle tavern.
Here the dog, frantic with excitement, turned down through the side
gate into the enclosure, where the sawyers were already at work. On
the dog raced through sawdust and shavings, down an alley, round
a passage, between two wood-piles, and finally, with a triumphant
yelp, sprang upon a large barrel which still stood upon the hand-
trolley on which it had been brought. With lolling tongue and blinking eyes, Toby stood upon the cask, looking from one to the other
of us for some sign of appreciation. The staves of the barrel and the
wheels of the trolley were smeared with a dark liquid, and the whole
air was heavy with the smell of creosote.

Sherlock Holmes and I looked blankly at each other, and then
burst simultaneously into an uncontrollable fit of laughter.

CHAPTER 8

THE BAKER STREET IRREGULARS

'WHAT now?' I asked. 'Toby has lost his character for infallibility.'

'He acted according to his lights,' said Holmes, lifting him down
from the barrel and walking him out of the timber-yard. 'If you

consider how much creosote is carted about London in one day, it is
no great wonder that our trail should have been crossed. It is much
used now, especially for the seasoning of wood. Poor Toby is not to
blame.'

'We must get on the main scent again, I suppose.'

'Yes. And, fortunately, we have no distance to go. Evidently what
puzzled the dog at the corner of Knight's Place was that there were
two different trails running in opposite directions. We took the wrong
one. It only remains to follow the other.'

There was no difficulty about this. On leading Toby to the place
where he had committed his fault, he cast about in a wide circle and
finally dashed off in a fresh direction.

'We must take care that he does not now bring us to the place where
the creosote-barrel came from,' I observed.

'I had thought of that. But you notice that he keeps on the pavement, whereas the barrel passed down the roadway. No, we are on the
true scent now.'

It tended down towards the river-side, running through Belmont
Place and Prince's Street. At the end of Broad Street it ran right down
to the water's edge, where there was a small wooden wharf. Toby led
us to the very edge of this, and there stood whining, looking out on
the dark current beyond.

'We are out of luck,' said Holmes. 'They have taken to a boat here.'

Several small punts* and skiffs* were lying about in the water and
on the edge of the wharf. We took Toby round to each in turn, but,
though he sniffed earnestly, he made no sign.

Close to the rude landing-stage was a small brick house, with
a wooden placard slung out through the second window. 'Mordecai
Smith' was printed across it in large letters, and, underneath, 'Boats
to hire by the hour or day'. A second inscription above the door
informed us that a steam launch was kept—a statement which was
confirmed by a great pile of coke* upon the jetty. Sherlock Holmes
looked slowly round, and his face assumed an ominous expression.

'This looks bad,' said he. 'These fellows are sharper than I
expected. They seem to have covered their tracks. There has, I fear,
been preconcerted management here.'

He was approaching the door of the house, when it opened, and
a little curly-headed lad of six came running out, followed by a stout-
ish, red-faced woman with a large sponge in her hand.

'You come back and be washed, Jack,' she shouted. 'Come back, you young imp; for if your father comes home and finds you like that, he'll let us hear of it.'

'Dear little chap!' said Holmes strategically. 'What a rosy-cheeked young rascal! Now, Jack, is there anything you would like?'

The youth pondered for a moment.

'I'd like a shillin',' said he.

'Nothing you would like better?'

'I'd like two shillin' better,' the prodigy answered, after some thought.

'Here you are, then! Catch!—A fine child, Mrs Smith!'

'Lor' bless you, sir, he is that, and forward. He gets a'most too much for me to manage, 'specially when my man is away days at a time.'

'Away, is he?' said Holmes, in a disappointed voice. 'I am sorry for that, for I wanted to speak to Mr Smith.'

'He's been away since yesterday mornin', sir, and, truth to tell, I am beginnin' to feel frightened about him. But if it was about a boat, sir, maybe I could serve as well.'

'I wanted to hire his steam launch.'

'Why, bless you, sir, it is in the steam launch that he has gone. That's what puzzles me; for I know there ain't more coals in her than would take her to about Woolwich and back. If he'd been away in the barge I'd ha' thought nothin'; for many a time a job has taken him as far as Gravesend, and then if there was much doin' there he might ha' stayed over. But what good is a steam launch without coals?'

'He might have bought some at a wharf down the river.'

'He might, sir, but it weren't his way. Many a time I've heard him call out at the prices they charge for a few odd bags. Besides, I don't like that wooden-legged man, wi' his ugly face and outlandish talk. What did he want always knockin' about here for?'

'A wooden-legged man?' said Holmes with bland surprise.

'Yes, sir, a brown, monkey-faced chap that's called more'n once for my old man. It was him that roused him up yesternight, and, what's more, my man knew he was comin', for he had steam up in the launch. I tell you straight, sir, I don't feel easy in my mind about it.'

'But, my dear Mrs Smith,' said Holmes, shrugging his shoulders, 'you are frightening yourself about nothing. How could you possibly tell that it was the wooden-legged man who came in the night? I don't quite understand how you can be so sure.'

'His voice, sir. I knew his voice, which is kind o' thick and foggy. He tapped at the winder—about three it would be. "Show a leg, matey," says he: "time to turn out guard." My old man woke up Jim—that's my eldest—and away they went without so much as a word to me. I could hear the wooden leg clackin' on the stones.'

'And was this wooden-legged man alone?'

'Couldn't say, I am sure, sir. I didn't hear no one else.'

'I am sorry, Mrs Smith, for I wanted a steam launch, and I have heard good reports of the—Let me see, what is her name?'

'The *Aurora*, sir.'

'Ah! She's not that old green launch with a yellow line, very broad in the beam?'

'No, indeed. She's as trim a little thing as any on the river. She's been fresh painted, black with two red streaks.'

'Thanks. I hope that you will hear soon from Mr Smith. I am going down the river, and if I should see anything of the *Aurora* I shall let him know that you are uneasy. A black funnel, you say?'

'No, sir. Black with a white band.'

'Ah, of course. It was the sides which were black. Good morning, Mrs Smith. There is a boatman here with a wherry,* Watson. We shall take it and cross the river.'

'The main thing with people of that sort', said Holmes, as we sat in the sheets* of the wherry, 'is never to let them think that their information can be of the slightest importance to you. If you do, they will instantly shut up like an oyster. If you listen to them under protest, as it were, you are very likely to get what you want.'

'Our course now seems pretty clear,' said I.

'What would you do, then?'

'I would engage a launch and go down the river on the track of the *Aurora*.'

'My dear fellow, it would be a colossal task. She may have touched at any wharf on either side of the stream between here and Greenwich. Below the bridge there is a perfect labyrinth of landing-places for miles. It would take you days and days to exhaust them, if you set about it alone.'

'Employ the police, then.'

'No. I shall probably call Athelney Jones in at the last moment.

He is not a bad fellow, and I should not like to do anything which would injure him professionally. But I have a fancy for working it out myself, now that we have gone so far.'

'Could we advertise, then, asking for information from wharf-ingers?'*

'Worse and worse! Our men would know that the chase was hot at their heels, and they would be off out of the country. As it is, they are likely enough to leave, but as long as they think they are perfectly safe they will be in no hurry. Jones's energy will be of use to us there, for his view of the case is sure to push itself into the daily press, and the runaways will think that everyone is off on the wrong scent.'

'What are we to do, then?' I asked as we landed near Millbank Penitentiary.*

'Take this hansom, drive home, have some breakfast, and get an hour's sleep. It is quite on the cards that we may be afoot to-night again. Stop at a telegraph office, cabby! We will keep Toby, for he may be of use to us yet.'

We pulled up at the Great Peter Street post-office, and Holmes despatched his wire.

'Whom do you think that is to?' he asked as we resumed our journey.

'I am sure I don't know.'

'You remember the Baker Street division of the detective police force whom I employed in the Jefferson Hope case?'

'Well,' said I, laughing.

'This is just the case where they might be invaluable. If they fail I have other resources, but I shall try them first. That wire was to my dirty little lieutenant, Wiggins, and I expect that he and his gang will be with us before we have finished our breakfast.'

It was between eight and nine o'clock now, and I was conscious of a strong reaction after the successive excitements of the night. I was limp and weary, befogged in mind and fatigued in body. I had not the professional enthusiasm which carried my companion on, nor could I look at the matter as a mere abstract intellectual problem. As far as the death of Bartholomew Sholto went, I had heard little good of him, and could feel no intense antipathy to his murderers. The treasure, however, was a different matter. That, or part of it, belonged rightfully to Miss Morstan. While there was a chance of recovering it, I was ready to devote my life to the one object. True, if I found it, it would probably put her forever beyond my reach. Yet it would be a petty and selfish love which would be influenced by such a thought as that. If Holmes could work to find the criminals, I had a tenfold stronger reason to urge me on to find the treasure.

A bath at Baker Street and a complete change freshened me up wonderfully. When I came down to our room I found the breakfast laid and Holmes pouring out the coffee.

'Here it is,' said he, laughing and pointing to an open newspaper. 'The energetic Jones and the ubiquitous reporter have fixed it up between them. But you have had enough of the case. Better have your ham and eggs first.'

I took the paper from him and read the short notice, which was headed 'Mysterious Business at Upper Norwood'.

About twelve o'clock last night [said the *Standard*] Mr Bartholomew Sholto, of Pondicherry Lodge, Upper Norwood, was found dead in his room under circumstances which point to foul play. As far as we can learn, no actual traces of violence were found upon Mr Sholto's person, but a valuable collection of Indian gems which the deceased gentleman had inherited from his father has been carried off. The discovery was first made by Mr Sherlock Holmes and Dr Watson, who had called at the house with Mr Thaddeus Sholto, brother of the deceased. By a singular piece of good fortune, Mr Athelney Jones, the well-known member of the detective police force, happened to be at the Norwood Police Station, and was on the ground within half an hour of the first alarm. His trained and experienced faculties were at once directed towards the detection of the criminals, with the gratifying result that the brother, Thaddeus Sholto, has already been arrested, together with the housekeeper, Mrs Bernstone, an Indian butler named Lal Rao, and a porter, or gatekeeper, named McMurdo. It is quite certain that the thief or thieves were well acquainted with the house, for Mr Jones's well-known technical knowledge and his powers of minute observation have enabled him to prove conclusively that the miscreants could not have entered by the door or by the window, but must have made their way across the roof of the building, and so through a trap-door into a room which communicated with that in which the body was found. This fact, which has been very clearly made out, proves conclusively that it was no mere haphazard burglary. The prompt and energetic action of the officers of the law shows the great advantage of the presence on such occasions of a single vigorous and masterful mind. We cannot but think that it supplies an argument to those who would wish to see our detectives more decentralized, and so brought into closer and more effective touch with the cases which it is their duty to investigate.

'Isn't it gorgeous!' said Holmes, grinning over his coffee cup. 'What do you think of it?'

'I think that we have had a close shave ourselves of being arrested for the crime.'

'So do I. I wouldn't answer for our safety now, if he should happen to have another of his attacks of energy.'

At this moment there was a loud ring at the bell, and I could hear Mrs Hudson, our landlady, raising her voice in a wail of expostulation and dismay.

'By heavens, Holmes,' I said, half rising, 'I believe that they are really after us.'

'No, it's not quite so bad as that. It is the unofficial force—the Baker Street irregulars.'

As he spoke, there came a swift pattering of naked feet upon the stairs, a clatter of high voices, and in rushed a dozen dirty and ragged little street arabs. There was some show of discipline among them, despite their tumultuous entry, for they instantly drew up in line and stood facing us with expectant faces. One of their number, taller and older than the others, stood forward with an air of lounging superiority which was very funny in such a disreputable little scarecrow.

'Got your message, sir,' said he, 'and brought 'em on sharp. Three bob and a tanner* for tickets.'

'Here you are,' said Holmes, producing some silver. 'In future they can report to you, Wiggins, and you to me. I cannot have the house invaded in this way. However, it is just as well that you should all hear the instructions. I want to find the whereabouts of a steam launch called the *Aurora*, owner Mordecai Smith, black with two red streaks, funnel black with a white band. She is down the river somewhere. I want one boy to be at Mordecai Smith's landing-stage opposite Millbank to say if the boat comes back. You must divide it out among yourselves and do both banks thoroughly. Let me know the moment you have news. Is that all clear?'

'Yes, guv'nor,' said Wiggins.

'The old scale of pay, and a guinea to the boy who finds the boat. Here's a day in advance. Now off you go!'

He handed them a shilling each, and away they buzzed down the stairs, and I saw them a moment later streaming down the street.

'If the launch is above water they will find her,' said Holmes, as he rose from the table and lit his pipe. 'They can go everywhere, see everything, overhear everyone. I expect to hear before evening that they have spotted her. In the meanwhile, we can do nothing but await results. We cannot pick up the broken trail until we find either the *Aurora* or Mr Mordecai Smith.'

'Toby could eat these scraps, I dare say. Are you going to bed, Holmes?'

'No: I am not tired. I have a curious constitution. I never remember feeling tired by work, though idleness exhausts me completely. I am going to smoke and to think over this queer business to which my fair client has introduced us. If ever man had an easy task, this of ours ought to be. Wooden-legged men are not so common, but the other man must, I should think, be absolutely unique.'

'That other man again!'

'I have no wish to make a mystery of him to you, anyway. But you must have formed your own opinion. Now, do consider the data. Diminutive foot-marks, toes never fettered by boots, naked feet, stone-headed wooden mace, great agility, small poisoned darts. What do you make of all this?'

'A savage!' I exclaimed. 'Perhaps one of those Indians who were the associates of Jonathan Small.'

'Hardly that,' said he. 'When first I saw signs of strange weapons, I was inclined to think so; but the remarkable character of the foot-marks caused me to reconsider my views. Some of the inhabitants of the Indian Peninsula are small men, but none could have left such marks as that. The Hindoo proper has long and thin feet. The sandal-wearing Mohammedan has the great toe well separated from the others, because the thong is commonly passed between. These little darts, too, could only be shot in one way. They are from a blow-pipe. Now, then, where are we to find our savage?'

'South America,' I hazarded.

He stretched his hand up, and took down a bulky volume from the shelf.

'This is the first volume of a gazetteer which is now being published. It may be looked upon as the very latest authority. What have we here? "Andaman Islands, situated 340 miles to the north of Sumatra, in the Bay of Bengal." Hum! hum! What's all this? Moist climate, coral reefs, sharks, Port Blair,* convict barracks, Rutland Island,* cotton-woods—Ah, here we are! "The aborigines of the Andaman Islands may perhaps claim the distinction of being the smallest race upon this earth, though some anthropologists prefer the Bushmen of Africa, the Digger Indians of America,* and the Terra del Fuegians.* The average height is rather below four feet, although many full-grown adults may be found who are very much smaller than this. They are a fierce, morose, and intractable people, though capable of forming most devoted friendships when their confidence has once been gained." Mark that, Watson. Now, then listen to this. "They are naturally hideous, having large, misshapen heads, small fierce eyes, and distorted features. Their feet and hands, however, are remarkably small. So intractable and fierce are they, that all the efforts of the British officials have failed to win them over in any degree. They have always been a terror to shipwrecked crews, braining the survivors with their stone-headed clubs, or shooting them with their poisoned arrows. These massacres are invariably concluded by a cannibal feast."* Nice, amiable people, Watson! If this fellow had been left to his own unaided devices, this affair might have taken an even more ghastly turn. I fancy that, even as it is, Jonathan Small would give a good deal not to have employed him.'

'But how came he to have so singular a companion?'

'Ah, that is more than I can tell. Since, however, we had already determined that Small had come from the Andamans, it is not so very wonderful that this islander should be with him. No doubt we shall know all about it in time. Look here, Watson; you look regularly done. Lie down there on the sofa, and see if I can put you to sleep.'

He took up his violin from the corner, and as I stretched myself out he began to play some low, dreamy, melodious air—his own, no doubt, for he had a remarkable gift for improvisation. I have a vague remembrance of his gaunt limbs, his earnest face, and the rise and fall of his bow. Then I seemed to be floated peacefully away upon a soft sea of sound, until I found myself in dreamland, with the sweet face of Mary Morstan looking down upon me.

CHAPTER 9

A BREAK IN THE CHAIN

IT was late in the afternoon before I woke, strengthened and refreshed. Sherlock Holmes still sat exactly as I had left him, save that he had laid aside his violin and was deep in a book. He looked across at me as I stirred, and I noticed that his face was dark and troubled.

'You have slept soundly,' he said. 'I feared that our talk would wake you.'

'I heard nothing,' I answered. 'Have you had fresh news, then?'

'Unfortunately, no. I confess that I am surprised and disappointed. I expected something definite by this time. Wiggins has just been up to report. He says that no trace can be found of the launch. It is a provoking check, for every hour is of importance.'

'Can I do anything? I am perfectly fresh now, and quite ready for another night's outing.'

'No; we can do nothing. We can only wait. If we go ourselves, the message might come in our absence and delay be caused. You can do what you will, but I must remain on guard.'

'Then I shall run over to Camberwell and call upon Mrs Cecil Forrester. She asked me to, yesterday.'

'On Mrs Cecil Forrester?' asked Holmes, with the twinkle of a smile in his eyes.

'Well, of course on Miss Morstan, too. They were anxious to hear what happened.'

'I would not tell them too much,' said Holmes. 'Women are never to be entirely trusted—not the best of them.'

I did not pause to argue over this atrocious sentiment.

'I shall be back in an hour or two,' I remarked.

'All right! Good luck! But, I say, if you are crossing the river you may as well return Toby, for I don't think it is at all likely that we shall have any use for him now.'

I took our mongrel accordingly and left him, together with a half-sovereign, at the old naturalist's in Pinchin Lane. At Camberwell I found Miss Morstan a little weary after her night's adventures, but very eager to hear the news. Mrs Forrester, too, was full of curiosity. I told them all that we had done, suppressing, however, the more dreadful parts of the tragedy. Thus, although I spoke of Mr Sholto's death, I said nothing of the exact manner and method of it. With all my omissions, however, there was enough to startle and amaze them.

'It is a romance!' cried Mrs Forrester. 'An injured lady, half a million in treasure, a black cannibal, and a wooden-legged ruffian. They take the place of the conventional dragon or wicked earl.'

'And two knight-errants to the rescue,' added Miss Morstan, with a bright glance at me.

'Why, Mary, your fortune depends upon the issue of this search. I don't think that you are nearly excited enough. Just imagine what it must be to be so rich, and to have the world at your feet!'

It sent a little thrill of joy to my heart to notice that she showed no sign of elation at the prospect. On the contrary, she gave a toss of her proud head, as though the matter were one in which she took small interest.

'It is for Mr Thaddeus Sholto that I am anxious,' she said. 'Nothing else is of any consequence; but I think that he has behaved most kindly and honourably throughout. It is our duty to clear him of this dreadful and unfounded charge.'

It was evening before I left Camberwell, and quite dark by the time I reached home. My companion's book and pipe lay by his chair, but he had disappeared. I looked about in the hope of seeing a note, but there was none.

'I suppose that Mr Sherlock Holmes has gone out,' I said to Mrs Hudson as she came up to lower the blinds.

'No, sir. He has gone to his room, sir. Do you know, sir,' sinking her voice into an impressive whisper, 'I am afraid for his health?'

'Why so, Mrs Hudson?'

'Well, he's that strange, sir. After you was gone he walked and he walked, up and down, and up and down, until I was weary of the sound of his footstep. Then I heard him talking to himself and muttering, and every time the bell rang out he came on the stair-head, with "What is that, Mrs Hudson?" And now he has slammed off to his room, but I can hear him walking away the same as ever. I hope he's not going to be ill, sir. I ventured to say something to him about cooling medicine,* but he turned on me, sir, with such a look that I don't know how ever I got out of the room.'

'I don't think that you have any cause to be uneasy, Mrs Hudson,' I answered. 'I have seen him like this before. He has some small matter upon his mind which makes him restless.'

I tried to speak lightly to our worthy landlady, but I was myself somewhat uneasy when through the long night I still from time to time heard the dull sound of his tread, and knew how his keen spirit was chafing against this involuntary inaction.

At breakfast-time he looked worn and haggard, with a little fleck of feverish colour upon either cheek.

'You are knocking yourself up, old man,' I remarked. 'I heard you marching about in the night.'

'No, I could not sleep,' he answered. 'This infernal problem is consuming me. It is too much to be balked by so petty an obstacle, when all else had been overcome. I know the men, the launch, everything; and yet I can get no news. I have set other agencies at work, and used every means at my disposal. The whole river has been searched on either side, but there is no news, nor has Mrs Smith heard of her husband. I shall come to the conclusion soon that they have scuttled the craft. But there are objections to that.'

'Or that Mrs Smith has put us on a wrong scent.'

'No, I think that may be dismissed. I had inquiries made, and there is a launch of that description.'

'Could it have gone up the river?'

'I have considered that possibility, too, and there is a search-party who will work up as far as Richmond. If no news comes to-day I shall start off myself tomorrow and go for the men rather than the boat. But surely, surely, we shall hear something.'

We did not, however. Not a word came to us either from Wiggins or from the other agencies. There were articles in most of the papers upon the Norwood tragedy. They all appeared to be rather hostile to the unfortunate Thaddeus Sholto. No fresh details were to be found, however, in any of them, save that an inquest was to be held upon the following day. I walked over to Camberwell in the evening to report our ill-success to the ladies, and on my return I found Holmes dejected and somewhat morose. He would hardly reply to my questions, and busied himself all the evening in an abstruse chemical analysis which involved much heating of retorts* and distilling of vapours, ending at last in a smell which fairly drove me out of the apartment. Up to the small hours of the morning I could hear the clinking of his test-tubes which told me that he was still engaged in his malodorous experiment.

In the early dawn I woke with a start and was surprised to find him standing by my bedside, clad in a rude sailor dress with a pea-jacket,* and a coarse red scarf round his neck.

'I am off down the river, Watson,' said he. 'I have been turning it over in my mind, and I can see only one way out of it. It is worth trying, at all events.'

'Surely I can come with you, then?' said I.

'No; you can be much more useful if you will remain here as my representative. I am loath to go, for it is quite on the cards that some message may come during the day, though Wiggins was despondent about it last night. I want you to open all notes and telegrams, and to act on your own judgment if any news should come. Can I rely upon you?'

'Most certainly.'

'I am afraid that you will not be able to wire me, for I can hardly tell yet where I may find myself. If I am in luck, however, I may not be gone so very long. I shall have news of some sort or other before I get back.'

I had heard nothing of him by breakfast-time. On opening the *Standard*, however, I found that there was a fresh allusion to the business.

With reference to the Upper Norwood tragedy [it remarked] we have reason to believe that the matter promises to be even more complex and mysterious than was originally supposed. Fresh evidence has shown that it is quite impossible that Mr Thaddeus Sholto could have been in any way concerned in the matter. He and the housekeeper, Mrs Bernstone, were both released yesterday evening. It is believed, however, that the police have a clue as to the real culprits, and that it is being prosecuted by Mr Athelney Jones, of Scotland Yard, with all his well-known energy and sagacity. Further arrests may be expected at any moment.

'That is satisfactory so far as it goes,' thought I. 'Friend Sholto is safe, at any rate. I wonder what the fresh clue may be, though it seems to be a stereotyped form whenever the police have made a blunder.'

I tossed the paper down upon the table, but at that moment my eye caught an advertisement in the agony column. It ran in this way:

LOST—Whereas Mordecai Smith, boatman, and his son Jim, left Smith's Wharf at or about three o'clock last Tuesday morning in the steam launch *Aurora*, black with two red stripes, funnel black with a white band, the sum of five pounds will be paid to anyone who can give information to Mrs Smith, at Smith's Wharf, or at 221B, Baker Street, as to the whereabouts of the said Mordecai Smith and the launch *Aurora*.

This was clearly Holmes's doing. The Baker Street address was enough to prove that. It struck me as rather ingenious, because it might be read by the fugitives without their seeing in it more than the natural anxiety of a wife for her missing husband.

It was a long day. Every time that a knock came to the door, or a sharp step passed in the street, I imagined that it was either Holmes returning or an answer to his advertisement. I tried to read, but my thoughts would wander off to our strange quest and to the ill-assorted and villainous pair whom we were pursuing. Could there be, I wondered, some radical flaw in my companion's reasoning? Might he not be suffering from some huge self-deception? Was it not possible that his nimble and speculative mind had built up this wild theory upon faulty premises? I had never known him to be wrong, and yet the keenest reasoner may occasionally be deceived. He was likely, I thought, to fall into error through the over-refinement of his logic—his preference for a subtle and bizarre explanation when a plainer and more commonplace one lay ready to his hand. Yet, on the other hand, I had myself seen the evidence, and I had heard the reasons for his deductions. When I looked back on the long chain of curious circumstances, many of them trivial in themselves, but all tending in the same direction, I could not disguise from myself that even if Holmes's explanation were incorrect the true theory must be equally *outré** and startling.

At three o'clock on the afternoon there was a loud peal at the bell, an authoritative voice in the hall, and, to my surprise, no less a person than Mr Athelney Jones was shown up to me. Very different was he, however, from the brusque and masterful professor of common sense who had taken over the case so confidently at Upper Norwood. His expression was downcast, and his bearing meek and even apologetic.

'Good-day, sir; good-day,' said he. 'Mr Sherlock Holmes is out, I understand.'

'Yes, and I cannot be sure when he will be back. But perhaps you would care to wait. Take that chair and try one of these cigars.'

'Thank you; I don't mind if I do,' said he, mopping his face with a red bandanna* handkerchief.

'And a whisky and soda?'

'Well, half a glass. It is very hot for the time of year; and I have had a good deal to worry and try me. You know my theory about this Norwood case?'

'I remember that you expressed one.'

'Well, I have been obliged to reconsider it. I had my net drawn tightly round Mr Sholto, sir, when pop he went through a hole in the middle of it. He was able to prove an alibi which could not be shaken. From the time that he left his brother's room he was never out of sight of someone or other. So it could not be he who climbed over roofs and through trap-doors. It's a very dark case, and my professional credit is at stake. I should be very glad of a little assistance.'

'We all need help sometimes,' said I.

'Your friend, Mr Sherlock Holmes, is a wonderful man, sir,' said he, in a husky and confidential voice. 'He's a man who is not to be beat. I have known that young man go into a good many cases, but I never saw the case yet that he could not throw a light upon. He is irregular in his methods and a little quick perhaps in jumping at theories, but, on the whole, I think he would have made a most promising officer, and I don't care who knows it. I have had a wire from him this morning, by which I understand that he has got some clue to this Sholto business. Here is his message.'

He took the telegram out of his pocket, and handed it to me. It was dated from Poplar at twelve o'clock.

Go to Baker Street at once [it said]. If I have not returned, wait for me. I am close on the track of the Sholto gang. You can come with us to-night if you want to be in at the finish.

'This sounds well. He has evidently picked up the scent again,' said I.

'Ah, then he has been at fault too,' exclaimed Jones with evident satisfaction. 'Even the best of us are thrown off sometimes. Of course this may prove to be a false alarm; but it is my duty as an officer of the law to allow no chance to slip. But there is someone at the door. Perhaps this is he.'

A heavy step was heard ascending the stair, with a great wheezing and rattling as from a man who was sorely put to it for breath. Once or twice he stopped, as though the climb were too much for him, but at last he made his way to our door and entered. His appearance corresponded to the sounds which we had heard. He was an aged man, clad in seafaring garb, with an old pea-jacket buttoned up to his throat. His back was bowed, his knees were shaky, and his breathing was painfully asthmatic. As he leaned upon a thick oaken cudgel his shoulders heaved in the effort to draw the air into his lungs. He had a coloured scarf round his chin, and I could see little of his face save a pair of keen dark eyes, overhung by bushy white brows, and long gray side-whiskers. Altogether he gave me the impression of a respectable master mariner who had fallen into years and poverty.

'What is it, my man?' I asked.

He looked about him in the slow methodical fashion of old age.

'Is Mr Sherlock Holmes here?' said he.

'No; but I am acting for him. You can tell me any message you have for him.'

'It was to him himself I was to tell it,' said he.

'But I tell you that I am acting for him. Was it about Mordecai Smith's boat?'

'Yes. I knows well where it is. An' I knows where the men he is after are. An' I knows where the treasure is. I knows all about it.'

'Then tell me, and I shall let him know.'

'It was to him I was to tell it,' he repeated with the petulant obstinacy of a very old man.

'Well, you must wait for him.'

'No, no; I ain't goin' to lose a whole day to please no one. If Mr Holmes ain't here, then Mr Holmes must find it all out for himself. I don't care about the look of either of you, and I won't tell a word.'

He shuffled towards the door, but Athelney Jones got in front of him.

'Wait a bit, my friend,' said he. 'You have important information, and you must not walk off. We shall keep you, whether you like it or not, until our friend returns.'

The old man made a little run towards the door, but, as Athelney Jones put his broad back up against it, he recognized the uselessness of resistance.

'Pretty sort o' treatment this!' he cried, stamping his stick. 'I come here to see a gentleman, and you two, who I never saw in my life, seize me and treat me in this fashion!'

'You will be none the worse,' I said. 'We shall recompense you for the loss of your time. Sit over here on the sofa, and you will not have long to wait.'

He came across sullenly enough and seated himself with his face resting on his hands. Jones and I resumed our cigars and our talk. Suddenly, however, Holmes's voice broke in upon us.

'I think that you might offer me a cigar too,' he said.

We both started in our chairs. There was Holmes sitting close to us with an air of quiet amusement.

'Holmes!' I exclaimed. 'You here! But where is the old man?'

'Here is the old man,' said he, holding out a heap of white hair. 'Here he is—wig, whiskers, eyebrows, and all. I thought my disguise was pretty good, but I hardly expected that it would stand that test.'

'Ah, you rogue!' cried Jones, highly delighted. 'You would have made an actor and a rare one. You had the proper workhouse cough, and those weak legs of yours are worth ten pound a week. I thought I knew the glint of your eye, though. You didn't get away from us so easily, you see.'

'I have been working in that get-up all day,' said he, lighting his cigar. 'You see, a good many of the criminal classes begin to know me—especially since our friend here took to publishing some of my cases: so I can only go on the war-path under some simple disguise like this. You got my wire?'

'Yes; that was what brought me here.'

'How has your case prospered?'

'It has all come to nothing. I have had to release two of my prisoners, and there is no evidence against the other two.'

'Never mind. We shall give you two others in the place of them. But you must put yourself under my orders. You are welcome to all the official credit, but you must act on the lines that I point out. Is that agreed?'

'Entirely, if you will help me to the men.'

'Well, then, in the first place I shall want a fast police-boat*— a steam launch—to be at the Westminster Stairs at seven o'clock.'

'That is easily managed. There is always one about there; but I can step across the road and telephone to make sure.'

'Then I shall want two staunch men, in case of resistance.'

'There will be two or three in the boat. What else?'

'When we secure the men we shall get the treasure. I think that it would be a pleasure to my friend here to take the box round to the young lady to whom half of it rightfully belongs. Let her be the first to open it. Eh, Watson?'

'It would be a great pleasure to me.'

'Rather an irregular proceeding,' said Jones, shaking his head. 'However, the whole thing is irregular, and I suppose we must wink at it. The treasure must afterwards be handed over to the authorities until after the official investigation.'

'Certainly. That is easily managed. One other point. I should much like to have a few details about this matter from the lips of Jonathan Small himself. You know I like to work the details of my cases out. There is no objection to my having an unofficial interview with him, either here in my rooms or elsewhere, as long as he is efficiently guarded?'

'Well, you are master of the situation. I have had no proof yet of the existence of this Jonathan Small. However, if you can catch him, I don't see how I can refuse you an interview with him.'

'That is understood, then?'

'Perfectly. Is there anything else?'

'Only that I insist upon your dining with us. It will be ready in half an hour. I have oysters and a brace of grouse, with something a little choice in white wines.—Watson, you have never yet recognized my merits as a housekeeper.'

CHAPTER 10

THE END OF THE ISLANDER

OUR meal was a merry one. Holmes could talk exceedingly well when he chose, and that night he did choose. He appeared to be in a state of nervous exaltation. I have never known him so brilliant. He spoke on a quick succession of subjects—on miracle plays,* on medieval pottery, on Stradivarius violins,* on the Buddhism of Ceylon,* and on the warships of the future—handling each as though he had made a special study of it. His bright humour marked the reaction from his black depression of the preceding days. Athelney Jones proved to be a sociable soul in his hours of relaxation, and faced his dinner with the air of a *bon vivant*.* For myself, I felt elated at the thought that we were nearing the end of our task, and I caught something of Holmes's gaiety. None of us alluded during dinner to the cause which had brought us together.

When the cloth was cleared Holmes glanced at his watch, and filled up three glasses with port.

'One bumper,'* said he, 'to the success of our little expedition. And now it is high time we were off. Have you a pistol, Watson?'

'I have my old service-revolver in my desk.'

'You had best take it, then. It is well to be prepared. I see that the cab is at the door. I ordered it for half-past six.'

It was a little past seven before we reached the Westminster wharf and found our launch awaiting us. Holmes eyed it critically.

'Is there anything to mark it as a police-boat?'

'Yes, that green lamp at the side.'

'Then take it off.'

The small change was made, we stepped on board, and the ropes were cast off. Jones, Holmes, and I sat in the stern. There was one man at the rudder, one to tend the engines, and two burly police-inspectors forward.

'Where to?' asked Jones.

'To the Tower.* Tell them to stop opposite to Jacobson's Yard.'

Our craft was evidently a very fast one. We shot past the long lines of loaded barges as though they were stationary. Holmes smiled with satisfaction as we overhauled a river steamer and left her behind us.

'We ought to be able to catch anything on the river,' he said.

'Well, hardly that. But there are not many launches to beat us.'

'We shall have to catch the *Aurora*, and she has a name for being a clipper.* I will tell you how the land lies, Watson. You recollect how annoyed I was at being baulked by so small a thing?'

'Yes.'

'Well, I gave my mind a thorough rest by plunging into a chemical analysis. One of our greatest statesmen has said that a change of work is the best rest.* So it is. When I had succeeded in dissolving the hydrocarbon which I was at work at, I came back to our problem of the Sholtos, and thought the whole matter out again. My boys had been up the river and down the river without result. The launch was not at any landing-stage or wharf, nor had it returned. Yet it could hardly have been scuttled to hide their traces, though that always remained as a possible hypothesis if all else failed. I knew that this man Small had a certain degree of low cunning, but I did not think him capable of anything in the nature of delicate finesse. That is usually a product of higher education. I then reflected that since he had certainly been in London some time—as we had evidence that he maintained a continual watch over Pondicherry Lodge—he could hardly leave at a moment's notice, but would need some little time, if it were only a day, to arrange his affairs. That was the balance of probability, at any rate.'

'It seems to me to be a little weak,' said I; 'it is more probable that he had arranged his affairs before ever he set out upon his expedition.'

'No, I hardly think so. This lair of his would be too valuable a retreat in case of need for him to give it up until he was sure that he could do without it. But a second consideration struck me. Jonathan Small must have felt that the peculiar appearance of his companion, however much he may have top-coated him, would give rise to gossip, and possibly be associated with this Norwood tragedy. He was quite sharp enough to see that. They had started from their headquarters under cover of darkness, and he would wish to get back before it was broad light. Now, it was past three o'clock, according to Mrs Smith, when they got the boat. It would be quite bright, and people would be about in an hour or so. Therefore, I argued, they did not go very far. They paid Smith well to hold his tongue, reserved his launch for the final escape, and hurried to their lodgings with the treasure-box. In a couple of nights, when they had time to see what view the papers took, and whether there was any suspicion, they would make their way under cover of darkness to some ship at Gravesend or in the Downs,* where no doubt they had already arranged for passages to America or the Colonies.'

'But the launch? They could not have taken that to their lodgings.'

'Quite so. I argued that the launch must be no great way off, in spite of its invisibility. I then put myself in the place of Small and looked at it as a man of his capacity would. He would probably consider that to send back the launch or to keep it at a wharf would make pursuit easy if the police did happen to get on his track. How, then, could he conceal the launch and yet have her at hand when wanted? I wondered what I should do myself if I were in his shoes. I could only think of one way of doing it. I might hand the launch over to some boat-builder or repairer, with directions to make a trifling change in her. She would then be removed to his shed or yard, and so be effectually concealed, while at the same time I could have her at a few hours' notice.'

'That seems simple enough.'

'It is just these very simple things which are extremely liable to be overlooked. However, I determined to act on the idea. I started at once in this harmless seaman's rig and enquired at all the yards down the river. I drew blank at fifteen, but at the sixteenth—Jacobson's—I learned that the *Aurora* had been handed over to them two days ago by a wooden-legged man, with some trivial directions as to her rudder. "There ain't naught amiss with her rudder," said the fore-man. "There she lies, with the red streaks." At that moment who should come down but Mordecai Smith, the missing owner. He was rather the worse for liquor. I should not, of course, have known him, but he bellowed out his name and the name of his launch. "I want her tonight at eight o'clock," said he—"eight o'clock sharp, mind, for I have two gentlemen who won't be kept waiting." They had evidently paid him well, for he was very flush of money, chucking shillings about to the men. I followed him some distance, but he subsided into an alehouse; so I went back to the yard, and, happening to pick up one of my boys on the way, I stationed him as a sentry over the launch. He is to stand at the water's edge and wave his handkerchief to us when they start. We shall be lying off in the stream, and it will be a strange thing if we do not take men, treasure, and all.'

'You have planned it all very neatly, whether they are the right men or not,' said Jones; 'but if the affair were in my hands I should have had a body of police in Jacobson's Yard, and arrested them when they came down.'

'Which would have been never. This man Small is a pretty shrewd fellow. He would send a scout on ahead, and if anything made him suspicious he would lie snug for another week.'

'But you might have stuck to Mordecai Smith, and so been led to their hiding-place,' said I.

'In that case I should have wasted my day. I think that it is a hundred to one against Smith knowing where they live. As long as he has liquor and good pay, why should he ask questions? They send him messages what to do. No, I thought over every possible course, and this is the best.'

While this conversation had been proceeding, we had been shooting the long series of bridges which span the Thames. As we passed the City the last rays of the sun were gilding the cross upon the summit of St Paul's. It was twilight before we reached the Tower.

'That is Jacobson's Yard,' said Holmes, pointing to a bristle of masts and rigging on the Surrey side. 'Cruise gently up and down here under cover of this string of lighters.'* He took a pair of night-glasses* from his pocket and gazed some time at the shore. 'I see my sentry at his post,' he remarked, 'but no sign of a handkerchief.'

'Suppose we go downstream a short way and lie in wait for them,' said Jones eagerly.

We were all eager by this time, even the policemen and stokers, who had a very vague idea of what was going forward.

'We have no right to take anything for granted,' Holmes answered. 'It is certainly ten to one that they go downstream, but we cannot be certain. From this point we can see the entrance of the yard, and they can hardly see us. It will be a clear night and plenty of light. We must stay where we are. See how the folk swarm over yonder in the gaslight.'

'They are coming from work in the yard.'

'Dirty-looking rascals, but I suppose every one has some little immortal spark concealed about him. You would not think it, to look at them. There is no *a priori** probability about it. A strange enigma is man!'

'Someone calls him a soul concealed in an animal,' I suggested.

'Winwood Reade is good upon the subject,' said Holmes. 'He remarks that, while the individual man is an insoluble puzzle, in the aggregate he becomes a mathematical certainty. You can, for example, never foretell what any one man will do, but you can say with precision what an average number will be up to. Individuals vary, but percentages remain constant. So says the statistician. But do I see a handkerchief? Surely there is a white flutter over yonder.'

'Yes, it is your boy,' I cried. 'I can see him plainly.'

'And there is the *Aurora*,' exclaimed Holmes, 'and going like the devil! Full speed ahead, engineer. Make after that launch with the yellow light. By heaven, I shall never forgive myself if she proves to have the heels of us!'

She had slipped unseen through the yard-entrance, and passed between two or three small craft, so that she had fairly got her speed up before we saw her. Now she was flying down the stream, near in to the shore, going at a tremendous rate. Jones looked gravely at her and shook his head.

'She is very fast,' he said. 'I doubt if we shall catch her.'

'We *must* catch her!' cried Holmes, between his teeth. 'Heap it on, stokers! Make her do all she can! If we burn the boat we must have them!'

We were fairly after her now. The furnaces roared, and the powerful engines whizzed and clanked, like a great metallic heart. Her sharp, steep prow cut through the still river-water and sent two rolling waves to right and to left of us. With every throb of the engines we sprang and quivered like a living thing. One great yellow lantern in our bows threw a long, flickering funnel of light in front of us. Right ahead a dark blur upon the water showed where the *Aurora* lay, and the swirl of white foam behind her spoke of the pace at which she was going. We flashed past barges, steamers, merchant-vessels, in and out, behind this one and round the other. Voices hailed us out of the darkness, but still the *Aurora* thundered on, and still we followed close upon her track.

'Pile it on, men, pile it on!' cried Holmes, looking down into the engine-room, while the fierce glow from below beat upon his eager, aquiline face. 'Get every pound of steam you can.'

'I think we gain a little,' said Jones, with his eyes on the *Aurora*.

'I am sure of it,' said I. 'We shall be up with her in a very few minutes.'

At that moment, however, as our evil fate would have it, a tug with three barges in tow blundered in between us. It was only by putting our helm hard down that we avoided a collision, and before we could round them and recover our way the *Aurora* had gained a good two hundred yards. She was still, however, well in view, and the murky, uncertain twilight was settling into a clear, starlit night. Our boilers were strained to their utmost, and the frail shell vibrated and creaked with the fierce energy which was driving us along. We had shot through the pool, past the West India Docks, down the long Deptford Reach, and up again after rounding the Isle of Dogs. The dull blur in front of us resolved itself now clearly enough into the dainty *Aurora*. Jones turned our searchlight upon her, so that we could plainly see the figures upon her deck. One man sat by the stern, with something black between his knees, over which he stooped. Beside him lay a dark mass, which looked like a Newfoundland dog.* The boy held the tiller, while against the red glare of the furnace I could see old Smith, stripped to the waist, and shovelling coals for dear life. They may have had some doubt at first as to whether we were really pursuing them, but now as we followed every winding and turning which they took there could no longer be any question about it. At Greenwich we were about three hundred paces behind them. At Blackwall we could not have been more than two hundred and fifty. I have coursed* many creatures in many countries during my chequered career, but never did sport give me such a wild thrill as this mad, flying man-hunt down the Thames. Steadily we drew in upon them, yard by yard. In the silence of the night we could hear the panting and clanking of their machinery. The man in the stern still crouched upon the deck, and his arms were moving as though he were busy, while every now and then he would look up and measure with a glance the distance which still separated us. Nearer we came and nearer. Jones yelled to them to stop. We were not more than four boat's-lengths behind them, both boats flying at a tremendous pace. It was a clear reach of the river, with Barking Level upon one side and the melancholy Plumstead Marshes upon the other. At our hail the man in the stern sprang up from the deck and shook his two clenched fists at us, cursing the while in a high, cracked voice. He was a good-sized, powerful man, and as he stood poising himself with legs astride, I could see that from the thigh downward there was but a wooden stump upon the right side. At the sound of his strident, angry cries, there was movement in the huddled bundle upon the deck. It straightened itself into a little black man—the smallest I have ever seen—with a great, misshapen head and a shock of tangled, dishevelled hair. Holmes had already drawn his revolver, and I whipped out mine at the sight of this savage, distorted creature. He was wrapped in some sort of dark ulster* or blanket, which left only his face exposed, but that face was enough to give a man a sleepless night. Never have I seen features so deeply marked with all bestiality and cruelty. His small eyes glowed and burned with a sombre light, and his thick lips were writhed back from his teeth, which grinned and chattered at us with half animal fury.

'Fire if he raises his hand,' said Holmes quietly.

We were within a boat's-length by this time, and almost within touch of our quarry. I can see the two of them now as they stood, the white man with his legs far apart, shrieking out curses, and the unhallowed dwarf with his hideous face, and his strong yellow teeth gnashing at us in the light of our lantern.

It was well that we had so clear a view of him. Even as we looked he plucked out from under his covering a short, round piece of wood, like a school-ruler, and clapped it to his lips. Our pistols rang out together. He whirled round, threw up his arms, and, with a kind of choking cough, fell sideways into the stream. I caught one glimpse of his venomous, menacing eyes amid the white swirl of the waters. At the same moment the wooden-legged man threw himself upon the rudder and put it hard down, so that his boat made straight for the southern bank, while we shot past her stern, only clearing her by a few feet. We were round after her in an instant, but she was already nearly at the bank. It was a wild and desolate place, where the moon glimmered upon a wide expanse of marsh-land, with pools of stagnant water and beds of decaying vegetation. The launch, with a dull thud, ran up upon the mud-bank, with her bow in the air and her stern flush with the water. The fugitive sprang out, but his stump instantly sank its whole length into the sodden soil. In vain he struggled and writhed. Not one step could he possibly take either forward or backwards. He yelled in impotent rage and kicked frantically into the mud with his other foot; but his struggles only bored his wooden pin the deeper into the sticky bank. When we brought our launch alongside he was so firmly anchored that it was only by throwing the end of a rope over his shoulders that we were able to haul him out and to drag him, like some evil fish, over our side. The two Smiths, father and son, sat sullenly in their launch but came aboard meekly enough when commanded. The *Aurora* herself we hauled off and made fast to our stern. A solid iron chest of Indian workmanship stood upon the deck. This, there could be no question, was the same that had contained the ill-omened treasure of the Sholtos. There was no key, but it was of considerable weight, so we transferred it carefully to our own little cabin. As we steamed slowly up-stream again, we flashed our searchlight in every direction, but there was no sign of the Islander. Somewhere in the dark ooze at the bottom of the Thames lie the bones of that strange visitor to our shores.

'See here,' said Holmes, pointing to the wooden hatchway. 'We were hardly quick enough with our pistols.' There, sure enough, just behind where we had been standing, stuck one of those murderous darts which we knew so well. It must have whizzed between us at the instant we fired. Holmes smiled at it and shrugged his shoulders in his easy fashion, but I confess that it turned me sick to think of the horrible death which had passed so close to us that night.

CHAPTER 11

THE GREAT AGRA TREASURE

OUR captive sat in the cabin opposite to the iron box which he had done so much and waited so long to gain. He was a sunburned, reckless-eyed fellow, with a network of lines and wrinkles all over his mahogany features, which told of a hard, open-air life. There was a singular prominence about his bearded chin which marked a man who was not to be easily turned from his purpose. His age may have been fifty or thereabouts, for his black, curly hair was thickly shot with gray. His face in repose was not an unpleasing one, though his heavy brows and aggressive chin gave him, as I had lately seen, a terrible expression when moved to anger. He sat now with his handcuffed hands upon his lap, and his head sunk upon his breast, while he looked with his keen, twinkling eyes at the box which had been the cause of his ill-doings. It seemed to me that there was more sorrow than anger in his rigid and contained countenance. Once he looked up at me with a gleam of something like humour in his eyes.

'Well, Jonathan Small,' said Holmes, lighting a cigar, 'I am sorry that it has come to this.'

'And so am I, sir,' he answered frankly. 'I don't believe that I can swing over the job.* I give you my word on the book that I never raised hand against Mr Sholto. It was that little hell-hound, Tonga, who shot one of his cursed darts into him. I had no part in it, sir. I was as grieved as if it had been my blood-relation. I welted the little devil with the slack end of the rope for it, but it was done, and I could not undo it again.'

'Have a cigar,' said Holmes; 'and you had best take a pull out of my flask, for you are very wet. How could you expect so small and weak a man as this black fellow to overpower Mr Sholto and hold him while you were climbing the rope?'

'You seem to know as much about it as if you were there, sir. The truth is that I hoped to find the room clear. I knew the habits of the house pretty well, and it was the time when Mr Sholto usually went down to his supper. I shall make no secret of the business. The best defence that I can make is just the simple truth. Now, if it had been the old major I would have swung for him with a light heart. I would have thought no more of knifing him than of smoking this cigar. But it's cursed hard that I should be lagged* over this young Sholto, with whom I had no quarrel whatever.'

'You are under the charge of Mr Athelney Jones, of Scotland Yard. He is going to bring you up to my rooms, and I shall ask you for a true account of the matter. You must make a clean breast of it, for if you do I hope that I may be of use to you. I think I can prove that the poison acts so quickly that the man was dead before ever you reached the room.'

'That he was, sir. I never got such a turn in my life as when I saw him grinning at me with his head on his shoulder as I climbed through the window. It fairly shook me, sir. I'd have half killed Tonga for it if he had not scrambled off. That was how he came to leave his club, and some of his darts too, as he tells me, which I dare say helped to put you on our track; though how you kept on it is more than I can tell. I don't feel no malice against you for it. But it does seem a queer thing,' he added, with a bitter smile, 'that I, who have a fair claim to half a million of money, should spend the first half of my life building a breakwater in the Andamans, and am like to spend the other half digging drains at Dartmoor.* It was an evil day for me when first I clapped eyes upon the merchant Achmet and had to do with the Agra treasure, which never brought anything but a curse yet upon the man who owned it. To him it brought murder, to Major Sholto it brought fear and guilt, to me it has meant slavery for life.'

At this moment Athelney Jones thrust his broad face and heavy shoulders into the tiny cabin.

'Quite a family party,' he remarked. 'I think I shall have a pull at that flask, Holmes. Well, I think we may all congratulate each other. Pity we didn't take the other alive; but there was no choice. I say, Holmes, you must confess that you cut it rather fine. It was all we could do to overhaul her.'

'All is well that ends well,' said Holmes. 'But I certainly did not know that the *Aurora* was such a clipper.'

'Smith says she is one of the fastest launches on the river, and that if he had had another man to help him with the engines we should never have caught her. He swears he knew nothing of this Norwood business.'

'Neither he did,' cried our prisoner—'not a word. I chose his launch because I heard that she was a flier. We told him nothing; but we paid him well, and he was to get something handsome if we reached our vessel, the *Esmeralda*, at Gravesend, outward bound for the Brazils.'*

'Well, if he has done no wrong we shall see that no wrong comes to him. If we are pretty quick in catching our men, we are not so quick in condemning them.' It was amusing to notice how the consequential Jones was already beginning to give himself airs on the strength of the capture. From the slight smile which played over Sherlock Holmes's face, I could see that the speech had not been lost upon him.

'We will be at Vauxhall Bridge presently,' said Jones, 'and shall land you, Dr Watson, with the treasure-box. I need hardly tell you that I am taking a very grave responsibility upon myself in doing this. It is most irregular, but of course an agreement is an agreement. I must, however, as a matter of duty, send an inspector with you, since you have so valuable a charge. You will drive, no doubt?'

'Yes, I shall drive.'

'It is a pity there is no key, that we may make an inventory first. You will have to break it open. Where is the key, my man?'

'At the bottom of the river,' said Small shortly.

'Hum! There was no use your giving this unnecessary trouble. We have had work enough already through you. However, Doctor, I need not warn you to be careful. Bring the box back with you to the Baker Street rooms. You will find us there, on our way to the station.'

They landed me at Vauxhall, with my heavy iron box, and with a bluff, genial inspector as my companion. A quarter of an hour's drive brought us to Mrs Cecil Forrester's. The servant seemed surprised at so late a visitor. Mrs Cecil Forrester was out for the evening, she explained, and likely to be very late. Miss Morstan, however, was in the drawing-room; so to the drawing-room I went, box in hand, leaving the obliging inspector in the cab.

She was seated by the open window, dressed in some sort of white diaphanous material, with a little touch of scarlet at the neck and waist. The soft light of a shaded lamp fell upon her as she leaned back in the basket chair, playing over her sweet grave face, and tinting with a dull, metallic sparkle the rich coils of her luxuriant hair. One white arm and hand drooped over the side of the chair, and her whole pose and figure spoke of an absorbing melancholy. At the sound of my footfall she sprang to her feet, however, and a bright flush of surprise and of pleasure coloured her pale cheeks.

'I heard a cab drive up,' she said. 'I thought that Mrs Forrester had come back very early, but I never dreamed that it might be you. What news have you brought me?'

'I have brought something better than news,' said I, putting down the box upon the table and speaking jovially and boisterously, though my heart was heavy within me. 'I have brought you something which is worth all the news in the world. I have brought you a fortune.'

She glanced at the iron box.

'Is that the treasure then?' she asked, coolly enough.

'Yes, this is the great Agra treasure. Half of it is yours and half is Thaddeus Sholto's. You will have a couple of hundred thousand each. Think of that! An annuity of ten thousand pounds. There will be few richer young ladies in England. Is it not glorious?'

I think I must have been rather over-acting my delight, and that she detected a hollow ring in my congratulations, for I saw her eyebrows rise a little, and she glanced at me curiously.

'If I have it,' said she, 'I owe it to you.'

'No, no,' I answered, 'not to me but to my friend Sherlock Holmes. With all the will in the world, I could never have followed up a clue which has taxed even his analytical genius. As it was, we very nearly lost it at the last moment.'

'Pray sit down and tell me all about it, Dr Watson,' said she.

I narrated briefly what had occurred since I had seen her last. Holmes's new method of search, the discovery of the *Aurora*, the appearance of Athelney Jones, our expedition in the evening, and the wild chase down the Thames. She listened with parted lips and shining eyes to my recital of our adventures. When I spoke of the dart which had so narrowly missed us, she turned so white that I feared that she was about to faint.

'It is nothing,' she said as I hastened to pour her out some water. 'I am all right again. It was a shock to me to hear that I had placed my friends in such horrible peril.'

'That is all over,' I answered. 'It was nothing. I will tell you no more gloomy details. Let us turn to something brighter. There is the treasure. What could be brighter than that? I got leave to bring it with me, thinking that it would interest you to be the first to see it.'

'It would be of the greatest interest to me,' she said. There was no eagerness in her voice, however. It had struck her, doubtless, that it might seem ungracious upon her part to be indifferent to a prize which had cost so much to win.

'What a pretty box!' she said, stooping over it. 'This is Indian work, I suppose?'

'Yes; it is Benares metal-work.'*

'And so heavy!' she exclaimed, trying to raise it. 'The box alone must be of some value. Where is the key?'

'Small threw it into the Thames,' I answered. 'I must borrow Mrs Forrester's poker.'

There was in the front a thick and broad hasp,* wrought in the image of a sitting Buddha. Under this I thrust the end of the poker and twisted it outward as a lever. The hasp sprang open with a loud snap. With trembling fingers I flung back the lid. We both stood gazing in astonishment. The box was empty!

No wonder that it was heavy. The ironwork was two-thirds of an inch thick all round. It was massive, well made, and solid, like a chest constructed to carry things of great price, but not one shred or crumb of metal or jewellery lay within it. It was absolutely and completely empty.

'The treasure is lost,' said Miss Morstan calmly.

As I listened to the words and realized what they meant, a great shadow seemed to pass from my soul. I did not know how this Agra treasure had weighed me down, until now that it was finally removed. It was selfish, no doubt, disloyal, wrong, but I could realize nothing save that the golden barrier was gone from between us.

'Thank God!' I ejaculated from my very heart.

She looked at me with a quick, questioning smile.

'Why do you say that?' she asked.

'Because you are within my reach again,' I said, taking her hand. She did not withdraw it. 'Because I love you, Mary, as truly as ever a man loved a woman. Because this treasure, these riches, sealed my lips. Now that they are gone I can tell you how I love you. That is why I said, "Thank God".'

'Then I say "Thank God", too,' she whispered, as I drew her to my side.

Whoever had lost a treasure, I knew that night that I had gained one.

CHAPTER 12

THE STRANGE STORY OF JONATHAN SMALL

A VERY patient man was that inspector in the cab, for it was a weary time before I rejoined him. His face clouded over when I showed him the empty box.

'There goes the reward!' said he gloomily. 'Where there is no money there is no pay. This night's work would have been worth a tenner* each to Sam Brown and me if the treasure had been there.'

'Mr Thaddeus Sholto is a rich man,' I said; 'he will see that you are rewarded, treasure or no.'

The inspector shook his head despondently, however.

'It's a bad job,' he repeated; 'and so Mr Athelney Jones will think.'

His forecast proved to be correct, for the detective looked blank enough when I got to Baker Street and showed him the empty box. They had only just arrived, Holmes, the prisoner, and he, for they had changed their plans so far as to report themselves at a station upon the way. My companion lounged in his armchair with his usual listless expression, while Small sat stolidly opposite to him with his wooden leg cocked over his sound one. As I exhibited the empty box he leaned back in his chair and laughed aloud.

'This is your doing, Small,' said Athelney Jones angrily.

'Yes, I have put it away where you shall never lay hand upon it,' he cried exultantly. 'It is my treasure, and if I can't have the loot I'll take darned good care that no one else does. I tell you that no living man has any right to it, unless it is three men who are in the Andaman convict-barracks and myself. I know now that I cannot have the use of it, and I know that they cannot. I have acted all through for them as much as for myself. It's been the sign of four with us always. Well, I know that they would have had me do just what I have done, and throw the treasure into the Thames rather than let it go to kith or kin of Sholto or Morstan. It was not to make them rich that we did for Achmet. You'll find the treasure where the key is, and where little Tonga is. When I saw that your launch must catch us, I put the loot away in a safe place. There are no rupees for you this journey.'

'You are deceiving us, Small,' said Athelney Jones sternly; 'if you had wished to throw the treasure into the Thames, it would have been easier for you to have thrown box and all.'

'Easier for me to throw and easier for you to recover,' he answered with a shrewd, side-long look. 'The man that was clever enough to hunt me down is clever enough to pick an iron box from the bottom of a river. Now that they are scattered over five miles or so, it may be a harder job. It went to my heart to do it, though. I was half mad when you came up with us. However, there's no good grieving over it. I've had ups in my life, and I've had downs, but I've learned not to cry over spilled milk.'

'This is a very serious matter, Small,' said the detective. 'If you had helped justice, instead of thwarting it in this way, you would have had a better chance at your trial.'

'Justice!' snarled the ex-convict. 'A pretty justice! Whose loot is this, if it is not ours? Where is the justice that I should give it up to those who have never earned it? Look how I have earned it! Twenty long years in that fever-ridden swamp, all day at work under the mangrove-tree, all night chained up in the filthy convict-huts, bitten by mosquitoes, racked with ague,* bullied by every cursed black-faced policeman who loved to take it out of a white man. That was how I earned the Agra treasure, and you talk to me of justice because I cannot bear to feel that I have paid this price only that another may enjoy it! I would rather swing a score of times, or have one of Tonga's darts in my hide, than live in a convict's cell and feel that another man is at his ease in a palace with the money that should be mine.'

Small had dropped his mask of stoicism, and all this came out in a wild whirl of words, while his eyes blazed, and the handcuffs clanked together with the impassioned movement of his hands. I could understand, as I saw the fury and the passion of the man, that it was no groundless or unnatural terror which had possessed Major Sholto when he first learned that the injured convict was upon his track.

'You forget that we know nothing of all this,' said Holmes quietly. 'We have not heard your story, and we cannot tell how far justice may originally have been on your side.'

'Well, sir, you have been very fair-spoken to me, though I can see that I have you to thank that I have these bracelets upon my wrists. Still, I bear no grudge for that. It is all fair and above-board. If you want to hear my story, I have no wish to hold it back. What I say to you is God's truth, every word of it. Thank you, you can put the glass beside me here, and I'll put my lips to it if I am dry.

'I am a Worcestershire man myself, born near Pershore. I dare say you would find a heap of Smalls living there now if you were to look. I have often thought of taking a look round there, but the truth is that I was never much of a credit to the family, and I doubt if they would be so very glad to see me. They were all steady, chapel-going folk, small farmers, well known and respected over the countryside, while I was always a bit of a rover. At last, however, when I was about eighteen, I gave them no more trouble, for I got into a mess over a girl, and could only get out of it again by taking the Queen's shilling* and joining the 3rd Buffs,* which was just starting for India.

'I wasn't destined to do much soldiering, however. I had just got past the goose-step, and learned to handle my musket, when I was fool enough to go swimming in the Ganges. Luckily for me, my company sergeant, John Holder, was in the water at the same time, and he was one of the finest swimmers in the service. A crocodile took me, just as I was half-way across, and nipped off my right leg as clean as a surgeon could have done it, just above the knee. What with the shock and the loss of blood, I fainted, and should have been drowned if Holder had not caught hold of me and paddled for the bank. I was five months in hospital over it, and when at last I was able to limp out of it with this timber-toe strapped to my stump, I found myself invalided out of the Army and unfitted for any active occupation.

'I was, as you can imagine, pretty down on my luck at this time, for I was a useless cripple, though not yet in my twentieth year. However, my misfortune soon proved to be a blessing in disguise. A man named Abel White, who had come out there as an indigo-planter,* wanted an overseer to look after his coolies* and keep them up to their work. He happened to be a friend of our colonel's, who had taken an interest in me since the accident. To make a long story short, the colonel recommended me strongly for the post, and, as the work was mostly to be done on horseback, my leg was no great obstacle, for I had enough knee left to keep a good grip on the saddle. What I had to do was to ride over the plantation, to keep an eye on the men as they worked, and to report the idlers. The pay was fair, I had comfortable quarters, and altogether I was content to spend the remainder of my life in indigo-planting. Mr Abel White was a kind man, and he would often drop into my little shanty and smoke a pipe with me, for white folk out there feel their hearts warm to each other as they never do here at home.

'Well, I was never in luck's way long. Suddenly, without a note of warning, the great mutiny* broke upon us. One month India lay as still and peaceful, to all appearance, as Surrey or Kent; the next there were two hundred thousand black devils let loose, and the country was a perfect hell. Of course you know all about it, gentlemen— a deal more than I do, very like, since reading is not in my line. I only know what I saw with my own eyes. Our plantation was at a place called Muttra, near the border of the North-west Provinces.* Night after night the whole sky was alight with the burning bungalows, and day after day we had small companies of Europeans passing through our estate with their wives and children, on their way to Agra, where were the nearest troops. Mr Abel White was an obstinate man. He had it in his head that the affair had been exaggerated, and that it would blow over as suddenly as it had sprung up. There he sat on his veranda, drinking whisky-pegs* and smoking cheroots,* while the country was in a blaze about him. Of course we stuck by him, I and Dawson, who, with his wife, used to do the book-work and the managing. Well, one fine day the crash came. I had been away on a distant plantation, and was riding slowly home in the evening, when my eye fell upon something all huddled together at the bottom of a steep nullah.* I rode down to see what it was, and the cold struck through my heart when I found it was Dawson's wife, all cut into ribbons, and half eaten by jackals and native dogs. A little farther up the road Dawson himself was lying on his face, quite dead, with an empty revolver in his hand, and four Sepoys* lying across each other in front of him. I reined up my horse, wondering which way I should turn; but at that moment I saw thick smoke curling up from Abel White's bungalow, and the flames beginning to burst through the roof. I knew then that I could do my employer no good, but would only throw my own life away if I meddled in the matter. From where I stood I could see hundreds of the black fiends, with their red coats still on their backs, dancing and howling round the burning house. Some of them pointed at me, and a couple of bullets sang past my head: so I broke away across the paddy-fields, and found myself at night safe within the walls at Agra.

'As it proved, however, there was no great safety there, either. The whole country was up like a swarm of bees. Wherever the English could collect in little bands they held just the ground that their guns commanded. Everywhere else they were helpless fugitives. It was a fight of the millions against the hundreds; and the cruellest part of it was that these men that we fought against, foot, horse, and gunners, were our own picked troops, whom we had taught and trained, handling our own weapons and blowing our own bugle-calls. At Agra there were the 3rd Bengal Fusiliers,* some Sikhs, two troops of horse, and a battery of artillery. A volunteer corps of clerks and merchants had been formed, and this I joined, wooden leg and all. We went out to meet the rebels at Shahgunge* early in July, and we beat them back, for a time, but our powder gave out, and we had to fall back upon the city.

'Nothing but the worst news came to us from every side—which is not to be wondered at, for if you look at the map you will see that we were right in the heart of it. Lucknow* is rather better than a hundred miles to the east, and Cawnpore* about as far to the south. From every point on the compass there was nothing but torture and murder and outrage.

'The city of Agra is a great place, swarming with fanatics and fierce devil-worshippers of all sorts. Our handful of men were lost among the narrow, winding streets. Our leader moved across the river, therefore, and took up his position in the old fort of Agra. I don't know if any of you gentlemen have ever read or heard anything of that old fort. It is a very queer place—the queerest that ever I was in, and I have been in some rum corners, too. First of all it is enormous in size. I should think that the enclosure must be acres and acres. There is a modern part, which took all our garrison, women, children, stores, and everything else, with plenty of room over. But the modern part is nothing like the size of the old quarter, where nobody goes, and which is given over to the scorpions and the centipedes. It is all full of great deserted halls, and winding passages, and long corridors twisting in and out, so that it is easy enough for folk to get lost in it. For this reason it was seldom that anyone went into it, though now and again a party with torches might go exploring.

'The river washes along the front of the old fort, and so protects it, but on the sides and behind there are many doors, and these had to be guarded, of course, in the old quarter as well as in that which was actually held by our troops. We were short-handed, with hardly men enough to man the angles of the building and to serve the guns. It was impossible for us, therefore, to station a strong guard at every one of the innumerable gates. What we did was to organize a central guard-house in the middle of the fort, and to leave each gate under the charge of one white man and two or three natives. I was selected to take charge during certain hours of the night of a small isolated door upon the south-west side of the building. Two Sikh troopers were placed under my command, and I was instructed if anything went wrong to fire my musket, when I might rely upon help coming at once from the central guard. As the guard was a good two hundred paces away, however, and as the space between was cut up into a labyrinth of passages and corridors, I had great doubts as to whether they could arrive in time to be of any use in case of an actual attack.

'Well, I was pretty proud at having this small command given me, since I was a raw recruit, and a game-legged one at that. For two nights I kept the watch with my Punjaubees.* They were tall, fierce-looking chaps, Mahomet Singh and Abdullah Khan by name, both old fighting men, who had borne arms against us at Chilian Wallah.* They could talk English pretty well, but I could get little out of them. They preferred to stand together and jabber all night in their queer Sikh lingo. For myself, I used to stand outside the gateway, looking down on the broad, winding river and on the twinkling lights of the great city. The beating of drums, the rattle of tomtoms, and the yells and howls of the rebels, drunk with opium and with bang,* were enough to remind us all night of our dangerous neighbours across the stream. Every two hours the officer of the night used to come round to all the posts, to make sure that all was well.

'The third night of my watch was dark and dirty, with a small driving rain. It was dreary work standing in the gateway hour after hour in such weather. I tried again and again to make my Sikhs talk, but without much success. At two in the morning the rounds passed, and broke for a moment the weariness of the night. Finding that my companions would not be led into conversation, I took out my pipe, and laid down my musket to strike the match. In an instant the two Sikhs were upon me. One of them snatched my firelock* up and levelled it at my head, while the other held a great knife to my throat and swore between his teeth that he would plunge it into me if I moved a step.

'My first thought was that these fellows were in league with the rebels, and that this was the beginning of an assault. If our door were in the hands of the Sepoys the place must fall, and the women and children be treated as they were in Cawnpore. Maybe you gentlemen think that I am just making out a case for myself, but I give you my word that when I thought of that, though I felt the point, of the knife at my throat, I opened my mouth with the intention of giving a scream, if it was my last one, which might alarm the main guard. The man who held me seemed to know my thoughts; for, even as I braced myself to it, he whispered: "Don't make a noise. The fort is safe enough. There are no rebel dogs on this side of the river." There was the ring of truth in what he said, and I knew that if I raised my voice I was a dead man. I could read it in the fellow's brown eyes. I waited, therefore, in silence, to see what it was that they wanted from me.

' "Listen to me, Sahib," said the taller and fiercer of the pair, the one whom they called Abdullah Khan. "You must either be with us now, or you must be silenced for ever. The thing is too great a one for us to hesitate. Either you are heart and soul with us on your oath on the cross of the Christians, or your body this night shall be thrown into the ditch, and we shall pass over to our brothers in the rebel army. There is no middle way. Which is it to be—death or life? We can only give you three minutes to decide, for the time is passing, and all must be done before the rounds come again."

' "How can I decide?" said I. "You have not told me what you want of me. But I tell you now that if it is anything against the safety of the fort I will have no truck with it, so you can drive home your knife and welcome."

' "It is nothing against the fort," said he. "We only ask you to do that which your countrymen come to this land for. We ask you to be rich. If you will be one of us this night, we will swear to you upon the naked knife, and by the threefold oath which no Sikh was ever known to break, that you shall have your fair share of the loot. A quarter of the treasure shall be yours. We can say no fairer."

' "But what is the treasure, then?" I asked. "I am as ready to be rich as you can be, if you will but show me how it can be done."

' "You will swear, then," said he, "by the bones of your father, by the honour of your mother, by the cross of your faith, to raise no hand and speak no word against us, either now or afterwards?"

' "I will swear it," I answered, "provided that the fort is not endangered."

' "Then my comrade and I will swear that you shall have a quarter of the treasure which shall be equally divided among the four of us."

' "There are but three," said I.

' "No; Dost Akbar must have his share. We can tell the tale to you while we wait them. Do you stand at the gate, Mahomet Singh, and give notice of their coming. The thing stands thus, Sahib, and I tell it to you because I know that an oath is binding upon a Feringhee,* and that we may trust you. Had you been a lying Hindoo, though you had sworn by all the gods in their false temples, your blood would have been upon the knife and your body in the water. But the Sikh knows the Englishman, and the Englishman knows the Sikh. Hearken, then, to what I have to say.

' "There is a rajah* in the northern provinces who has much

wealth, though his lands are small. Much has come to him from his
father, and more still he has set by himself, for he is of a low nature,
and hoards his gold rather than spend it. When the troubles broke
out he would be friends both with the lion and the tiger—with the
Sepoy and with the Company's *Raj*.* Soon, however, it seemed to
him that the white men's day was come, for through all the land he
could hear of nothing but of their death and their overthrow. Yet,
being a careful man, he made such plans that, come what might,
half at least of his treasure should be left to him. That which was
in gold and silver he kept by him in the vaults of his palace, but the
most precious stones and the choicest pearls that he had he put in
an iron box, and sent it by a trusty servant, who, under the guise of
a merchant, should take it to the fort at Agra, there to lie until the
land is at peace. Thus, if the rebels won he would have his money,
but if the Company conquered, his jewels would be saved to him.
Having thus divided his hoard, he threw himself into the cause of
the Sepoys, since they were strong upon his borders. By his doing
this, mark you, Sahib, his property becomes the due of those who
have been true to their salt.

' "This pretended merchant, who travels under the name of
Achmet, is now in the city of Agra, and desires to gain his way into
the fort. He has with him as travelling-companion my foster-brother
Dost Akbar, who knows his secret. Dost Akbar has promised this
night to lead him to a side-postern of the fort, and has chosen this
one for his purpose. Here he will come presently, and here he will find
Mahomet Singh and myself awaiting him. The place is lonely, and
none shall know of his coming. The world shall know of the merchant
Achmet no more, but the great treasure of the rajah shall be divided
among us. What say you to it, Sahib?"

'In Worcestershire the life of a man seems a great and a sacred
thing; but it is very different when there is fire and blood all round
you, and you have been used to meeting death at every turn. Whether
Achmet the merchant lived or died was a thing as light as air to me,
but at the talk about the treasure my heart turned to it, and I thought
of what I might do in the old country with it, and how my folk would
stare when they saw their ne'er-do-weel coming back with his pockets
full of gold moidores.* I had, therefore, already made up my mind.
Abdullah Khan, however, thinking that I hesitated, pressed the matter more closely.

' "Consider, Sahib," said he, "that if this man is taken by the commandant he will be hung or shot, and his jewels taken by the Government, so that no man will be a rupee the better for them. Now, since we do the taking of him, why should we not do the rest as well? The jewels will be as well with us as in the Company's coffers. There will be enough to make every one of us rich men and great chiefs. No one can know about the matter, for here we are cut off from all men. What could be better for the purpose? Say again, then, Sahib, whether you are with us, or if we must look upon you as an enemy."

' "I am with you heart and soul," said I.

' "It is well," he answered, handing me back my firelock. "You see that we trust you, for your word, like ours, is not to be broken. We have now only to wait for my brother and the merchant."

' "Does your brother know, then, of what you will do?" I asked.

' "The plan is his. He has devised it. We will go to the gate and share the watch with Mahomet Singh."

'The rain was still falling steadily, for it was just the beginning of the wet season. Brown, heavy clouds were drifting across the sky, and it was hard to see more than a stone-cast. A deep moat lay in front of our door, but the water was in places nearly dried up, and it could easily be crossed. It was strange to me to be standing there with those two wild Punjaubees waiting for the man who was coming to his death.

'Suddenly my eye caught the glint of a shaded lantern at the other side of the moat. It vanished among the mound-heaps, and then appeared again coming slowly in our direction.

' "Here they are!" I exclaimed.

' "You will challenge him, Sahib, as usual," whispered Abdullah. "Give him no cause for fear. Send us in with him, and we shall do the rest while you stay here on guard. Have the lantern ready to uncover, that we may be sure that it is indeed the man."

'The light had flickered onwards, now stopping and now advancing, until I could see two dark figures upon the other side of the moat. I let them scramble down the sloping bank, splash through the mire, and climb half-way up to the gate, before I challenged them.

' "Who goes there?" said I, in a subdued voice.

' "Friends," came the answer. I uncovered my lantern and threw a flood of light upon them. The first was an enormous Sikh, with a black beard which swept nearly down to his cummerbund. Outside of a show I have never seen so tall a man. The other was a little fat, round fellow, with a great yellow turban, and a bundle in his hand, done up in a shawl. He seemed to be all in a quiver with fear, for his hands twitched as if he had the ague, and his head kept turning to left and right with two bright little twinkling eyes, like a mouse when he ventures out from his hole. It gave me the chills to think of killing him, but I thought of the treasure, and my heart set as hard as a flint within me. When he saw my white face he gave a little chirrup of joy and came running up towards me.

' "Your protection, Sahib," he panted, "your protection for the unhappy merchant Achmet. I have travelled across Rajpootana* that I might seek the shelter of the fort at Agra. I have been robbed and beaten and abused because I have been the friend of the Company. It is a blessed night this when I am once more in safety—I and my poor possessions."

' "What have you in the bundle?" I asked.

' "An iron box," he answered, "which contains one or two little family matters which are of no value to others, but which I should be sorry to lose. Yet I am not a beggar; and I shall reward you, young Sahib, and your governor also, if he will give me the shelter I ask."

'I could not trust myself to speak longer with the man. The more I looked at his fat, frightened face, the harder did it seem that we should slay him in cold blood. It was best to get it over.

' "Take him to the main guard," said I. The two Sikhs closed in upon him on each side, and the giant walked behind, while they marched in through the dark gateway. Never was a man so compassed round with death. I remained at the gateway with the lantern.

'I could hear the measured tramp of their footsteps sounding through the lonely corridors. Suddenly it ceased, and I heard voices, and a scuffle, with the sound of blows. A moment later there came, to my horror, a rush of footsteps coming in my direction, with a loud breathing of a running man. I turned my lantern down the long straight passage, and there was the fat man, running like the wind, with a smear of blood across his face, and close at his heels, bounding like a tiger, the great black-bearded Sikh, with a knife flashing in his hand. I have never seen a man run so fast as that little merchant. He was gaining on the Sikh, and I could see that if he once passed me and got to the open air he would save himself yet. My heart softened to him, but again the thought of his treasure turned me hard and bitter. I cast my firelock between his legs as he raced past, and he rolled twice over like a shot rabbit. Ere he could stagger to his feet the Sikh was upon him, and buried his knife twice in his side. The man never uttered moan nor moved muscle, but lay where he had fallen. I think myself that he may have broken his neck with the fall. You see, gentlemen, that I am keeping my promise. I am telling you every word of the business just exactly as it happened, whether it is in my favour or not.'

He stopped and held out his manacled hands for the whisky-and-water which Holmes had brewed for him. For myself, I confess that I had now conceived the utmost horror of the man, not only for this cold-blooded business in which he had been concerned, but even more for the somewhat flippant and careless way in which he narrated it. Whatever punishment was in store for him, I felt that he might expect no sympathy from me. Sherlock Holmes and Jones sat with their hands upon their knees, deeply interested in the story, but with the same disgust written upon their faces. He may have observed it, for there was a touch of defiance in his voice and manner as he proceeded.

'It was all very bad, no doubt,' said he. 'I should like to know how many fellows in my shoes would have refused a share of this loot when they knew that they would have their throats cut for their pains. Besides, it was my life or his when once he was in the fort. If he had got out, the whole business would come to light, and I should have been court-martialled and shot as likely as not; for people were not very lenient at a time like that.'

'Go on with your story,' said Holmes shortly.

'Well, we carried him in, Abdullah, Akbar, and I. A fine weight he was, too, for all that he was so short. Mahomet Singh was left to guard the door. We took him to a place which the Sikhs had already prepared. It was some distance off, where a winding passage leads to a great empty hall, the brick walls of which were all crumbling to pieces. The earth floor had sunk in at one place, making a natural grave, so we left Achmet the merchant there, having first covered him over with loose bricks. This done, we all went back to the treasure.

'It lay where he had dropped it when he was first attacked. The box was the same which now lies open upon your table. A key was hung by a silken cord to that carved handle upon the top. We opened it, and the light of the lantern gleamed upon a collection of gems such as I have read of and thought about when I was a little lad at Pershore.

It was blinding to look upon them. When we had feasted our eyes we took them all out and made a list of them. There were one hundred and forty-three diamonds of the first water,* including one which has been called, I believe, "the Great Mogul",* and is said to be the second largest stone in existence. Then there were ninety-seven very fine emeralds, and one hundred and seventy rubies, some of which, however, were small. There were forty carbuncles, two hundred and ten sapphires, sixty-one agates, and a great quantity of beryls, onyxes, cats'-eyes, turquoises, and other stones, the very names of which I did not know at the time, though I have become more familiar with them since. Besides this, there were nearly three hundred very fine pearls, twelve of which were set in a gold coronet. By the way, these last had been taken out of the chest, and were not there when I recovered it.

'After we had counted our treasures we put them back into the chest and carried them to the gateway to show them to Mahomet Singh. Then we solemnly renewed our oath to stand by each other and be true to our secret. We agreed to conceal our loot in a safe place until the country should be at peace again, and then to divide it equally among ourselves. There was no use dividing it at present, for if gems of such value were found upon us it would cause suspicion, and there was no privacy in the fort nor any place where we could keep them. We carried the box, therefore, into the same hall where we had buried the body, and there, under certain bricks in the best-preserved wall, we made a hollow and put our treasure. We made careful note of the place, and next day I drew four plans, one for each of us, and put the sign of the four of us at the bottom, for we had sworn that we should each always act for all, so that none might take advantage. This is an oath that I can put my hand to my heart and swear that I have never broken.

'Well, there's no use my telling you gentlemen what came of the Indian mutiny. After Wilson* took Delhi and Sir Colin* relieved Lucknow the back of the business was broken. Fresh troops came pouring in, and Nana Sahib made himself scarce over the frontier. A flying column under Colonel Greathed* came round to Agra and cleared the Pandies* away from it. Peace seemed to be settling upon the country, and we four were beginning to hope that the time was at hand when we might safely go off with our shares of the plunder. In a moment, however, our hopes were shattered by our being arrested as the murderers of Achmet.

'It came about in this way. When the rajah put his jewels into the hands of Achmet he did it because he knew that he was a trusty man. They are suspicious folk in the East, however: so what does this rajah do but take a second even more trusty servant and set him to play the spy upon the first. This second man was ordered never to let Achmet out of his sight, and he followed him like his shadow. He went after him that night and saw him pass through the doorway. Of course he thought he had taken refuge in the fort, and applied for admission there himself next day, but could find no trace of Achmet. This seemed to him so strange that he spoke about it to a sergeant of guides,* who brought it to the ears of the commandant. A thorough search was quickly made, and the body was discovered. Thus at the very moment that we thought that all was safe we were all four seized and brought to trial on a charge of murder—three of us because we had held the gate that night, and the fourth because he was known to have been in the company of the murdered man. Not a word about the jewels came out at the trial, for the rajah had been deposed and driven out of India: so no one had any particular interest in them. The murder, however, was clearly made out, and it was certain that we must all have been concerned in it. The three Sikhs got penal servitude for life, and I was condemned to death, though my sentence was afterwards commuted to the same as the others.

'It was rather a queer position that we found ourselves in then. There we were all four tied by the leg and with precious little chance of ever getting out again, while we each held a secret which might have put each of us in a palace if we could only have made use of it. It was enough to make a man eat his heart out to have to stand the kick and the cuff of every petty jack-in-office,* to have rice to eat and water to drink, when that gorgeous fortune was ready for him outside, just waiting to be picked up. It might have driven me mad; but I was always a pretty stubborn one, so I just held on and bided my time.

'At last it seemed to me to have come. I was changed from Agra to Madras, and from there to Blair Island* in the Andamans. There are very few white convicts at this settlement, and, as I had behaved well from the first, I soon found myself a sort of privileged person. I was given a hut in Hope Town, which is a small place on the slopes of Mount Harriet, and I was left pretty much to myself. It is a dreary, fever-stricken place, and all beyond our little clearings was infested with wild cannibal natives, who were ready enough to blow a poisoned dart at us if they saw a chance. There was digging and ditching and yam-planting, and a dozen other things to be done, so we were busy enough all day; though in the evening we had a little time to ourselves. Among other things, I learned to dispense drugs for the surgeon, and picked up a smattering of his knowledge. All the time I was on the lookout for a chance of escape; but it is hundreds of miles from any other land, and there is little or no wind in those seas: so it was a terribly difficult job to get away.

'The surgeon, Dr Somerton, was a fast, sporting young chap, and the other young officers would meet in his rooms of an evening and play cards. The surgery, where I used to make up my drugs, was next to his sitting-room, with a small window between us. Often, if I felt lonesome, I used to turn out the lamp in the surgery, and then, standing there, I could hear their talk and watch their play. I am fond of a hand at cards myself, and it was almost as good as having one to watch the others. There was Major Sholto, Captain Morstan, and Lieutenant Bromley Brown, who were in command of the native troops, and there was the surgeon himself, and two or three prison-officials, crafty old hands who played a nice, sly, safe game. A very snug little party they used to make.

'Well, there was one thing which very soon struck me, and that was that the soldiers used always to lose and the civilians to win. Mind, I don't say there was anything unfair, but so it was. These prison-chaps had done little else than play cards ever since they had been at the Andamans, and they knew each other's game to a point, while the others just played to pass the time and threw their cards down anyhow. Night after night the soldiers got up poorer men, and the poorer they got the more keen they were to play. Major Sholto was the hardest hit. He used to pay in notes and gold at first, but soon it came to notes of hand and for big sums. He sometimes would win for a few deals just to give him heart, and then the luck would set in against him worse than ever. All day he would wander about as black as thunder, and he took to drinking a deal more than was good for him.

'One night he lost even more heavily than usual. I was sitting in my hut when he and Captain Morstan came stumbling along on the way to their quarters. They were bosom friends, those two, and never far apart. The major was raving about his losses.

' "It's all up, Morstan," he was saying as they passed my hut. "I shall have to send in my papers.* I am a ruined man."

' "Nonsense, old chap!" said the other, slapping him upon the shoulder. "I've had a nasty facer* myself, but—" That was all I could hear, but it was enough to set me thinking.

'A couple of days later Major Sholto was strolling on the beach: so I took the chance of speaking to him.

' "I wish to have your advice, Major," said I.

' "Well, Small, what is it?" he asked, taking his cheroot from his lips.

' "I wanted to ask you, sir," said I, "who is the proper person to whom hidden treasure should be handed over. I know where half a million worth lies, and, as I cannot use it myself, I thought perhaps the best thing that I could do would be to hand it over to the proper authorities, and then perhaps they would get my sentence shortened for me."

' "Half a million, Small?" he gasped, looking hard at me to see if I was in earnest.

' "Quite that, sir—in jewels and pearls. It lies there ready for anyone. And the queer thing about it is that the real owner is outlawed and cannot hold property, so that it belongs to the first comer."

' "To Government, Small," he stammered, "to Government." But he said it in a halting fashion, and I knew in my heart that I had got him.

' "You think, then, sir, that I should give the information to the Governor-General?" said I quietly.

' "Well, well, you must not do anything rash, or that you might repent. Let me hear all about it, Small. Give me the facts."

'I told him the whole story, with small changes, so that he could not identify the places. When I had finished he stood stock still and full of thought. I could see by the twitch of his lip that there was a struggle going on within him.

' "This is a very important matter, Small," he said at last. "You must not say a word to anyone about it, and I shall see you again soon."

'Two nights later he and his friend, Captain Morstan, came to my hut in the dead of the night with a lantern.

' "I want you just to let Captain Morstan hear that story from your own lips, Small," said he.

'I repeated it as I had told it before.

' "It rings true, eh?" said he. "It's good enough to act upon?"

'Captain Morstan nodded.

' "Look here, Small," said the major. "We have been talking it over, my friend here and I, and we have come to the conclusion that this secret of yours is hardly a Government matter, after all, but is a private concern of your own, which of course you have the power of disposing of as you think best. Now the question is, What price would you ask for it? We might be inclined to take it up, and at least look into it, if we could agree as to terms." He tried to speak in a cool, careless way, but his eyes were shining with excitement and greed.

'"Why, as to that, gentlemen," I answered, trying also to be cool, but feeling as excited as he did, "there is only one bargain which, a man in my position can make. I shall want you to help me to my freedom, and to help my three companions to theirs. We shall then take you into partnership, and give you a fifth share to divide between you."

'"Hum!" said he. "A fifth share! That is not very tempting."

'"It would come to fifty thousand apiece," said I.

'"But how can we gain your freedom? You know very well that you ask an impossibility."

'"Nothing of the sort," I answered. "I have thought it all out to the last detail. The only bar to our escape is that we can get no boat fit for the voyage, and no provisions to last us for so long a time. There are plenty of little yachts and yawls at Calcutta or Madras which would serve our turn well. Do you bring one over. We shall engage to get aboard her by night, and if you will drop us on any part of the Indian coast you will have done your part of the bargain."

'"If there were only one," he said.

'"None or all," I answered. "We have sworn it. The four of us must always act together."

'"You see, Morstan," said he, "Small is a man of his word. He does not flinch from his friends. I think we may very well trust him."

'"It's a dirty business," the other answered. "Yet, as you say, the money will save our commissions handsomely."

'"Well, Small," said the major, "we must, I suppose, try and meet you. We must first, of course, test the truth of your story. Tell me where the box is hid, and I shall get leave of absence and go back to India in the monthly relief-boat to inquire into the affair."

'"Not so fast," said I, growing colder as he got hot. "I must have the consent of my three comrades. I tell you that it is four or none with us."

'"Nonsense!" he broke in. "What have three black fellows to do with our agreement?"

' "Black or blue," said I, "they are in with me, and we all go together."

'Well, the matter ended by a second meeting, at which Mahomet Singh, Abdullah Khan, and Dost Akbar* were all present. We talked the matter over again, and at last we came to an arrangement. We were to provide both the officers with charts of the part of the Agra fort, and mark the place in the wall where the treasure was hid. Major Sholto was to go to India to test our story. If he found the box he was to leave it there, to send out a small yacht provisioned for a voyage, which was to lie off Rutland Island, and to which we were to make our way, and finally to return to his duties. Captain Morstan was then to apply for leave of absence, to meet us at Agra, and there we were to have a final division of the treasure, he taking the major's share as well as his own. All this we sealed by the most solemn oaths that the mind could think or the lips utter. I sat up all night with paper and ink, and by the morning I had the two charts all ready, signed with the sign of four—that is, of Abdullah, Akbar, Mahomet, and myself.

'Well, gentlemen, I weary you with my long story, and I know that my friend Mr Jones is impatient to get me safely stowed in chokey.* I'll make it as short as I can. The villain Sholto went off to India, but he never came back again. Captain Morstan showed me his name among a list of passengers in one of the mail-boats very shortly afterwards. His uncle had died leaving him a fortune, and he had left the Army; yet he could stoop to treat five men as he had treated us. Morstan went over to Agra shortly afterwards, and found, as we expected, that the treasure was indeed gone. The scoundrel had stolen it all without carrying out one of the conditions on which we had sold him the secret. From that time I lived only for vengeance. I thought of it by day and I nursed it by night. It became an overpowering, absorbing passion with me. I cared nothing for the law—nothing for the gallows. To escape, to track down Sholto, to have my hand upon his throat—that was my one thought. Even the Agra treasure had come to be a smaller thing in my mind than the slaying of Sholto.

'Well, I have set my mind on many things in this life, and never one which I did not carry out. But it was weary years before my time came. I have told you that I had picked up something of medicine. One day when Dr Somerton was down with a fever a little Andaman Islander was picked up by a convict-gang in the woods. He was sick to death, and had gone to a lonely place to die. I took him in hand, though he was as venomous as a young snake, and after a couple of months I got him all right and able to walk. He took a kind of fancy to me then, and would hardly go back to his woods, but was always hanging about my hut. I learned a little of his lingo from him, and this made him all the fonder of me.

'Tonga—for that was his name—was a fine boatman, and owned a big, roomy canoe of his own. When I found that he was devoted to me and would do anything to serve me, I saw my chance of escape. I talked it over with him. He was to bring his boat round on a certain night to an old wharf which was never guarded, and there he was to pick me up. I gave him directions to have several gourds of water and a lot of yams, cocoa-nuts, and sweet potatoes.

'He was staunch and true, was little Tonga. No man ever had a more faithful mate. At the night named he had his boat at the wharf. As it chanced, however, there was one of the convict-guard down there—a vile Pathan* who had never missed a chance of insulting and injuring me. I had always vowed vengeance, and now I had my chance. It was as if fate had placed him in my way that I might pay my debt before I left the island. He stood on the bank with his back to me, and his carbine on his shoulder. I looked about for a stone to beat out his brains with, but none could I see.

'Then a queer thought came into my head, and showed me where I could lay my hand on a weapon. I sat down in the darkness and unstrapped my wooden leg. With three long hops I was on him. He put his carbine to his shoulder, but I struck him full, and knocked the whole front of his skull in. You can see the split in the wood now where I hit him. We both went down together, for I could not keep my balance; but when I got up I found him still lying quiet enough. I made for the boat, and in an hour we were well out at sea. Tonga had brought all his earthly possessions with him, his arms and his gods. Among other things, he had a long bamboo spear, and some Andaman cocoa-nut matting, with which I made a sort of a sail. For ten days we were beating about, trusting to luck, and on the eleventh we were picked up by a trader which was going from Singapore to Jiddah* with a cargo of Malay pilgrims. They were a rum crowd, and Tonga and I soon managed to settle down among them. They had one very good quality: they let you alone and asked no questions.

'Well, if I were to tell you all the adventures that my little chum and I went through, you would not thank me, for I would have you here until the sun was shining. Here and there we drifted about the world, something always turning up to keep us from London. All the time, however, I never lost sight of my purpose. I would dream of Sholto at night. A hundred times I have killed him in my sleep. At last, however, some three or four years ago, we found ourselves in England. I had no great difficulty in finding where Sholto lived, and I set to work to discover whether he had realized the treasure, or if he still had it. I made friends with someone who could help me—I name no names, for I don't want to get anyone else in a hole—and I soon found that he still had the jewels. Then I tried to get at him in many ways; but he was pretty sly, and had always two prize-fighters, besides his sons and his *khitmutgar*, on guard over him.

'One day, however, I got word that he was dying. I hurried at once to the garden, mad that he should slip out of my clutches like that, and, looking through the window, I saw him lying in his bed, with his sons on each side of him. I'd have come through and taken my chance with the three of them, only even as I looked at him his jaw dropped, and I knew that he was gone. I got into his room that same night, though, and I searched his papers to see if there was any record of where he had hidden our jewels. There was not a line, however, so I came away, bitter and savage as a man could be. Before I left I bethought me that if I ever met my Sikh friends again it would be a satisfaction to know that I had left some mark of our hatred; so I scrawled down the sign of the four of us, as it had been on the chart, and I pinned it on his bosom. It was too much that he should be taken to the grave without some token from the men whom he had robbed and befooled.

'We earned a living at this time by my exhibiting poor Tonga at fairs and other such places as the black cannibal. He would eat raw meat and dance his war-dance: so we always had a hatful of pennies after a day's work. I still heard all the news from Pondicherry Lodge, and for some years there was no news to hear, except that they were hunting for the treasure. At last, however, came what we had waited for so long. The treasure had been found. It was up at the top of the house in Mr Bartholomew Sholto's chemical laboratory. I came at once and had a look at the place, but I could not see how, with my wooden leg, I was to make my way up to it. I learned, however, about a trap-door in the roof, and also about Mr Sholto's supper-hour. It seemed to me that I could manage the thing easily through Tonga. I brought him out with me with a long rope wound round his waist. He could climb like a cat, and he soon made his way through the roof, but, as ill luck would have it, Bartholomew Sholto was still in the room, to his cost. Tonga thought he had done something very clever in killing him, for when I came up by the rope I found him strutting about as proud as a peacock. Very much surprised was he when I made at him with the rope's end and cursed him for a little bloodthirsty imp. I took the treasure-box and let it down, and then slid down myself, having first left the sign of the four upon the table, to show that the jewels had come back at last to those who had most right to them. Tonga then pulled up the rope, closed the window, and made off the way that he had come.

'I don't know that I have anything else to tell you. I had heard a waterman speak of the speed of Smith's launch, the *Aurora*, so I thought she would be a handy craft for our escape. I engaged with old Smith, and was to give him a big sum if he got us safe to our ship. He knew, no doubt, that there was some screw loose, but he was not in our secrets. All this is the truth, and if I tell it to you, gentlemen, it is not to amuse you—for you have not done me a very good turn—but it is because I believe the best defence I can make is just to hold back nothing, but let all the world know how badly I have myself been served by Major Sholto, and how innocent I am of the death of his son.'

'A very remarkable account,' said Sherlock Holmes. 'A fitting wind-up to an extremely interesting case. There is nothing at all new to me in the latter part of your narrative, except that you brought your own rope. That I did not know. By the way, I had hoped that Tonga had lost all his darts; yet he managed to shoot one at us in the boat.'

'He had lost them all, sir, except the one which was in his blow-pipe at the time.'

'Ah, of course,' said Holmes. 'I had not thought of that.'

'Is there any other point which you would like to ask about?' asked the convict affably.

'I think not, thank you,' my companion answered.

'Well, Holmes,' said Athelney Jones, 'you are a man to be humoured, and we all know that you are a connoisseur of crime; but duty is duty, and I have gone rather far in doing what you and your friend asked me. I shall feel more at ease when we have our story-teller here safe under lock and key. The cab still waits, and there are two inspectors downstairs. I am much obliged to you both for your assistance. Of course you will be wanted at the trial. Good-night to you.'

'Good-night, gentlemen both,' said Jonathan Small.

'You first, Small,' remarked the wary Jones as they left the room. 'I'll take particular care that you don't club me with your wooden leg, whatever you may have done to the gentleman at the Andaman Isles.'

'Well, and there is the end of our little drama,' I remarked, after we had sat some time smoking in silence. 'I fear that it may be the last investigation in which I shall have the chance of studying your methods. Miss Morstan has done me the honour to accept me as a husband in prospective.'

He gave a most dismal groan.

'I feared as much,' said he. 'I really cannot congratulate you.'

I was a little hurt.

'Have you any reason to be dissatisfied with my choice?' I asked.

'Not at all. I think she is one of the most charming young ladies I ever met, and might have been most useful in such work as we have been doing. She had a decided genius that way; witness the way in which she preserved that Agra plan from all the other papers of her father. But love is an emotional thing, and whatever is emotional is opposed to that true cold reason which I place above all things. I should never marry myself, lest I bias my judgment.'

'I trust,' said I, laughing, 'that my judgment may survive the ordeal. But you look weary.'

'Yes, the reaction is already upon me. I shall be as limp as a rag for a week.'

'Strange,' said I, 'how terms of what in another man I should call laziness alternate with your fits of splendid energy and vigour.'

'Yes,' he answered, 'there are in me the makings of a very fine loafer, and also of a pretty spry sort of fellow. I often think of those lines of old Goethe:

> Schade dass die Natur nur *einen* Mensch aus dir schuf,
> Denn zum würdigen Mann war und zum Schelmen der Stoff.*

By the way, *à propos* of this Norwood business, you see that they had, as I surmised, a confederate in the house, who could be none other than Lal Rao, the butler: so Jones actually has the undivided honour of having caught one fish in his great haul.'

'The division seems rather unfair,' I remarked. 'You have done all the work in this business. I get a wife out of it, Jones gets the credit, pray what remains for you?'

'For me,' said Sherlock Holmes, 'there still remains the cocaine-bottle.' And he stretched his long white hand up for it.

A SCANDAL IN BOHEMIA

To Sherlock Holmes she is always *the* woman. I have seldom heard him mention her under any other name. In his eyes she eclipses and predominates the whole of her sex. It was not that he felt any emotion akin to love for Irene Adler. All emotions, and that one particularly, were abhorrent to his cold, precise, but admirably balanced mind. He was, I take it, the most perfect reasoning and observing machine that the world has seen; but, as a lover, he would have placed himself in a false position. He never spoke of the softer passions, save with a gibe and a sneer. They were admirable things for the observer— excellent for drawing the veil from men's motives and actions. But for the trained reasoner to admit such intrusions into his own delicate and finely adjusted temperament was to introduce a distracting factor which might throw a doubt upon all his mental results. Grit in a sensitive instrument, or a crack in one of his own high-power lenses, would not be more disturbing than a strong emotion in a nature such as his. And yet there was but one woman to him, and that woman was the late Irene Adler, of dubious and questionable memory.

I had seen little of Holmes since the singular chain of events which I have already narrated in a bold fashion under the heading of *The Sign of the Four*. My marriage had, as he foretold, drifted us away from each other. My own complete happiness, and the home-centred interests which rise up around the man who first finds himself master of his own establishment, were sufficient to absorb all my attention; while Holmes, who loathed every form of society with his whole Bohemian soul, remained in our lodgings in Baker Street, buried among his old books, and alternating from week to week between cocaine and ambition, the drowsiness of the drug, and the fierce energy of his own keen nature. He was still, as ever, deeply attracted by the study of crime, and occupied his immense faculties and extraordinary powers of observation in following out those clues, and clearing up those mysteries, which had been abandoned as hopeless by the official police. From time to time I heard some vague account of his doings: of his summons to Odessa in the case of the Trepoff murder, of his clearing up of the singular tragedy of the Atkinson brothers at Trincomalee,* and finally of the mission which he had accomplished so delicately and successfully for the reigning family of Holland. Beyond these signs of his activity, however, which I merely shared with all the readers of the daily press, I knew little of my former friend and companion.

One night—it was on the 20th of March, 1888—I was returning from a journey to a patient (for I had now returned to civil practice*), when my way led me through Baker Street. As I passed the well-remembered door, which must always be associated in my mind with my wooing, and with the dark incidents of the Study in Scarlet, I was seized with a keen desire to see Holmes again, and to know how he was employing his extraordinary powers. His rooms were brilliantly lit, and, even as I looked up, I saw his tall spare figure pass twice in a dark silhouette against the blind. He was pacing the room swiftly, eagerly, with his head sunk upon his chest, and his hands clasped behind him. To me, who knew his every mood and habit, his attitude and manner told their own story. He was at work again. He had risen out of his drug-created dreams, and was hot upon the scent of some new problem. I rang the bell, and was shown up to the chamber which had formerly been in part my own.

His manner was not effusive. It seldom was; but he was glad, I think, to see me. With hardly a word spoken, but with a kindly eye, he waved me to an armchair, threw across his case of cigars, and indicated a spirit case* and a gasogene* in the corner. Then he stood before the fire, and looked me over in his singular introspective fashion.

'Wedlock suits you,' he remarked. 'I think, Watson, that you have put on seven and a half pounds since I saw you.'

'Seven,' I answered.

'Indeed, I should have thought a little more. Just a trifle more, I fancy, Watson. And in practice again, I observe. You did not tell me that you intended to go into harness.'*

'Then, how do you know?'

'I see it, I deduce it. How do I know that you have been getting yourself very wet lately, and that you have a most clumsy and careless servant girl?'

'My dear Holmes,' said I, 'this is too much. You would certainly have been burned had you lived a few centuries ago. It is true that I had a country walk on Thursday and came home in a dreadful mess; but, as I have changed my clothes, I can't imagine how you deduce it. As to Mary Jane, she is incorrigible, and my wife has given her notice; but there again I fail to see how you work it out.'

He chuckled to himself and rubbed his long nervous hands together.

'It is simplicity itself,' said he; 'my eyes tell me that on the inside of your left shoe, just where the firelight strikes it, the leather is scored by six almost parallel cuts. Obviously they have been caused by someone who has very carelessly scraped round the edges of the sole in order to remove crusted mud from it. Hence, you see, my double deduction that you had been out in vile weather, and that you had a particularly malignant boot-slitting specimen of the London slavey.* As to your practice, if a gentleman walks into my rooms smelling of iodoform,* with a black mark of nitrate of silver* upon his right fore-finger, and a bulge on the side of his top hat to show where he has secreted his stethoscope, I must be dull indeed if I do not pronounce him to be an active member of the medical profession.'

I could not help laughing at the ease with which he explained his process of deduction. 'When I hear you give your reasons,' I remarked, 'the thing always appears to me to be so ridiculously simple that I could easily do it myself, though at each successive instance of your reasoning I am baffled, until you explain your process. And yet I believe that my eyes are as good as yours.'

'Quite so,' he answered, lighting a cigarette, and throwing himself down into an armchair. 'You see, but you do not observe. The distinction is clear. For example, you have frequently seen the steps which lead up from the hall to this room.'

'Frequently.'

'How often?'

'Well, some hundreds of times.'

'Then how many are there?'

'How many! I don't know.'

'Quite so. You have not observed. And yet you have seen. That is just my point. Now, I know that there are seventeen steps, because I have both seen and observed. By the way, since you are interested in these little problems, and since you are good enough to chronicle one or two of my trifling experiences, you may be interested in this.' He threw over a sheet of thick, pink-tinted note-paper which had been lying open upon the table. 'It came by the last post,'* said he. 'Read it aloud.'

The note was undated, and without either signature or address.

'There will call upon you tonight, at a quarter to eight o'clock,' it said, 'a gentleman who desires to consult you upon a matter of the very deepest moment. Your recent services to one of the Royal Houses of Europe have shown that you are one who may safely be trusted with matters which are of an importance which can hardly be exaggerated. This account of you we have from all quarters received. Be in your chamber then at that hour, and do not take it amiss if your visitor wear a mask.'

'This is indeed a mystery,' I remarked. 'What do you imagine that it means?'

'I have no data yet. It is a capital mistake to theorize before one has data. Insensibly one begins to twist facts to suit theories, instead of theories to suit facts. But the note itself. What do you deduce from it?'

I carefully examined the writing, and the paper upon which it was written.

'The man who wrote it was presumably well-to-do,' I remarked, endeavouring to imitate my companion's processes. 'Such paper could not be bought under half-a-crown a packet. It is peculiarly strong and stiff.'

'Peculiar—that is the very word,' said Holmes. 'It is not an English paper at all. Hold it up to the light.'

I did so, and saw a large *E* with a small *g*, a *P*, and a large *G* with a small *t* woven into the texture of the paper.

'What do you make of that?' asked Holmes.

'The name of the maker, no doubt; or his monogram, rather.'

'Not at all. The *G* with the small *t* stands for "Gesellschaft", which is the German for "Company". It is a customary contraction like our "Co.". *P*, of course, stands for "Papier". Now for the *Eg*. Let us glance at our Continental Gazetteer.'* He took down a heavy brown volume from his shelves. 'Eglow, Eglonitz—here we are, Egria. It is in a German-speaking country—in Bohemia, not far from Carlsbad.* "Remarkable as being the scene of the death of Wallenstein,* and for its numerous glass factories and paper mills." Ha, ha, my boy, what do you make of that?' His eyes sparkled, and he sent up a great blue triumphant cloud from his cigarette.

'The paper was made in Bohemia,' I said.

'Precisely. And the man who wrote the note is a German. Do you note the peculiar construction of the sentence—"This account of you we have from all quarters received". A Frenchman or Russian

could not have written that. It is the German who is so uncourteous
to his verbs. It only remains, therefore, to discover what is wanted by
this German who writes upon Bohemian paper, and prefers wearing
a mask to showing his face. And here he comes, if I am not mistaken,
to resolve all our doubts.'

As he spoke there was the sharp sound of horses' hoofs and grating
wheels against the kerb, followed by a sharp pull at the bell. Holmes
whistled.

'A pair, by the sound,' said he. 'Yes,' he continued, glancing out of
the window. 'A nice little brougham* and a pair of beauties. A hundred and fifty guineas apiece. There's money in this case, Watson, if
there is nothing else.'

'I think that I had better go, Holmes.'

'Not a bit, Doctor. Stay where you are. I am lost without my
Boswell.* And this promises to be interesting. It would be a pity to
miss it.'

'But your client—'

'Never mind him. I may want your help, and so may he. Here
he comes. Sit down in that armchair, Doctor, and give us your best
attention.'

A slow and heavy step, which had been heard upon the stairs and
in the passage, paused immediately outside the door. Then there was
a loud and authoritative tap.

'Come in!' said Holmes.

A man entered who could hardly have been less than six feet
six inches in height, with the chest and limbs of a Hercules. His
dress was rich with a richness which would, in England, be looked
upon as akin to bad taste. Heavy bands of astrakhan* were slashed
across the sleeves and fronts of his double-breasted coat, while the
deep blue cloak which was thrown over his shoulders was lined
with flame-coloured silk, and secured at the neck with a brooch
which consisted of a single flaming beryl.* Boots which extended
half-way up his calves, and which were trimmed at the tops with
a rich brown fur, completed the impression of barbaric opulence
which was suggested by his whole appearance. He carried a broad-
brimmed hat in his hand, while he wore across the upper part of his
face, extending down past the cheek-bones, a black vizard mask,*
which he had apparently adjusted that very moment, for his hand
was still raised to it as he entered. From the lower part of the face

he appeared to be a man of strong character, with a thick, hanging lip, and a long straight chin, suggestive of resolution pushed to the length of obstinacy.

'You had my note?' he asked, with a deep, harsh voice and a strongly marked German accent. 'I told you that I would call.' He looked from one to the other of us, as if uncertain which to address.

'Pray take a seat,' said Holmes. 'This is my friend and colleague, Dr Watson, who is occasionally good enough to help me in my cases. Whom have I the honour to address?'

'You may address me as the Count von Kramm, a Bohemian nobleman. I understand that this gentleman, your friend, is a man of honour and discretion, whom I may trust with a matter of the most extreme importance. If not, I should much prefer to communicate with you alone.'

I rose to go, but Holmes caught me by the wrist and pushed me back into my chair. 'It is both, or none,' said he. 'You may say before this gentleman anything which you may say to me.'

The Count shrugged his broad shoulders. 'Then I must begin,' said he, 'by binding you both to absolute secrecy for two years, at the end of that time the matter will be of no importance. At present it is not too much to say that it is of such weight that it may have an influence upon European history.'

'I promise,' said Holmes.

'And I.'

'You will excuse this mask,' continued our strange visitor. 'The august person who employs me wishes his agent to be unknown to you, and I may confess at once that the title by which I have just called myself is not exactly my own.'

'I was aware of it,' said Holmes dryly.

'The circumstances are of great delicacy, and every precaution has to be taken to quench what might grow to be an immense scandal and seriously compromise one of the reigning families of Europe. To speak plainly, the matter implicates the great House of Ormstein, hereditary kings of Bohemia.'

'I was also aware of that,' murmured Holmes, settling himself down in his armchair, and closing his eyes.

Our visitor glanced with some apparent surprise at the languid, lounging figure of the man who had been no doubt depicted to him as the most incisive reasoner, and most energetic agent in Europe.

Holmes slowly reopened his eyes, and looked impatiently at his gigantic client.

'If your Majesty would condescend to state your case,' he remarked, 'I should be better able to advise you.'

The man sprang from his chair, and paced up and down the room in uncontrollable agitation. Then, with a gesture of desperation, he tore the mask from his face and hurled it upon the ground. 'You are right,' he cried, 'I am the King. Why should I attempt to conceal it?'

'Why, indeed?' murmured Holmes. 'Your Majesty had not spoken before I was aware that I was addressing Wilhelm Gottsreich Sigismond von Ormstein, Grand Duke of Cassel-Felstein, and hereditary King of Bohemia.'

'But you can understand,' said our strange visitor, sitting down once more and passing his hand over his high, white forehead, 'you can understand that I am not accustomed to doing such business in my own person. Yet the matter was so delicate that I could not confide it to an agent without putting myself in his power. I have come *incognito* from Prague for the purpose of consulting you.'

'Then, pray consult,' said Holmes, shutting his eyes once more.

'The facts are briefly these: Some five years ago, during a lengthy visit to Warsaw, I made the acquaintance of the well-known adventuress Irene Adler. The name is no doubt familiar to you.'

'Kindly look her up in my index, Doctor,' murmured Holmes, without opening his eyes. For many years he had adopted a system of docketing all paragraphs concerning men and things, so that it was difficult to name a subject or a person on which he could not at once furnish information. In this case I found her biography sandwiched in between that of a Hebrew Rabbi and that of a staff-commander who had written a monograph upon the deep-sea fishes.

'Let me see,' said Holmes. 'Hum! Born in New Jersey in the year 1858. Contralto—hum! La Scala,* hum! Prima donna Imperial Opera of Warsaw—Yes! Retired from operatic stage—ha! Living in London—quite so! Your Majesty, as I understand, became entangled with this young person, wrote her some compromising letters, and is now desirous of getting those letters back.'

'Precisely so. But how—'

'Was there a secret marriage?'

'None.'

'No legal papers or certificates?'

'None.'

'Then I fail to follow your Majesty. If this young person should produce her letters for blackmailing or other purposes, how is she to prove their authenticity?'

'There is the writing.'

'Pooh, pooh! Forgery.'

'My private note-paper.'

'Stolen.'

'My own seal.'

'Imitated.'

'My photograph.'

'Bought.'

'We were both in the photograph.'

'Oh, dear! That is very bad! Your Majesty has indeed committed an indiscretion.'

'I was mad—insane.'

'You have compromised yourself seriously.'

'I was only Crown Prince then. I was young. I am but thirty now.'

'It must be recovered.'

'We have tried and failed.'

'Your Majesty must pay. It must be bought.'

'She will not sell.'

'Stolen, then.'

'Five attempts have been made. Twice burglars in my pay ransacked her house. Once we diverted her luggage when she travelled. Twice she has been waylaid. There has been no result.'

'No sign of it?'

'Absolutely none.'

Holmes laughed. 'It is quite a pretty little problem,' said he.

'But a very serious one to me,' returned the King, reproachfully.

'Very, indeed. And what does she propose to do with the photograph?'

'To ruin me.'

'But how?'

'I am about to be married.'

'So I have heard.'

'To Clotilde Lothman von Saxe-Meningen, second daughter of the King of Scandinavia. You may know the strict principles of her family. She is herself the very soul of delicacy. A shadow of a doubt as to my conduct would bring the matter to an end.'

'And Irene Adler?'

'Threatens to send them the photograph. And she will do it. I know that she will do it. You do not know her, but she has a soul of steel. She has the face of the most beautiful of women, and the mind of the most resolute of men. Rather than I should marry another woman, there are no lengths to which she would not go—none.'

'You are sure that she has not sent it yet?'

'I am sure.'

'And why?'

'Because she has said that she would send it on the day when the betrothal was publicly proclaimed. That will be next Monday.'

'Oh, then, we have three days yet,' said Holmes, with a yawn. 'That is very fortunate, as I have one or two matters of importance to look into just at present. Your Majesty will, of course, stay in London for the present?'

'Certainly. You will find me at the Langham,* under the name of the Count von Kramm.'

'Then I shall drop you a line to let you know how we progress.'

'Pray do so. I shall be all anxiety.'

'Then, as to money?'

'You have *carte blanche.*'

'Absolutely?'

'I tell you that I would give one of the provinces of my kingdom to have that photograph.'

'And for present expenses?'

The King took a heavy chamois leather bag from under his cloak, and laid it on the table.

'There are three hundred pounds in gold, and seven hundred in notes,' he said.

Holmes scribbled a receipt upon a sheet of his note-book, and handed it to him.

'And mademoiselle's address?' he asked.

'Is Briony Lodge, Serpentine Avenue, St John's Wood.'

Holmes took a note of it. 'One other question,' said he. 'Was the photograph a cabinet?'*

'It was.'

'Then, good-night, your Majesty, and I trust that we shall soon have some good news for you. And good night, Watson,' he added, as the wheels of the Royal brougham rolled down the street. 'If you will be good enough to call tomorrow afternoon, at three o'clock, I should like to chat this little matter over with you.'

At three o'clock precisely I was at Baker Street, but Holmes had not yet returned. The landlady informed me that he had left the house shortly after eight o'clock in the morning. I sat down beside the fire, however, with the intention of awaiting him, however long he might be. I was already deeply interested in his inquiry, for, though it was surrounded by none of the grim and strange features which were associated with the two crimes which I have elsewhere recorded,* still, the nature of the case and the exalted station of his client gave it a character of its own. Indeed, apart from the nature of the investigation which my friend had on hand, there was something in his masterly grasp of a situation, and his keen, incisive reasoning, which made it a pleasure to me to study his system of work, and to follow the quick, subtle methods by which he disentangled the most inextricable mysteries. So accustomed was I to his invariable success that the very possibility of his failing had ceased to enter into my head.

It was close upon four before the door opened, and a drunken-looking groom,* ill-kempt and side-whiskered with an inflamed face and disreputable clothes, walked into the room. Accustomed as I was to my friend's amazing powers in the use of disguises, I had to look three times before I was certain that it was indeed he. With a nod he vanished into the bedroom, whence he emerged in five minutes tweed-suited and respectable, as of old. Putting his hands into his pockets, he stretched out his legs in front of the fire, and laughed heartily for some minutes.

'Well, really!' he cried, and then he choked; and laughed again until he was obliged to lie back, limp and helpless, in the chair.

'What is it?'

'It's quite too funny. I am sure you could never guess how I employed my morning, or what I ended by doing.'

'I can't imagine. I suppose that you have been watching the habits, and perhaps the house, of Miss Irene Adler.'

'Quite so, but the sequel was rather unusual. I will tell you, how-ever. I left the house a little after eight o'clock this morning, in the character of a groom out of work. There is a wonderful sympathy and freemasonry among horsey men. Be one of them, and you will know all that there is to know. I soon found Briony Lodge. It is a *bijou* villa, with a garden at the back, but built out in front right up to the road, two stories. Chubb lock* to the door. Large sitting-room on the right side, well-furnished, with long windows almost to the floor, and those preposterous English window fasteners which a child could open. Behind there was nothing remarkable, save that the passage window could be reached from the top of the coach-house. I walked round it and examined it closely from every point of view, but without noting anything else of interest.

'I then lounged down the street, and found, as I expected, that there was a mews in a lane which runs down by one wall of the garden. I lent the ostlers* a hand in rubbing down their horses, and I received in exchange twopence, a glass of half-and-half,* two fills of shag tobacco,* and as much information as I could desire about Miss Adler, to say nothing of half a dozen other people in the neighbourhood in whom I was not in the least interested, but whose biographies I was compelled to listen to.'

'And what of Irene Adler?' I asked.

'Oh, she has turned all the men's heads down in that part. She is the daintiest thing under a bonnet on this planet. So say the Serpentine Mews, to a man. She lives quietly, sings at concerts, drives out at five every day, and returns at seven sharp for dinner. Seldom goes out at other times, except when she sings. Has only one male visitor, but a good deal of him. He is dark, handsome, and dashing; never calls less than once a day, and often twice. He is a Mr Godfrey Norton, of the Inner Temple.* See the advantages of a cabman as a confidant. They had driven him home a dozen times from Serpentine Mews, and knew all about him. When I had listened to all that they had to tell, I began to walk up and down near Briony Lodge once more, and to think over my plan of campaign.

'This Godfrey Norton was evidently an important factor in the matter. He was a lawyer. That sounded ominous. What was the relation between them, and what the object of his repeated visits? Was she his client, his friend, or his mistress? If the former, she had probably transferred the photograph to his keeping. If the latter, it was less likely. On the issue of this question depended whether I should continue my work at Briony Lodge, or turn my attention to the gentleman's chambers in the Temple. It was a delicate point, and it widened the field of my inquiry. I fear that I bore you with these details, but I have to let you see my little difficulties, if you are to understand the situation.'

'I am following you closely,' I answered.

'I was still balancing the matter in my mind when a hansom cab* drove up to Briony Lodge, and a gentleman sprang out. He was a remarkably handsome man, dark, aquiline, and moustached— evidently the man of whom I had heard. He appeared to be in a great hurry, shouted to the cabman to wait, and brushed past the maid who opened the door with the air of a man who was thoroughly at home.

'He was in the house about half an hour, and I could catch glimpses of him, in the windows of the sitting-room, pacing up and down, talking excitedly and waving his arms. Of her I could see nothing. Presently he emerged, looking even more flurried than before. As he stepped up to the cab, he pulled a gold watch from his pocket and looked at it earnestly, "Drive like the devil," he shouted, "first to Gross and Hankey's in Regent Street, and then to the church of St Monica in the Edgware Road. Half a guinea if you do it in twenty minutes!"

'Away they went, and I was just wondering whether I should not do well to follow them, when up the lane came a neat little landau,* the coachman with his coat only half buttoned, and his tie under his ear, while all the tags of his harness were sticking out of the buckles. It hadn't pulled up before she shot out of the hall door and into it. I only caught a glimpse of her at the moment, but she was a lovely woman, with a face that a man might die for.

'"The Church of St Monica, John," she cried, "and half a sovereign if you reach it in twenty minutes."

'This was quite too good to lose, Watson. I was just balancing whether I should run for it, or whether I should perch behind her landau, when a cab came through the street. The driver looked twice at such a shabby fare; but I jumped in before he could object. "The Church of St Monica," said I, "and half a sovereign if you reach it in twenty minutes." It was twenty-five minutes to twelve,* and of course it was clear enough what was in the wind.

'My cabby drove fast. I don't think I ever drove faster, but the others were there before us. The cab and the landau with their steaming horses were in front of the door when I arrived. I paid the man, and hurried into the church. There was not a soul there save the two whom I had followed, and a surpliced clergyman, who seemed to be expostulating with them. They were all three standing in a knot in front of the altar. I lounged up the side aisle like any other idler who has dropped into a church. Suddenly, to my surprise, the three at the altar faced round to me, and Godfrey Norton came running as hard as he could towards me.

' "Thank God!" he cried. "You'll do. Come! Come!"

' "What then?" I asked.

' "Come, man, come, only three minutes, or it won't be legal."

'I was half dragged up to the altar, and before I knew where I was, I found myself mumbling responses which were whispered in my ear, and vouching for things of which I knew nothing, and generally assisting in the secure tying up of Irene Adler, spinster, to Godfrey Norton, bachelor. It was all done in an instant, and there was the gentleman thanking me on the one side and the lady on the other, while the clergyman beamed on me in front. It was the most pre-posterous position in which I ever found myself in my life, and it was the thought of it that started me laughing just now. It seems that there had been some informality about their licence, that the clergy-man absolutely refused to marry them without a witness of some sort, and that my lucky appearance saved the bridegroom from having to sally out into the streets in search of a best man. The bride gave me a sovereign, and I mean to wear it on my watch-chain in memory of the occasion.'

'This is a very unexpected turn of affairs,' said I; 'and what then?'

'Well, I found my plans very seriously menaced. It looked as if the pair might take an immediate departure, and so necessitate very prompt and energetic measures on my part. At the church door, how-ever, they separated, he driving back to the Temple, and she to her own house. "I shall drive out in the Park at five as usual," she said as she left him. I heard no more. They drove away in different direc-tions, and I went off to make my own arrangements.'

'Which are?'

'Some cold beef and a glass of beer,' he answered, ringing the bell. 'I have been too busy to think of food, and I am likely to be busier still this evening. By the way, Doctor, I shall want your co-operation.'

'I shall be delighted.'

'You don't mind breaking the law?'

'Not in the least.'

'Nor running a chance of arrest?'

'Not in a good cause.'

'Oh, the cause is excellent!'

'Then I am your man.'

'I was sure that I might rely on you.'

'But what is it you wish?'

'When Mrs Turner* has brought in the tray I will make it clear to you. Now,' he said, as he turned hungrily on the simple fare that our landlady had provided, 'I must discuss it while I eat, for I have not much time. It is nearly five now. In two hours we must be on the scene of action. Miss Irene, or Madame, rather, returns from her drive at seven. We must be at Briony Lodge to meet her.'

'And what then?'

'You must leave that to me. I have already arranged what is to occur. There is only one point on which I must insist. You must not interfere, come what may. You understand?'

'I am to be neutral?'

'To do nothing whatever. There will probably be some small unpleasantness. Do not join in it. It will end in my being conveyed into the house. Four or five minutes afterwards the sitting-room window will open. You are to station yourself close to that open window.'

'Yes.'

'You are to watch me, for I will be visible to you.'

'Yes.'

'And when I raise my hand—so—you will throw into the room what I give you to throw, and will, at the same time, raise the cry of fire. You quite follow me?'

'Entirely.'

'It is nothing very formidable,' he said, taking a long cigar-shaped roll from his pocket. 'It is an ordinary plumber's smoke rocket,* fitted with a cap* at either end to make it self-lighting. Your task is confined to that. When you raise your cry of fire, it will be taken up by quite a number of people. You may then walk to the end of the street, and I will rejoin you in ten minutes. I hope that I have made myself clear?'

'I am to remain neutral, to get near the window, to watch you, and, at the signal, to throw in this object, then to raise the cry of fire, and to await you at the corner of the street.'

'Precisely.'

'Then you may entirely rely on me.'

'That is excellent. I think perhaps it is almost time that I prepared for the new *rôle* I have to play.'

He disappeared into his bedroom, and returned in a few minutes in the character of an amiable and simple-minded Non-conformist clergyman. His broad black hat, his baggy trousers, his white tie, his sympathetic smile, and general look of peering and benevolent curiosity, were such as Mr John Hare* alone could have equalled. It was not merely that Holmes changed his costume. His expression, his manner, his very soul seemed to vary with every fresh part that he assumed. The stage lost a fine actor, even as science lost an acute reasoner, when he became a specialist in crime.

It was a quarter past six when we left Baker Street, and it still wanted ten minutes to the hour when we found ourselves in Serpentine Avenue. It was already dusk, and the lamps were just being lighted as we paced up and down in front of Briony Lodge, waiting for the coming of its occupant. The house was just such as I had pictured it from Sherlock Holmes's succinct description, but the locality appeared to be less private than I expected. On the contrary, for a small street in a quiet neighbourhood, it was remarkably animated. There was a group of shabbily-dressed men smoking and laughing in a corner, a scissors-grinder* with his wheel, two guardsmen who were flirting with a nurse-girl, and several well-dressed young men who were lounging up and down with cigars in their mouths.

'You see,' remarked Holmes, as we paced to and fro in front of the house, 'this marriage rather simplifies matters. The photograph becomes a double-edged weapon now. The chances are that she would be as averse to its being seen by Mr Godfrey Norton, as our client is to its coming to the eyes of his Princess. Now the question is—Where are we to find the photograph?'

'Where, indeed?'

'It is most unlikely that she carries it about with her. It is cabinet size. Too large for easy concealment about a woman's dress. She knows that the King is capable of having her waylaid and searched. Two attempts of the sort have already been made. We may take it then that she does not carry it about with her.'

'Where, then?'

'Her banker or her lawyer. There is that double possibility. But I am inclined to think neither. Women are naturally secretive, and they like to do their own secreting. Why should she hand it over to anyone else? She could trust her own guardianship, but she could not tell what indirect or political influence might be brought to bear upon a business man. Besides, remember that she had resolved to use it within a few days. It must be where she can lay her hands upon it. It must be in her own house.'

'But it has twice been burgled.'

'Pshaw! They did not know how to look.'

'But how will you look?'

'I will not look.'

'What then?'

'I will get her to show me.'

'But she will refuse.'

'She will not be able to. But I hear the rumble of wheels. It is her carriage. Now carry out my orders to the letter.'

As he spoke, the gleam of the sidelights of a carriage came round the curve of the avenue. It was a smart little landau which rattled up to the door of Briony Lodge. As it pulled up, one of the loafing men at the corner dashed forward to open the door in the hope of earning a copper, but was elbowed away by another loafer who had rushed up with the same intention. A fierce quarrel broke out, which was increased by the two guardsmen, who took sides with one of the loungers, and by the scissors-grinder, who was equally hot upon the other side. A blow was struck, and in an instant the lady, who had stepped from her carriage, was the centre of a little knot of flushed and struggling men who struck savagely at each other with their fists and sticks. Holmes dashed into the crowd to protect the lady; but just as he reached her, he gave a cry and dropped to the ground, with the blood running freely down his face. At his fall the guardsmen took to their heels in one direction and the loungers in the other, while a number of better dressed people who had watched the scuffle without taking part in it, crowded in to help the lady and to attend to the injured man. Irene Adler, as I will still call her, had hurried up the steps; but she stood at the top with her superb figure outlined against the lights of the hall, looking back into the street.

'Is the poor gentleman much hurt?' she asked.

'He is dead,' cried several voices.

'No, no, there's life in him,' shouted another. 'But he'll be gone before you can get him to hospital.'

'He's a brave fellow,' said a woman. 'They would have had the lady's purse and watch if it hadn't been for him. They were a gang, and a rough one, too. Ah, he's breathing now.'

'He can't lie in the street. May we bring him in, marm?'

'Surely. Bring him into the sitting-room. There is a comfortable sofa. This way, please!'

Slowly and solemnly he was borne into Briony Lodge, and laid out in the principal room, while I still observed the proceedings from my post by the window. The lamps had been lit, but the blinds had not been drawn, so that I could see Holmes as he lay upon the couch. I do not know whether he was seized with compunction at that moment for the part he was playing, but I know that I never felt more heartily ashamed of myself in my life than when I saw the beautiful creature against whom I was conspiring, or the grace and kindliness with which she waited upon the injured man. And yet it would be the blackest treachery to Holmes to draw back now from the part which he had entrusted to me. I hardened my heart and took the smoke-rocket from under my ulster.* After all, I thought, we are not injuring her. We are but preventing her from injuring another.

Holmes had sat up upon the couch, and I saw him motion like a man who is in want of air. A maid rushed across and threw open the window. At the same instant I saw him raise his hand, and at the signal I tossed my rocket into the room with a cry of 'Fire'. The word was no sooner out of my mouth than the whole crowd of spectators, well dressed and ill—gentlemen, ostlers, and servant maids—joined in a general shriek of 'Fire'. Thick clouds of smoke curled into the room, and out at the open window. I caught a glimpse of rushing figures, and a moment later the voice of Holmes from within, assuring them that it was a false alarm. Slipping through the shouting crowd I made my way to the corner of the street, and in ten minutes was rejoiced to find my friend's arm in mine, and to get away from the scene of the uproar. He walked swiftly and in silence for some few minutes, until we had turned down one of the quiet streets which lead towards the Edgware Road.

'You did it very nicely, Doctor,' he remarked. 'Nothing could have been better. It is all right.'

'You have the photograph!'

'I know where it is.'

'And how did you find out?'

'She showed me, as I told you she would.'

'I am still in the dark.'

'I do not wish to make a mystery,' said he, laughing. 'The matter was perfectly simple. You, of course, saw that everyone in the street was an accomplice. They were all engaged for the evening.'

'I guessed as much.'

'Then, when the row broke out, I had a little moist red paint in the palm of my hand. I rushed forward, fell down, clapped my hand to my face, and became a piteous spectacle. It is an old trick.'

'That also I could fathom.'

'Then they carried me in. She was bound to have me in. What else could she do? And into her sitting-room which was the very room which I suspected. It lay between that and her bedroom, and I was determined to see which. They laid me on a couch, I motioned for air, they were compelled to open the window, and you had your chance.'

'How did that help you?'

'It was all-important. When a woman thinks that her house is on fire, her instinct is at once to rush to the thing which she values most. It is a perfectly overpowering impulse, and I have more than once taken advantage of it. In the case of the Darlington Substitution Scandal it was of use to me, and also in the Arnsworth Castle business. A married woman grabs at her baby—an unmarried one reaches for her jewel box. Now it was clear to me that our lady of to-day had nothing in the house more precious to her than what we are in quest of. She would rush to secure it. The alarm of fire was admirably done. The smoke and shouting was enough to shake nerves of steel. She responded beautifully. The photograph is in a recess behind a sliding panel just above the right bell-pull. She was there in an instant, and I caught a glimpse of it as she half drew it out. When I cried out that it was a false alarm, she replaced it, glanced at the rocket, rushed from the room, and I have not seen her since. I rose, and, making my excuses, escaped from the house. I hesitated whether to attempt to secure the photograph at once; but the coachman had come in, and as he was watching me narrowly, it seemed safer to wait. A little over-precipitance may ruin all.'

'And now?' I asked.

'Our quest is practically finished. I shall call with the King tomorrow, and with you, if you care to come with us. We will be shown into the sitting-room to wait for the lady, but it is probable that when she comes she may find neither us nor the photograph. It might be a satisfaction to His Majesty to regain it with his own hands.'

'And when will you call?'

'At eight in the morning. She will not be up, so that we shall have a clear field. Besides, we must be prompt, for this marriage may mean a complete change in her life and habits. I must wire to the King without delay.'

We had reached Baker Street, and had stopped at the door. He was searching his pockets for the key, when some one passing said:

'Good night, Mister Sherlock Holmes.'

There were several people on the pavement at the time, but the greeting appeared to come from a slim youth in an ulster who had hurried by.

'I've heard that voice before,' said Holmes, staring down the dimly lit street. 'Now, I wonder who the deuce that could have been.'

I slept at Baker Street that night, and we were engaged upon our toast and coffee when the King of Bohemia rushed into the room.

'You have really got it!' he cried, grasping Sherlock Holmes by either shoulder, and looking eagerly into his face.

'Not yet.'

'But you have hopes?'

'I have hopes.'

'Then, come. I am all impatience to be gone.'

'We must have a cab.'

'No, my brougham is waiting.'

'Then that will simplify matters.'

We descended, and started off once more for Briony Lodge.

'Irene Adler is married,' remarked Holmes.

'Married! When?'

'Yesterday.'

'But to whom?'

'To an English lawyer named Norton.'

'But she could not love him?'

'I am in hopes that she does.'

'And why in hopes?'

'Because it would spare your Majesty all fear of future annoyance. If the lady loves her husband, she does not love your Majesty. If she does not love your Majesty there is no reason why she should interfere with your Majesty's plan.'

'It is true. And yet——! Well! I wish she had been of my own station! What a queen she would have made!' He relapsed into a moody silence which was not broken until we drew up in Serpentine Avenue.

The door of Briony Lodge was open, and an elderly woman stood upon the steps. She watched us with a sardonic eye as we stepped from the brougham.

'Mr Sherlock Holmes, I believe?' said she.

'I am Mr Holmes,' answered my companion, looking at her with a questioning and rather startled gaze.

'Indeed! My mistress told me that you were likely to call. She left this morning with her husband, by the 5.15 train from Charing Cross, for the Continent.'

'What!' Sherlock Holmes staggered back, white with chagrin and surprise. 'Do you mean that she has left England?'

'Never to return.'

'And the papers?' asked the King, hoarsely. 'All is lost.'

'We shall see.' He pushed past the servant, and rushed into the drawing-room, followed by the King and myself. The furniture was scattered about in every direction, with dismantled shelves, and open drawers, as if the lady had hurriedly ransacked them before her flight. Holmes rushed at the bell-pull, tore back a small sliding shutter, and, plunging in his hand, pulled out a photograph and a letter. The photograph was of Irene Adler herself in evening dress, the letter was superscribed to 'Sherlock Holmes, Esq. To be left till called for.' My friend tore it open and we all three read it together. It was dated at midnight of the preceding night, and ran in this way:

MY DEAR MR SHERLOCK HOLMES,

You really did it very well. You took me in completely. Until after the alarm of fire, I had not a suspicion. But then, when I found how I had betrayed myself, I began to think. I had been warned against you months ago. I had been told that if the King employed an agent, it would certainly be you. And your address had been given me. Yet, with all this, you made me reveal what you wanted to know. Even after I became suspicious, I found it hard to think evil of such a dear, kind old clergyman. But, you know, I have been trained as an actress myself. Male costume is nothing new to me. I often take advantage of the freedom which it gives. I sent John, the coachman, to watch you, ran upstairs, got into my walking clothes, as I call them, and came down just as you departed.

Well, I followed you to your door and so made sure that I was really an object of interest to the celebrated Mr Sherlock Holmes. Then I, rather imprudently, wished you good-night, and started for the Temple to see my husband.

We both thought the best resource was flight when pursued by so formidable an antagonist; so you will find the nest empty when you call to-morrow. As to the photograph, your client may rest in peace. I love and am loved by a better man than he. The King may do what he will without hindrance from one whom he has cruelly wronged. I keep it only to safeguard myself, and to preserve a weapon which will always secure me from any steps which he might take in the future. I leave a photograph which he might care to possess; and I remain, dear Mr Sherlock Holmes, very truly yours, IRENE NORTON, *née* ADLER

'What a woman—oh, what a woman!' cried the King of Bohemia, when we had all three read this epistle. 'Did I not tell you how quick and resolute she was? Would she not have made an admirable queen? Is it not a pity she was not on my level?'

'From what I have seen of the lady, she seems, indeed, to be on a very different level to your Majesty,' said Holmes, coldly. 'I am sorry that I have not been able to bring your Majesty's business to a more successful conclusion.'

'On the contrary, my dear sir,' cried the King. 'Nothing could be more successful. I know that her word is inviolate. The photograph is now as safe as if it were in the fire.'

'I am glad to hear your Majesty say so.'

'I am immensely indebted to you. Pray tell me in what way I can reward you. This ring—' He slipped an emerald snake ring from his finger and held it out upon the palm of his hand.

'Your Majesty has something which I should value even more highly,' said Holmes.

'You have but to name it.'

'This photograph!'

The King stared at him in amazement.

'Irene's photograph!' he cried. 'Certainly, if you wish it.'

'I thank your Majesty. Then there is no more to be done in the matter. I have the honour to wish you a very good morning.'

He bowed, and, turning away without observing the hand which the King stretched out to him, he set off in my company for his chambers.

And that was how a great scandal threatened to affect the kingdom of Bohemia, and how the best plans of Mr Sherlock Holmes were beaten by a woman's wit. He used to make merry over the cleverness of women, but I have not heard him do it of late. And when he speaks of Irene Adler, or when he refers to her photograph, it is always under the honourable title of *the* woman.

A CASE OF IDENTITY

'My dear fellow,' said Sherlock Holmes, as we sat on either side of the fire in his lodgings at Baker Street, 'life is infinitely stranger than anything which the mind of man could invent. We would not dare to conceive the things which are really mere commonplaces of existence. If we could fly out of that window hand in hand, hover over this great city, gently remove the roofs, and peep in at the queer things which are going on, the strange coincidences, the plannings, the cross-purposes, the wonderful chains of events, working through generations, and leading to the most *outré*** results, it would make all fiction with its conventionalities and foreseen conclusions most stale and unprofitable.'*

'And yet I am not convinced of it,' I answered. 'The cases which come to light in the papers are, as a rule, bald enough, and vulgar enough. We have in our police reports realism pushed to its extreme limits, and yet the result is, it must be confessed, neither fascinating nor artistic.'

'A certain selection and discretion must be used in producing a realistic effect,' remarked Holmes. 'This is wanting in the police report, where more stress is laid perhaps upon the platitudes of the magistrate than upon the details, which to an observer contain the vital essence of the whole matter. Depend upon it there is nothing so unnatural as the commonplace.'

I smiled and shook my head. 'I can quite understand you thinking so,' I said. 'Of course, in your position of unofficial adviser and helper to everybody who is absolutely puzzled, throughout three continents, you are brought in contact with all that is strange and bizarre. But here'—I picked up the morning paper from the ground—'let us put it to a practical test. Here is the first heading upon which I come. "A husband's cruelty to his wife." There is half a column of print, but I know without reading it that it is all perfectly familiar to me. There is, of course, the other woman, the drink, the push, the blow, the bruise, the sympathetic sister or landlady. The crudest of writers could invent nothing more crude.'

'Indeed, your example is an unfortunate one for your argument,' said Holmes, taking the paper, and glancing his eye down it. 'This is the Dundas separation case, and, as it happens, I was engaged in clearing up some small points in connection with it. The husband was a teetotaller, there was no other woman, and the conduct complained of was that he had drifted into the habit of winding up every meal by taking out his false teeth and hurling them at his wife, which you will allow is not an action likely to occur to the imagination of the average story-teller. Take a pinch of snuff, Doctor, and acknowledge that I have scored over you in your example.'

He held out his snuff-box of old gold, with a great amethyst in the centre of the lid. Its splendour was in such contrast to his homely ways and simple life that I could not help commenting upon it.

'Ah,' said he, 'I forgot that I had not seen you for some weeks. It is a little souvenir from the King of Bohemia in return for my assistance in the case of the Irene Adler papers.'

'And the ring?' I asked, glancing at a remarkable brilliant* which sparkled upon his finger.

'It was from the reigning family of Holland, though the matter in which I served them was of such delicacy that I cannot confide it even to you, who have been good enough to chronicle one or two of my little problems.'

'And have you any on hand just now?' I asked with interest.

'Some ten or twelve, but none which presents any feature of interest. They are important, you understand, without being interesting. Indeed, I have found that it is usually in unimportant matters that there is a field for observation, and for the quick analysis of cause and effect which gives the charm to an investigation. The larger crimes are apt to be the simpler, for the bigger the crime, the more obvious, as a rule, is the motive. In these cases, save for one rather intricate matter which has been referred to me from Marseilles, there is nothing which presents any features of interest. It is possible, however, that I may have something better before very many minutes are over, for this is one of my clients, or I am much mistaken.'

He had risen from his chair, and was standing between the parted blinds, gazing down into the dull, neutral-tinted London street. Looking over his shoulder I saw that on the pavement opposite there stood a large woman with a heavy fur boa round her neck, and a large curling red feather in a broad-brimmed hat which was tilted in a coquettish Duchess-of-Devonshire fashion* over her ear. From under this great panoply she peeped up in a nervous, hesitating fashion at our windows, while her body oscillated backwards and forwards, and her fingers fidgeted with her glove buttons. Suddenly, with a plunge, as of the swimmer who leaves the bank, she hurried across the road, and we heard the sharp clang of the bell.

'I have seen those symptoms before,' said Holmes, throwing his cigarette into the fire. 'Oscillation upon the pavement always means an *affaire du cœur*. She would like advice, but is not sure that the matter is not too delicate for communication. And yet even here we may discriminate. When a woman has been seriously wronged by a man she no longer oscillates, and the usual symptom is a broken bell wire. Here we may take it that there is a love matter, but that the maiden is not so much angry as perplexed, or grieved. But here she comes in person to resolve our doubts.'

As he spoke there was a tap at the door, and the boy in buttons entered to announce Miss Mary Sutherland, while the lady herself loomed behind his small black figure like a full-sailed merchantman behind a tiny pilot boat. Sherlock Holmes welcomed her with the easy courtesy for which he was remarkable, and having closed the door, and bowed her into an armchair, he looked over her in the minute and yet abstracted fashion which was peculiar to him.

'Do you not find,' he said, 'that with your short sight it is a little trying to do so much typewriting?'

'I did at first,' she answered, 'but now I know where the letters are without looking.' Then, suddenly realizing the full purport of his words, she gave a violent start, and looked up with fear and astonishment upon her broad, good-humoured face. 'You've heard about me, Mr Holmes,' she cried, 'else how could you know all that?'

'Never mind,' said Holmes, laughing, 'it is my business to know things. Perhaps I have trained myself to see what others overlook. If not, why should you come to consult me?'

'I came to you, sir, because I heard of you from Mrs Etherege, whose husband you found so easy when the police and everyone had given him up for dead. Oh, Mr Holmes, I wish you would do as much for me. I'm not rich, but still I have a hundred a year in my own right, besides the little that I make by the machine, and I would give it all to know what has become of Mr Hosmer Angel.'

'Why did you come away to consult me in such a hurry?' asked Sherlock Holmes, with his finger-tips together, and his eyes to the ceiling.

Again a startled look came over the somewhat vacuous face of Miss Mary Sutherland. 'Yes, I did bang out of the house,' she said, 'for it made me angry to see the easy way in which Mr Windibank—that is, my father—took it all. He would not go to the police, and he would not go to you, and so at last, as he would do nothing, and kept on saying that there was no harm done, it made me mad, and I just on with my things and came right away to you.'

'Your father?' said Holmes. 'Your step-father, surely, since the name is different?'

'Yes, my step-father. I call him father, though it sounds funny, too, for he is only five years and two months older than myself.'

'And your mother is alive?'

'Oh, yes, mother is alive and well. I wasn't best pleased, Mr Holmes, when she married again so soon after father's death, and a man who was nearly fifteen years younger than herself. Father was a plumber in the Tottenham Court Road, and he left a tidy business behind him, which mother carried on with Mr Hardy, the foreman, but when Mr Windibank came he made her sell the business, for he was very superior, being a traveller in wines. They got four thousand seven hundred for goodwill and interest, which wasn't near as much as father could have got if he had been alive.'

I had expected to see Sherlock Holmes impatient under this rambling and inconsequential narrative, but, on the contrary, he had listened with the greatest concentration of attention.

'Your own little income,' he asked, 'does it come out of the business?'

'Oh, no, sir, it is quite separate, and was left me by my uncle Ned in Auckland. It is in New Zealand Stock, paying 4½ per cent. Two thousand five hundred pounds was the amount, but I can only touch the interest.'

'You interest me extremely,' said Holmes. 'And since you draw so large a sum as a hundred a year, with what you earn into the bargain, you no doubt travel a little and indulge yourself in every way. I believe that a single lady can get on very nicely upon an income of about sixty pounds.'

'I could do with much less than that, Mr Holmes, but you understand that as long as I live at home I don't wish to be a burden to them, and so they have the use of the money just while I am staying with them. Of course that is only just for the time. Mr Windibank

draws my interest every quarter, and pays it over to mother, and I find
that I can do pretty well with what I earn at typewriting. It brings me
twopence a sheet, and I can often do from fifteen to twenty sheets in
a day.'

'You have made your position very clear to me,' said Holmes.
'This is my friend, Dr Watson, before whom you can speak as freely
as before myself. Kindly tell us now all about your connection with
Mr Hosmer Angel.'

A flush stole over Miss Sutherland's face, and she picked nervously at the fringe of her jacket. 'I met him first at the gasfitters'
ball,' she said. 'They used to send father tickets when he was alive,
and then afterwards they remembered us, and sent them to mother.
Mr Windibank did not wish us to go. He never did wish us to go
anywhere. He would get quite mad if I wanted so much as to join
a Sunday-school treat. But this time I was set on going, and I would
go, for what right had he to prevent? He said the folk were not fit for
us to know, when all father's friends were to be there. And he said that
I had nothing fit to wear, when I had my purple plush that I had never
so much as taken out of the drawer. At last, when nothing else would
do, he went off to France upon the business of the firm, but we went,
mother and I, with Mr Hardy, who used to be our foreman, and it was
there I met Mr Hosmer Angel.'

'I suppose,' said Holmes, 'that when Mr Windibank came back
from France, he was very annoyed at your having gone to the ball.'

'Oh, well, he was very good about it. He laughed, I remember, and
shrugged his shoulders, and said there was no use denying anything
to a woman, for she would have her way.'

'I see. Then at the gasfitters' ball you met, as I understand, a gentleman called Mr Hosmer Angel.'

'Yes, sir. I met him that night, and he called next day to ask if
we had got home all safe, and after that we met him—that is to say,
Mr Holmes, I met him twice for walks, but after that father came back
again, and Mr Hosmer Angel could not come to the house any more.'

'No?'

'Well, you know, father didn't like anything of the sort. He wouldn't
have any visitors if he could help it, and he used to say that a woman
should be happy in her own family circle. But then, as I used to say
to mother, a woman wants her own circle to begin with, and I had not
got mine yet.'

'But how about Mr Hosmer Angel? Did he make no attempt to see you?'

'Well, father was going off to France again in a week, and Hosmer wrote and said that it would be safer and better not to see each other until he had gone. We would write in the meantime, and he used to write every day. I took the letters in in the morning, so there was no need for father to know.'

'Were you engaged to the gentleman at this time?'

'Oh, yes, Mr Holmes. We were engaged after the first walk that we took. Hosmer—Mr Angel—was a cashier in an office in Leadenhall Street—and—'

'What office?'

'That's the worst of it, Mr Holmes, I don't know.'

'Where did he live then?'

'He slept on the premises.'

'And you don't know his address?'

'No—except that it was Leadenhall Street.'

'Where did you address your letters, then?'

'To the Leadenhall Street Post Office, to be left till called for. He said that if they were sent to the office he would be chaffed by all the other clerks about having letters from a lady, so I offered to typewrite them, like he did his, but he wouldn't have that, for he said that when I wrote them they seemed to come from me but when they were type-written he always felt that the machine had come between us. That will just show you how fond he was of me, Mr Holmes, and the little things that he would think of.'

'It was most suggestive,' said Holmes. 'It has long been an axiom of mine that the little things are infinitely the most important. Can you remember any other little things about Mr Hosmer Angel?'

'He was a very shy man, Mr Holmes. He would rather walk with me in the evening than in the daylight, for he said that he hated to be conspicuous. Very retiring and gentlemanly he was. Even his voice was gentle. He'd had the quinsy and swollen glands when he was young, he told me, and it had left him with a weak throat, and a hesitating, whispering fashion of speech. He was always well-dressed, very neat and plain, but his eyes were weak, just as mine are, and he wore tinted glasses against the glare.'

'Well, and what happened when Mr Windibank, your step-father, returned to France?'

'Mr Hosmer Angel came to the house again, and proposed that we should marry before father came back. He was in dreadful earnest, and made me swear, with my hands on the Testament, that whatever happened I would always be true to him. Mother said he was quite right to make me swear, and that it was a sign of his passion. Mother was all in his favour from the first, and was even fonder of him than I was. Then, when they talked of marrying within the week, I began to ask about father; but they both said never to mind about father, but just to tell him afterwards, and mother said she would make it all right with him. I didn't quite like that, Mr Holmes. It seemed funny that I should ask his leave, as he was only a few years older than me; but I didn't want to do anything on the sly, so I wrote to father at Bordeaux, where the Company has its French offices, but the letter came back to me on the very morning of the wedding.'

'It missed him then?'

'Yes, sir, for he had started to England just before it arrived.'

'Ha! that was unfortunate. Your wedding was arranged, then, for the Friday. Was it to be in church?'

'Yes, sir, but very quietly. It was to be at St Saviour's, near King's Cross, and we were to have breakfast afterwards at the St Pancras Hotel. Hosmer came for us in a hansom, but as there were two of us, he put us both into it, and stepped himself into a four-wheeler which happened to be the only other cab in the street. We got to the church first, and when the four-wheeler drove up we waited for him to step out, but he never did, and when the cabman got down from the box and looked, there was no one there! The cabman said he could not imagine what had become of him, for he had seen him get in with his own eyes. That was last Friday, Mr Holmes, and I have never seen or heard anything since then to throw any light upon what became of him.'

'It seems to me that you have been very shamefully treated,' said Holmes.

'Oh no, sir! He was too good and kind to leave me so. Why, all the morning he was saying to me that, whatever happened, I was to be true; and that even if something quite unforeseen occurred to separate us, I was always to remember that I was pledged to him, and that he would claim his pledge sooner or later. It seemed strange talk for a wedding morning, but what has happened since gives a meaning to it.'

'Most certainly it does. Your own opinion is, then, that some unforeseen catastrophe has occurred to him?'

'Yes, sir. I believe that he foresaw some danger, or else he would not have talked so. And then I think that what he foresaw happened.'

'But you have no notion as to what it could have been?'

'None.'

'One more question. How did your mother take the matter?'

'She was angry, and said that I was never to speak of the matter again.'

'And your father? Did you tell him?'

'Yes, and he seemed to think, with me, that something had happened, and that I should hear of Hosmer again. As he said, what interest could anyone have in bringing me to the doors of the church, and then leaving me? Now, if he had borrowed my money, or if he had married me and got my money settled on him, there might be some reason; but Hosmer was very independent about money, and never would look at a shilling of mine. And yet what could have happened? And why could he not write? Oh, it drives me half mad to think of! and I can't sleep a wink at night.' She pulled a little handkerchief out of her muff, and began to sob heavily into it.

'I shall glance into the case for you,' said Holmes, rising, 'and I have no doubt that we shall reach some definite result. Let the weight of the matter rest upon me now, and do not let your mind dwell upon it further. Above all, try to let Mr Hosmer Angel vanish from your memory, as he has done from your life.'

'Then you don't think I'll see him again?'

'I fear not.'

'Then what has happened to him?'

'You will leave that question in my hands. I should like an accurate description of him, and any letters of his which you can spare.'

'I advertised for him in last Saturday's *Chronicle*,' said she. 'Here is the slip, and here are four letters from him.'

'Thank you. And your address?'

'31 Lyon Place, Camberwell.'

'Mr Angel's address you never had, I understand. Where is your father's place of business?'

'He travels for Westhouse & Marbank, the great claret importers of Fenchurch Street.'

'Thank you. You have made your statement very clearly. You will leave the papers here, and remember the advice which I have given you. Let the whole incident be a sealed book, and do not allow it to affect your life.'

'You are very kind, Mr Holmes, but I cannot do that. I shall be true to Hosmer. He shall find me ready when he comes back.'

For all the preposterous hat and the vacuous face, there was something noble in the simple faith of our visitor which compelled our respect. She laid her little bundle of papers upon the table, and went her way, with a promise to come again whenever she might be summoned.

Sherlock Holmes sat silent for a few minutes with his fingertips still pressed together, his legs stretched out in front of him, and his gaze directed upwards to the ceiling. Then he took down from the rack the old and oily clay pipe, which was to him as a counsellor, and, having lit it, he leaned back in his chair, with the thick blue cloud-wreaths spinning up from him, and a look of infinite languor in his face.

'Quite an interesting study, that maiden,' he observed. 'I found her more interesting than her little problem, which, by the way, is rather a trite one. You will find parallel cases, if you consult my index, in Andover in '77, and there was something of the sort at The Hague last year. Old as is the idea, however, there were one or two details which were new to me. But the maiden herself was most instructive.'

'You appear to read a good deal upon her which was quite invisible to me,' I remarked.

'Not invisible, but unnoticed, Watson. You did not know where to look, and so you missed all that was important. I can never bring you to realize the importance of sleeves, the suggestiveness of thumb-nails, or the great issues that may hang from a bootlace. Now what did you gather from that woman's appearance? Describe it.'

'Well, she had a slate-coloured, broad-brimmed straw hat, with a feather of a brickish red. Her jacket was black, with black beads sewn upon it, and a fringe of little black jet ornaments. Her dress was brown, rather darker than coffee colour, with a little purple plush at the neck and sleeves. Her gloves were greyish, and were worn through at the right forefinger. Her boots I didn't observe. She had small, round, hanging gold ear-rings, and a general air of being fairly well to do, in a vulgar, comfortable, easy-going way.'

Sherlock Holmes clapped his hands softly together and chuckled.

''Pon my word, Watson, you are coming along wonderfully. You have really done very well indeed. It is true that you have missed everything of importance, but you have hit upon the method, and you have a quick eye for colour. Never trust to general impressions, my boy, but concentrate yourself upon details. My first glance is always at a woman's sleeve. In a man it is perhaps better first to take the knee of the trouser. As you observe, this woman had plush upon her sleeves, which is a most useful material for showing traces. The double line a little above the wrist, where the typewritist presses against the table, was beautifully defined. The sewing-machine, of the hand type, leaves a similar mark, but only on the left arm, and on the side of it farthest from the thumb, instead of being right across the broadest part, as this was. I then glanced at her face, and observing the dint of a pince-nez at either side of her nose, I ventured a remark upon short sight and typewriting, which seemed to surprise her.'

'It surprised me.'

'But, surely, it was very obvious. I was then much surprised and interested on glancing down to observe that, though the boots which she was wearing were not unlike each other, they were really odd ones, the one having a slightly decorated toe-cap, and the other a plain one. One was buttoned only in the two lower buttons out of five, and the other at the first, third, and fifth. Now, when you see that a young lady, otherwise neatly dressed, has come away from home with odd boots, half-buttoned, it is no great deduction to say that she came away in a hurry.'

'And what else?' I asked, keenly interested, as I always was, by my friend's incisive reasoning.

'I noted, in passing, that she had written a note before leaving home, but after being fully dressed. You observed that her right glove was torn at the forefinger, but you did not apparently see that both glove and finger were stained with violet ink. She had written in a hurry, and dipped her pen too deep. It must have been this morning, or the mark would not remain clear upon the finger. All this is amusing, though rather elementary, but I must go back to business, Watson. Would you mind reading me the advertised description of Mr Hosmer Angel?'

I held the little printed slip to the light. 'Missing,' it said, 'on the morning of the 14th, a gentleman named Hosmer Angel. About 5 ft

7 in in height; strongly built, sallow complexion, black hair, a little bald in the centre, bushy, black side whiskers and moustache; tinted glasses, slight infirmity of speech. Was dressed, when last seen, in black frock-coat faced with silk, black waistcoat, gold Albert chain, and grey Harris tweed trousers, with brown gaiters over elastic-sided boots. Known to have been employed in an office in Leadenhall Street. Anybody bringing, etc., etc.'

'That will do,' said Holmes. 'As to the letters,' he continued, glancing over them, 'they are very commonplace. Absolutely no clue in them to Mr Angel, save that he quotes Balzac once. There is one remarkable point, however, which will no doubt strike you.'

'They are typewritten,' I remarked.

'Not only that, but the signature is typewritten. Look at the neat little "Hosmer Angel" at the bottom. There is a date you see, but no superscription, except Leadenhall Street, which is rather vague. The point about the signature is very suggestive—in fact, we may call it conclusive.'

'Of what?'

'My dear fellow, is it possible you do not see how strongly it bears upon the case?'

'I cannot say that I do, unless it were that he wished to be able to deny his signature if an action for breach of promise were instituted.'

'No, that was not the point. However, I shall write two letters which should settle the matter. One is to a firm in the City, the other is to the young lady's step-father, Mr Windibank, asking him whether he could meet us here at six o'clock to-morrow evening. It is just as well that we should do business with the male relatives. And now, Doctor, we can do nothing until the answers to those letters come, so we may put our little problem upon the shelf for the interim.'

I had had so many reasons to believe in my friend's subtle powers of reasoning, and extraordinary energy in action, that I felt that he must have some solid grounds for the assured and easy demeanour with which he treated the singular mystery which he had been called upon to fathom. Only once had I known him to fail, in the case of the King of Bohemia and of the Irene Adler photograph, but when I looked back to the weird business of the Sign of Four, and the extraordinary circumstances connected with the Study in Scarlet, I felt that it would be a strange tangle indeed which he could not unravel.

I left him then, still puffing at his black clay pipe, with the conviction that when I came again on the next evening I would find that he held in his hands all the clues which would lead up to the identity of the disappearing bridegroom of Miss Mary Sutherland.

A professional case of great gravity was engaging my own attention at the time, and the whole of next day I was busy at the bedside of the sufferer. It was not until close upon six o'clock that I found myself free, and was able to spring into a hansom and drive to Baker Street, half afraid that I might be too late to assist at the *dénouement* of the little mystery. I found Sherlock Holmes alone, however, half asleep, with his long, thin form curled up in the recesses of his armchair. A formidable array of bottles and test-tubes, with the pungent cleanly smell of hydrochloric acid, told me that he had spent his day in the chemical work which was so dear to him.

'Well, have you solved it?' I asked as I entered.

'Yes. It was the bisulphate of baryta.'*

'No, no, the mystery!' I cried.

'Oh, that! I thought of the salt that I have been working upon. There was never any mystery in the matter, though, as I said yesterday, some of the details are of interest. The only drawback is that there is no law, I fear, that can touch the scoundrel.'

'Who was he, then, and what was his object in deserting Miss Sutherland?'

The question was hardly out of my mouth, and Holmes had not yet opened his lips to reply, when we heard a heavy footfall in the passage, and a tap at the door.

'This is the girl's step-father, Mr James Windibank,' said Holmes. 'He has written to me to say that he would be here at six. Come in!'

The man who entered was a sturdy middle-sized fellow, some thirty years of age, clean shaven, and sallow skinned, with a bland, insinuating manner, and a pair of wonderfully sharp and penetrating grey eyes. He shot a questioning glance at each of us, placed his shiny top-hat upon the sideboard, and with a slight bow, sidled down into the nearest chair.

'Good evening, Mr James Windibank,' said Holmes. 'I think that this typewritten letter is from you, in which you made an appointment with me for six o'clock!'

'Yes, sir. I am afraid that I am a little late, but I am not quite my own master, you know. I am sorry that Miss Sutherland has troubled you about this little matter, for I think it is far better not to wash linen of this sort in public. It was quite against my wishes that she came, but she is a very excitable, impulsive girl, as you may have noticed, and she is not easily controlled when she has made up her mind on a point. Of course, I do not mind you so much, as you are not connected with the official police, but it is not pleasant to have a family misfortune like this noised abroad. Besides, it is a useless expense, for how could you possibly find this Hosmer Angel?'

'On the contrary,' said Holmes quietly; 'I have every reason to believe that I will succeed in discovering Mr Hosmer Angel.'

Mr Windibank gave a violent start, and dropped his gloves. 'I am delighted to hear it,' he said.

'It is a curious thing,' remarked Holmes, 'that a typewriter has really quite as much individuality as a man's handwriting. Unless they are quite new, no two of them write exactly alike. Some letters get more worn than others, and some wear only on one side. Now, you remark in this note of yours, Mr Windibank, that in every case there is some little slurring over of the "e", and a slight defect in the tail of the "r". There are fourteen other characteristics, but those are the more obvious.'

'We do all our correspondence with this machine at the office, and no doubt it is a little worn,' our visitor answered, glancing keenly at Holmes with his bright little eyes.

'And now I will show you what is really a very interesting study, Mr Windibank,' Holmes continued. 'I think of writing another little monograph some of these days on the typewriter and its relation to crime. It is a subject to which I have devoted some little attention. I have here four letters which purport to come from the missing man. They are all typewritten. In each case, not only are the "e's" slurred and the "r's" tailless, but you will observe, if you care to use my magnifying lens, that the fourteen other characteristics to which I have alluded are there as well.'

Mr Windibank sprang out of his chair, and picked up his hat. 'I cannot waste time over this sort of fantastic talk, Mr Holmes,' he said. 'If you can catch the man, catch him, and let me know when you have done it.'

'Certainly,' said Holmes, stepping over and turning the key in the door. 'I let you know, then, that I have caught him!'

'What! where?' shouted Mr Windibank, turning white to his lips, and glancing about him like a rat in a trap.

'Oh, it won't do—really it won't,' said Holmes, suavely. 'There is no possible getting out of it, Mr Windibank. It is quite too transparent, and it was a very bad compliment when you said it was impossible for me to solve so simple a question. That's right! Sit down, and let us talk it over.'

Our visitor collapsed into a chair with a ghastly face and a glitter of moisture on his brow. 'It—it's not actionable,' he stammered.

'I am very much afraid that it is not. But between ourselves, Windibank, it was as cruel, and selfish, and heartless a trick in a petty way as ever came before me. Now, let me just run over the course of events, and you will contradict me if I go wrong.'

The man sat huddled up in his chair, with his head sunk upon his breast, like one who is utterly crushed. Holmes stuck his feet up on the corner of the mantelpiece, and leaning back with his hands in his pockets, began talking, rather to himself, as it seemed, than to us.

'The man married a woman very much older than himself for her money,' said he, 'and he enjoyed the use of the money of the daughter as long as she lived with them. It was a considerable sum for people in their position, and the loss of it would have made a serious difference. It was worth an effort to preserve it. The daughter was of a good, amiable disposition, but affectionate and warm-hearted in her ways, so that it was evident that with her fair personal advantages, and her little income, she would not be allowed to remain single long. Now her marriage would mean, of course, the loss of a hundred a year, so what does her step-father do to prevent it? He takes the obvious course of keeping her at home, and forbidding her to seek the company of people of her own age. But soon he found that that would not answer for ever. She became restive, insisted upon her rights, and finally announced her positive intention of going to a certain ball. What does her clever step-father do then? He conceives an idea more creditable to his head than to his heart. With the connivance and assistance of his wife he disguised himself, covered those keen eyes with tinted glasses, masked the face with a moustache and a pair of bushy whiskers, sunk that clear voice into an insinuating whisper, and doubly secure on account of the girl's short sight, he appears as Mr Hosmer Angel, and keeps off other lovers by making love himself.'

'It was only a joke at first,' groaned our visitor. 'We never thought that she would have been so carried away.'

'Very likely not. However that may be, the young lady was very decidedly carried away, and having quite made up her mind that her step-father was in France, the suspicion of treachery never for an instant entered her mind. She was flattered by the gentleman's attentions, and the effect was increased by the loudly expressed admiration of her mother. Then Mr Angel began to call, for it was obvious that the matter should be pushed as far as it would go, if a real effect were to be produced. There were meetings, and an engagement, which would finally secure the girl's affections from turning towards anyone else. But the deception could not be kept up for ever. These pretended journeys to France were rather cumbrous. The thing to do was clearly to bring the business to an end in such a dramatic manner that it would leave a permanent impression upon the young lady's mind, and prevent her from looking upon any other suitor for some time to come. Hence those vows of fidelity exacted upon a Testament, and hence also the allusions to a possibility of something happening on the very morning of the wedding. James Windibank wished Miss Sutherland to be so bound to Hosmer Angel, and so uncertain as to his fate, that for ten years to come, at any rate, she would not listen to another man. As far as the church door he brought her, and then, as he could go no further, he conveniently vanished away by the old trick of stepping in at one door of a four-wheeler, and out at the other. I think that that was the chain of events, Mr Windibank!'

Our visitor had recovered something of his assurance while Holmes had been talking, and he rose from his chair now with a cold sneer upon his pale face.

'It may be so, or it may not, Mr Holmes,' said he, 'but if you are so very sharp you ought to be sharp enough to know that it is you who are breaking the law now, and not me. I have done nothing actionable from the first, but as long as you keep that door locked you lay yourself open to an action for assault and illegal constraint.'

'The law cannot, as you say, touch you,' said Holmes, unlocking and throwing open the door, 'yet there never was a man who deserved punishment more. If the young lady has a brother or a friend he ought to lay a whip across your shoulders. By Jove!' he continued, flushing up at the sight of the bitter sneer upon the man's face, 'it is not part of my duties to my client, but here's a hunting-crop handy, and I think I shall just treat myself to—' He took two swift steps to the whip, but before he could grasp it there was a wild clatter of steps upon the stairs, the heavy hall door banged, and from the window we could see Mr James Windibank running at the top of his speed down the road.

'There's a cold-blooded scoundrel!' said Holmes, laughing, as he threw himself down into his chair once more. 'That fellow will rise from crime to crime until he does something very bad and ends on a gallows. The case has, in some respects, been not entirely devoid of interest.'

'I cannot now entirely see all the steps of your reasoning,' I remarked.

'Well, of course it was obvious from the first that this Mr Hosmer Angel must have some strong object for his curious conduct, and it was equally clear that the only man who really profited by the incident, as far as we could see, was the step-father. Then the fact that the two men were never together, but that the one always appeared when the other was away, was suggestive. So were the tinted spectacles and the curious voice, which both hinted at a disguise, as did the bushy whiskers. My suspicions were all confirmed by his peculiar action in typewriting his signature, which of course inferred that his handwriting was so familiar to her that she would recognize even the smallest sample of it. You see all these isolated facts, together with many minor ones, all pointed in the same direction.'

'And how did you verify them?'

'Having once spotted my man, it was easy to get corroboration. I knew the firm for which this man worked. Having taken the printed description, I eliminated everything from it which could be the result of a disguise—the whiskers, the glasses, the voice, and I sent it to the firm, with a request that they would inform me whether it answered the description of any of their travellers. I had already noticed the peculiarities of the typewriter, and I wrote to the man himself at his business address, asking him if he would come here. As I expected, his reply was typewritten, and revealed the same trivial but characteristic defects. The same post brought me a letter from Westhouse & Marbank, of Fenchurch Street, to say that the description tallied in every respect with that of their employee, James Windibank. *Voilà tout*!'

'And Miss Sutherland?'

'If I tell her she will not believe me. You may remember the old Persian saying, "There is danger for him who taketh the tiger cub, and danger also for whoso snatches a delusion from a woman." There is as much sense in Hafiz as in Horace, and as much knowledge of the world.'

THE RED-HEADED LEAGUE

I HAD called upon my friend, Mr Sherlock Holmes, one day in the autumn of last year, and found him in deep conversation with a very stout, florid-faced, elderly gentleman, with fiery red hair. With an apology for my intrusion, I was about to withdraw, when Holmes pulled me abruptly into the room, and closed the door behind me.

'You could not possibly have come at a better time, my dear Watson,' he said, cordially.

'I was afraid that you were engaged.'

'So I am. Very much so.'

'Then I can wait in the next room.'

'Not at all. This gentleman, Mr Wilson, has been my partner and helper in many of my most successful cases, and I have no doubt that he will be of the utmost use to me in yours also.'

The stout gentleman half rose from his chair, and gave a bob of greeting, with a quick little questioning glance from his small, fat-encircled eyes.

'Try the settee,' said Holmes, relapsing into his armchair, and putting his fingertips together, as was his custom when in judicial moods. 'I know, my dear Watson, that you share my love of all that is bizarre and outside the conventions and humdrum routine of every-day life. You have shown your relish for it by the enthusiasm which has prompted you to chronicle, and, if you will excuse my saying so, somewhat to embellish so many of my own little adventures.'

'Your cases have indeed been of the greatest interest to me,' I observed.

'You will remember that I remarked the other day, just before we went into the very simple problem presented by Miss Mary Sutherland,* that for strange effects and extraordinary combinations we must go to life itself, which is always far more daring than any effort of the imagination.'

'A proposition which I took the liberty of doubting.'

'You did, Doctor, but none the less you must come round to my view, for otherwise I shall keep piling fact upon fact on you, until your reason breaks down under them and acknowledges me to be right. Now, Mr Jabez Wilson here has been good enough to call upon me this morning, and to begin a narrative which promises to be one of the most singular which I have listened to for some time. You have heard me remark that the strangest and most unique things are very often connected not with the larger but with the smaller crimes, and occasionally, indeed, where there is room for doubt whether any positive crime has been committed. As far as I have heard, it is impossible for me to say whether the present case is an instance of crime or not, but the course of events is certainly among the most singular that I have ever listened to. Perhaps, Mr Wilson, you would have the great kindness to recommence your narrative. I ask you not merely because my friend Dr Watson has not heard the opening part, but also because the peculiar nature of the story makes me anxious to have every possible detail from your lips. As a rule, when I have heard some slight indication of the course of events I am able to guide myself by the thousands of other similar cases which occur to my memory. In the present instance I am forced to admit that the facts are, to the best of my belief, unique.'

The portly client puffed out his chest with an appearance of some little pride, and pulled a dirty and wrinkled newspaper from the inside pocket of his greatcoat. As he glanced down the advertisement column, with his head thrust forward, and the paper flattened out upon his knee, I took a good look at the man, and endeavoured after the fashion of my companion to read the indications which might be presented by his dress or appearance.

I did not gain very much, however, by my inspection. Our visitor bore every mark of being an average commonplace British tradesman, obese, pompous, and slow.* He wore rather baggy grey shepherd's check trousers,* a not over-clean black frock-coat, unbuttoned in the front, and a drab waist-coat with a heavy brassy Albert chain,* and a square pierced bit of metal dangling down as an ornament. A frayed top-hat, and a faded brown overcoat with a wrinkled velvet collar lay upon a chair beside him. Altogether, look as I would, there was nothing remarkable about the man save his blazing red head, and the expression of extreme chagrin and discontent upon his features.

Sherlock Holmes's quick eye took in my occupation, and he shook his head with a smile as he noticed my questioning glances. 'Beyond the obvious facts that he has at some time done manual labour, that he takes snuff, that he is a Freemason,* that he has been in China, and that he has done a considerable amount of writing lately, I can deduce nothing else.'

Mr Jabez Wilson started up in his chair, with his forefinger upon the paper, but his eyes upon my companion.

'How, in the name of good fortune, did you know that, Mr Holmes?' he asked. 'How did you know, for example, that I did manual labour? It's as true as gospel, and I began as a ship's carpenter.'

'Your hands, my dear sir. Your right hand is quite a size larger then your left. You have worked with it, and the muscles are more developed.'

'Well, the snuff, then, and the Freemasonry?'

'I won't insult your intelligence by telling you how I read that, especially as, rather against the strict rules of your order,* you use an arc and compass breastpin.'*

'Ah, of course, I forgot that. But the writing?'

'What else can be indicated by that right cuff so very shiny for five inches, and the left one with the smooth patch near the elbow where you rest it upon the desk.'

'Well, but China?'

'The fish which you have tattooed immediately above your right wrist could only have been done in China. I have made a small study of tattoo marks, and have even contributed to the literature of the subject. That trick of staining the fishes' scales of a delicate pink is quite peculiar to China. When, in addition, I see a Chinese coin hanging from your watch-chain, the matter becomes even more simple.'

Mr Jabez Wilson laughed heavily. 'Well, I never!' said he. 'I thought at first you had done something clever, but I see that there was nothing in it after all.'

'I begin to think, Watson,' said Holmes, 'that I make a mistake in explaining. "Omne ignotum pro magnifico,"* you know, and my poor little reputation, such as it is, will suffer shipwreck if I am so candid. Can you not find the advertisement, Mr Wilson?'

'Yes, I have got it now,' he answered, with his thick, red finger planted half-way down the column. 'Here it is. This is what began it all. You must read it for yourself, sir.'

I took the paper from him and read as follows:

To the Red-Headed League—On account of the bequest of the late Ezekiah Hopkins, of Lebanon, Penn., U.S.A., there is now another vacancy open which entitles a member of the League to a salary of four pounds a week for purely nominal services. All red-headed men who are sound in body and mind, and above the age of twenty-one years, are eligible. Apply in person on Monday, at eleven o'clock, to Duncan Ross, at the offices of the League, 7, Pope's Court, Fleet Street.

'What on earth does this mean?' I ejaculated, after I had twice read over the extraordinary announcement.

Holmes chuckled, and wriggled in his chair, as was his habit when in high spirits. 'It is a little off the beaten track, isn't it?' said he. 'And now, Mr Wilson, off you go at scratch,* and tell us all about yourself, your household, and the effect which this advertisement had upon your fortunes. You will first make a note, Doctor, of the paper and the date.'

'It is the *Morning Chronicle*,* of April 27, 1890. Just two months ago.'

'Very good. Now, Mr Wilson?'

'Well, it is just as I have been telling you, Mr Sherlock Holmes,' said Jabez Wilson, mopping his forehead, 'I have a small pawn-broker's business* at Coburg Square, near the City.* It's not a very large affair, and of late years it has not done more than just give me a living. I used to be able to keep two assistants, but now I only keep one; and I would have a job to pay him, but that he is willing to come for half wages, so as to learn the business.'

'What is the name of this obliging youth?' asked Sherlock Holmes.

'His name is Vincent Spaulding, and he's not such a youth either. It's hard to say his age. I should not wish a smarter assistant, Mr Holmes; and I know very well that he could better himself, and earn twice what I am able to give him. But after all, if he is satisfied, why should I put ideas in his head?'

'Why, indeed? You seem most fortunate in having an employee who comes under the full market price. It is not a common experience among employers in this age. I don't know that your assistant is not as remarkable as your advertisement.'

'Oh, he has his faults, too,' said Mr Wilson. 'Never was such a fellow for photography. Snapping away with a camera when he ought to be improving his mind, and then diving down into the cellar like a rabbit into its hole to develop his pictures. That is his main fault; but on the whole, he's a good worker. There's no vice in him.'

'He is still with you, I presume?'

'Yes, sir. He and a girl of fourteen, who does a bit of simple cooking, and keeps the place clean—that's all I have in the house, for I am a widower, and never had any family. We live very quietly, sir, the three of us; and we keep a roof over our heads, and pay our debts, if we do nothing more.

'The first thing that put us out was that advertisement. Spaulding, he came down into the office just this day eight weeks with this very paper in his hand, and he says:

'"I wish to the Lord, Mr Wilson, that I was a red-headed man."

'"Why that?" I asks.

'"Why," says he, "here's another vacancy on the League of the Red-Headed Men. It's worth quite a little fortune to any man who gets it, and I understand that there are more vacancies than there are men, so that the trustees are at their wits' end what to do with the money. If my hair would only change colour, here's a nice little crib* all ready for me to step into."

'"Why, what is it, then?" I asked. You see, Mr Holmes, I am a very stay-at-home man, and, as my business came to me instead of my having to go to it, I was often weeks on end without putting my foot over the door-mat. In that way I didn't know much of what was going on outside, and I was always glad of a bit of news.

'"Have you never heard of the League of the Red-Headed Men?" he asked, with his eyes open.

'"Never."

'"Why, I wonder at that, for you are eligible yourself for one of the vacancies."

'"And what are they worth?" I asked.

'"Oh, merely a couple of hundred a year, but the work is slight, and it need not interfere much with one's other occupations."

'Well, you can easily think that that made me prick up my ears, for the business has not been over good for some years, and an extra couple of hundred would have been very handy.

'"Tell me all about it," said I.

'"Well," said he, showing me the advertisement, "you can see for yourself that the League has a vacancy, and there is the address where you should apply for particulars. As far as I can make out, the League was founded by an American millionaire, Ezekiah Hopkins, who was very peculiar in his ways. He was himself red-headed, and he had a great sympathy for all red-headed men; so, when he died, it was found that he had left his enormous fortune in the hands of trustees, with instructions to apply the interest to the providing of easy berths to men whose hair is of that colour. From all I hear it is splendid pay, and very little to do."

' "But," said I, "there would be millions of red-headed men who would apply."

' "Not so many as you might think," he answered. "You see, it is really confined to Londoners, and to grown men. This American had started from London when he was young, and he wanted to do the old town a good turn. Then, again, I have heard it is no use your applying if your hair is light red, or dark red, or anything but real, bright, blazing, fiery red. Now, if you cared to apply, Mr Wilson, you would just walk in; but perhaps it would hardly be worth your while to put yourself out of the way for the sake of a few hundred pounds."

'Now, it is a fact, gentlemen, as you may see for yourselves, that my hair is of a very full and rich tint, so that it seemed to me that, if there was to be any competition in the matter, I stood as good a chance as any man that I had ever met. Vincent Spaulding seemed to know so much about it that I thought he might prove useful, so I just ordered him to put up the shutters for the day, and to come right away with me. He was very willing to have a holiday, so we shut the business up, and started off for the address that was given us in the advertisement.

'I never hope to see such a sight as that again, Mr Holmes. From north, south, east, and west every man who had a shade of red in his hair had tramped into the City to answer the advertisement. Fleet Street was choked with red-headed folk, and Pope's Court looked like a coster's orange barrow.* I should not have thought there were so many in the whole country as were brought together by that single advertisement. Every shade of colour they were—straw, lemon, orange, brick, Irish-setter, liver, clay; but, as Spaulding said, there were not many who had the real vivid flame-coloured tint. When I saw how many were waiting I would have given it up in despair; but Spaulding would not hear of it. How he did it I could not imagine, but he pushed and pulled and butted until he got me through the crowd, and right up to the steps which led to the office. There was a double stream upon the stair, some going up in hope, and some coming back dejected; but we wedged in as well as we could, and soon found ourselves in the office.'

'Your experience has been a most entertaining one,' remarked Holmes, as his client paused and refreshed his memory with a huge pinch of snuff. 'Pray continue your very interesting statement.'

'There was nothing in the office but a couple of wooden chairs and a deal table, behind which sat a small man, with a head that was even redder than mine. He said a few words to each candidate as he came up, and then he always managed to find some fault in them which would disqualify them. Getting a vacancy did not seem to be such a very easy matter after all. However, when our turn came, the little man was more favourable to me than to any of the others, and he closed the door as we entered, so that he might have a private word with us.

' "This is Mr Jabez Wilson," said my assistant, "and he is willing to fill a vacancy in the League."

' "And he is admirably suited for it," the other answered. "He has every requirement. I cannot recall when I have seen anything so fine." He took a step backwards, cocked his head on one side, and gazed at my hair until I felt quite bashful. Then suddenly he plunged forward, wrung my hand, and congratulated me warmly on my success.

' "It would be injustice to hesitate," said he. "You will, however, I am sure, excuse me for taking an obvious precaution." With that he seized my hair in both his hands, and tugged until I yelled with the pain. "There is water in your eyes," said he, as he released me. "I perceive that all is as it should be. But we have to be careful, for we have twice been deceived by wigs and once by paint. I could tell you tales of cobbler's wax* which would disgust you with human nature." He stepped over to the window, and shouted through it at the top of his voice that the vacancy was filled. A groan of disappointment came up from below, and the folk all trooped away in different directions, until there was not a red head to be seen except my own and that of the manager.

' "My name," said he, "is Mr Duncan Ross, and I am myself one of the pensioners upon the fund left by our noble benefactor. Are you a married man, Mr Wilson? Have you a family?"

'I answered that I had not.

'His face fell immediately.

' "Dear me!" he said gravely, "that is very serious indeed! I am sorry to hear you say that. The fund was, of course, for the propagation and spread of the red-heads as well as for their maintenance. It is exceedingly unfortunate that you should be a bachelor."

'My face lengthened at this, Mr Holmes, for I thought that I was not to have the vacancy after all; but after thinking it over for a few minutes, he said that it would be all right.

'"In the case of another," said he, "the objection might be fatal, but we must stretch a point in favour of a man with such a head of hair as yours. When shall you be able to enter upon your new duties?"

'"Well, it is a little awkward, for I have a business already," said I.

'"Oh, never mind about that, Mr Wilson!" said Vincent Spaulding. "I shall be able to look after that for you."

'"What would be the hours?" I asked.

'"Ten to two."

'Now a pawnbroker's business is mostly done of an evening, Mr Holmes, especially Thursday and Friday evening, which is just before pay-day; so it would suit me very well to earn a little in the mornings. Besides, I knew that my assistant was a good man, and that he would see to anything that turned up.

'"That would suit me very well," said I. "And the pay?"

'"Is four pounds a week."*

'"And the work?"

'"Is purely nominal."

'"What do you call purely nominal?"

'"Well, you have to be in the office, or at least in the building, the whole time. If you leave, you forfeit your whole position for ever. The will is very clear upon that point. You don't comply with the conditions if you budge from the office during that time."

'"It's only four hours a day, and I should not think of leaving," said I.

'"No excuse will avail," said Mr Duncan Ross, "neither sickness, nor business, nor anything else. There you must stay, or you lose your billet."*

'"And the work?"

'"Is to copy out the *Encyclopedia Britannica*. There is the first volume of it in that press.* You must find your own ink, pens, and blotting-paper, but we provide this table and chair. Will you be ready to-morrow?"

'"Certainly," I answered.

' "Then good-bye, Mr Jabez Wilson, and let me congratulate you once more on the important position which you have been fortunate enough to gain." He bowed me out of the room, and I went home with my assistant, hardly knowing what to say or do, I was so pleased at my own good fortune.

'Well, I thought over the matter all day, and by evening I was in low spirits again; for I had quite persuaded myself that the whole affair must be some great hoax or fraud, though what its object might be I could not imagine. It seemed altogether past belief that anyone could make such a will, or that they would pay a sum for doing anything so simple as copying out the *Encyclopedia Britannica*. Vincent Spaulding did what he could to cheer me up, but by bedtime I had reasoned myself out of the whole thing. However, in the morning I determined to have a look at it anyhow, so I bought a penny bottle of ink, and with a quill pen, and seven sheets of foolscap paper,* I started off for Pope's Court.

'Well, to my surprise and delight everything was as right as possible. The table was set out ready for me, and Mr Duncan Ross was there to see that I got fairly to work. He started me off upon the letter A, and then he left me; but he would drop in from time to time to see that all was right with me. At two o'clock he bade me good-day, complimented me upon the amount that I had written, and locked the door of the office after me.

'This went on day after day, Mr Holmes, and on Saturday the manager came in and planked down* four golden sovereigns for my week's work. It was the same next week, and the same the week after. Every morning I was there at ten, and every afternoon I left at two. By degrees Mr Duncan Ross took to coming in only once of a morning, and then, after a time, he did not come in at all. Still, of course, I never dared to leave the room for an instant, for I was not sure when he might come, and the billet was such a good one, and suited me so well, that I would not risk the loss of it.

'Eight weeks passed away like this, and I had written about Abbots, and Archery, and Armour, and Architecture, and Attica, and hoped with diligence that I might get on to the B's before very long. It cost me something in foolscap, and I had pretty nearly filled a shelf with my writings. And then suddenly the whole business came to an end.'

'To an end?'

'Yes, sir. And no later than this morning. I went to my work as usual at ten o'clock, but the door was shut and locked, with a little square of cardboard hammered on to the middle of the panel with a tack. Here it is, and you can read for yourself.'

He held up a piece of white cardboard, about the size of a sheet of note-paper. It read in this fashion:

THE RED-HEADED LEAGUE IS DISSOLVED.
OCT. 9, 1890.*

Sherlock Holmes and I surveyed this curt announcement and the rueful face behind it, until the comical side of the affair so completely overtopped every other consideration that we both burst out into a roar of laughter.

'I cannot see that there is anything very funny,' cried our client, flushing up to the roots of his flaming head. 'If you can do nothing better than laugh at me, I can go elsewhere.'

'No, no,' cried Holmes, shoving him back into the chair from which he had half risen. 'I really wouldn't miss your case for the world. It is most refreshingly unusual. But there is, if you will excuse me saying so, something just a little funny about it. Pray what steps did you take when you found the card upon the door?'

'I was staggered, sir. I did not know what to do. Then I called at the offices round, but none of them seemed to know anything about it. Finally, I went to the landlord, who is an accountant living on the ground floor, and I asked him if he could tell me what had become of the Red-Headed League. He said that he had never heard of any such body. Then I asked him who Mr Duncan Ross was. He answered that the name was new to him.

' "Well," said I, "the gentleman at No. 4."

' "What, the red-headed man?"

' "Yes."

' "Oh," said he, "his name was William Morris. He was a solicitor, and was using my room as a temporary convenience until his new premises were ready. He moved out yesterday."

' "Where could I find him?"

' "Oh, at his new offices. He did tell me the address. Yes, 17 King Edward Street, near St Paul's."

'I started off, Mr Holmes, but when I got to that address it was a manufactory of artificial knee-caps, and no one in it had ever heard of either Mr William Morris, or Mr Duncan Ross.'

'And what did you do then?' asked Holmes.

'I went home to Saxe-Coburg Square, and I took the advice of my assistant. But he could not help me in any way. He could only say that if I waited I should hear by post. But that was not quite good enough, Mr Holmes. I did not wish to lose such a place without a struggle, so, as I had heard that you were good enough to give advice to poor folk who were in need of it, I came right away to you.'

'And you did very wisely,' said Holmes. 'Your case is an exceedingly remarkable one, and I shall be happy to look into it. From what you have told me I think that it is possible that graver issues hang from it than might at first sight appear.'

'Grave enough!' said Mr Jabez Wilson. 'Why, I have lost four pounds a week.'

'As far as you are personally concerned,' remarked Holmes, 'I do not see that you have any grievance against this extraordinary league. On the contrary, you are, as I understand, richer by some thirty pounds, to say nothing of the minute knowledge which you have gained on every subject which comes under the letter A. You have lost nothing by them.'

'No, sir. But I want to find out about them, and who they are, and what their object was in playing this prank—if it was a prank—upon me. It was a pretty expensive joke for them, for it cost them two-and-thirty pounds.'

'We shall endeavour to clear up these points for you. And, first, one or two questions, Mr Wilson. This assistant of yours who first called your attention to the advertisement—how long had he been with you?'

'About a month then.'

'How did he come?'

'In answer to an advertisement.'

'Was he the only applicant?'

'No, I had a dozen.'

'Why did you pick him?'

'Because he was handy, and would come cheap.'

'At half wages, in fact.'

'Yes.'

'What is he like, this Vincent Spaulding?'

'Small, stout-built, very quick in his ways, no hair on his face, though he's not short of thirty. Has a white splash of acid upon his forehead.'

Holmes sat up in his chair in considerable excitement. 'I thought as much,' said he. 'Have you ever observed that his ears are pierced for ear-rings?'

'Yes, sir. He told me that a gipsy had done it for him when he was a lad.'

'Hum!' said Holmes, sinking back in deep thought. 'He is still with you?'

'Oh, yes, sir; I have only just left him.'

'And has your business been attended to in your absence?'

'Nothing to complain of, sir. There's never very much to do of a morning.'

'That will do, Mr Wilson. I shall be happy to give you an opinion upon the subject in the course of a day or two. To-day is Saturday, and I hope that by Monday we may come to a conclusion.'

'Well, Watson,' said Holmes, when our visitor had left us, 'what do you make of it all?'

'I make nothing of it,' I answered, frankly. 'It is a most mysterious business.'

'As a rule,' said Holmes, 'the more bizarre a thing is the less mysterious it proves to be. It is your commonplace, featureless crimes which are really puzzling, just as a commonplace face is the most difficult to identify. But I must be prompt over this matter.'

'What are you going to do, then?' I asked.

'To smoke,' he answered. 'It is quite a three-pipe problem, and I beg that you won't speak to me for fifty minutes.' He curled himself up in his chair, with his thin knees drawn up to his hawk-like nose, and there he sat with his eyes closed and his black clay pipe thrusting out like the bill of some strange bird. I had come to the conclusion that he had dropped asleep, and indeed was nodding myself, when he suddenly sprang out of his chair with the gesture of a man who had made up his mind, and put his pipe down upon the mantelpiece.

'Sarasate* plays at the St James's Hall this afternoon,' he remarked. 'What do you think, Watson? Could your patients spare you for a few hours?'

'I have nothing to do to-day. My practice is never very absorbing.'

'Then put on your hat, and come. I am going through the City first, and we can have some lunch on the way. I observe that there is a good deal of German music on the programme which is rather more to my taste than Italian or French. It is introspective, and I want to introspect. Come along!'

We travelled by the Underground as far as Aldersgate;* and a short walk took us to Saxe-Coburg Square, the scene of the singular story which we had listened to in the morning. It was a pokey, little, shabby-genteel place, where four lines of dingy two-storied brick houses looked out into a small railed-in enclosure, where a lawn of weedy grass and a few clumps of faded laurel bushes made a hard fight against a smoke-laden and uncongenial atmosphere. Three gilt balls* and a brown board with 'JABEZ WILSON' in white letters upon a corner house, announced the place where our red-headed client carried on his business. Sherlock Holmes stopped in front of it with his head on one side and looked it all over, with his eyes shining brightly between puckered lids. Then he walked slowly up the street and then down again to the corner, still looking keenly at the houses. Finally he returned to the pawnbroker's, and, having thumped vigorously upon the pavement with his stick two or three times, he went up to the door and knocked. It was instantly opened by a bright-looking, clean-shaven young fellow, who asked him to step in.

'Thank you,' said Holmes, 'I only wished to ask you how you would go from here to the Strand.'

'Third right, fourth left,' answered the assistant promptly, closing the door.

'Smart fellow, that,' observed Holmes as we walked away. 'He is, in my judgement, the fourth smartest man in London, and for daring I am not sure that he has not a claim to be third. I have known something of him before.'

'Evidently,' said I, 'Mr Wilson's assistant counts for a good deal in this mystery of the Red-Headed League. I am sure that you inquired your way merely in order that you might see him.'

'Not him.'

'What then?'

'The knees of his trousers.'

'And what did you see?'

'What I expected to see.'

'Why did you beat the pavement?'

'My dear Doctor, this is a time for observation, not for talk. We are spies in an enemy's country. We know something of Saxe-Coburg Square. Let us now explore the paths which lie behind it.'

The road in which we found ourselves as we turned round the corner from the retired Saxe-Coburg Square presented as great a contrast to it as the front of a picture does to the back. It was one of the main arteries which convey the traffic of the City to the north and west. The roadway was blocked with the immense stream of commerce flowing in a double tide inwards and outwards, while the footpaths were black with the hurrying swarm of pedestrians. It was difficult to realize as we looked at the line of fine shops and stately business premises that they really abutted on the other side upon the faded and stagnant square which we had just quitted.

'Let me see,' said Holmes, standing at the corner, and glancing along the line, 'I should like just to remember the order of the houses here. It is a hobby of mine to have an exact knowledge of London. There is Mortimer's, the tobacconist, the little newspaper shop, the Coburg branch of the City and Suburban Bank, the Vegetarian Restaurant, and McFarlane's carriage-building *depôt*. That carries us right on to the other block. And now, Doctor, we've done our work, so it's time we had some play. A sandwich and a cup of coffee, and then off to violin-land, where all is sweetness, and delicacy, and harmony, and there are no red-headed clients to vex us with their conundrums.'

My friend was an enthusiastic musician being himself not only a very capable performer, but a composer of no ordinary merit. All the afternoon he sat in the stalls wrapped in the most perfect happiness, gently waving his long thin fingers in time to the music, while his gently smiling face and his languid, dreamy eyes were as unlike those of Holmes the sleuth-hound, Holmes the relentless, keen-witted, ready-handed criminal agent, as it was possible to conceive. In his singular character the dual nature alternately asserted itself and his extreme exactness and astuteness represented, as I have often thought, the reaction against the poetic and contemplative mood which occasionally predominated in him. The swing of his nature took him from extreme languor to devouring energy; and, as I knew well, he was never so truly formidable as when, for days on end, he had been lounging in his arm-chair amid his improvisations and his black-letter editions.* Then it was that the lust of the chase would suddenly come upon him, and that his brilliant reasoning power would rise to the level of intuition, until those who were unacquainted with his methods would look askance at him as on a man whose knowledge was not that of other mortals. When I saw him that afternoon so enwrapped in the music at St James's Hall I felt that an evil time might be coming upon those whom he had set himself to hunt down.

'You want to go home, no doubt, Doctor,' he remarked, as we emerged.

'Yes, it would be as well.'

'And I have some business to do which will take some hours. This business at Coburg Square is serious.'

'Why serious?'

'A considerable crime is in contemplation. I have every reason to believe that we shall be in time to stop it. But to-day being Saturday rather complicates matters. I shall want your help to-night.'

'At what time?'

'Ten will be early enough.'

'I shall be at Baker Street at ten.'

'Very well. And I say, Doctor! there may be some little danger, so kindly put your army revolver in your pocket.' He waved his hand, turned on his heel, and disappeared in an instant among the crowd.

I trust that I am not more dense than my neighbours, but I was always oppressed with a sense of my own stupidity in my dealings with Sherlock Holmes. Here I had heard what he had heard, I had seen what he had seen, and yet from his words it was evident that he saw clearly not only what had happened, but what was about to happen, while to me the whole business was still confused and grotesque. As I drove home to my house in Kensington I thought over it all, from the extraordinary story of the red-headed copier of the *Encyclopedia* down to the visit to Saxe-Coburg Square, and the ominous words with which he had parted from me. What was this nocturnal expedition, and why should I go armed? Where were we going, and what were we to do? I had the hint from Holmes that this smooth-faced pawnbroker's assistant was a formidable man—a man who might play a deep game. I tried to puzzle it out, but gave it up in despair, and set the matter aside until night should bring an explanation.

It was a quarter past nine when I started from home and made my way across the Park, and so through Oxford Street to Baker Street. Two hansoms* were standing at the door, and, as I entered the passage, I heard the sound of voices from above. On entering his room, I found Holmes in animated conversation with two men, one of whom I recognized as Peter Jones, the official police agent; while the other was a long, thin, sad-faced man, with a very shiny hat and oppressively respectable frock-coat.

'Ha! our party is complete,' said Holmes, buttoning up his pea-jacket,* and taking his heavy hunting-crop* from the rack. 'Watson, I think you know Mr Jones, of Scotland Yard? Let me introduce you to Mr Merryweather, who is to be our companion in tonight's adventure.'

'We're hunting in couples again, Doctor, you see,' said Jones in his consequential way. 'Our friend here is a wonderful man for starting a chase. All he wants is an old dog to help him to do the running down.'

'I hope a wild goose may not prove to be the end of our chase,' observed Mr Merryweather gloomily.

'You may place considerable confidence in Mr Holmes, sir,' said the police agent loftily. 'He has his own little methods, which are, if he won't mind my saying so, just a little too theoretical and fantastic, but he has the makings of a detective in him. It is not too much to say that once or twice, as in that business of the Sholto murder and the Agra treasure,* he has been more nearly correct than the official force.'

'Oh, if you say so, Mr Jones, it is all right!' said the stranger, with deference. 'Still, I confess that I miss my rubber.* It is the first Saturday night for seven-and-thirty years that I have not had my rubber.'

'I think you will find,' said Sherlock Holmes, 'that you will play for a higher stake tonight than you have ever done yet, and that the play will be more exciting. For you, Mr Merryweather, the stake will be some thirty thousand pounds; and for you, Jones, it will be the man upon whom you wish to lay your hands.'

'John Clay, the murderer, thief, smasher,* and forger. He's a young man, Mr Merryweather, but he is at the head of his profession, and I would rather have my bracelets on him than on any criminal in London. He's a remarkable man, is young John Clay. His grandfather was a Royal Duke, and he himself has been to Eton and Oxford. His brain is as cunning as his fingers, and though we meet signs of him at every turn, we never know where to find the man himself. He'll crack a crib* in Scotland one week, and be raising money to build an orphanage in Cornwall the next. I've been on his track for years, and have never set eyes on him yet.'

'I hope that I may have the pleasure of introducing you tonight. I've had one or two little turns also with Mr John Clay, and I agree with you that he is at the head of his profession. It is past ten, however, and quite time that we started. If you two will take the first hansom, Watson and I will follow in the second.'

Sherlock Holmes was not very communicative during the long drive, and lay back in the cab humming the tunes which he had heard in the afternoon. We rattled through an endless labyrinth of gas-lit streets until we emerged into Farringdon Street.

'We are close there now,' my friend remarked. 'This fellow Merryweather is a bank director and personally interested in the matter. I thought it as well to have Jones with us also. He is not a bad fellow, though an absolute imbecile in his profession. He has one positive virtue. He is as brave as a bulldog, and as tenacious as a lobster if he gets his claws upon anyone. Here we are, and they are waiting for us.'

We had reached the same crowded thoroughfare in which we had found ourselves in the morning. Our cabs were dismissed, and, following the guidance of Mr Merryweather, we passed down a narrow passage, and through a side door, which he opened for us. Within there was a small corridor, which ended in a very massive iron gate. This also was opened, and led down a flight of winding stone steps, which terminated at another formidable gate. Mr Merryweather stopped to light a lantern, and then conducted us down a dark, earth-smelling passage, and so, after opening a third door, into a huge vault or cellar, which was piled all round with crates and massive boxes.

'You are not very vulnerable from above,' Holmes remarked, as he held up the lantern and gazed about him.

'Nor from below,' said Mr Merryweather, striking his stick upon the flags which lined the floor. 'Why, dear me, it sounds quite hollow!' he remarked, looking up in surprise.

'I must really ask you to be a little more quiet,' said Holmes severely. 'You have already imperilled the whole success of our expedition. Might I beg that you would have the goodness to sit down upon one of those boxes, and not to interfere?'

The solemn Mr Merryweather perched himself upon a crate, with a very injured expression upon his face, while Holmes fell upon his knees upon the floor, and, with the lantern and a magnifying lens, began to examine minutely the cracks between the stones. A few seconds sufficed to satisfy him for he sprang to his feet again, and put his glass in his pocket.

'We have at least an hour before us,' he remarked, 'for they can hardly take any steps until the good pawnbroker is safely in bed. Then they will not lose a minute, for the sooner they do their work the longer time they will have for their escape. We are at present, Doctor—as no doubt you have divined—in the cellar of the City branch of one of the principal London banks. Mr Merryweather is the chairman of directors, and he will explain to you that there are reasons why the more daring criminals of London should take a considerable interest in this cellar at present.'

'It is our French gold,' whispered the director. 'We have had several warnings that an attempt might be made upon it.'

'Your French gold?'

'Yes. We had occasion some months ago to strengthen our resources, and borrowed, for that purpose, thirty thousand napoleons* from the Bank of France. It has become known that we have never had occasion to unpack the money, and that it is still lying in our cellar. The crate upon which I sit contains two thousand napoleons packed between layers of lead foil. Our reserve of bullion is much larger at present than is usually kept in a single branch office, and the directors have had misgivings upon the subject.'

'Which were very well justified,' observed Holmes. 'And now it is time that we arranged our little plans. I expect that within an hour matters will come to a head. In the meantime, Mr Merryweather, we must put the screen over that dark lantern.'*

'And sit in the dark?'

'I am afraid so. I had brought a pack of cards in my pocket, and I thought that, as we were a *partie carrée*,* you might have your rubber after all. But I see that the enemy's preparations have gone so far that we cannot risk the presence of a light. And, first of all, we must choose our positions. These are daring men, and, though we shall take them at a disadvantage they may do us some harm, unless we are careful. I shall stand behind this crate, and do you conceal yourself behind those. Then, when I flash a light upon them, close in swiftly. If they fire, Watson, have no compunction about shooting them down.'

I placed my revolver, cocked, upon the top of the wooden case behind which I crouched. Holmes shot the slide across the front of his lantern, and left us in pitch darkness—such an absolute darkness as I have never before experienced. The smell of hot metal remained to assure us that the light was still there, ready to flash out at a moment's notice. To me, with my nerves worked up to a pitch of expectancy, there was something depressing and subduing in the sudden gloom, and in the cold, dank air of the vault.

'They have but one retreat,' whispered Holmes. 'That is back through the house into Saxe-Coburg Square. I hope that you have done what I asked you, Jones?'

'I have an inspector and two officers waiting at the front door.'

'Then we have stopped all the holes. And now we must be silent and wait.'

What a time it seemed! From comparing notes afterwards it was but an hour and a quarter, yet it appeared to me that the night must have almost gone, and the dawn be breaking above us. My limbs were weary and stiff, for I feared to change my position, yet my nerves were worked up to the highest pitch of tension, and my hearing was so acute that I could not only hear the gentle breathing of my companions, but I could distinguish the deeper, heavier in-breath of the bulky Jones from the thin sighing note of the bank director. From my position I could look over the case in the direction of the floor. Suddenly my eyes caught the glint of a light.

At first it was but a lurid spark upon the stone pavement. Then it lengthened out until it became a yellow line, and then, without any warning or sound, a gash seemed to open and a hand appeared, a white, almost womanly hand, which felt about in the centre of the little area of light. For a minute or more the hand, with its writhing fingers, protruded out of the floor. Then it was withdrawn as suddenly as it appeared, and all was dark again save the single lurid spark, which marked a chink between the stones.

Its disappearance, however, was but momentary. With a rending, tearing sound, one of the broad, white stones turned over upon its side and left a square gaping hole through which streamed the light of a lantern. Over the edge there peeped a clean-cut, boyish face, which looked keenly about it, and then, with a hand on either side of the aperture, drew itself shoulder high and waist high until one knee rested upon the edge. In another instant he stood at the side of the hole, and was hauling after him a companion, lithe and small like himself, with a pale face and a shock of very red hair.

'It's all clear,' he whispered. 'Have you the chisel and the bags? Great Scott! Jump,* Archie, jump, and I'll swing for it!'*

Sherlock Holmes had sprung out and seized the intruder by the collar. The other dived down the hole, and I heard the sound of rending cloth as Jones clutched at his skirts.* The light flashed upon the barrel of a revolver, but Holmes's hunting-crop came down on the man's wrist, and the pistol clinked upon the stone floor.

'It's no use, John Clay,' said Holmes blandly; 'you have no chance at all.'

'So I see,' the other answered, with the utmost coolness. 'I fancy that my pal is all right, though I see you have got his coat-tails.'

'There are three men waiting for him at the door,' said Holmes.

'Oh, indeed. You seem to have done the thing very completely. I must compliment you.'

'And I you,' Holmes answered. 'Your red-headed idea was very new and effective.'

'You'll see your pal again presently,' said Jones. 'He's quicker at climbing down holes than I am. Just hold out while I fix the derbies.'*

'I beg that you will not touch me with your filthy hands,' remarked our prisoner, as the handcuffs clattered upon his wrists. 'You may not be aware that I have royal blood in my veins. Have the goodness also when you address me always to say "sir" and "please".'

'All right,' said Jones, with a stare and a snigger. 'Well, would you please, sir, march upstairs, where we can get a cab to carry your highness to the police-station.'

'That is better,' said John Clay, serenely. He made a sweeping bow to the three of us, and walked quietly off in the custody of the detective.

'Really, Mr Holmes,' said Mr Merryweather, as we followed them from the cellar, 'I do not know how the bank can thank you or repay you. There is no doubt that you have detected and defeated in the most complete manner one of the most determined attempts at bank robbery that have ever come within my experience.'

'I have had one or two little scores of my own to settle with Mr John Clay,' said Holmes. 'I have been at some small expense over this matter, which I shall expect the bank to refund, but beyond that I am amply repaid by having had an experience which is in many ways unique, and by hearing the very remarkable narrative of the Red-Headed League.'

'You see, Watson,' he explained in the early hours of the morning, as we sat over a glass of whisky-and-soda in Baker Street, 'it was perfectly obvious from the first that the only possible object of this rather fantastic business of the advertisement of the League, and the copying of the *Encyclopedia*, must be to get this not over-bright pawnbroker out of the way for a number of hours every day. It was a curious way of managing it, but really it would be difficult to suggest a better. The method was no doubt suggested to Clay's ingenious mind by the colour of his accomplice's hair. The four pounds a week was a lure which must draw him, and what was it to them, who were playing for thousands? They put in the advertisement; one rogue has the temporary office, the other rogue incites the man to apply for it, and together they manage to secure his absence every morning in the week. From the time that I heard of the assistant having come for half-wages, it was obvious to me that he had some strong motive for securing the situation.'

'But how could you guess what the motive was?'

'Had there been women in the house, I should have suspected a mere vulgar intrigue. That, however, was out of the question. The man's business was a small one, and there was nothing in his house which could account for such elaborate preparations and such an expenditure as they were at. It must then be something out of the house. What could it be? I thought of the assistant's fondness for photography, and his trick of vanishing into the cellar. The cellar! There was the end of this tangled clue. Then I made inquiries as to this mysterious assistant, and found that I had to deal with one of the coolest and most daring criminals in London. He was doing something in the cellar—something which took many hours a day for months on end. What could it be, once more? I could think of nothing save that he was running a tunnel to some other building.

'So far I had got when we went to visit the scene of action. I surprised you by beating upon the pavement with my stick. I was ascertaining whether the cellar stretched out in front or behind. It was not in front. Then I rang the bell, and, as I hoped, the assistant answered it. We have had some skirmishes, but we had never set eyes on each other before. I hardly looked at his face. His knees were what I wished to see. You must yourself have remarked how worn, wrinkled and stained they were. They spoke of those hours of burrowing. The only remaining point was what they were burrowing for. I walked round the corner, saw the City and Suburban Bank abutted on our friend's premises, and felt that I had solved my problem. When you drove home after the concert I called upon Scotland Yard, and upon the chairman of the bank directors, with the result that you have seen.'

'And how could you tell that they would make their attempt to-night?' I asked.

'Well, when they closed their League offices that was a sign that they cared no longer about Mr Jabez Wilson's presence; in other words, that they had completed their tunnel. But it was essential that they should use it soon, as it might be discovered, or the bullion might be removed. Saturday would suit them better than any other day, as it would give them two days for their escape. For all these reasons I expected them to come to-night.'

'You reasoned it out beautifully,' I exclaimed in unfeigned admiration. 'It is so long a chain, and yet every link rings true.'

'It saved me from ennui,' he answered, yawning. 'Alas, I already feel it closing in upon me! My life is spent in one long effort to escape from the commonplaces of existence. These little problems help me to do so.'

'And you are a benefactor of the race,' said I.

He shrugged his shoulders. 'Well, perhaps, after all, it is of some little use,' he remarked. ' "L'homme c'est rien—l'œuvre c'est tout,"* as Gustave Flaubert wrote to George Sand.'

THE MAN WITH THE TWISTED LIP

ISA WHITNEY, brother of the late Elias Whitney, D.D., Principal of the Theological College of St George's, was much addicted to opium.* The habit grew upon him, as I understand, from some foolish freak when he was at college, for having read De Quincey's description of his dreams and sensations,* he had drenched his tobacco with laudanum* in an attempt to produce the same effects. He found, as so many more have done, that the practice is easier to attain than to get rid of, and for many years he continued to be a slave to the drug, an object of mingled horror and pity to his friends and relatives. I can see him now, with yellow, pasty face, drooping lids and pin-point pupils, all huddled in a chair, the wreck and ruin of a noble man.

One night—it was in June, '89—there came a ring to my bell, about the hour when a man gives his first yawn, and glances at the clock. I sat up in my chair, and my wife laid her needlework down in her lap and made a little face of disappointment.

'A patient!' said she. 'You'll have to go out.'

I groaned, for I was newly come back from a weary day.

We heard the door open, a few hurried words, and then quick steps upon the linoleum. Our own door flew open, and a lady, clad in some dark-coloured stuff with a black veil, entered the room.

'You will excuse my calling so late,' she began, and then, suddenly losing her self-control, she ran forward, threw her arms about my wife's neck, and sobbed upon her shoulder. 'Oh! I'm in such trouble!' she cried; 'I do so want a little help.'

'Why,' said my wife, pulling up her veil, 'It is Kate Whitney. How you startled me, Kate! I had not an idea who you were when you came in.'

'I didn't know what to do, so I came straight to you.' That was always the way. Folk who were in grief came to my wife like birds to a lighthouse.

'It was very sweet of you to come. Now, you must have some wine and water, and sit here comfortably and tell us all about it. Or should you rather that I sent James* off to bed?'

'Oh, no, no. I want the Doctor's advice and help too. It's about Isa. He has not been home for two days. I am so frightened about him!'

It was not the first time that she had spoken to us of her husband's trouble, to me as a doctor, to my wife as an old friend and school companion. We soothed and comforted her by such words as we could find. Did she know where her husband was? Was it possible that we could bring him back to her?

It seemed that it was. She had the surest information that of late he had, when the fit was on him, made use of an opium den* in the furthest east of the City. Hitherto his orgies had always been confined to one day, and he had come back, twitching and shattered, in the evening. But now the spell had been upon him eight-and-forty hours, and he lay there, doubtless, among the dregs of the docks, breathing in the poison or sleeping off the effects. There he was to be found, she was sure of it, at the 'Bar of Gold', in Upper Swandam Lane. But what was she to do? How could she, a young and timid woman, make her way into such a place, and pluck her husband out from among the ruffians who surrounded him?

There was the case, and of course there was but one way out of it. Might I not escort her to this place? And then, as a second thought, why should she come at all? I was Isa Whitney's medical adviser, and as such I had influence over him. I could manage it better if I were alone. I promised her on my word that I would send him home in a cab within two hours if he were indeed at the address which she had given me. And so in ten minutes I had left my armchair and cheery sitting-room behind me, and was speeding eastward in a hansom* on a strange errand, as it seemed to me at the time, though the future only could show how strange it was to be.

But there was no great difficulty in the first stage of my adventure. Upper Swandam Lane is a vile alley lurking behind the high wharves which line the north side of the river to the east of London Bridge. Between a slop shop,* and a gin shop,* approached by a steep flight of steps leading down to a black gap like the mouth of a cave, I found the den of which I was in search. Ordering my cab to wait, I passed down the steps, worn hollow in the centre by the ceaseless tread of drunken feet, and by the light of a flickering oil lamp above the door I found the latch and made my way into a long, low room, thick and heavy with the brown opium smoke, and terraced with wooden berths, like the forecastle of an emigrant ship.

Through the gloom one could dimly catch a glimpse of bodies lying in strange fantastic poses, bowed shoulders, bent knees, heads thrown back and chins pointing upwards, with here and there a dark, lack-lustre eye turned upon the newcomer. Out of the black shadows there glimmered little red circles of light, now bright, now faint, as the burning poison waxed or waned in the bowls of the metal pipes. The most lay silent, but some muttered to themselves, and others talked together in a strange, low, monotonous voice, their conversation coming in gushes, and then suddenly tailing off into silence, each mumbling out his own thoughts, and paying little heed to the words of his neighbour. At the further end was a small brazier of burning charcoal,* beside which on a three-legged wooden stool there sat a tall, thin old man, with his jaw resting upon his two fists, and his elbows upon his knees, staring into the fire.

As I entered, a sallow Malay attendant had hurried up with a pipe for me and a supply of the drug, beckoning me to an empty berth.

'Thank you, I have not come to stay,' said I. 'There is a friend of mine here, Mr Isa Whitney, and I wish to speak with him.'

There was a movement and an exclamation from my right, and, peering through the gloom, I saw Whitney, pale, haggard, and unkempt, staring out at me.

'My God! It's Watson,' said he. He was in a pitiable state of reaction, with every nerve in a twitter. 'I say, Watson, what o'clock is it?'

'Nearly eleven.'

'Of what day?'

'Of Friday, June 19th.'

'Good heavens! I thought it was Wednesday. It *is* Wednesday. What d'you want to frighten a chap for?' He sank his face on to his arms, and began to sob in a high treble key.

'I tell you that it is Friday, man. Your wife has been waiting this two days for you. You should be ashamed of yourself!'

'So I am. But you've got mixed, Watson, for I have only been here a few hours, three pipes, four pipes—I forget how many. But I'll go home with you. I wouldn't frighten Kate—poor little Kate. Give me your hand! Have you a cab?'

'Yes, I have one waiting.'

'Then I shall go in it. But I must owe something. Find what I owe, Watson. I am all off colour. I can do nothing for myself.'

I walked down the narrow passage between the double row of sleepers, holding my breath to keep out the vile, stupefying fumes of the drug, and looking about for the manager. As I passed the tall man who sat by the brazier I felt a sudden pluck at my skirt,* and a low voice whispered, 'Walk past me, and then look back at me.' The words fell quite distinctly upon my ear. I glanced down. They could only have come from the old man at my side, and yet he sat now as absorbed as ever, very thin, very wrinkled, bent with age, an opium pipe* dangling down from between his knees, as though it had dropped in sheer lassitude from his fingers. I took two steps forward and looked back. It took all my self-control to prevent me from breaking out into a cry of astonishment. He had turned his back so that none could see him but I. His form had filled out, his wrinkles were gone, the dull eyes had regained their fire, and there, sitting by the fire, and grinning at my surprise, was none other than Sherlock Holmes. He made a slight motion to me to approach him, and instantly, as he turned his face half round to the company once more, subsided into a doddering, loose-lipped senility.

'Holmes!' I whispered, 'what on earth are you doing in this den?'

'As low as you can,' he answered, 'I have excellent ears. If you would have the great kindness to get rid of that sottish friend of yours, I should be exceedingly glad to have a little talk with you.'

'I have a cab outside.'

'Then pray send him home in it. You may safely trust him, for he appears to be too limp to get into any mischief. I should recommend you also to send a note by the cabman to your wife to say that you have thrown in your lot with me. If you will wait outside, I shall be with you in five minutes.'

It was difficult to refuse any of Sherlock Holmes's requests, for they were always so exceedingly definite, and put forward with such an air of mastery. I felt, however, that when Whitney was once confined in the cab, my mission was practically accomplished; and for the rest, I could not wish anything better than to be associated with my friend in one of those singular adventures which were the normal condition of his existence. In a few minutes I had written my note, paid Whitney's bill, led him out to the cab, and seen him driven through the darkness. In a very short time a decrepit figure had emerged from the opium den, and I was walking down the street with Sherlock Holmes. For two streets he shuffled along with a bent back and an uncertain foot. Then, glancing quickly round, he straightened himself out and burst into a hearty fit of laughter.

'I suppose, Watson,' said he, 'that you imagine that I have added opium-smoking to cocaine injections and all the other little weak-nesses on which you have favoured me with your medical views.'

'I was certainly surprised to find you there.'

'But not more so than I to find you.'

'I came to find a friend.'

'And I to find an enemy!'

'An enemy?'

'Yes, one of my natural enemies, or, shall I say, my natural prey. Briefly, Watson, I am in the midst of a very serious inquiry, and I have hoped to find a clue in the incoherent ramblings of these sots, as I have done before now. Had I been recognized in that den my life would not have been worth an hour's purchase, for I have used it before now for my own purposes, and the rascally Lascar* who runs it has sworn vengeance upon me. There is a trap-door at the back of that building, near the corner of Paul's Wharf, which could tell some strange tales of what has passed through it upon the moonless nights.'

'What! You do not mean bodies?'

'Aye, bodies, Watson. We should be rich men if we had a thousand pounds for every poor devil who has been done to death in that den. It is the vilest murder-trap on the whole riverside, and I fear Neville St Clair has entered it never to leave it more. But our trap should be here!' He put his two fore-fingers between his teeth and whistled shrilly, a signal which was answered by a similar whistle from the dis-tance, followed shortly by the rattle of wheels and the clink of horse's hoofs.

'Now, Watson,' said Holmes, as a tall dog-cart* dashed up through the gloom, throwing out two golden tunnels of yellow light from its side-lanterns, 'you'll come with me, won't you?'

'If I can be of use.'

'Oh, a trusty comrade is always of use. And a chronicler still more so. My room at The Cedars is a double-bedded one.'

'The Cedars?'

'Yes; that is Mr St Clair's house. I am staying there while I conduct the inquiry.'

'Where is it, then?'

'Near Lee, in Kent. We have a seven-mile drive before us.'

'But I am all in the dark.'

'Of course you are. You'll know all about it presently. Jump up here!

All right, John, we shall not need you. Here's half-a-crown. Look out for me to-morrow about eleven. Give her her head! So long, then!'

He flicked the horse with his whip, and we dashed away through the endless succession of sombre and deserted streets, which widened gradually, until we were flying across a broad balustraded bridge, with the murky river flowing sluggishly beneath us. Beyond lay another broad wilderness of bricks and mortar, its silence broken only by the heavy, regular footfall of the policeman, or the songs and shouts of some belated party of revellers. A dull wrack* was drifting slowly across the sky, and a star or two twinkled dimly here and there through the rifts of the clouds. Holmes drove in silence, with his head sunk upon his breast, and the air of a man who is lost in thought, whilst I sat beside him curious to learn what this new quest might be which seemed to tax his powers so sorely, and yet afraid to break in upon the current of his thoughts. We had driven several miles, and were beginning to get to the fringe of the belt of suburban villas, when he shook himself, shrugged his shoulders, and lit up his pipe with the air of a man who has satisfied himself that he is acting for the best.

'You have a grand gift of silence, Watson,' said he. 'It makes you quite invaluable as a companion. 'Pon my word, it is a great thing for me to have someone to talk to, for my own thoughts are not over-pleasant. I was wondering what I should say to this dear little woman to-night when she meets me at the door.'

'You forget that I know nothing about it.'

'I shall just have time to tell you the facts of the case before we get to Lee. It seems absurdly simple, and yet, somehow, I can get nothing to go upon. There's plenty of thread, no doubt, but I can't get the end of it in my hand. Now, I'll state the case clearly and concisely to you, Watson, and maybe you may see a spark where all is dark to me.'

'Proceed, then.'

'Some years ago—to be definite, in May, 1884—there came to Lee a gentleman, Neville St Clair by name, who appeared to have plenty of money. He took a large villa, laid out the grounds very nicely, and lived generally in good style. By degrees he made friends in the neighbourhood, and in 1887 he married the daughter of a local brewer, by whom he has now had two children. He had no occupation, but was interested in several companies, and went into town as a rule in the morning, returning by the 5.14 from Cannon Street* every night. Mr St Clair is now 37 years of age, is a man of temperate habits, a good husband, a very affectionate father, and a man who is popular with all who know him. I may add that his whole debts at the present moment, as far as we have been able to ascertain, amount to £88 10s., while he has £220 standing to his credit in the Capital and Counties Bank. There is no reason, therefore, to think that money troubles have been weighing upon his mind.

'Last Monday Mr Neville St Clair went into town rather earlier than usual, remarking before he started that he had two important commissions to perform, and that he would bring his little boy home a box of bricks.* Now, by the merest chance his wife received a telegram upon this same Monday, very shortly after his departure, to the effect that a small parcel of considerable value which she had been expecting was waiting for her at the offices of the Aberdeen Shipping Company. Now, if you are well up in your London, you will know that the office of the company is in Fresno Street, which branches out of Upper Swandam Lane, where you found me to-night. Mrs St Clair had her lunch, started for the City, did some shopping, proceeded to the Company's office, got her packet, and found herself exactly at 4.35 walking through Swandam Lane on her way back to the station. Have you followed me so far?'

'It is very clear.'

'If you remember, Monday was an exceedingly hot day, and Mrs St Clair walked slowly, glancing about in the hope of seeing a cab, as she did not like the neighbourhood in which she found herself. While she walked in this way down Swandam Lane she suddenly heard an ejaculation or cry, and was struck cold to see her husband looking down at her, and, as it seemed to her, beckoning to her from a second-floor window. The window was open, and she distinctly saw his face, which she describes as being terribly agitated. He waved his hands frantically to her, and then vanished from the window so suddenly that it seemed to her that he had been plucked back by some irresistible force from behind. One singular point which struck her quick feminine eye was that, although he wore some dark coat, such as he had started to town in, he had on neither collar nor necktie.

'Convinced that something was amiss with him, she rushed down the steps—for the house was none other than the opium den in which you found me to-night—and, running through the front room, she attempted to ascend the stairs which led to the first floor. At the foot of the stairs, however, she met this Lascar scoundrel, of whom I have spoken, who thrust her back, and, aided by a Dane, who acts as assistant there, pushed her out into the street. Filled with the most maddening doubts and fears, she rushed down the lane, and, by rare good fortune, met, in Fresno Street, a number of constables with an inspector, all on their way to their beat. The inspector and two men accompanied her back, and, in spite of the continued resistance of the proprietor, they made their way to the room in which Mr St Clair had last been seen. There was no sign of him there. In fact, in the whole of that floor there was no one to be found, save a crippled wretch of hideous aspect, who, it seems, made his home there. Both he and the Lascar stoutly swore that no one else had been in the front room during that afternoon. So determined was their denial that the inspector was staggered, and had almost come to believe that Mrs St Clair had been deluded when, with a cry, she sprang at a small deal box* which lay upon the table, and tore the lid from it. Out there fell a cascade of children's bricks. It was the toy which he had promised to bring home.

'This discovery, and the evident confusion which the cripple showed, made the inspector realize that the matter was serious. The rooms were carefully examined, and results all pointed to an abominable crime. The front room was plainly furnished as a sitting-room, and led into a small bedroom, which looked out upon the back of one of the wharves. Between the wharf and the bedroom window is a narrow strip, which is dry at low tide, but is covered at high tide with at least four and a half feet of water. The bedroom window was a broad one, and opened from below. On examination traces of blood were to be seen upon the window-sill, and several scattered drops were visible upon the wooden floor of the bedroom. Thrust away behind a curtain in the front room were all the clothes of Mr Neville St Clair, with the exception of his coat. His boots, his socks, his hat, and his watch—all were there. There were no signs of violence upon any of these garments, and there were no other traces of Mr Neville St Clair. Out of the window he must apparently have gone, for no other exit could be discovered, and the ominous bloodstains upon the sill gave little promise that he could save himself by swimming, for the tide was at its very highest at the moment of the tragedy.

'And now as to the villains who seemed to be immediately implicated in the matter. The Lascar was known to be a man of the vilest antecedents, but as by Mrs St Clair's story he was known to have been at the foot of the stair within a few seconds of her husband's appearance at the window, he could hardly have been more than an accessory to the crime. His defence was one of absolute ignorance, and he protested that he had no knowledge as to the doings of Hugh Boone, his lodger, and that he could not account in any way for the presence of the missing gentleman's clothes.

'So much for the Lascar manager. Now for the sinister cripple who lives upon the second floor of the opium den, and who was certainly the last human being whose eyes rested upon Neville St Clair. His name is Hugh Boone, and his hideous face is one which is familiar to every man who goes much to the City. He is a professional beggar, though in order to avoid the police regulations he pretends to a small trade in wax vestas.* Some little distance down Threadneedle Street* upon the left hand side there is, as you may have remarked, a small angle in the wall. Here it is that the creature takes his daily seat, cross-legged, with his tiny stock of matches on his lap, and as he is a piteous spectacle a small rain of charity descends into the greasy leather cap which lies upon the pavement before him. I have watched this fellow more than once, before ever I thought of making his professional acquaintance, and I have been surprised at the harvest which he has reaped in so short a time. His appearance, you see, is so remarkable that no one can pass him without observing him. A shock of orange hair, a pale face disfigured by a horrible scar, which, by its contraction, has turned up the outer edge of his upper lip, a bull-dog chin, and a pair of very penetrating dark eyes, which present a singular contrast to the colour of his hair, all mark him out from amid the common crowd of mendicants, and so, too, does his wit, for he is ever ready with a reply to any piece of chaff which may be thrown at him by the passers-by. This is the man whom we now learn to have been the lodger at the opium den, and to have been the last man to see the gentleman of whom we are in quest.'

'But a cripple!' said I. 'What could he have done single-handed against a man in the prime of life?'

'He is a cripple in the sense that he walks with a limp; but, in other respects, he appears to be a powerful and well-nurtured man. Surely your medical experience would tell you, Watson, that weakness in one limb is often compensated for by exceptional strength in the others.'

'Pray continue your narrative.'

'Mrs St Clair had fainted at the sight of the blood upon the window, and she was escorted home in a cab by the police, as her presence could be of no help to them in their investigations. Inspector Barton, who had charge of the case, made a very careful examination of the premises, but without finding anything which threw any light upon the matter. One mistake had been made in not arresting Boone instantly, as he was allowed some few minutes during which he might have communicated with his friend the Lascar, but this fault was soon remedied, and he was seized and searched, without anything being found which could incriminate him. There were, it is true, some bloodstains upon his right shirt-sleeve, but he pointed to his ring finger, which had been cut near the nail, and explained that the bleeding came from there, adding that he had been to the window not long before, and that the stains which had been observed there came doubtless from the same source. He denied strenuously having ever seen Mr Neville St Clair, and swore that the presence of the clothes in his room was as much a mystery to him as to the police. As to Mrs St Clair's assertion, that she had actually seen her husband at the window, he declared that she must have been either mad or dreaming. He was removed, loudly protesting, to the police station, while the inspector remained upon the premises in the hope that the ebbing tide might afford some fresh clue.

'And it did, though they hardly found upon the mudbank what they had feared to find. It was Neville St Clair's coat, and not Neville St Clair, which lay uncovered as the tide receded. And what do you think they found in the pockets?'

'I cannot imagine.'

'No, I don't think you will guess. Every pocket stuffed with pennies and halfpennies—four hundred and twenty-one pennies, and two hundred and seventy halfpennies. It was no wonder that it had not been swept away by the tide. But a human body is a different matter. There is a fierce eddy between the wharf and the house. It seemed likely enough that the weighted coat had remained when the stripped body had been sucked away into the river.'

'But I understand that all the other clothes were found in the room. Would the body be dressed in a coat alone?'

'No, sir, but the facts might be met speciously enough. Suppose that this man Boone had thrust Neville St Clair through the window, there is no human eye which could have seen the deed. What would he do then? It would of course instantly strike him that he must get rid of the tell-tale garments. He would seize the coat then, and be in the act of throwing it out when it would occur to him that it would swim and not sink. He has little time, for he had heard the scuffle downstairs when the wife tried to force her way up, and perhaps he has already heard from his Lascar confederate that the police are hurrying up the street. There is not an instant to be lost. He rushes to some secret hoard, where he has accumulated the fruits of his beggary, and he stuffs all the coins upon which he can lay his hands into the pockets to make sure of the coat's sinking. He throws it out, and would have done the same with the other garments had not he heard the rush of steps below, and only just had time to close the window when the police appeared.'

'It certainly sounds feasible.'

'Well, we will take it as a working hypothesis for want of a better. Boone, as I have told you, was arrested and taken to the station, but it could not be shown that there had ever before been anything against him. He had for years been known as a professional beggar, but his life appeared to have been a very quiet and innocent one. There the matter stands at present, and the questions which have to be solved, what Neville St Clair was doing in the opium den, what happened to him when there, where he is now, and what Hugh Boone had to do with his disappearance, are all as far from solution as ever. I confess that I cannot recall any case within my experience which looked at the first glance so simple, and yet which presented such difficulties.'

Whilst Sherlock Holmes had been detailing this singular series of events we had been whirling through the outskirts of the great town until the last straggling houses had been left behind, and we rattled along with a country hedge upon either side of us. Just as he finished, however, we drove through two scattered villages, where a few lights still glimmered in the windows.

'We are on the outskirts of Lee,' said my companion. 'We have touched on three English counties in our short drive, starting in Middlesex, passing over an angle of Surrey, and ending in Kent. See that light among the trees? That is The Cedars, and beside that lamp sits a woman whose anxious ears have already, I have little doubt, caught the clink of our horse's feet.'

'But why are you not conducting the case from Baker Street?' I asked.

'Because there are many inquiries which must be made out here. Mrs St Clair has most kindly put two rooms at my disposal, and you may rest assured that she will have nothing but a welcome for my friend and colleague. I hate to meet her, Watson, when I have no news of her husband. Here we are. Whoa, there, whoa!'

We had pulled up in front of a large villa which stood within its own grounds. A stable-boy had run out to the horse's head, and, springing down, I followed Holmes up the small, winding gravel drive which led to the house. As we approached, the door flew open, and a little blonde woman stood in the opening, clad in some sort of light *mousseline-de-soie*,* with a touch of fluffy pink chiffon at her neck and wrists. She stood with her figure outlined against the flood of light, one hand upon the door, one half raised in eagerness, her body slightly bent, her head and face protruded, with eager eyes and parted lips, a standing question.

'Well?' she cried, 'well?' And then, seeing that there were two of us, she gave a cry of hope which sank into a groan as she saw that my companion shook his head and shrugged his shoulders.

'No good news?'

'None.'

'No bad?'

'No.'

'Thank God for that. But come in. You must be weary, for you have had a long day.'

'This is my friend, Dr Watson. He has been of most vital use to me in several of my cases, and a lucky chance has made it possible for me to bring him out and associate him with this investigation.'

'I am delighted to see you,' said she, pressing my hand warmly. 'You will, I am sure, forgive anything which may be wanting in our arrangements, when you consider the blow which has come so suddenly upon us.'

'My dear madam,' said I, 'I am an old campaigner,* and if I were not, I can very well see that no apology is needed. If I can be of any assistance, either to you or to my friend here, I shall be indeed happy.'

'Now, Mr Sherlock Holmes,' said the lady as we entered a well-lit dining-room, upon the table of which a cold supper had been laid out. 'I should very much like to ask you one or two plain questions, to which I beg that you will give a plain answer.'

'Certainly, madam.'

'Do not trouble about my feelings. I am not hysterical, nor given to fainting. I simply wish to hear your real, real opinion.'

'Upon what point?'

'In your heart of hearts, do you think that Neville is alive?'

Sherlock Holmes seemed to be embarrassed by the question. 'Frankly now!' she repeated, standing upon the rug, and looking keenly down at him, as he leaned back in a basket chair.

'Frankly, then, madam, I do not.'

'You think that he is dead?'

'I do.'

'Murdered?'

'I don't say that. Perhaps.'

'And on what day did he meet his death?'

'On Monday.'

'Then perhaps, Mr Holmes, you will be good enough to explain how it is that I have received this letter from him today?'

Sherlock Holmes sprang out of his chair as if he had been galvanized.*

'What!' he roared.

'Yes, today.' She stood smiling, holding up a little slip of paper in the air.

'May I see it?'

'Certainly.'

He snatched it from her in his eagerness, and smoothing it out upon the table, he drew over the lamp, and examined it intently. I had left my chair, and was gazing at it over his shoulder. The envelope was a very coarse one, and was stamped with the Gravesend post-mark, and with the date of that very day, or rather of the day before, for it was considerably after midnight.

'Coarse writing!' murmured Holmes. 'Surely this is not your husband's writing, madam.'

'No, but the enclosure is.'

'I perceive also that whoever addressed the envelope had to go and inquire as to the address.'

'How can you tell that?'

'The name, you see, is in perfectly black ink, which has dried itself. The rest is of the greyish colour which shows that blotting-paper has been used. If it had been written straight off, and then blotted, none would be of a deep black shade. This man has written the name, and there has then been a pause before he wrote the address, which can only mean that he was not familiar with it. It is, of course, a trifle, but there is nothing so important as trifles. Let us now see the letter! Ha! there has been an enclosure here!'

'Yes, there was a ring. His signet ring.'

'And you are sure that this is your husband's hand?'

'One of his hands.'

'One?'

'His hand when he wrote hurriedly. It is very unlike his usual writing, and yet I know it well.'

' "Dearest, do not be frightened. All will come well. There is a huge error which it may take some little time to rectify. Wait in patience.— Neville." Written in pencil upon a flyleaf of a book,* octavo size,* no watermark. Hum!—Posted to-day in Gravesend by a man with a dirty thumb. Ha! And the flap has been gummed, if I am not very much in error, by a person who has been chewing tobacco. And you have no doubt that it is your husband's hand, madam?'

'None. Neville wrote those words.'

'And they were posted to-day at Gravesend. Well, Mrs St Clair, the clouds lighten, though I should not venture to say that the danger is over.'

'But he must be alive, Mr Holmes.'

'Unless this is a clever forgery to put us on the wrong scent. The ring, after all, proves nothing. It may have been taken from him.'

'No, no; it is, it is, it is his very own writing!'

'Very well. It may, however, have been written on Monday, and only posted to-day.'

'That is possible.'

'If so, much may have happened between.'

'Oh, you must not discourage me, Mr Holmes. I know that all is well with him. There is so keen a sympathy between us that I should know if evil came upon him. On the very day that I saw him last he cut himself in the bedroom, and yet I in the dining-room rushed upstairs instantly with the utmost certainty that something had happened. Do you think that I would respond to such a trifle, and yet be ignorant of his death?'

'I have seen too much not to know that the impression of a woman may be more valuable than the conclusion of an analytical reasoner.

And in this letter you certainly have a very strong piece of evidence to corroborate your view. But if your husband is alive and able to write letters, why should he remain away from you?'

'I cannot imagine. It is unthinkable.'

'And on Monday he made no remarks before leaving you?'

'No.'

'And you were surprised to see him in Swandam Lane?'

'Very much so.'

'Was the window open?'

'Yes.'

'Then he might have called to you?'

'He might.'

'He only, as I understand, gave an inarticulate cry?'

'Yes.'

'A call for help, you thought?'

'Yes. He waved his hands.'

'But it might have been a cry of surprise. Astonishment at the unexpected sight of you might cause him to throw up his hands.'

'It is possible.'

'And you thought he was pulled back?'

'He disappeared so suddenly.'

'He might have leaped back. You did not see anyone else in the room?'

'No, but this horrible man confessed to having been there, and the Lascar was at the foot of the stairs.'

'Quite so. Your husband, as far as you could see, had his ordinary clothes on?'

'But without his collar or tie. I distinctly saw his bare throat.'

'Had he ever spoken of Swandam Lane?'

'Never.'

'Had he ever shown any signs of having taken opium?'

'Never.'

'Thank you, Mrs St Clair. Those are the principal points about which I wished to be absolutely clear. We shall now have a little supper and then retire, for we may have a very busy day to-morrow.'

A large and comfortable double-bedded room had been placed at our disposal, and I was quickly between the sheets, for I was weary after my night of adventure. Sherlock Holmes was a man, however, who when he had an unsolved problem upon his mind would go for days, and even for a week, without rest, turning it over, rearranging his facts, looking at it from every point of view, until he had either fathomed it, or convinced himself that his data were insufficient. It was soon evident to me that he was now preparing for an all-night sitting. He took off his coat and waistcoat, put on a large blue dressing-gown, and then wandered about the room collecting pillows from his bed, and cushions from the sofa and armchairs. With these he constructed a sort of Eastern divan,* upon which he perched himself cross-legged, with an ounce of shag tobacco* and a box of matches laid out in front of him. In the dim light of the lamp I saw him sitting there, an old brier pipe* between his lips, his eyes fixed vacantly upon the corner of the ceiling, the blue smoke curling up from him, silent, motionless, with the light shining upon his strong-set aquiline features. So he sat as I dropped off to sleep, and so he sat when a sudden ejaculation caused me to wake up, and I found the summer sun shining into the apartment. The pipe was still between his lips, the smoke still curled upwards, and the room was full of a dense tobacco haze, but nothing remained of the heap of shag which I had seen upon the previous night.

'Awake, Watson?' he asked.

'Yes.'

'Game for a morning drive?'

'Certainly.'

'Then dress. No one is stirring yet, but I know where the stable-boy sleeps, and we shall soon have the trap out.' He chuckled to himself as he spoke, his eyes twinkled, and he seemed a different man to the sombre thinker of the previous night.

As I dressed I glanced at my watch. It was no wonder that no one was stirring. It was twenty-five minutes past four. I had hardly finished when Holmes returned with the news that the boy was putting in the horse.

'I want to test a little theory of mine,' said he, pulling on his boots. 'I think, Watson, that you are now standing in the presence of one of the most absolute fools in Europe. I deserve to be kicked from here to Charing Cross. But I think I have the key of the affair now.'

'And where is it?' I asked, smiling.

'In the bath-room,' he answered. 'Oh, yes, I am not joking,' he continued, seeing my look of incredulity. 'I have just been there, and I have taken it out, and I have got it in this Gladstone bag.* Come on, my boy, and we shall see whether it will not fit the lock.'

We made our way downstairs as quietly as possible; and out into the bright morning sunshine. In the road stood our horse and trap, with the half-clad stable-boy waiting at the head. We both sprang in, and away we dashed down the London road. A few country carts were stirring, bearing in vegetables to the metropolis, but the lines of villas on either side were as silent and lifeless as some city in a dream.

'It has been in some points a singular case,' said Holmes, flicking the horse on into a gallop. 'I confess that I have been as blind as a mole, but it is better to learn wisdom late, than never to learn it at all.'

In town, the earliest risers were just beginning to look sleepily from their windows as we drove through the streets of the Surrey side.* Passing down the Waterloo Bridge Road we crossed over the river, and dashing up Wellington Street wheeled sharply to the right, and found ourselves in Bow Street.* Sherlock Holmes was well known to the Force, and the two constables at the door saluted him. One of them held the horse's head while the other led us in.

'Who is on duty?' asked Holmes.

'Inspector Bradstreet, sir.'

'Ah, Bradstreet, how are you?' A tall, stout official had come down the stone-flagged passage, in a peaked cap and frogged jacket.* 'I wish to have a word with you, Bradstreet.'

'Certainly, Mr Holmes. Step into my room here.'

It was a small office-like room, with a huge ledger upon the table, and a telephone projecting from the wall. The inspector sat down at his desk.

'What can I do for you, Mr Holmes?'

'I called about that beggarman, Boone—the one who was charged with being concerned in the disappearance of Mr Neville St Clair, of Lee.'

'Yes. He was brought up and remanded for further inquiries.'

'So I heard. You have him here?'

'In the cells.'

'Is he quiet?'

'Oh, he gives no trouble. But he is a dirty scoundrel.'

'Dirty?'

'Yes, it is all we can do to make him wash his hands, and his face is as black as a tinker's. Well, when once his case has been settled he will have a regular prison bath; and I think, if you saw him you would agree with me that he needed it.'

'I should like to see him very much.'

'Would you? That is easily done. Come this way. You can leave your bag.'

'No, I think that I'll take it.'

'Very good. Come this way, if you please.' He led us down a passage, opened a barred door, passed down a winding stair, and brought us to a white-washed corridor with a line of doors on each side.

'The third on the right is his,' said the inspector. 'Here it is!' He quietly shot back a panel in the upper part of the door, and glanced through.

'He is asleep,' said he. 'You can see him very well.'

We both put our eyes to the grating. The prisoner lay with his face towards us, in a very deep sleep, breathing slowly and heavily. He was a middle-sized man, coarsely clad as became his calling, with a coloured shirt protruding through the rent in his tattered coat. He was, as the inspector had said, extremely dirty, but the grime which covered his face could not conceal its repulsive ugliness. A broad weal from an old scar ran across it from eye to chin, and by its contraction had turned up one side of the upper lip, so that three teeth were exposed in a perpetual snarl. A shock of very bright red hair grew low over his eyes and forehead.

'He's a beauty, isn't he?' said the inspector.

'He certainly needs a wash,' remarked Holmes. 'I had an idea that he might, and I took the liberty of bringing the tools with me.' He opened his Gladstone bag as he spoke, and took out, to my astonishment, a very large bath sponge.

'He! he! You are a funny one,' chuckled the inspector.

'Now, if you will have the great goodness to open that door very quietly, we will soon make him cut a much more respectable figure.'

'Well, I don't know why not,' said the inspector. 'He doesn't look a credit to the Bow Street cells, does he?' He slipped his key into the lock, and we all very quietly entered the cell. The sleeper half turned, and then settled down once more into a deep slumber. Holmes stooped to the water jug, moistened his sponge, and then rubbed it twice vigorously across and down the prisoner's face.

'Let me introduce you,' he shouted, 'to Mr Neville St Clair, of Lee, in the county of Kent.'

Never in my life have I seen such a sight. The man's face peeled off under the sponge like the bark from a tree. Gone was the coarse brown tint! Gone, too, the horrid scar which had seamed it across, and the twisted lip which had given the repulsive sneer to the face! A twitch brought away the tangled red hair, and there, sitting up in his bed, was a pale, sad-faced, refined-looking man, black-haired and smooth-skinned, rubbing his eyes, and staring about him with sleepy bewilderment. Then suddenly realizing the exposure, he broke into a scream, and threw himself down with his face to the pillow.

'Great heaven!' cried the inspector, 'it is, indeed, the missing man. I know him from the photograph.'

The prisoner turned with the reckless air of a man who abandons himself to his destiny. 'Be it so,' said he. 'And pray what am I charged with?'

'With making away with Mr Neville St—Oh, come, you can't be charged with that, unless they make a case of attempted suicide of it,' said the inspector, with a grin. 'Well, I have been twenty-seven years in the Force, but this really takes the cake.'

'If I am Mr Neville St Clair, then it is obvious that no crime has been committed, and that, therefore, I am illegally detained.'

'No crime, but a very great error has been committed,' said Holmes. 'You would have done better to have trusted your wife.'

'It was not the wife, it was the children,' groaned the prisoner. 'God help me, I would not have them ashamed of their father. My God! What an exposure! What can I do?'

Sherlock Holmes sat down beside him on the couch, and patted him kindly on the shoulder.

'If you leave it to a court of law to clear the matter up,' said he, 'of course you can hardly avoid publicity. On the other hand, if you convince the police authorities that there is no possible case against you, I do not know that there is any reason that the details should find their way into the papers. Inspector Bradstreet would, I am sure, make notes upon anything which you might tell us, and submit it to the proper authorities. The case would then never go into court at all.'

'God bless you!' cried the prisoner passionately. 'I would have endured imprisonment, aye, even execution, rather than have left my miserable secret as a family blot to my children.

'You are the first who have ever heard my story. My father was a schoolmaster in Chesterfield, where I received an excellent education. I travelled in my youth, took to the stage, and finally became a reporter on an evening paper in London. One day my editor wished to have a series of articles upon begging in the metropolis, and I volunteered to supply them. There was the point from which all my adventures started. It was only by trying begging as an amateur that I could get the facts upon which to base my articles. When an actor I had, of course, learned all the secrets of making up, and had been famous in the greenroom* for my skill. I took advantage now of my attainments. I painted my face, and to make myself as pitiable as possible I made a good scar and fixed one side of my lip in a twist by the aid of a small slip of flesh-coloured plaster. Then with a red head of hair, and an appropriate dress, I took my station in the busiest part of the City, ostensibly as a match-seller, but really as a beggar. For seven hours I plied my trade, and when I returned home in the evening I found, to my surprise, that I had received no less than twenty-six shillings and fourpence.

'I wrote my articles, and thought little more of the matter until, some time later, I backed a bill* for a friend, and had a writ served upon me for £25. I was at my wits' end where to get the money, but a sudden idea came to me. I begged a fortnight's grace from the creditor, asked for a holiday from my employers, and spent the time in begging in the City under my disguise. In ten days I had the money, and had paid the debt.

'Well, you can imagine how hard it was to settle down to arduous work at two pounds a week, when I knew that I could earn as much in a day by smearing my face with a little paint, laying my cap on the ground, and sitting still. It was a long fight between my pride and the money, but the dollars* won at last, and I threw up reporting, and sat day after day in the corner which I had first chosen, inspiring pity by my ghastly face, and filling my pockets with coppers. Only one man knew my secret. He was the keeper of a low den in which I used to lodge in Swandam Lane, where I could every morning emerge as a squalid beggar and in the evening transform myself into a well-dressed man about town. This fellow, a Lascar, was well paid by me for his rooms, so that I knew that my secret was safe in his possession.

'Well, very soon I found that I was saving considerable sums of money. I do not mean that any beggar in the streets of London could earn seven hundred pounds a year—which is less than my average takings—but I had exceptional advantages in my power of making up, and also in a facility in repartee, which improved by practice, and made me quite a recognized character in the City. All day a stream of pennies, varied by silver, poured in upon me, and it was a very bad day upon which I failed to take two pounds.

'As I grew richer I grew more ambitious, took a house in the country, and eventually married, without anyone having a suspicion as to my real occupation. My dear wife knew that I had business in the City. She little knew what.

'Last Monday I had finished for the day, and was dressing in my room above the opium den, when I looked out of the window, and saw, to my horror and astonishment, that my wife was standing in the street, with her eyes fixed full upon me. I gave a cry of surprise, threw up my arms to cover my face, and rushing to my confidant, the Lascar, entreated him to prevent anyone from coming up to me. I heard her voice downstairs, but I knew that she could not ascend. Swiftly I threw off my clothes, pulled on those of a beggar, and put on my pigments and wig. Even a wife's eyes could not pierce so complete a disguise. But then it occurred to me that there might be a search in the room and that the clothes might betray me. I threw open the window, re-opening by my violence a small cut which I had inflicted upon myself in the bedroom that morning. Then I seized my coat, which was weighted by the coppers which I had just transferred to it from the leather bag in which I carried my takings. I hurled it out of the window, and it disappeared into the Thames. The other clothes would have followed, but at that moment there was a rush of constables up the stair, and a few minutes after I found, rather, I confess, to my relief, that instead of being identified as Mr Neville St Clair, I was arrested as his murderer.

'I do not know that there is anything else for me to explain. I was determined to preserve my disguise as long as possible, and hence my preference for a dirty face. Knowing that my wife would be terribly anxious, I slipped off my ring, and confided it to the Lascar at a moment when no constable was watching me, together with a hurried scrawl, telling her that she had no cause to fear.'

'That note only reached her yesterday,' said Holmes.

'Good God! What a week she must have spent.'

'The police have watched this Lascar,' said Inspector Bradstreet, 'and I can quite understand that he might find it difficult to post a letter unobserved. Probably he handed it to some sailor customer of his, who forgot all about it for some days.'

'That was it,' said Holmes, nodding approvingly, 'I have no doubt of it. But have you never been prosecuted for begging?'

'Many times; but what was a fine to me?'

'It must stop here, however,' said Bradstreet. 'If the police are to hush this thing up, there must be no more of Hugh Boone.'

'I have sworn it by the most solemn oaths which a man can take.'

'In that case I think that it is probable that no further steps may be taken. But if you are found again, then all must come out. I am sure, Mr Holmes, that we are very much indebted to you for having cleared the matter up. I wish I knew how you reach your results.'

'I reached this one,' said my friend, 'by sitting upon five pillows and consuming an ounce of shag. I think, Watson, that if we drive to Baker Street we shall just be in time for breakfast.'

THE BLUE CARBUNCLE

I HAD called upon my friend Sherlock Holmes upon the second morning after Christmas, with the intention of wishing him the compliments of the season. He was lounging upon the sofa in a purple dressing gown, a pipe-rack within his reach upon the right, and a pile of crumpled morning papers, evidently newly studied, near at hand. Beside the couch was a wooden chair, and on the angle of the back hung a very seedy and disreputable hard felt hat, much the worse for wear, and cracked in several places. A lens and a forceps lying upon the seat of the chair suggested that the hat had been suspended in this manner for the purpose of examination.

'You are engaged,' said I; 'perhaps I interrupt you.'

'Not at all. I am glad to have a friend with whom I can discuss my results. The matter is a perfectly trivial one' (he jerked his thumb in the direction of the old hat), 'but there are points in connection with it which are not entirely devoid of interest, and even of instruction.'

I seated myself in his armchair, and warmed my hands before his crackling fire, for a sharp frost had set in, and the windows were thick with the ice crystals. 'I suppose,' I remarked, 'that, homely as it looks, this thing has some deadly story linked on to it—that it is the clue which will guide you in the solution of some mystery, and the punishment of some crime.'

'No, no. No crime,' said Sherlock Holmes, laughing. 'Only one of those whimsical little incidents which will happen when you have four million human beings all jostling each other within the space of a few square miles.* Amid the action and reaction of so dense a swarm of humanity, every possible combination of events may be expected to take place, and many a little problem will be presented which may be striking and bizarre without being criminal. We have already had experience of such.'

'So much so,' I remarked, 'that, of the last six cases which I have added to my notes, three have been entirely free of any legal crime.'

'Precisely. You allude to my attempt to recover the Irene Adler papers, to the singular case of Miss Mary Sutherland, and to the adventure of the man with the twisted lip. Well, I have no doubt that this small matter will fall into the same innocent category. You know Peterson, the commissionaire?'*

'Yes.'

'It is to him that this trophy belongs.'

'It is his hat.'

'No, no; he found it. Its owner is unknown. I beg that you will look upon it, not as a battered billycock,* but as an intellectual problem. And, first, as to how it came here. It arrived upon Christmas morning, in company with a good fat goose, which is, I have no doubt, roasting at this moment in front of Peterson's fire. The facts are these. About four o'clock on Christmas morning, Peterson, who, as you know, is a very honest fellow, was returning from some small jollification, and was making his way homewards down Tottenham Court Road. In front of him he saw, in the gaslight, a tallish man, walking with a slight stagger, and carrying a white goose slung over his shoulder. As he reached the corner of Goodge Street a row broke out between this stranger and a little knot of roughs. One of the latter knocked off the man's hat, on which he raised his stick to defend himself, and, swinging it over his head, smashed the shop window behind him. Peterson had rushed forward to protect the stranger from his assailants, but the man, shocked at having broken the window, and seeing an official-looking person in uniform rushing towards him, dropped his goose, took to his heels and vanished amid the labyrinth of small streets which lie at the back of Tottenham Court Road. The roughs had also fled at the appearance of Peterson, so that he was left in possession of the field of battle, and also of the spoils of victory in the shape of this battered hat and a most unimpeachable Christmas goose.'

'Which surely he restored to their owner?'

'My dear fellow, there lies the problem. It is true that "For Mrs Henry Baker" was printed upon a small card which was tied to the bird's left leg, and it is also true that the initials "H. B." are legible upon the lining of this hat; but, as there are some thousands of Bakers, and some hundreds of Henry Bakers in this city of ours, it is not easy to restore lost property to any one of them.'

'What, then, did Peterson do?'

'He brought round both hat and goose to me on Christmas morning, knowing that even the smallest problems are of interest to me. The goose we retained until this morning, when there were signs that, in spite of the slight frost, it would be well that it should be eaten without unnecessary delay. Its finder has carried it off, therefore, to fulfil the ultimate destiny of a goose, while I continue to retain the hat of the unknown gentleman who lost his Christmas dinner.'

'Did he not advertise?'

'No.'

'Then, what clue could you have as to his identity?'

'Only as much as we can deduce.'

'From his hat?'

'Precisely.'

'But you are joking. What can you gather from this old battered felt?'

'Here is my lens. You know my methods. What can you gather yourself as to the individuality of the man who has worn this article?'

I took the tattered object in my hands, and turned it over rather ruefully. It was a very ordinary black hat of the usual round shape, hard and much the worse for wear. The lining had been of red silk, but was a good deal discoloured. There was no maker's name; but, as Holmes had remarked, the initials 'H. B.' were scrawled upon one side. It was pierced in the brim for a hat-securer, but the elastic was missing. For the rest, it was cracked, exceedingly dusty, and spotted in several places, although there seemed to have been some attempt to hide the discoloured patches by smearing them with ink.

'I can see nothing,' said I, handing it back to my friend.

'On the contrary, Watson, you can see everything. You fail, however, to reason from what you see. You are too timid in drawing your inferences.'

'Then, pray tell me what it is that you can infer from this hat?'

He picked it up, and gazed at it in the peculiar introspective fashion which was characteristic of him. 'It is perhaps less suggestive than it might have been,' he remarked, 'and yet there are a few inferences which are very distinct, and a few others which represent at least a strong balance of probability. That the man was highly intellectual is of course obvious upon the face of it, and also that he was fairly well-to-do within the last three years, although he has now fallen upon evil days. He had foresight, but has less now than formerly, pointing to a moral retrogression, which, when taken with the decline of his fortunes, seems to indicate some evil influence, probably drink, at work upon him. This may account also for the obvious fact that his wife has ceased to love him.'

'My dear Holmes!'

'He has, however, retained some degree of self-respect,' he continued, disregarding my remonstrance. 'He is a man who leads a sedentary life, goes out little, is out of training entirely, is middle-aged, has grizzled hair which he has had cut within the last few days, and which he anoints with lime-cream.* These are the more patent facts which are to be deduced from his hat. Also, by the way, that it is extremely improbable that he has gas laid on his house.'

'You are certainly joking, Holmes.'

'Not in the least. Is it possible that even now when I give you these results you are unable to see how they are attained?'

'I have no doubt that I am very stupid; but I must confess that I am unable to follow you. For example, how did you deduce that this man was intellectual?'

For answer Holmes clapped the hat upon his head. It came right over the forehead and settled upon the bridge of his nose. 'It is a question of cubic capacity,' said he: 'a man with so large a brain must have something in it.'*

'The decline of his fortunes, then?'

'This hat is three years old. These flat brims curled at the edge came in then. It is a hat of the very best quality. Look at the band of ribbed silk, and the excellent lining. If this man could afford to buy so expensive a hat three years ago, and has had no hat since, then he has assuredly gone down in the world.'

'Well, that is clear enough, certainly. But how about the foresight, and the moral retrogression?'

Sherlock Holmes laughed. 'Here is the foresight,' said he, putting his finger upon the little disc and loop of the hat-securer. 'They are never sold upon hats. If this man ordered one, it is a sign of a certain amount of foresight, since he went out of his way to take this precaution against the wind. But since we see that he has broken the elastic, and has not troubled to replace it, it is obvious that he has less foresight now than formerly, which is a distinct proof of a weakening nature. On the other hand, he has endeavoured to conceal some of these stains upon the felt by daubing them with ink, which is a sign that he has not entirely lost his self-respect.'

'Your reasoning is certainly plausible.'

'The further points, that he is middle-aged, that his hair is grizzled, that it has been recently cut, and that he uses lime-cream, are all to be gathered from a close examination of the lower part of the lining. The lens discloses a large number of hair ends, clean cut by the scissors of the barber. They all appear to be adhesive, and there is a distinct odour of lime-cream. This dust, you will observe, is not the gritty, grey dust of the street, but the fluffy brown dust of the house, showing that it has been hung up indoors most of the time; while the marks of moisture upon the inside are proof positive that the wearer perspired very freely, and could, therefore, hardly be in the best of training.'

'But his wife—you said that she had ceased to love him.'

'This hat has not been brushed for weeks. When I see you, my dear Watson, with a week's accumulation of dust upon your hat, and when your wife allows you to go out in such a state, I shall fear that you also have been unfortunate enough to lose your wife's affection.'

'But he might be a bachelor.'

'Nay, he was bringing home the goose as a peace-offering to his wife. Remember the card upon the bird's leg.'

'You have an answer to everything. But how on earth do you deduce that the gas is not laid on in the house?'

'One tallow stain, or even two, might come by chance; but, when I see no less than five, I think that there can be little doubt that the individual must be brought into frequent contact with burning tallow—walks upstairs at night probably with his hat in one hand and a guttering candle in the other. Anyhow, he never got tallow stains from a gas jet. Are you satisfied?'

'Well, it is very ingenious,' said I, laughing; 'but since, as you said just now, there has been no crime committed, and no harm done save the loss of a goose, all this seems to be rather a waste of energy.'

Sherlock Holmes had opened his mouth to reply, when the door flew open, and Peterson the commissionaire rushed into the apartment with flushed cheeks and the face of a man who is dazed with astonishment.

'The goose, Mr Holmes! The goose, sir!' he gasped.

'Eh! What of it, then? Has it returned to life, and flapped off through the kitchen window?' Holmes twisted himself round upon the sofa to get a fairer view of the man's excited face.

'See here, sir! See what my wife found in its crop!'* He held out his hand, and displayed upon the centre of the palm a brilliantly scintillating blue stone, rather smaller than a bean in size, but of such purity and radiance that it twinkled like an electric point in the dark hollow of his hand.

Sherlock Holmes sat up with a whistle. 'By Jove, Peterson,' said he, 'this is treasure-trove indeed! I suppose you know what you have got?'

'A diamond, sir! A precious stone! It cuts into glass as though it were putty.'

'It's more than a precious stone. It's *the* precious stone.'

'Not the Countess of Morcar's blue carbuncle?'* I ejaculated.

'Precisely so. I ought to know its size and shape, seeing that I have read the advertisement about it in *The Times* every day lately. It is absolutely unique, and its value can only be conjectured, but the reward offered of a thousand pounds is certainly not within a twentieth part of the market price.'

'A thousand pounds! Great Lord of mercy!' The commissionaire plumped down into a chair, and stared from one to the other of us.

'That is the reward, and I have reason to know that there are sentimental considerations in the background which would induce the Countess to part with half of her fortune if she could but recover the gem.'

'It was lost, if I remember aright, at the Hotel Cosmopolitan,' I remarked.

'Precisely so, on the 22nd of December, just five days ago. John Horner, a plumber, was accused of having abstracted it from the lady's jewel-case. The evidence against him was so strong that the case has been referred to the Assizes.* I have some account of the matter here, I believe.' He rummaged amid his newspapers, glancing over the dates, until at last he smoothed one out, doubled it over, and read the following paragraph:

'"Hotel Cosmopolitan Jewel Robbery. John Horner, 26, plumber, was brought up upon the charge of having upon the 22nd inst., abstracted from the jewel-case of the Countess of Morcar the valuable gem known as the blue carbuncle. James Ryder, upper-attendant* at the hotel, gave his evidence to the effect that he had shown Horner up to the dressing-room of the Countess of Morcar upon the day of the robbery, in order that he might solder the second bar of the grate, which was loose. He had remained with Horner some little time but had finally been called away. On returning, he found that Horner had disappeared, that the bureau had been forced open, and that the small morocco casket* in which, as it afterwards transpired, the Countess was accustomed to keep her jewel, was lying empty upon the dressing-table. Ryder instantly gave the alarm, and Horner was arrested the same evening; but the stone could not be found either upon his person or in his rooms. Catherine Cusack, maid to the Countess, deposed to having heard Ryder's cry of dismay on discovering the robbery, and to having rushed into the room, where she found matters were as described by the last witness. Inspector Bradstreet, B Division,* gave evidence as to the arrest of Horner, who struggled frantically, and protested his innocence in the strongest terms. Evidence of a previous conviction for robbery having been given against the prisoner, the magistrate refused to deal summarily with the offence, but referred it to the Assizes. Horner, who had shown signs of intense emotion during the proceedings, fainted away at the conclusion, and was carried out of court."

'Hum! So much for the police-court,' said Holmes thoughtfully, tossing aside his paper. 'The question for us now to solve is the sequence of events from a rifled jewel-case at one end to the crop of a goose in Tottenham Court Road at the other. You see, Watson, our little deductions have suddenly assumed a much more important and less innocent aspect. Here is the stone; the stone came from the goose, and the goose came from Mr Henry Baker, the gentleman with the bad hat and all the other characteristics with which I have bored you. So now we must set ourselves very seriously to finding this gentleman, and ascertaining what part he has played in this little mystery. To do this, we must try the simplest means first, and these lie undoubtedly in an advertisement in all the evening papers. If this fail, I shall have recourse to other methods.'

'What will you say?'

'Give me a pencil, and that slip of paper. Now, then: "Found at the corner of Goodge Street, a goose and a black felt hat. Mr Henry Baker can have the same by applying at 6.30 this evening at 221B Baker Street." That is clear and concise.'

'Very. But will he see it?'

'Well, he is sure to keep an eye on the papers, since, to a poor man, the loss was a heavy one. He was clearly so scared by his mischance in breaking the window, and by the approach of Peterson, that he thought of nothing but flight; but since then he must have bitterly regretted the impulse which caused him to drop his bird. Then, again, the introduction of his name will cause him to see it, for every one who knows him will direct his attention to it. Here you are, Peterson, run down to the advertising agency, and have this put in the evening papers.'

'In which, sir?'

'Oh, in the *Globe, Star, Pall Mall, St James's Gazette, Evening News, Standard, Echo*,* and any others that occur to you.'

'Very well, sir. And this stone?'

'Ah, yes. I shall keep the stone. Thank you. And, I say, Peterson, just buy a goose on your way back, and leave it here with me, for we must have one to give to this gentleman in place of the one which your family is now devouring.'

When the commissionaire had gone, Holmes took up the stone and held it against the light. 'It's a bonny thing,' said he. 'Just see how it glints and sparkles. Of course it is a nucleus and focus of crime. Every good stone is. They are the devil's pet baits. In the larger and older jewels every facet may stand for a bloody deed. This stone is not yet twenty years old. It was found in the banks of the Amoy River in Southern China,* and is remarkable in having every characteristic of the carbuncle, save that it is blue in shade, instead of ruby red. In spite of its youth, it has already a sinister history. There have been two murders, a vitriol-throwing,* a suicide, and several robberies brought about for the sake of this forty-grain weight* of crystallized charcoal.* Who would think that so pretty a toy would be a purveyor to the gallows and the prison? I'll lock it up in my strong-box, now, and drop a line to the Countess to say that we have it.'

'Do you think this man Horner is innocent?'

'I cannot tell.'

'Well, then, do you imagine that this other one, Henry Baker, had anything to do with the matter?'

'It is, I think, much more likely that Henry Baker is an absolutely innocent man, who had no idea that the bird which he was carrying was of considerably more value than if it were made of solid gold. That, however, I shall determine by a very simple test, if we have an answer to our advertisement.'

'And you can do nothing until then?'

'Nothing.'

'In that case I shall continue my professional round. But I shall come back in the evening at the hour you have mentioned, for I should like to see the solution of so tangled a business.'

'Very glad to see you. I dine at seven. There is a woodcock, I believe. By the way, in view of recent occurrences, perhaps I ought to ask Mrs Hudson to examine its crop.'

I had been delayed at a case, and it was a little after half-past six when I found myself in Baker Street once more. As I approached the house I saw a tall man in a Scotch bonnet,* with a coat which was buttoned up to his chin, waiting outside in the bright semicircle which was thrown from the fanlight. Just as I arrived, the door was opened, and we were shown up together to Holmes's room.

'Mr Henry Baker, I believe,' said he, rising from his armchair, and greeting his visitor with the easy air of geniality which he could so readily assume. 'Pray take this chair by the fire, Mr Baker. It is a cold night, and I observe that your circulation is more adapted for summer than for winter. Ah, Watson, you have just come at the right time. Is that your hat, Mr Baker?'

'Yes, sir, that is undoubtedly my hat.'

He was a large man, with rounded shoulders, a massive head, and a broad, intelligent face, sloping down to a pointed beard of grizzled brown. A touch of red in nose and cheeks, with a slight tremor of his extended hand, recalled Holmes's surmise as to his habits. His rusty black frock-coat was buttoned right up in front, with the collar turned up, and his lank wrists protruded from his sleeves without a sign of cuff or shirt. He spoke in a low staccato fashion, choosing his words with care, and gave the impression generally of a man of learning and letters who had had ill-usage at the hands of fortune.

'We have retained these things for some days,' said Holmes, 'because we expected to see an advertisement from you giving your address. I am at a loss to know now why you did not advertise.'

Our visitor gave a rather shame-faced laugh. 'Shillings have not been so plentiful with me as they once were,' he remarked. 'I had no doubt that the gang of roughs who assaulted me had carried off both my hat and the bird. I did not care to spend more money in a hopeless attempt at recovering them.'

'Very naturally. By the way, about the bird—we were compelled to eat it.'

'To eat it!' Our visitor half rose from his chair in his excitement.

'Yes; it would have been no use to anyone had we not done so. But

I presume that this other goose upon the sideboard, which is about the same weight and perfectly fresh, will answer your purpose equally well?'

'Oh, certainly, certainly!' answered Mr Baker, with a sigh of relief.

'Of course, we still have the feathers, legs, crop, and so on of your own bird, if you so wish—'

The man burst into a hearty laugh. 'They might be useful to me as relics of my adventure,' said he, 'but beyond that I can hardly see what use the *disjecta membra** of my late acquaintance are going to be to me. No, sir, I think that, with your permission, I will confine my attentions to the excellent bird which I perceive upon the sideboard.'

Sherlock Holmes glanced sharply across at me with a slight shrug of his shoulders.

'There is your hat, then, and there your bird,' said he. 'By the way, would it bore you to tell me where you got the other one from? I am somewhat of a fowl fancier, and I have seldom seen a better-grown goose.'

'Certainly, sir,' said Baker, who had risen and tucked his newly-gained property under his arm. 'There are a few of us who frequent the "Alpha" Inn near the Museum*—we are to be found in the Museum itself during the day, you understand. This year our good host, Windigate by name, instituted a goose-club, by which, on consideration of some few pence every week, we were each to receive a bird at Christmas. My pence were duly paid, and the rest is familiar to you. I am much indebted to you, sir, for a Scotch bonnet is fitted neither to my years nor my gravity.' With a comical pomposity of manner he bowed solemnly to both of us, and strode off upon his way.

'So much for Mr Henry Baker,' said Holmes, when he had closed the door behind him. 'It is quite certain that he knows nothing whatever about the matter. Are you hungry, Watson?'

'Not particularly.'

'Then I suggest that we turn our dinner into a supper, and follow up this clue while it is still hot.'

'By all means.'

It was a bitter night, so we drew on our ulsters and wrapped cravats about our throats. Outside, the stars were shining coldly in a cloudless sky, and the breath of the passers-by blew out into smoke like so many pistol shots. Our footfalls rang out crisply and loudly as we swung through the doctors' quarter, Wimpole Street, Harley Street, and so through Wigmore Street into Oxford Street. In a quarter of an hour we were in Bloomsbury at the "Alpha" Inn, which is a small public-house at the corner of one of the streets which run down into Holborn. Holmes pushed open the door of the private bar, and ordered two glasses of beer from the ruddy-faced, white-aproned landlord.

'Your beer should be excellent if it is as good as your geese,' he said.

'My geese!' The man seemed surprised.

'Yes. I was speaking only half an hour ago to Mr Henry Baker, who was a member of your goose-club.'

'Ah! yes. I see. But you see, sir, them's not *our* geese.'

'Indeed! Whose, then?'

'Well, I got the two dozen from a salesman in Covent Garden.'*

'Indeed! I know some of them. Which was it?'

'Breckinridge is his name.'

'Ah! I don't know him. Well, here's your good health, landlord, and prosperity to your house. Good-night!

'Now for Mr Breckinridge,' he continued, buttoning up his coat, as we came out into the frosty air. 'Remember, Watson, that though we have so homely a thing as a goose at one end of this chain, we have at the other a man who will certainly get seven years' penal servitude,* unless we can establish his innocence. It is possible that our inquiry may but confirm his guilt; but, in any case, we have a line of investigation which has been missed by the police, and which a singular chance has placed in our hands. Let us follow it out to the bitter end. Faces to the south, then, and quick march!'

We passed across Holborn, down Endell Street, and so through a zigzag of slums of Covent Garden Market. One of the largest stalls bore the name of Breckinridge upon it, and the proprietor, a horsey-looking man* with a sharp face and trim side-whiskers, was helping a boy to put up the shutters.

'Good evening, it's a cold night,' said Holmes.

The salesman nodded, and shot a questioning glance at my companion.

'Sold out of geese, I see,' continued Holmes, pointing at the bare slabs of marble.

'Let you have five hundred to-morrow morning.'

'That's no good.'

'Well, there are some on the stall with the gas flare.'

'Oh, but I was recommended to you.'

'Who by?'

'The landlord of the "Alpha".'

'Ah, yes; I sent him a couple of dozen.'

'Fine birds they were, too. Now where did you get them from?'

To my surprise the question provoked a burst of anger from the salesman.

'Now then, mister,' said he, with his head cocked and his arms akimbo, 'what are you driving at? Let's have it straight, now.'

'It is straight enough. I should like to know who sold you the geese which you supplied to the "Alpha".'

'Well, then, I shan't tell you. So now!'

'Oh, it is a matter of no importance; but I don't know why you should be so warm over such a trifle.'*

'Warm! You'd be as warm, maybe, if you were pestered as I am. When I pay good money for a good article there should be an end of the business; but it's "Where are the geese?" and "Who did you sell the geese to?" and "What will you take for the geese?" One would think they were the only geese in the world, to hear the fuss that is made over them.'

'Well, I have no connection with any other people who have been making inquiries,' said Holmes carelessly. 'If you won't tell us the bet is off, that is all. But I'm always ready to back my opinion on a matter of fowls, and I have a fiver on it that the bird I ate is country bred.'

'Well, then, you've lost your fiver, for it's town bred,' snapped the salesman.

'It's nothing of the kind.'

'I say it is.'

'I don't believe you.'

'D'you think you know more about fowls than I, who have handled them ever since I was a nipper? I tell you, all those birds that went to the "Alpha" were town bred.'

'You'll never persuade me to believe that.'

'Will you bet, then?'

'It's merely taking your money, for I know that I am right. But I'll have a sovereign on with you, just to teach you not to be obstinate.'

The salesman chuckled grimly. 'Bring me the books, Bill,' said he.

The small boy brought round a small thin volume and a great greasy-backed one, laying them out together beneath the hanging lamp.

'Now then, Mr Cocksure,' said the salesman, 'I thought that I was out of geese, but before I finish you'll find that there is still one left in my shop. You see this little book?'

'Well?'

'That's the list of the folk from whom I buy. D'you see? Well, then, here on this page are the country folk, and the numbers after their names are where their accounts are in the big ledger. Now, then! You see this other page in red ink? Well, that is a list of my town suppliers. Now, look at that third name. Just read it out to me.'

'Mrs Oakshott, 117, Brixton Road—249,' read Holmes.

'Quite so. Now turn that up in the ledger.'

Holmes turned to the page indicated. 'Here you are, "Mrs Oakshott, 117, Brixton Road, egg and poultry supplier." '

'Now, then, what's the last entry?'

' "December 22. Twenty-four geese at 7*s* 6*d*." '

'Quite so. There you are. And underneath?'

' "Sold to Mr Windigate of the 'Alpha' at 12*s*." '

'What have you to say now?'

Sherlock Holmes looked deeply chagrined. He drew a sovereign from his pocket and threw it down upon the slab, turning away with the air of a man whose disgust is too deep for words. A few yards off he stopped under a lamp-post, and laughed in the hearty, noiseless fashion which was peculiar to him.

'When you see a man with whiskers of that cut and the "*Pink 'Un*"* protruding out of his pocket, you can always draw him by a bet,' said he. 'I dare say that if I had put a hundred pounds down in front of him that man would not have given me such complete information as was drawn from him by the idea that he was doing me on a wager. Well, Watson, we are, I fancy, nearing the end of our quest, and the only point which remains to be determined is whether we should go on to this Mrs Oakshott tonight, or whether we should reserve it for to-morrow. It is clear from what that surly fellow said that there are others besides ourselves who are anxious about the matter, and I should—'

His remarks were suddenly cut short by a loud hubbub which broke out from the stall which we had just left. Turning round we saw a little rat-faced fellow, standing in the centre of the circle of yellow light which was thrown by the swinging lamp, while Breckinridge the salesman, framed in the door of his stall, was shaking his fists fiercely at the cringing figure.

'I've had enough of you and your geese,' he shouted. 'I wish you were all at the devil together. If you come pestering me any more with your silly talk I'll set the dog at you. You bring Mrs Oakshott here and I'll answer her, but what have you to do with it? Did I buy the geese off you?'

'No: but one of them was mine all the same,' whined the little man.

'Well, then, ask Mrs Oakshott for it.'

'She told me to ask you.'

'Well, you can ask the King of Proosia,* for all I care. I've had enough of it. Get out of this!' He rushed fiercely forward, and the inquirer flitted away into the darkness.

'Ha, this may save us a visit to Brixton Road,' whispered Holmes. 'Come with me, and we will see what is to be made of this fellow.' Striding through the scattered knots of people who lounged round the flaring stalls, my companion speedily overtook the little man and touched him upon the shoulder. He sprang round, and I could see in the gaslight that every vestige of colour had been driven from his face.

'Who are you, then? What do you want?' he asked in a quavering voice.

'You will excuse me,' said Holmes, blandly, 'but I could not help overhearing the questions which you put to the salesman just now. I think that I could be of assistance to you.'

'You? Who are you? How could you know anything of the matter?'

'My name is Sherlock Holmes. It is my business to know what other people don't know.'

'But you can know nothing of this?'

'Excuse me, I know everything of it. You are endeavouring to trace some geese which were sold by Mrs Oakshott, of Brixton Road, to a salesman named Breckinridge, by him in turn to Mr Windigate, of the "Alpha", and by him to his club, of which Mr Henry Baker is a member.'

'Oh, sir, you are the very man whom I have longed to meet,' cried the little fellow, with outstretched hands and quivering fingers. 'I can hardly explain to you how interested I am in this matter.'

Sherlock Holmes hailed a four-wheeler* which was passing. 'In that case we had better discuss it in a cosy room rather than in this windswept market-place,' said he. 'But pray tell me, before we go further, who it is that I have the pleasure of assisting.'

The man hesitated for an instant. 'My name is John Robinson,' he answered, with a sidelong glance.

'No, no; the real name,' said Holmes sweetly. 'It is always awkward doing business with an *alias*.'

A flush sprang to the white cheeks of the stranger. 'Well, then,' said he, 'my real name is James Ryder.'

'Precisely so. Head attendant at the Hotel Cosmopolitan. Pray step into the cab, and I shall soon be able to tell you everything which you would wish to know.'

The little man stood glancing from one to the other of us with half-frightened, half-hopeful eyes, as one who is not sure whether he is on the verge of a windfall or of a catastrophe. Then he stepped into the cab, and in half an hour we were back in the sitting-room at Baker Street. Nothing had been said during our drive, but the high, thin breathing of our new companion, and the claspings and unclaspings of his hands, spoke of the nervous tension within him.

'Here we are!' said Holmes cheerily, as we filed into the room. 'The fire looks very seasonable in this weather. You look cold, Mr Ryder. Pray take the basket chair.* I will just put on my slippers before we settle this little matter of yours. Now, then! You want to know what became of those geese?'

'Yes, sir.'

'Or rather, I fancy, of that goose. It was one bird, I imagine, in which you were interested—white, with a black bar across the tail.'

Ryder quivered with emotion. 'Oh, sir,' he cried, 'can you tell me where it went to?'

'It came here.'

'Here?'

'Yes, and a most remarkable bird it proved. I don't wonder that you should take an interest in it. It laid an egg after it was dead—the bonniest, brightest little blue egg that was ever seen. I have it here in my museum.'

Our visitor staggered to his feet, and clutched the mantelpiece with his right hand. Holmes unlocked his strong-box, and held up the blue carbuncle, which shone out like a star, with a cold, brilliant, many-pointed radiance. Ryder stood glaring with a drawn face, uncertain whether to claim or to disown it.

'The game's up, Ryder,' said Holmes quietly. 'Hold up, man, or you'll be into the fire. Give him an arm back into his chair, Watson.

He's not got blood enough to go in for felony with impunity. Give him a dash of brandy. So! Now he looks a little more human. What a shrimp it is, to be sure!'

For a moment he had staggered and nearly fallen, but the brandy brought a tinge of colour into his cheeks, and he sat staring with frightened eyes at his accuser.

'I have almost every link in my hands, and all the proofs which I could possibly need, so there is little which you need tell me. Still, that little may as well be cleared up to make the case complete. You had heard, Ryder, of this blue stone of the Countess of Morcar's?'

'It was Catherine Cusack who told me of it,' said he, in a crackling voice.

'I see. Her ladyship's waiting-maid. Well the temptation of sudden wealth so easily acquired was too much for you, as it has been for better men before you; but you were not very scrupulous in the means you used. It seems to me, Ryder, that there is the making of a very pretty villain in you. You knew that this man Horner, the plumber, had been concerned in some such matter before, and that suspicion would rest the more readily upon him. What did you do, then? You made some small job in my lady's room—you and your confederate Cusack—and you managed that he should be the man sent for. Then, when he had left, you rifled the jewel-case, raised the alarm, and had this unfortunate man arrested. You then—'

Ryder threw himself down suddenly upon the rug, and clutched at my companion's knees. 'For God's sake, have mercy!' he shrieked. 'Think of my father! Of my mother! It would break their hearts. I never went wrong before! I never will again. I swear it. I'll swear it on a Bible. Oh, don't bring it into court! For Christ's sake, don't!'

'Get back into your chair!' said Holmes sternly. 'It is very well to cringe and crawl now, but you thought little enough of this poor Horner in the dock for a crime of which he knew nothing.'

'I will fly, Mr Holmes. I will leave the country, sir. Then the charge against him will break down.'

'Hum! We will talk about that. And now let us hear a true account of the next act. How came the stone into the goose, and how came the goose into the open market? Tell us the truth, for there lies your only hope of safety.'

Ryder passed his tongue over his parched lips. 'I will tell you it just as it happened, sir,' said he. 'When Horner had been arrested, it seemed to me that it would be best for me to get away with the stone at once, for I did not know at what moment the police might not take it into their heads to search me and my room. There was no place about the hotel where it would be safe. I went out, as if on some commission, and I made for my sister's house. She had married a man named Oakshott, and lived in Brixton Road, where she fattened fowls for the market. All the way there every man I met seemed to me to be a policeman or a detective, and for all that it was a cold night, the sweat was pouring down my face before I came to the Brixton Road. My sister asked me what was the matter, and why I was so pale; but I told her that I had been upset by the jewel robbery at the hotel. Then I went into the backyard, and smoked a pipe, and wondered what it would be best to do.

'I had a friend once called Maudsley, who went to the bad, and has just been serving his time in Pentonville.* One day he had met me, and fell into talk about the ways of thieves and how they could get rid of what they stole. I knew that he would be true to me, for I knew one or two things about him, so I made up my mind to go right on to Kilburn, where he lived and take him into my confidence. He would show me how to turn the stone into money. But how to get to him in safety? I thought of the agonies I had gone through in coming from the hotel. I might at any moment be seized and searched, and there would be the stone in my waistcoat pocket. I was leaning against the wall at the time, and looking at the geese which were waddling about round my feet, and suddenly an idea came into my head which showed me how I could beat the best detective that ever lived.

'My sister had told me some weeks before that I might have the pick of her geese for a Christmas present, and I knew that she was always as good as her word. I would take my goose now, and in it I would carry my stone to Kilburn. There was a little shed in the yard, and behind this I drove one of the birds, a fine big one, white, with a barred tail. I caught it, and, prising its bill open, I thrust the stone down its throat as far as my finger could reach. The bird gave a gulp, and I felt the stone pass along its gullet and down into its crop. But the creature flapped and struggled, and out came my sister to know what was the matter. As I turned to speak to her the brute broke loose, and fluttered off among the others.

'"Whatever were you doing with that bird, Jem?" says she.

' "Well," said I, "you said you'd give me one for Christmas, and I was feeling which was the fattest."

' "Oh," says she, "we've set yours aside for you. Jem's bird, we call it. It's the big, white one over yonder. There's twenty-six of them, which makes one for you, and one for us, and two dozen for the market."

' "Thank you, Maggie," says I; "but if it is all the same to you I'd rather have that one I was handling just now."

' "The other is a good three pound heavier," she said, "and we fattened it expressly for you."

' "Never mind. I'll have the other, and I'll take it now," said I.

' "Oh, just as you like," said she, a little huffed. "Which is it you want, then?"

' "That white one, with the barred tail, right in the middle of the flock."

' "Oh, very well. Kill it and take it with you."

'Well, I did what she said, Mr Holmes, and I carried the bird all the way to Kilburn. I told my pal what I had done, for he was a man that it was easy to tell a thing like that to. He laughed until he choked, and we got a knife and opened the goose. My heart turned to water, for there was no sign of the stone, and I knew that some terrible mistake had occurred. I left the bird, rushed back to my sister's, and hurried into the back yard. There was not a bird to be seen there.

' "Where are they all, Maggie?" I cried.

' "Gone to the dealer's."

' "Which dealer's?"

' "Breckinridge, of Covent Garden."

' "But was there another with a barred tail?" I asked, "the same as the one I chose?"

' "Yes, Jem, there were two barred-tailed ones, and I could never tell them apart."

'Well, then, of course, I saw it all, and I ran off as hard as my feet would carry me to this man Breckinridge; but he had sold the lot at once, and not one word would he tell me as to where they had gone. You heard him yourselves tonight. Well, he has always answered me like that. My sister thinks that I am going mad. Sometimes I think that I am myself. And now—now I am myself a branded thief, without ever having touched the wealth for which I sold my character. God help me! God help me!' He burst into convulsive sobbing, with his face buried in his hands.

There was a long silence, broken only by his heavy breathing, and by the measured tapping of Sherlock Holmes's finger-tips upon the edge of the table. Then my friend rose, and threw open the door.

'Get out!' said he.

'What, sir! Oh, heaven bless you!'

'No more words. Get out!'

And no more words were needed. There was a rush, a clatter upon the stairs, the bang of a door, and the crisp rattle of running footfalls from the street.

'After all, Watson,' said Holmes, reaching up his hand for his clay pipe, 'I am not retained by the police to supply their deficiencies. If Horner were in danger it would be another thing, but this fellow will not appear against him, and the case must collapse. I suppose that I am commuting a felony, but it is just possible that I am saving a soul. This fellow will not go wrong again. He is too terribly frightened. Send him to gaol now, and you make him a gaol-bird for life. Besides, it is the season of forgiveness. Chance has put in our way a most singular and whimsical problem, and its solution is its own reward. If you will have the goodness to touch the bell, Doctor, we will begin another investigation, in which also a bird will be the chief feature.'

THE SPECKLED BAND

In glancing over my notes of the seventy odd cases in which I have during the last eight years studied the methods of my friend Sherlock Holmes, I find many tragic, some comic, a large number merely strange, but none commonplace; for, working as he did rather for the love of his art than for the acquirement of wealth, he refused to associate himself with any investigation which did not tend towards the unusual, and even the fantastic. Of all these varied cases, however, I cannot recall any which presented more singular features than that which was associated with the well-known Surrey family of the Roylotts of Stoke Moran. The events in question occurred in the early days of my association with Holmes, when we were sharing rooms as bachelors, in Baker Street. It is possible that I might have placed them upon record before, but a promise of secrecy was made at the time, from which I have only been freed during the last month by the untimely death of the lady to whom the pledge was given. It is perhaps as well that the facts should now come to light, for I have reasons to know there are widespread rumours as to the death of Dr Grimesby Roylott which tend to make the matter even more terrible than the truth.

It was early in April, in the year '83, that I woke one morning to find Sherlock Holmes standing, fully dressed, by the side of my bed. He was a late riser as a rule, and, as the clock on the mantelpiece showed me that it was only a quarter past seven, I blinked up at him in some surprise, and perhaps just a little resentment, for I was myself regular in my habits.

'Very sorry to knock you up, Watson,' said he, 'but it's the common lot this morning. Mrs Hudson has been knocked up, she retorted upon me, and I on you.'

'What is it, then? A fire?'

'No, a client. It seems that a young lady has arrived in a considerable state of excitement, who insists upon seeing me. She is waiting now in the sitting-room. Now, when young ladies wander about the metropolis at this hour of the morning, and knock sleepy people up out of their beds, I presume that it is something very pressing which they have to communicate. Should it prove to be an interesting case, you would, I am sure, wish to follow it from the outset. I thought at any rate that I should call you, and give you the chance.'

'My dear fellow, I would not miss it for anything.'

I had no keener pleasure than in following Holmes in his professional investigations, and in admiring the rapid deductions, as swift as intuitions, and yet always founded on a logical basis, with which he unravelled the problems which were submitted to him. I rapidly threw on my clothes, and was ready in a few minutes to accompany my friend down to the sitting-room. A lady dressed in black and heavily veiled, who had been sitting in the window, rose as we entered.

'Good morning, madam,' said Holmes, cheerily. 'My name is Sherlock Holmes. This is my intimate friend and associate, Dr Watson, before whom you can speak as freely as before myself. Ha, I am glad to see that Mrs Hudson has had the good sense to light the fire. Pray draw up to it, and I shall order you a cup of hot coffee, for I observe that you are shivering.'

'It is not cold which makes me shiver,' said the woman in a low voice, changing her seat as requested.

'What then?'

'It is fear, Mr Holmes. It is terror.' She raised her veil as she spoke, and we could see that she was indeed in a pitiable state of agitation, her face all drawn and grey, with restless, frightened eyes, like those of some hunted animal. Her features and figure were those of a woman of thirty, but her hair was shot with premature grey, and her expression was weary and haggard. Sherlock Holmes ran her over with one of his quick, all-comprehensive glances.

'You must not fear,' said he, soothingly, bending forward and patting her forearm. 'We shall soon set matters right, I have no doubt. You have come in by train this morning, I see.'

'You know me, then?'

'No, but I observe the second half of a return ticket in the palm of your left glove. You must have started early and yet you had a good drive in a dog-cart,* along heavy roads, before you reached the station.'

The lady gave a violent start, and stared in bewilderment at my companion.

'There is no mystery, my dear madam,' said he, smiling. 'The left arm of your jacket is spattered with mud in no less than seven places. The marks are perfectly fresh. There is no vehicle save a dog-cart which throws up mud in that way, and then only when you sit on the left-hand side of the driver.'

'Whatever your reasons may be, you are perfectly correct,' said she. 'I started from home before six, reached Leatherhead at twenty past, and came in by the first train to Waterloo. Sir, I can stand this strain no longer, I shall go mad if it continues. I have no one to turn to—none, save only one, who cares for me, and he, poor fellow, can be of little aid. I have heard of you, Mr Holmes; I have heard of you from Mrs Farintosh, whom you helped in the hour of her sore need. It was from her that I had your address. Oh, sir, do you not think you could help me too, and at least throw a little light through the dense darkness which surrounds me? At present it is out of my power to reward you for your services, but in a month or two I shall be married, with the control of my own income, and then at least you shall not find me ungrateful.'

Holmes turned to his desk, and unlocking it, drew out a small case-book which he consulted.

'Farintosh,' said he. 'Ah, yes, I recall the case; it was concerned with an opal tiara. I think it was before your time, Watson. I can only say, madam, that I shall be happy to devote the same care to your case as I did to that of your friend. As to reward, my profession is its reward; but you are at liberty to defray whatever expenses I may be put to, at the time which suits you best. And now I beg that you will lay before us everything that may help us in forming an opinion upon the matter.'

'Alas!' replied our visitor. 'The very horror of my situation lies in the fact that my fears are so vague, and my suspicions depend so entirely upon small points, which might seem trivial to another, that even he to whom of all others I have a right to look for help and advice looks upon all that I tell him about it as the fancies of a nervous woman. He does not say so, but I can read it from his soothing answers and averted eyes. But I have heard, Mr Holmes, that you can see deeply into the manifold wickedness of the human heart. You may advise me how to walk amid the dangers which encompass me.'

'I am all attention, madam.'

'My name is Helen Stoner, and I am living with my step-father, who is the last survivor of one of the oldest Saxon families in England; the Roylotts of Stoke Moran, on the western border of Surrey.'

Holmes nodded his head. 'The name is familiar to me,' said he.

'The family was at one time among the richest in England, and the estate extended over the borders into Berkshire in the north, and Hampshire in the west. In the last century, however, four successive heirs were of a dissolute and wasteful disposition, and the family ruin was eventually completed by a gambler, in the days of the Regency.* Nothing was left save a few acres of ground, and the two-hundred-year-old house, which is itself crushed under a heavy mortgage. The last squire dragged out his existence there, living the horrible life of an aristocratic pauper; but his only son, my stepfather, seeing that he must adapt himself to the new conditions, obtained an advance from a relative, which enabled him to take a medical degree, and went out to Calcutta,* where, by his professional skill and his force of character, he established a large practice. In a fit of anger, however, caused by some robberies which had been perpetrated in the house, he beat his native butler to death, and narrowly escaped a capital sentence. As it was, he suffered a long term of imprisonment, and afterwards returned to England a morose and disappointed man.

'When Dr Roylott was in India he married my mother, Mrs Stoner, the young widow of Major-General Stoner, of the Bengal Artillery.* My sister Julia and I were twins, and we were only two years old at the time of my mother's re-marriage. She had a considerable sum of money, not less than a thousand a year, and this she bequeathed to Dr Roylott entirely whilst we resided with him, with a provision that a certain annual sum should be allowed to each of us in the event of our marriage. Shortly after our return to England my mother died—she was killed eight years ago in a railway accident near Crewe. Dr Roylott then abandoned his attempts to establish himself in practice in London, and took us to live with him in the ancestral house at Stoke Moran. The money which my mother had left was enough for all our wants, and there seemed no obstacle to our happiness.

'But a terrible change came over our stepfather about this time. Instead of making friends and exchanging visits with our neighbours, who had at first been overjoyed to see a Roylott of Stoke Moran back in the old family seat, he shut himself up in his house, and seldom came out save to indulge in ferocious quarrels with whoever might cross his path. Violence of temper approaching to mania has been hereditary in the men of the family, and in my stepfather's case it had, I believe, been intensified by his long residence in the tropics. A series of disgraceful brawls took place, two of which ended in the police-court, until at last he became the terror of the village, and the folks would fly at his approach, for he is a man of immense strength, and absolutely uncontrollable in his anger.

'Last week he hurled the local blacksmith over a parapet into a stream and it was only by paying over all the money that I could gather together that I was able to avert another public exposure. He had no friends at all save the wandering gipsies,* and he would give these vagabonds leave to encamp upon the few acres of bramble-covered land which represent the family estate, and would accept in return the hospitality of their tents, wandering away with them sometimes for weeks on end. He has a passion also for Indian animals, which are sent over to him by a correspondent,* and he has at this moment a cheetah and a baboon, which wander freely over his grounds, and are feared by the villagers almost as much as their master.

'You can imagine from what I say that my poor sister Julia and I had no great pleasure in our lives. No servant would stay with us, and for a long time we did all the work of the house. She was but thirty at the time of her death, and yet her hair had already begun to whiten, even as mine has.'

'Your sister is dead, then?'

'She died just two years ago, and it is of her death that I wish to speak to you. You can understand that, living the life which I have described, we were little likely to see anyone of our own age and position. We had, however, an aunt, my mother's maiden sister, Miss Honoria Westphail, who lives near Harrow, and we were occasionally allowed to pay short visits at this lady's house. Julia went there at Christmas two years ago, and met there a half-pay Major of Marines,* to whom she became engaged. My stepfather learned of the engagement when my sister returned, and offered no objection to the marriage; but within a fortnight of the day which had been fixed for the wedding, the terrible event occurred which has deprived me of my only companion.'

Sherlock Holmes had been leaning back in his chair with his eyes closed, and his head sunk in a cushion, but he half opened his lids now, and glanced across at his visitor.

'Pray be precise as to details,' said he.

'It is easy for me to be so, for every event of that dreadful time is seared into my memory. The manor house is, as I have already said, very old, and only one wing is now inhabited. The bedrooms in this wing are on the ground floor, the sitting-rooms being in the central block of the buildings. Of these bedrooms the first is Dr Roylott's, the second my sister's, and the third my own. There is no communication between them, but they all open out into the same corridor. Do I make myself plain?'

'Perfectly so.'

'The windows of the three rooms open out upon the lawn. That fatal night Dr Roylott had gone to his room early, though we knew that he had not retired to rest, for my sister was troubled by the smell of the strong Indian cigars which it was his custom to smoke. She left her room, therefore, and came into mine, where she sat for some time, chatting about her approaching wedding. At eleven o'clock she rose to leave me, but she paused at the door and looked back.

' "Tell me, Helen," said she, "have you ever heard anyone whistle in the dead of the night?"

' "Never," said I.

' "I suppose that you could not possibly whistle yourself in your sleep?"

' "Certainly not. But why?"

' "Because during the last few nights I have always, about three in the morning, heard a low clear whistle. I am a light sleeper, and it has awakened me. I cannot tell where it came from—perhaps from the next room, perhaps from the lawn. I thought that I would just ask you whether you had heard it."

' "No, I have not. It must be those wretched gipsies in the plantation."

' "Very likely. And yet if it were on the lawn I wonder that you did not hear it also."

' "Ah, but I sleep more heavily than you."

' "Well, it is of no great consequence, at any rate," she smiled back at me, closed my door, and a few moments later I heard her key turn in the lock.'

'Indeed,' said Holmes. 'Was it your custom always to lock yourselves in at night?'

'Always.'

'And why?'

'I think that I mentioned to you that the Doctor kept a cheetah and a baboon. We had no feeling of security unless our doors were locked.'

'Quite so. Pray proceed with your statement.'

'I could not sleep that night. A vague feeling of impending misfortune impressed me. My sister and I, you will recollect, were twins, and you know how subtle are the links which bind two souls which are so closely allied. It was a wild night. The wind was howling outside, and the rain was beating and splashing against the windows. Suddenly, amidst all the hubbub of the gale, there burst forth the wild scream of a terrified woman. I knew that it was my sister's voice. I sprang from my bed, wrapped a shawl round me, and rushed into the corridor. As I opened my door I seemed to hear a low whistle, such as my sister described, and a few moments later a clanging sound, as if a mass of metal had fallen. As I ran down the passage my sister's door was unlocked, and revolved slowly upon its hinges. I stared at it horror-stricken, not knowing what was about to issue from it. By the light of the corridor lamp I saw my sister appear at the opening, her face blanched with terror, her hands groping for help, her whole figure swaying to and fro like that of a drunkard. I ran to her and threw my arms round her, but at that moment her knees seemed to give way and she fell to the ground. She writhed as one who is in terrible pain, and her limbs were dreadfully convulsed. At first I thought that she had not recognized me, but as I bent over her she suddenly shrieked out in a voice which I shall never forget, "Oh, my God! Helen! It was the band! The speckled band!" There was something else which she would fain have said, and she stabbed with her finger into the air in the direction of the Doctor's room, but a fresh convulsion seized her and choked her words. I rushed out, calling loudly for my stepfather, and I met him hastening from his room in his dressing-gown. When he reached my sister's side she was unconscious, and though he poured brandy down her throat, and sent for medical aid from the village, all efforts were in vain, for she slowly sank and died without having recovered her consciousness. Such was the dreadful end of my beloved sister.'

'One moment,' said Holmes: 'are you sure about this whistle and metallic sound? Could you swear to it?'

'That was what the county coroner* asked me at the inquiry. It is my strong impression that I heard it, and yet among the crash of the gale, and the creaking of an old house, I may possibly have been deceived.'

'Was your sister dressed?'

'No, she was in her nightdress. In her right hand was found the charred stump of a match, and in her left a matchbox.'

'Showing that she had struck a light and looked about her when the alarm took place. That is important. And what conclusions did the coroner come to?'

'He investigated the case with great care, for Dr Roylott's conduct had long been notorious in the county, but he was unable to find any satisfactory cause of death. My evidence showed that the door had been fastened upon the inner side, and the windows were blocked by old-fashioned shutters with broad iron bars, which were secured every night. The walls were carefully sounded, and were shown to be quite solid all round, and the flooring was also thoroughly examined, with the same result. The chimney is wide, but is barred up by four large staples. It is certain, therefore, that my sister was quite alone when she met her end. Besides, there were no marks of any violence upon her.'

'How about poison?'

'The doctors examined her for it, but without success.'

'What do you think that this unfortunate lady died of, then?'

'It is my belief that she died of pure fear and nervous shock, though what it was which frightened her I cannot imagine.'

'Were there gipsies in the plantation at the time?'

'Yes, there are nearly always some there.'

'Ah, and what did you gather from this allusion to a band—a speckled band?'

'Sometimes I have thought that it was merely the wild talk of delirium, sometimes that it may have referred to some band of people, perhaps to these very gipsies in the plantation. I do not know whether the spotted handkerchiefs which so many of them wear over their heads might have suggested the strange adjective which she used.'

Holmes shook his head like a man who is far from being satisfied.

'These are very deep waters,' said he; 'pray go on with your narrative.'

'Two years have passed since then, and my life has been until lately lonelier than ever. A month ago, however, a dear friend, whom I have known for many years, has done me the honour to ask my hand in marriage. His name is Armitage—Percy Armitage—the second son of Mr Armitage, of Crane Water, near Reading. My stepfather has offered no opposition to the match, and we are to be married in the course of the spring. Two days ago some repairs were started in the west wing of the building, and my bedroom wall has been pierced, so that I have had to move into the chamber in which my sister died, and to sleep in the very bed in which she slept. Imagine, then, my thrill of terror when last night, as I lay awake, thinking over her terrible fate, I suddenly heard in the silence of the night the low whistle which had been the herald of her own death. I sprang up and lit the lamp, but nothing was to be seen in the room. I was too shaken to go to bed again, however, so I dressed, and as soon as it was daylight I slipped down, got a dog-cart at the Crown Inn, which is opposite, and drove to Leatherhead, from whence I have come on this morning, with the one object of seeing you and asking your advice.'

'You have done wisely,' said my friend. 'But have you told me all?'

'Yes, all.'

'Miss Stoner, you have not. You are screening your stepfather.'

'Why, what do you mean?'

For answer Holmes pushed back the frill of black lace which fringed the hand that lay upon our visitor's knee. Five little livid spots, the marks of four fingers and a thumb, were printed upon the white wrist.

'You have been cruelly used,' said Holmes.

The lady coloured deeply, and covered over her injured wrist. 'He is a hard man,' she said, 'and perhaps he hardly knows his own strength.'

There was a long silence, during which Holmes leaned his chin upon his hands and stared into the crackling fire.

'This is very deep business,' he said at last. 'There are a thousand details which I should desire to know before I decide upon our course of action. Yet we have not a moment to lose. If we were to come to Stoke Moran to-day, would it be possible for us to see over these rooms without the knowledge of your stepfather?'

'As it happens, he spoke of coming into town to-day upon some most important business. It is probable that he will be away all day, and that there would be nothing to disturb you. We have a housekeeper now, but she is old and foolish, and I could easily get her out of the way.'

'Excellent. You are not averse to this trip, Watson?'

'By no means.'

'Then we shall both come. What are you going to do yourself?'

'I have one or two things which I would wish to do now that I am in town. But I shall return by the twelve o'clock train, so as to be there in time for your coming.'

'And you may expect us early in the afternoon. I have myself some small business matters to attend to. Will you not wait and breakfast?'

'No, I must go. My heart is lightened already since I have confided my trouble to you. I shall look forward to seeing you again this afternoon.' She dropped her thick black veil over her face, and glided from the room.

'And what do you think of it all, Watson?' asked Sherlock Holmes, leaning back in his chair.

'It seems to me to be a most dark and sinister business.'

'Dark enough, and sinister enough.'

'Yet if the lady is correct in saying that the flooring and walls are sound, and that the door, window, and chimney are impassable, then her sister must have been undoubtedly alone when she met her mysterious end.'

'What becomes, then, of these nocturnal whistles, and what of the very peculiar words of the dying woman?'

'I cannot think.'

'When you combine the ideas of whistles at night, the presence of a band of gipsies who are on intimate terms with this old doctor, the fact that we have every reason to believe that the doctor has an interest in preventing his stepdaughter's marriage, the dying allusion to a band, and finally, the fact that Miss Helen Stoner heard a metallic clang, which might have been caused by one of those metal bars which secured the shutters falling back into their place, I think there is good ground to think that the mystery may be cleared along those lines.'

'But what, then, did the gipsies do?'

'I cannot imagine.'

'I see many objections to any such a theory.'

'And so do I. It is precisely for that reason that we are going to Stoke Moran this day. I want to see whether the objections are fatal, or if they may be explained away. But what, in the name of the devil!'

The ejaculation had been drawn from my companion by the fact that our door had been suddenly dashed open, and that a huge man framed himself in the aperture. His costume was a peculiar mixture of the professional and of the agricultural, having a black top-hat, a long frock-coat, and a pair of high gaiters,* with a hunting-crop* swinging in his hand. So tall was he that his hat actually brushed the cross bar of the doorway, and his breadth seemed to span it across from side to side. A large face, seared with a thousand wrinkles, burned yellow with the sun, and marked with every evil passion, was turned from one to the other of us, while his deep-set, bile-shot eyes,* and the high thin fleshless nose, gave him somewhat the resemblance to a fierce old bird of prey.

'Which of you is Holmes?' asked this apparition.

'My name, sir, but you have the advantage of me,' said my companion, quietly.

'I am Dr Grimesby Roylott, of Stoke Moran.'

'Indeed, Doctor,' said Holmes, blandly. 'Pray take a seat.'

'I will do nothing of the kind. My stepdaughter has been here. I have traced her. What has she been saying to you?'

'It is a little cold for the time of the year,' said Holmes.

'What has she been saying to you?' screamed the old man furiously.

'But I have heard that the crocuses promise well,' continued my companion imperturbably.

'Ha! You put me off, do you?' said our new visitor, taking a step forward, and shaking his hunting-crop. 'I know you, you scoundrel! I have heard of you before. You are Holmes the meddler.'

My friend smiled.

'Holmes the busybody!'

His smile broadened.

'Holmes the Scotland Yard jack-in-office.'*

Holmes chuckled heartily. 'Your conversation is most entertaining,' said he. 'When you go out close the door, for there is a decided draught.'

'I will go when I have had my say. Don't you dare to meddle with my affairs. I know that Miss Stoner has been here—I traced her! I am a dangerous man to fall foul of! See here.' He stepped swiftly forward, seized the poker, and bent it into a curve with his huge brown hands.

'See that you keep yourself out of my grip,' he snarled, and hurling the twisted poker into the fireplace, he strode out of the room.

'He seems a very amiable person,' said Holmes, laughing. 'I am not quite so bulky, but if he had remained I might have shown him that my grip was not much more feeble than his own.' As he spoke he picked up the steel poker, and with a sudden effort straightened it out again.

'Fancy his having the insolence to confound me with the official detective force! This incident gives zest to our investigation, however, and I only trust that our little friend will not suffer from her imprudence in allowing this brute to trace her. And now, Watson, we shall order breakfast, and afterwards I shall walk down to Doctors' Commons,* where I hope to get some data which may help us in this matter.'

It was nearly one o'clock when Sherlock Holmes returned from his excursion. He held in his hand a sheet of blue paper, scrawled over with notes and figures.

'I have seen the will of the deceased wife,' said he. 'To determine its exact meaning I have been obliged to work out the present prices of the investments with which it is concerned. The total income, which at the time of the wife's death was little short of £1,100, is now through the fall in agricultural prices* not more than £750. Each daughter can claim an income of £250,* in case of marriage. It is evident, therefore, that if both girls had married, this beauty would have had a mere pittance, while even one of them would cripple him to a serious extent. My morning's work has not been wasted, since it has proved that he has the very strongest motives for standing in the way of anything of the sort. And now, Watson, this is too serious for dawdling, especially as the old man is aware that we are interesting ourselves in his affairs, so if you are ready we shall call a cab and drive to Waterloo. I should be very much obliged if you would slip your revolver into your pocket. An Eley's No. 2* is an excellent argument with gentlemen who can twist steel pokers into knots. That and a tooth-brush are, I think, all that we need.'

At Waterloo we were fortunate in catching a train for Leatherhead, where we hired a trap at the station inn, and drove for four or five miles through the lovely Surrey lanes. It was a perfect day, with a bright sun and a few fleecy clouds in the heavens. The trees and wayside hedges were just throwing out their first green shoots, and the air was full of the pleasant smell of the moist earth. To me at least there was a strange contrast between the sweet promise of the spring and this sinister quest upon which we were engaged. My companion sat in front of the trap, his arms folded, his hat pulled down over his eyes, and his chin sunk upon his breast, buried in the deepest thought. Suddenly, however, he started, tapped me on the shoulder, and pointed over the meadows.

'Look there!' said he.

A heavily-timbered park stretched up in a gentle slope, thickening into a grove at the highest point. From amidst the branches there jutted out the grey gables and high roof-tree of a very old mansion.

'Stoke Moran?' said he.

'Yes, sir, that be the house of Dr Grimesby Roylott,' remarked the driver.

'There is some building going on there,' said Holmes: 'that is where we are going.'

'There's the village,' said the driver, pointing to a cluster of roofs some distance to the left; 'but if you want to get to the house, you'll find it shorter to go over this stile, and so by the footpath over the fields. There it is, where the lady is walking.'

'And the lady, I fancy, is Miss Stoner,' observed Holmes, shading his eyes. 'Yes, I think we had better do as you suggest.'

We got off, paid our fare, and the trap rattled back on its way to Leatherhead.

'I thought it as well,' said Holmes, as we climbed the stile, 'that this fellow should think we had come here as architects, or on some definite business. It may stop his gossip. Good afternoon, Miss Stoner. You see that we have been as good as our word.'

Our client of the morning had hurried forward to meet us with a face which spoke her joy. 'I have been waiting so eagerly for you,' she cried, shaking hands with us warmly. 'All has turned out splendidly. Dr Roylott has gone to town, and it is unlikely that he will be back before evening.'

'We have had the pleasure of making the Doctor's acquaintance,' said Holmes, and in a few words he sketched out what had occurred. Miss Stoner turned white to the lips as she listened.

'Good heavens!' she cried, 'he has followed me, then.'

'So it appears.'

'He is so cunning that I never know when I am safe from him. What will he say when he returns?'

'He must guard himself, for he may find that there is someone more cunning than himself upon his track. You must lock yourself from him to-night. If he is violent, we shall take you away to your

aunt's at Harrow. Now, we must make the best use of our time, so
kindly take us at once to the rooms which we are to examine.'

The building was of grey, lichen-blotched stone, with a high
central portion, and two curving wings, like the claws of a crab,
thrown out on each side. In one of these wings the windows were
broken, and blocked with wooden boards, while the roof was partly
caved in, a picture of ruin. The central portion was in little better
repair, but the right-hand block was comparatively modern, and
the blinds in the windows, with the blue smoke curling up from
the chimneys, showed that this was where the family resided. Some
scaffolding had been erected against the end wall, and the stonework had been broken into, but there were no signs of any workmen
at the moment of our visit. Holmes walked slowly up and down the
ill-trimmed lawn, and examined with deep attention the outsides of
the windows.

'This, I take it, belongs to the room in which you used to sleep, the
centre one to your sister's, and the one next to the main building to
Dr Roylott's chamber?'

'Exactly so. But I am now sleeping in the middle one.'

'Pending the alterations, as I understand. By the way, there does
not seem to be any very pressing need for repairs at that end wall.'

'There were none. I believe that it was an excuse to move me from
my room.'

'Ah! that is suggestive. Now, on the other side of this narrow wing
runs the corridor from which these three rooms open. There are windows in it, of course?'

'Yes, but very small ones. Too narrow for anyone to pass through.'

'As you both locked your doors at night, your rooms were unap-
proachable from that side. Now, would you have the kindness to go
into your room, and to bar your shutters.'

Miss Stoner did so, and Holmes, after a careful examination
through the open window, endeavoured in every way to force the
shutter open, but without success. There was no slit through which
a knife could be passed to raise the bar. Then with his lens he tested
the hinges, but they were of solid iron, built firmly into the massive
masonry. 'Hum!' said he, scratching his chin in some perplexity, 'my
theory certainly presents some difficulties. No one could pass these
shutters if they were bolted. Well, we shall see if the inside throws any
light upon the matter.'

A small side-door led into the whitewashed corridor from which the three bedrooms opened. Holmes refused to examine the third chamber, so we passed at once to the second, that in which Miss Stoner was now sleeping, and in which her sister had met her fate. It was a homely little room, with a low ceiling and a gaping fireplace, after the fashion of old country houses. A brown chest of drawers stood in one corner, a narrow white-counterpaned* bed in another, and a dressing-table on the left-hand side of the window. These articles, with two small wickerwork chairs, made up all the furniture in the room, save for a square of Wilton carpet* in the centre. The boards round and the panelling of the walls were brown, worm-eaten oak, so old and discoloured that it may have dated from the original building of the house. Holmes drew one of the chairs into a corner and sat silent, while his eyes travelled round and round and up and down, taking in every detail of the apartment.

'Where does that bell communicate with?' he asked at last, pointing to a thick bell-rope which hung down beside the bed, the tassel actually lying upon the pillow.

'It goes to the housekeeper's room.'

'It looks newer than the other things?'

'Yes, it was only put there a couple of years ago.'

'Your sister asked for it, I suppose?'

'No, I never heard of her using it. We used always to get what we wanted for ourselves.'

'Indeed, it seemed unnecessary to put so nice a bell-pull there. You will excuse me for a few minutes while I satisfy myself as to this floor.' He threw himself down upon his face with his lens in his hand, and crawled swiftly backwards and forwards, examining minutely the cracks between the boards. Then he did the same with the woodwork with which the chamber was panelled. Finally he walked over to the bed and spent some time in staring at it, and in running his eye up and down the wall. Finally he took the bell-rope in his hand and gave it a brisk tug.

'Why, it's a dummy,' said he.

'Won't it ring?'

'No, it is not even attached to a wire. This is very interesting. You can see now that it is fastened to a hook just above where the little opening of the ventilator is.'

'How very absurd! I never noticed that before.'

'Very strange!' muttered Holmes, pulling at the rope. 'There are one or two very singular points about this room. For example, what a fool a builder must be to open a ventilator into another room, when, with the same trouble, he might have communicated with the outside air!'

'That is also quite modern,' said the lady.

'Done about the same time as the bell-rope?' remarked Holmes.

'Yes, there were several little changes carried out about that time.'

'They seem to have been of a most interesting character—dummy bell-ropes, and ventilators which do not ventilate. With your permission, Miss Stoner, we shall now carry our researches into the inner apartment.'

Dr Grimesby Roylott's chamber was larger than that of his step-daughter, but was as plainly furnished. A camp bed,* a small wooden shelf full of books, mostly of a technical character, an armchair beside the bed, a plain wooden chair against the wall, a round table, and a large iron safe were the principal things which met the eye. Holmes walked slowly round and examined each and all of them with the keenest interest.

'What's in here?' he asked, tapping the safe.

'My stepfather's business papers.'

'Oh! you have seen inside then?'

'Only once, some years ago. I remember that it was full of papers.'

'There isn't a cat in it, for example?'

'No. What a strange idea!'

'Well, look at this!' He took up a small saucer of milk which stood on the top of it.

'No; we don't keep a cat. But there is a cheetah and a baboon.'

'Ah, yes, of course! Well, a cheetah is just a big cat, and yet a saucer of milk does not go very far in satisfying its wants, I daresay. There is one point which I should wish to determine.' He squatted down in front of the wooden chair, and examined the seat of it with the greatest attention.

'Thank you. That is quite settled,' said he, rising and putting his lens in his pocket. 'Hello! here is something interesting!'

The object which had caught his eye was a small dog lash hung on one corner of the bed. The lash, however, was curled upon itself, and tied so as to make a loop of whipcord.

'What do you make of that, Watson?'

'It's a common enough lash. But I don't know why it should be tied.'

'That is not quite so common, is it? Ah, me! it's a wicked world, and when a clever man turns his brain to crime it is the worst of all. I think that I have seen enough now, Miss Stoner, and, with your permission, we shall walk out upon the lawn.'

I had never seen my friend's face so grim, or his brow so dark, as it was when we turned from the scene of his investigation. We had walked several times up and down the lawn, neither Miss Stoner nor myself liking to break in upon his thoughts before he roused himself from his reverie.

'It is very essential, Miss Stoner,' said he, 'that you should absolutely follow my advice in every respect.'

'I shall most certainly do so.'

'The matter is too serious for any hesitation. Your life may depend upon your compliance.'

'I assure you that I am in your hands.'

'In the first place, both my friend and I must spend the night in your room.'

Both Miss Stoner and I gazed at him in astonishment.

'Yes, it must be so. Let me explain. I believe that that is the village inn over there?'

'Yes, that is the "Crown".'

'Very good. Your windows would be visible from there?'

'Certainly.'

'You must confine yourself to your room, on pretence of a headache, when your stepfather comes back. Then when you hear him retire for the night, you must open the shutters of your window, undo the hasp,* put your lamp there as a signal to us, and then withdraw with everything which you are likely to want into the room which you used to occupy. I have no doubt that, in spite of the repairs, you could manage there for one night.'

'Oh, yes, easily.'

'The rest you will leave in our hands.'

'But what will you do?'

'We shall spend the night in your room, and we shall investigate the cause of this noise which has disturbed you.'

'I believe, Mr Holmes, that you have already made up your mind,' said Miss Stoner, laying her hand upon my companion's sleeve.

'Perhaps I have.'

'Then for pity's sake tell me what was the cause of my sister's death.'

'I should prefer to have clearer proofs before I speak.'

'You can at least tell me whether my own thought is correct, and if she died from some sudden fright.'

'No, I do not think so. I think that there was probably some more tangible cause. And now, Miss Stoner, we must leave you, for if Dr Roylott returned and saw us, our journey would be in vain. Goodbye, and be brave, for if you will do what I have told you, you may rest assured that we shall soon drive away the dangers that threaten you.'

Sherlock Holmes and I had no difficulty in engaging a bedroom and sitting-room at the Crown Inn. They were on the upper floor, and from our window we could command a view of the avenue gate, and of the inhabited wing of Stoke Moran Manor House. At dusk we saw Dr Grimesby Roylott drive past, his huge form looming up beside the little figure of the lad who drove him. The boy had some slight difficulty in undoing the heavy iron gates, and we heard the hoarse roar of the Doctor's voice, and saw the fury with which he shook his clenched fists at him. The trap drove on, and a few minutes later we saw a sudden light spring up among the trees as the lamp was lit in one of the sitting-rooms.

'Do you know, Watson,' said Holmes, as we sat together in the gathering darkness, 'I have really some scruples as to taking you tonight. There is a distinct element of danger.'

'Can I be of assistance?'

'Your presence might be invaluable.'

'Then I shall certainly come.'

'It is very kind of you.'

'You speak of danger. You have evidently seen more in these rooms than was visible to me.'

'No, but I fancy that I may have deduced a little more. I imagine that you saw all that I did.'

'I saw nothing remarkable save the bell-rope, and what purpose that could answer I confess is more than I can imagine.'

'You saw the ventilator, too?'

'Yes, but I do not think that it is such a very unusual thing to have a small opening between two rooms. It was so small that a rat could hardly pass through.'

'I knew that we should find a ventilator before ever we came to Stoke Moran.'

'My dear Holmes!'

'Oh, yes, I did. You remember in her statement she said that her sister could smell Dr Roylott's cigar. Now, of course that suggests at once that there must be a communication between the two rooms. It could only be a small one, or it would have been remarked upon at the Coroner's inquiry. I deduced a ventilator.'

'But what harm can there be in that?'

'Well, there is at least a curious coincidence of dates. A ventilator is made, a cord is hung, and a lady who sleeps in the bed dies. Does not that strike you?'

'I cannot as yet see any connection.'

'Did you observe anything very peculiar about that bed?'

'No.'

'It was clamped to the floor. Did you ever see a bed fastened like that before?'

'I cannot say that I have.'

'The lady could not move her bed. It must always be in the same relative position to the ventilator and to the rope—for so we may call it, since it was clearly never meant for a bell-pull.'

'Holmes,' I cried, 'I seem to see dimly what you are hitting at. We are only just in time to prevent some subtle and horrible crime.'

'Subtle enough, and horrible enough. When a doctor does go wrong, he is the first of criminals. He has nerve and he has knowledge. Palmer and Pritchard* were among the heads of their profession. This man strikes even deeper, but, I think, Watson, that we shall be able to strike deeper still. But we shall have horrors enough before the night is over: for goodness' sake let us have a quiet pipe, and turn our minds for a few hours to something more cheerful.'

About nine o'clock the light among the trees was extinguished, and all was dark in the direction of the Manor House. Two hours passed slowly away, and then, suddenly, just at the stroke of eleven, a single bright light shone out right in front of us.

'That is our signal,' said Holmes, springing to his feet; 'it comes from the middle window.'

As we passed out he exchanged a few words with the landlord, explaining that we were going on a late visit to an acquaintance, and that it was possible that we might spend the night there. A moment later we were out on the dark road, a chill wind blowing in our faces, and one yellow light twinkling in front of us through the gloom to guide us on our sombre errand.

There was little difficulty in entering the grounds, for unrepaired breaches gaped in the old park wall. Making our way among the trees, we reached the lawn, crossed it, and were about to enter through the window, when out from a clump of laurel bushes there darted what seemed to be a hideous and distorted child, who threw itself on the grass with writhing limbs, and then ran swiftly across the lawn into the darkness.

'My God!' I whispered, 'did you see it?'

Holmes was for the moment as startled as I. His hand closed like a vice upon my wrist in his agitation. Then he broke into a low laugh, and put his lips to my ear.

'It is a nice household,' he murmured. 'That is the baboon.'

I had forgotten the strange pets which the doctor affected. There was a cheetah, too; perhaps we might find it upon our shoulders at any moment. I confess that I felt easier in my mind when, after following Holmes's example and slipping off my shoes, I found myself inside the bedroom. My companion noiselessly closed the shutters, moved the lamp on to the table, and cast his eyes round the room. All was as we had seen it in the day-time. Then creeping up to me and making a trumpet of his hand, he whispered into my ear again so gently that it was all that I could do to distinguish the words:

'The least sound would be fatal to our plans.'

I nodded to show that I had heard.

'We must sit without a light. He would see it through the ventilator.'

I nodded again.

'Do not go to sleep; your very life may depend upon it. Have your pistol ready in case we should need it. I will sit on the side of the bed, and you in that chair.'

I took out my revolver and laid it on the corner of the table.

Holmes had brought up a long thin cane, and this he placed upon the bed beside him. By it he laid the box of matches and the stump of a candle. Then he turned down the lamp and we were left in darkness.

How shall I ever forget that dreadful vigil? I could not hear a sound, not even the drawing of a breath, and yet I knew that my companion sat open-eyed, within a few feet of me, in the same state of nervous tension in which I was myself. The shutters cut off the least ray of light, and we waited in absolute darkness. From outside came the occasional cry of a night-bird, and once at our very window a long drawn, cat-like whine, which told us that the cheetah was indeed at liberty. Far away we could hear the deep tones of the parish clock, which boomed out every quarter of an hour. How long they seemed, those quarters! Twelve struck, and one, and two, and three, and still we sat waiting silently for whatever might befall.

Suddenly there was the momentary gleam of a light up in the direction of the ventilator, which vanished immediately, but was succeeded by a strong smell of burning oil and heated metal. Someone in the next room had lit a dark lantern.* I heard a gentle sound of movement, and then all was silent once more, though the smell grew stronger. For half an hour I sat with straining ears. Then suddenly another sound became audible—a very gentle, soothing sound, like that of a small jet of steam escaping continually from a kettle. The instant that we heard it, Holmes sprang from the bed, struck a match, and lashed furiously with his cane at the bell-pull.

'You see it. Watson?' he yelled. 'You see it?'

But I saw nothing. At the moment when Holmes struck the light I heard a low, clear whistle, but the sudden glare flashing into my weary eyes made it impossible for me to tell what it was at which my friend lashed so savagely. I could, however, see that his face was deadly pale, and filled with horror and loathing.

He had ceased to strike, and was gazing up at the ventilator, when suddenly there broke from the silence of the night the most horrible cry to which I have ever listened. It swelled up louder and louder, a hoarse yell of pain and fear and anger all mingled in the one dreadful shriek. They say that away down in the village, and even in the distant parsonage, that cry raised the sleepers from their beds. It struck cold to our hearts, and I stood gazing at Holmes, and he at me, until the last echoes of it had died away into the silence from which it rose.

'What can it mean?' I gasped.

'It means that it is all over,' Holmes answered. 'And perhaps, after all, it is for the best. Take your pistol, and we shall enter Dr Roylott's room.'

With a grave face he lit the lamp, and led the way down the corridor. Twice he struck at the chamber door without any reply from

within. Then he turned the handle and entered, I at his heels, with
the cocked pistol in my hand.

It was a singular sight which met our eyes. On the table stood
a dark lantern with the shutter half open, throwing a brilliant beam
of light upon the iron safe, the door of which was ajar. Beside this
table, on the wooden chair, sat Dr Grimesby Roylott, clad in a long
grey dressing-gown, his bare ankles protruding beneath, and his feet
thrust into red heelless Turkish slippers. Across his lap lay the short
stock with the long lash which we had noticed during the day. His
chin was cocked upwards, and his eyes were fixed in a dreadful rigid
stare at the corner of the ceiling. Round his brow he had a peculiar
yellow band, with brownish speckles, which seemed to be bound tight
round his head. As we entered he made neither sound nor motion.

'The band! the speckled band!' whispered Holmes,

I took a step forward: in an instant his strange headgear began to
move, and there reared itself from among his hair the squat diamond-
shaped head and puffed neck of a loathsome serpent.

'It is a swamp adder!'* cried Holmes—'the deadliest snake in
India. He has died within ten seconds of being bitten. Violence does,
in truth, recoil upon the violent, and the schemer falls into the pit
which he digs for another.* Let us thrust this creature back into its
den, and we can then remove Miss Stoner to some place of shelter,
and let the county police know what has happened.'

As he spoke he drew the dog whip swiftly from the dead man's lap,
and throwing the noose round the reptile's neck, he drew it from its
horrid perch, and carrying it at arm's length, threw it into the iron
safe, which he closed upon it.

Such are the true facts of the death of Dr Grimesby Roylott, of Stoke
Moran. It is not necessary that I should prolong a narrative which has
already run to too great a length, by telling how we broke the sad news
to the terrified girl, how we conveyed her by the morning train to the
care of her good aunt at Harrow, of how the slow process of official
inquiry came to the conclusion that the Doctor met his fate while
indiscreetly playing with a dangerous pet. The little which I had yet
to learn of the case was told me by Sherlock Holmes as we travelled
back next day.

'I had,' said he, 'come to an entirely erroneous conclusion, which
shows, my dear Watson, how dangerous it always is to reason from

insufficient data. The presence of the gipsies, and the use of the word "band", which was used by the poor girl, no doubt, to explain the appearance which she had caught a horrid glimpse of by the light of her match, were sufficient to put me upon an entirely wrong scent. I can only claim the merit that I instantly reconsidered my position when, however, it became clear to me that whatever danger threatened an occupant of the room could not come either from the window or the door. My attention was speedily drawn, as I have already remarked to you, to this ventilator, and to the bell-rope which hung down to the bed. The discovery that this was a dummy, and that the bed was clamped to the floor, instantly gave rise to the suspicion that the rope was there as a bridge for something passing through the hole, and coming to the bed. The idea of a snake instantly occurred to me, and when I coupled it with my knowledge that the Doctor was furnished with a supply of creatures from India, I felt that I was probably on the right track. The idea of using a form of poison which could not possibly be discovered by any chemical test was just such a one as would occur to a clever and ruthless man who had had an Eastern training. The rapidity with which such a poison would take effect would also, from his point of view, be an advantage. It would be a sharp-eyed coroner indeed who could distinguish the two little dark punctures which would show where the poison fangs had done their work. Then I thought of the whistle. Of course, he must recall the snake before the morning light revealed it to the victim. He had trained it, probably by the use of the milk which we saw, to return to him when summoned. He would put it through this ventilator at the hour that he thought best, with the certainty that it would crawl down the rope, and land on the bed. It might or might not bite the occupant, perhaps she might escape every night for a week, but sooner or later she must fall a victim.

'I had come to these conclusions before ever I had entered his room. An inspection of his chair showed me that he had been in the habit of standing on it, which, of course, would be necessary in order that he should reach the ventilator. The sight of the safe, the saucer of milk, and the loop of whipcord were really enough to finally dispel any doubts which may have remained. The metallic clang heard by Miss Stoner was obviously caused by her father hastily closing the door of his safe upon its terrible occupant. Having once made up my mind, you know the steps which I took in order to put the matter to the proof. I heard the creature hiss, as I have no doubt that you did also, and I instantly lit the light and attacked it.'

'With the result of driving it through the ventilator.'

'And also with the result of causing it to turn upon its master at the other side. Some of the blows of my cane came home, and roused its snakish temper, so that it flew upon the first person it saw. In this way I am no doubt indirectly responsible for Dr Grimesby Roylott's death, and I cannot say that it is likely to weigh very heavily upon my conscience.'

THE MUSGRAVE RITUAL

An anomaly which often struck me in the character of my friend Sherlock Holmes was that, although in his methods of thought he was the neatest and most methodical of mankind, and although also he affected a certain quiet primness of dress, he was none the less in his personal habits one of the most untidy men that ever drove a fellow-lodger to distraction. Not that I am in the least conventional in that respect myself. The rough-and-tumble work in Afghanistan,* coming on the top of a natural Bohemianism of disposition, has made me rather more lax than befits a medical man. But with me there is a limit, and when I find a man who keeps his cigars in the coal-scuttle, his tobacco in the toe end of a Persian slipper, and his unanswered correspondence transfixed by a jack-knife into the very centre of his wooden mantelpiece, then I begin to give myself virtuous airs. I have always held, too, that pistol practice should distinctly be an open-air pastime; and when Holmes in one of his queer humours would sit in an arm-chair, with his hair-trigger* and a hundred Boxer cartridges,* and proceed to adorn the opposite wall with a patriotic V. R.* done in bullet-pocks, I felt strongly that neither the atmosphere nor the appearance of our room was improved by it.

Our chambers were always full of chemicals and of criminal relics, which had a way of wandering into unlikely positions, and of turning up in the butter-dish, or in even less desirable places. But his papers were my great crux. He had a horror of destroying documents, especially those which were connected with his past cases, and yet it was only once in every year or two that he would muster energy to docket and arrange them, for, as I have mentioned somewhere in these incoherent memoirs, the outbursts of passionate energy when he performed the remarkable feats with which his name is associated were followed by reactions of lethargy, during which he would lie about with his violin and his books, hardly moving, save from the sofa to the table. Thus month after month his papers accumulated, until every corner of the room was stacked with bundles of manuscript which were on no account to be burned, and which could not be put away save by their owner.

One winter's night, as we sat together by the fire, I ventured to suggest to him that as he had finished pasting extracts into his commonplace book* he might employ the next two hours in making our room a little more habitable. He could not deny the justice of my request, so with a rather rueful face he went off to his bedroom, from which he returned presently pulling a large tin box behind him. This he placed in the middle of the floor, and squatting down upon a stool in front of it he threw back the lid. I could see that it was already a third full of bundles of paper tied up with red tape into separate packages.

'There are cases enough here, Watson,' said he, looking at me with mischievous eyes. 'I think that if you knew all that I have in this box you would ask me to pull some out instead of putting others in.'

'These are the records of your early work, then?' I asked. 'I have often wished that I had notes of those cases.'

'Yes, my boy; these were all done prematurely before my biographer had come to glorify me.' He lifted bundle after bundle in a tender, caressing sort of way. 'They are not all successes, Watson,' said he, 'but there are some pretty little problems among them. Here's the record of the Tarleton murders and the case of Vamberry, the wine merchant, and the adventure of the old Russian woman, and the singular affair of the aluminium crutch, as well as a full account of Ricoletti of the club foot and his abominable wife. And here—ah, now! this really is something a little *recherché*.'

He dived his arm down to the bottom of the chest, and brought up a small wooden box, with a sliding lid, such as children's toys are kept in. From within he produced a crumpled piece of paper, an old-fashioned brass key, a peg of wood with a ball of string attached to it, and three rusty old discs of metal.

'Well, my boy, what do you make of this lot?' he asked, smiling at my expression.

'It is a curious collection.'

'Very curious; and the story that hangs round it will strike you as being more curious still.'

'These relics have a history, then?'

'So much so that they *are* history.'

'What do you mean by that?'

Sherlock Holmes picked them up one by one, and laid them along the edge of the table. Then he re-seated himself in his chair, and looked them over with a gleam of satisfaction in his eyes.

'These,' said he, 'are all that I have left to remind me of the episode of the Musgrave Ritual.'

I had heard him mention the case more than once, though I had never been able to gather the details.

'I should be so glad,' said I, 'if you would give me an account of it.'

'And leave the litter as it is?' he cried, mischievously. 'Your tidiness won't bear much strain, after all, Watson. But I should be glad that you should add this case to your annals, for there are points in it which make it quite unique in the criminal records of this or, I believe, of any other country. A collection of my trifling achievements would certainly be incomplete which contained no account of this very singular business.

'You may remember how the affair of the *Gloria Scott*, and my conversation with the unhappy man whose fate I told you of, first turned my attention in the direction of the profession which has become my life's work. You see me now when my name has become known far and wide, and when I am generally recognized both by the public and by the official force as being a final court of appeal in doubtful cases. Even when you knew me first, at the time of the affair which you have commemorated in *A Study in Scarlet*, I had already established a considerable, though not a very lucrative, connection. You can hardly realize, then, how difficult I found it at first, and how long I had to wait before I succeeded in making any headway.

'When I first came up to London I had rooms in Montague Street, just round the corner from the British Museum, and there I waited, filling in my too abundant leisure time by studying all those branches of science which might make me more efficient. Now and again cases came in my way, principally through the introduction of old fellow students, for during my last years at the university there was a good deal of talk there about myself and my methods. The third of these cases was that of the Musgrave Ritual, and it is to the interest which was aroused by that singular chain of events, and the large issues which proved to be at stake, that I trace my first stride towards the position which I now hold.

'Reginald Musgrave had been in the same college as myself, and I had some slight acquaintance with him. He was not generally popular among the undergraduates, though it always seemed to me that what was set down as pride was really an attempt to cover extreme natural diffidence. In appearance he was a man of an exceedingly aristocratic type, thin, high-nosed, and large-eyed, with languid and yet courtly manners. He was indeed a scion of one of the very oldest families in the kingdom, though his branch was a cadet one* which had separated from the northern Musgraves some time in the sixteenth century, and had established itself in western Sussex, where the manor house of Hurlstone is perhaps the oldest inhabited building in the county. Something of his birthplace seemed to cling to the man, and I never looked at his pale, keen face, or the poise of his head, without associating him with grey archways and mullioned windows* and all the venerable wreckage of a feudal keep. Now and again we drifted into talk, and I can remember that more than once he expressed a keen interest in my methods of observation and inference.

'For four years I had seen nothing of him, until one morning he walked into my room in Montague Street. He had changed little, was dressed like a young man of fashion—he was always a bit of a dandy—and preserved the same quiet, suave manner which had formerly distinguished him.

'"How has all gone with you, Musgrave?" I asked, after we had cordially shaken hands.

'"You probably heard of my poor father's death," said he. "He was carried off about two years ago. Since then I have, of course, had the Hurlstone estates to manage, and as I am member for the district* as well, my life has been a busy one; but I understand, Holmes, that you are turning to practical ends those powers with which you used to amaze us."

'"Yes," said I, "I have taken to living by my wits."

'"I am delighted to hear it, for your advice at present would be exceedingly valuable to me. We have had some very strange doings at Hurlstone, and the police have been able to throw no light upon the matter. It is really the most extraordinary and inexplicable business."

'You can imagine with what eagerness I listened to him, Watson, for the very chance for which I had been panting during all those months of inaction seemed to have come within my reach. In my inmost heart I believed that I could succeed where others failed, and now I had the opportunity to test myself.

'"Pray let me have the details," I cried.

'Reginald Musgrave sat down opposite to me, and lit the cigarette which I had pushed towards him.

' "You must know," said he, "that though I am a bachelor I have to keep up a considerable staff of servants at Hurlstone, for it is a rambling old place, and takes a good deal of looking after. I preserve,* too, and in the pheasant months* I usually have a house party, so that it would not do to be short-handed. Altogether there are eight maids, the cook, the butler, two footmen, and a boy. The garden and the stables, of course, have a separate staff.

' "Of these servants the one who had been longest in our service was Brunton, the butler. He was a young schoolmaster out of place when he was first taken up by my father, but he was a man of great energy and character, and he soon became quite invaluable in the household. He was a well-grown, handsome man, with a splendid forehead, and though he has been with us for twenty years he cannot be more than forty now. With his personal advantages and his extraordinary gifts, for he can speak several languages and play nearly every musical instrument, it is wonderful that he should have been satisfied so long in such a position, but I suppose that he was comfortable and lacked energy to make any change. The butler of Hurlstone is always a thing that is remembered by all who visit us.

' "But this paragon has one fault. He is a bit of a Don Juan,* and you can imagine that for a man like him it is not a very difficult part to play in a quiet country district.

' "When he was married it was all right, but since he has been a widower we have had no end of trouble with him. A few months ago we were in hopes that he was about to settle down again, for he became engaged to Rachel Howells, our second housemaid, but he has thrown her over since then and taken up with Janet Tregellis, the daughter of the head gamekeeper. Rachel, who is a very good girl, but of an excitable Welsh temperament, had a sharp touch of brain fever, and goes about the house now—or did until yesterday—like a black-eyed shadow of her former self. That was our first drama at Hurlstone, but a second one came to drive it from our minds, and it was prefaced by the disgrace and dismissal of butler Brunton.

' "This is how it came about. I have said that the man was intelligent, and this very intelligence has caused his ruin, for it seems to have led to an insatiable curiosity about things which did not in the least concern him. I had no idea of the lengths to which this would carry him until the merest accident opened my eyes to it.

'"I have said that the house is a rambling one. One night last week—on Thursday night, to be more exact—I found that I could not sleep, having foolishly taken a cup of strong *café noir* after my dinner. After struggling against it until two in the morning I felt that it was quite hopeless, so I rose and lit the candle with the intention of continuing a novel which I was reading. The book, however, had been left in the billiard-room, so I pulled on my dressing-gown and started off to get it.

'"In order to reach the billiard-room I had to descend a flight of stairs, and then to cross the head of the passage which led to the library and the gun-room. You can imagine my surprise when as I looked down this corridor I saw a glimmer of light coming from the open door of the library. I had myself extinguished the lamp and closed the door before coming to bed. Naturally, my first thought was of burglars. The corridors at Hurlstone have their walls largely decorated with trophies of old weapons. From one of these I picked a battle-axe, and then, leaving my candle behind me, I crept on tip-toe down the passage and peeped in at the open door.

'"Brunton, the butler, was in the library. He was sitting, fully dressed, in an easy chair, with a slip of paper, which looked like a map, upon his knee, and his forehead sunk forward upon his hand in deep thought. I stood, dumb with astonishment, watching him from the darkness. A small taper on the edge of the table shed a feeble light, which sufficed to show me that he was fully dressed. Suddenly, as I looked, he rose from his chair, and walking over to a bureau at the side, he unlocked it and drew out one of the drawers. From this he took a paper, and, returning to his seat, he flattened it out beside the taper on the edge of the table, and began to study it with minute attention. My indignation at this calm examination of our family documents overcame me so far that I took a step forward, and Brunton looking up saw me standing in the doorway. He sprang to his feet, his face turned livid with fear, and he thrust into his breast the chart-like paper which he had been originally studying.

'"'So!' said I, 'this is how you repay the trust which we have reposed in you! You will leave my service tomorrow.'

'"He bowed with the look of a man who is utterly crushed, and slunk past me without a word. The taper was still on the table, and by its light I glanced to see what the paper was which Brunton had

taken from the bureau. To my surprise it was nothing of any importance at all, but simply a copy of the questions and answers in the
singular old observance called the Musgrave Ritual. It is a sort of
ceremony peculiar to our family, which each Musgrave for centuries
past has gone through upon his coming of age—a thing of private
interest, and perhaps of some little importance to the archaeolo-
gist, like our own blazonings and charges,* but of no practical use
whatever."

' "We had better come back to the paper afterwards," said I.

' "If you think it really necessary," he answered, with some hesitation. "To continue my statement, however, I re-locked the bureau,
using the key which Brunton had left, and I had turned to go, when
I was surprised to find that the butler had returned and was standing
before me.

' " 'Mr Musgrave, sir,' he cried, in a voice which was hoarse with
emotion, 'I can't bear disgrace, sir. I've always been proud above my
station in life, and disgrace would kill me. My blood will be on your
head, sir—it will, indeed—if you drive me to despair. If you cannot
keep me after what has passed, then for God's sake let me give you
notice and leave in a month, as if of my own free will. I could stand
that, Mr Musgrave, but not to be cast out before all the folk that
I know so well.'

' " 'You don't deserve much consideration, Brunton,' I answered.
'Your conduct has been most infamous. However, as you have been
a long time in the family, I have no wish to bring public disgrace upon
you. A month, however, is too long. Take yourself away in a week, and
give what reason you like for going.'

' " 'Only a week, sir?' he cried in a despairing voice. 'A fortnight—
say at least a fortnight.'

' " 'A week,' I repeated, 'and you may consider yourself to have
been very leniently dealt with.'

' "He crept away, his face sunk upon his breast, like a broken man,
while I put out the light and returned to my room.

' "For two days after this Brunton was most assiduous in his attention to his duties. I made no allusion to what had passed, and waited
with some curiosity to see how he would cover his disgrace. On the
third morning, however, he did not appear, as was his custom, after
breakfast to receive my instructions for the day. As I left the dining-
room I happened to meet Rachel Howells, the maid. I have told you

that she had only recently recovered from an illness, and was looking so wretchedly pale and wan that I remonstrated with her for being at work.

' "'You should be in bed,' I said. 'Come back to your duties when you are stronger.'

' "She looked at me with so strange an expression that I began to suspect that her brain was affected.

' "'I am strong enough, Mr Musgrave,' said she.

' "'We will see what the doctor says,' I answered. 'You must stop work now, and when you go downstairs just say that I wish to see Brunton.'

' "'The butler is gone,' said she.

' "'Gone! Gone where?'

' "'He is gone. No one has seen him. He is not in his room. Oh, yes, he is gone—he is gone!' She fell back against the wall with shriek after shriek of laughter, while I, horrified at this sudden hysterical attack, rushed to the bell to summon help. The girl was taken to her room, still screaming and sobbing, while I made inquiries about Brunton. There was no doubt about it that he had disappeared. His bed had not been slept in; he had been seen by no one since he had retired to his room the night before; and yet it was difficult to see how he could have left the house, as both windows and doors were found to be fastened in the morning. His clothes, his watch, and even his money were in his room—but the black suit which he usually wore was missing. His slippers, too, were gone, but his boots were left behind. Where, then, could butler Brunton have gone in the night, and what could have become of him now?

' "Of course we searched the house and the outhouses, but there was no trace of him. It is, as I have said, a labyrinth of an old building, especially the original wing, which is now practically uninhabited, but we ransacked every room and attic without discovering the least sign of the missing man. It was incredible to me that he could have gone away leaving all his property behind him, and yet where could he be? I called in the local police, but without success. Rain had fallen on the night before, and we examined the lawn and the paths all round the house, but in vain. Matters were in this state when a new development quite drew our attention away from the original mystery.

' "For two days Rachel Howells had been so ill, sometimes delirious, sometimes hysterical, that a nurse had been employed to sit up with her at night. On the third night after Brunton's disappearance, the nurse, finding her patient sleeping nicely, had dropped into a nap in the arm-chair, when she woke in the early morning to find the bed empty, the window open, and no signs of the invalid. I was instantly aroused, and with the two footmen started off at once in search of the missing girl. It was not difficult to tell the direction which she had taken, for, starting from under her window, we could follow her footmarks easily across the lawn to the edge of the mere,* where they vanished, close to the gravel path which leads out of the grounds. The lake there is 8 ft. deep, and you can imagine our feelings when we saw that the trail of the poor demented girl came to an end at the edge of it.

'"Of course, we had the drags at once, and set to work to recover the remains; but no trace of the body could we find. On the other hand, we brought to the surface an object of a most unexpected kind. It was a linen bag, which contained within it a mass of old rusted and discoloured metal and several dull-coloured pieces of pebble or glass. This strange find was all that we could get from the mere, and although we made every possible search and inquiry yesterday, we know nothing of the fate either of Rachel Howells or Richard Brunton. The county police are at their wits' end, and I have come up to you as a last resource."

'You can imagine, Watson, with what eagerness I listened to this extraordinary sequence of events, and endeavoured to piece them together, and to devise some common thread upon which they might all hang.

'The butler was gone. The maid was gone. The maid had loved the butler, but had afterwards had cause to hate him. She was of Welsh blood, fiery and passionate. She had been terribly excited immediately after his disappearance. She had flung into the lake a bag containing some curious contents. These were all factors which had to be taken into consideration, and yet none of them got quite to the heart of the matter. What was the starting-point of this chain of events? There lay the end of this tangled line.

'"I must see that paper, Musgrave," said I, "which this butler of yours thought it worth his while to consult, even at the risk of the loss of his place."

'"It is rather an absurd business, this Ritual of ours," he answered, "but it has at least the saving grace of antiquity to excuse it. I have a copy of the questions and answers here, if you care to run your eye over them."

'He handed me the very paper which I have here, Watson, and this is the strange catechism to which each Musgrave had to submit when he came to man's estate. I will read you the questions and answers as they stand:

' "Whose was it?*

' "His who is gone.

' "Who shall have it?

' "He who will come.

' "What was the month?

' "The sixth from the first.

' "Where was the sun?

' "Over the oak.

' "Where was the shadow?

' "Under the elm.

' "How was it stepped?

' "North by ten and by ten, east by five and by five, south by two and by two, west by one and by one, and so under.

' "What shall we give for it?

' "All that is ours.

' "Why should we give it?

' "For the sake of the trust."

' "The original has no date, but is in the spelling of the middle of the seventeenth century," remarked Musgrave. "I am afraid, however, that it can be of little help to you in solving this mystery."

' "At least," said I, "it gives us another mystery, and one which is even more interesting than the first. It may be that the solution of the one may prove to be the solution of the other. You will excuse me, Musgrave, if I say that your butler appears to me to have been a very clever man, and to have had a clearer insight than ten generations of his masters."

' "I hardly follow you," said Musgrave. "The paper seems to me to be of no practical importance."

' "But to me it seems immensely practical, and I fancy that Brunton took the same view. He had probably seen it before that night on which you caught him."

' "It is very possible. We took no pains to hide it."

' "He simply wished, I should imagine, to refresh his memory upon that last occasion. He had, as I understand, some sort of map or chart which he was comparing with the manuscript, and which he thrust into his pocket when you appeared?"

'"That is true. But what could he have to do with this old family custom of ours, and what does this rigmarole mean?"

'"I don't think that we should have much difficulty in determining that," said I. "With your permission we will take the first train down to Sussex and go a little more deeply into the matter upon the spot."

'The same afternoon saw us both at Hurlstone. Possibly you have seen pictures and read descriptions of the famous old building, so I will confine my account of it to saying that it is built in the shape of an L, the long arm being the more modern portion, and the shorter the ancient nucleus from which the other has developed. Over the low, heavy-lintelled door, in the centre of this old part, is chiselled the date 1607, but experts are agreed that the beams and stonework are really much older than this. The enormously thick walls and tiny windows of this part had in the last century driven the family into building the new wing, and the old one was used now as a storehouse and a cellar when it was used at all. A splendid park, with fine old timber, surrounded the house, and the lake, to which my client had referred, lay close to the avenue, about two hundred yards from the building.

'I was already firmly convinced, Watson, that there were not three separate mysteries here, but one only, and that if I could read the Musgrave Ritual aright, I should hold in my hand the clue which would lead me to the truth concerning both the butler Brunton, and the maid Howells. To that, then, I turned all my energies. Why should this servant be so anxious to master this old formula? Evidently because he saw something in it which had escaped all those generations of country squires, and from which he expected some personal advantage. What was it, then, and how had it affected his fate?

'It was perfectly obvious to me on reading the Ritual that the measurements must refer to some spot to which the rest of the document alluded, and that if we could find that spot we should be in a fair way towards knowing what the secret was which the old Musgraves had thought it necessary to embalm in so curious a fashion. There were two guides given us to start with, an oak and an elm. As to the oak, there could be no question at all. Right in front of the house, upon the left-hand side of the drive, there stood a patriarch among oaks, one of the most magnificent trees that I have ever seen.

' "That was there when your Ritual was drawn up?" said I, as we drove past it.

' "It was there at the Norman Conquest, in all probability," he answered. "It has a girth of 23 ft."

'Here was one of my fixed points secured.

' "Have you any old elms?" I asked.

' "There used to be a very old one over yonder, but it was struck by lightning ten years ago, and we cut down the stump."

' "You can see where it used to be?"

' "Oh, yes."

' "There are no other elms?"

' "No old ones, but plenty of beeches."

' "I should like to see where it grew."

'We had driven up in a dog-cart,* and my client led me away at once, without our entering the house, to the scar on the lawn where the elm had stood. It was nearly midway between the oak and the house. My investigation seemed to be progressing.

' "I suppose it is impossible to find out how high the elm was?" I asked.

' "I can give you it at once. It was 64 ft."

' "How do you come to know it?" I asked in surprise.

' "When my old tutor used to give me an exercise in trigonometry it always took the shape of measuring heights. When I was a lad I worked out every tree and building on the estate."

'This was an unexpected piece of luck. My data were coming more quickly than I could have reasonably hoped.

' "Tell me," I asked, "did your butler ever ask you such a question?"

'Reginald Musgrave looked at me in astonishment. "Now that you call it to my mind," he answered, "Brunton *did* ask me about the height of the tree some months ago, in connection with some little argument with the groom."

'This was excellent news, Watson, for it showed me that I was on the right road. I looked up at the sun. It was low in the heavens, and I calculated that in less than an hour it would lie just above the topmost branches of the old oak. One condition mentioned in the Ritual would then be fulfilled. And the shadow of the elm must mean the further end of the shadow, otherwise the trunk would have been chosen as the guide. I had then to find where the far end of the shadow would fall when the sun was just clear of the oak.'

'That must have been difficult, Holmes, when the elm was no longer there.'

'Well, at least, I knew that if Brunton could do it, I could also. Besides, there was no real difficulty. I went with Musgrave to his study and whittled myself this peg, to which I tied this long string, with a knot at each yard. Then I took two lengths of a fishing-rod, which came to just six feet, and I went back with my client to where the elm had been. The sun was just grazing the top of the oak. I fastened the rod on end, marked out the direction of the shadow, and measured it. It was 9 ft. in length.

'Of course, the calculation was now a simple one. If a rod of 6 ft. threw a shadow of 9 ft., a tree of 64 ft. would throw one of 96 ft., and the line of one would of course be the line of the other. I measured out the distance, which brought me almost to the wall of the house, and I thrust a peg into the spot. You can imagine my exultation, Watson, when within 2 in. of my peg I saw a conical depression in the ground. I knew that it was the mark made by Brunton in his measurements, and that I was still upon his trail.

'From this starting point I proceeded to step, having first taken the cardinal points by my pocket compass. Ten steps with each foot took me along parallel with the wall of the house, and again I marked my spot with a peg. Then I carefully paced off five to the east and two to the south. It brought me to the very threshold of the old door. Two steps to the west meant now that I was to go two paces down the stone-flagged passage, and this was the place indicated by the Ritual.

'Never have I felt such a cold chill of disappointment, Watson. For a moment it seemed to me that there must be some radical mistake in my calculations. The setting sun shone full upon the passage floor, and I could see that the old foot-worn grey stones, with which it was paved, were firmly cemented together, and had certainly not been moved for many a long year. Brunton had not been at work here. I tapped upon the floor, but it sounded the same all over, and there was no sign of any crack or crevice. But fortunately, Musgrave, who had begun to appreciate the meaning of my proceedings, and who was now as excited as myself, took out his manuscript to check my calculations.

' "And under," he cried: "you have omitted the 'and under'."

'I had thought that it meant that we were to dig, but now, of course,

I saw at once that I was wrong. "There is a cellar under this, then?" I cried.

' "Yes, and as old as the house. Down here, through this door."

'We went down a winding stone stair, and my companion, striking a match, lit a large lantern which stood on a barrel in the corner. In an instant it was obvious that we had at last come upon the true place, and that we had not been the only people to visit the spot recently.

'It had been used for the storage of wood, but the billets,* which had evidently been littered over the floor, were now piled at the sides so as to leave a clear space in the middle. In this space lay a large and heavy flagstone, with a rusted iron ring in the centre, to which a thick shepherd's check muffler was attached.

' "By Jove!" cried my client, "that's Brunton's muffler. I have seen it on him, and could swear to it. What has the villain been doing here?"

'At my suggestion a couple of the county police were summoned to be present, and I then endeavoured to raise the stone by pulling on the cravat. I could only move it slightly, and it was with the aid of one of the constables that I succeeded at last in carrying it to one side. A black hole yawned beneath, into which we all peered, while Musgrave, kneeling at the side, pushed down the lantern.

'A small chamber about 7 ft. deep and 4 ft. square lay open to us. At one side of this was a squat, brass-bound, wooden box, the lid of which was hinged upwards, with this curious, old-fashioned key projecting from the lock. It was furred outside by a thick layer of dust, and damp and worms had eaten through the wood so that a crop of livid fungi was growing on the inside of it. Several discs of metal—old coins apparently—such as I hold here, were scattered over the bottom of the box, but it contained nothing else.

'At that moment, however, we had no thought for the old chest, for our eyes were riveted upon that which crouched beside it. It was the figure of a man, clad in a suit of black, who squatted down upon his hams with his forehead sunk upon the edge of the box and his two arms thrown out on each side of it. The attitude had drawn all the stagnant blood to his face, and no man could have recognized that distorted, liver-coloured countenance; but his height, his dress, and his hair were all sufficient to show my client, when we had drawn the body up, that it was indeed his missing butler. He had been dead some days, but there was no wound or bruise upon his person to show how he had met his dreadful end. When his body had been carried from the cellar we found ourselves still confronted with a problem which was almost as formidable as that with which we had started.

'I confess that so far, Watson, I had been disappointed in my investigation. I had reckoned upon solving the matter when once I had found the place referred to in the Ritual; but now I was there, and was apparently as far as ever from knowing what it was which the family had concealed with such elaborate precautions. It is true that I had thrown a light upon the fate of Brunton, but now I had to ascertain how that fate had come upon him, and what part had been played in the matter by the woman who had disappeared. I sat down upon a keg in the corner and thought the whole matter carefully over.

'You know my methods in such cases, Watson: I put myself in the man's place, and having first gauged his intelligence, I try to imagine how I should myself have proceeded under the same circumstances. In this case the matter was simplified by Brunton's intelligence being quite first rate, so that it was unnecessary to make any allowance for the personal equation, as the astronomers have dubbed it. He knew that something valuable was concealed. He had spotted the place. He found that the stone which covered it was just too heavy for a man to move unaided. What would he do next? He could not get help from outside, even if he had someone whom he could trust, without the unbarring of doors, and considerable risk of detection. It was better, if he could, to have his helpmate inside the house. But whom could he ask? This girl had been devoted to him. A man always finds it hard to realize that he may have finally lost a woman's love, however badly he may have treated her. He would try by a few attentions to make his peace with the girl Howells, and then would engage her as his accomplice. Together they would come at night to the cellar, and their united force would suffice to raise the stone. So far I could follow their actions as if I had actually seen them.

'But for two of them, and one a woman, it must have been heavy work, the raising of that stone. A burly Sussex policeman and I had found it no light job. What would they do to assist them? Probably what I should have done myself. I rose and examined carefully the different billets of wood which were scattered round the floor. Almost at once I came upon what I expected. One piece, about 3 ft. in length, had a marked indentation at one end, while several were flattened at the sides as if they had been compressed by some considerable weight. Evidently, as they had dragged the stone up they had thrust the chunks of wood into the chink, until at last, when the opening was large enough to crawl through, they would hold it open by a billet placed lengthwise, which might very well become indented at the lower end, since the whole weight of the stone would press it down on to the edge of the other slab. So far I was still on safe ground.

'And now, how was I to proceed to reconstruct this midnight drama? Clearly only one could get into the hole, and that one was Brunton. The girl must have waited above. Brunton then unlocked the box, handed up the contents, presumably—since they were not to be found—and then—and then what happened?

'What smouldering fire of vengeance had suddenly sprung into flame in this passionate Celtic woman's soul when she saw the man who had wronged her—wronged her, perhaps, far more than we suspected—in her power? Was it a chance that the wood had slipped and that the stone had shut Brunton into what had become his sepulchre? Had she only been guilty of silence as to his fate? Or had some sudden blow from her hand dashed the support away and sent the slab crashing down into its place. Be that as it might, I seemed to see that woman's figure, still clutching at her treasure-trove, and flying wildly up the winding stair with her ears ringing perhaps with the muffled screams from behind her, and with the drumming of frenzied hands against the slab of stone which was choking her faithless lover's life out.

'Here was the secret of her blanched face, her shaken nerves, her peals of hysterical laughter on the next morning. But what had been in the box? What had she done with that? Of course, it must have been the old metal and pebbles which my client had dragged from the mere. She had thrown them in there at the first opportunity, to remove the last trace of her crime.

'For twenty minutes I had sat motionless thinking the matter out. Musgrave still stood with a very pale face swinging his lantern and peering down into the hole.

' "These are coins of Charles I,"* said he, holding out the few which had been left in the box. "You see we were right in fixing our date for the Ritual."

' "We may find something else of Charles I," I cried, as the probable meaning of the first two questions of the Ritual broke suddenly upon me. "Let me see the contents of the bag you fished from the mere."

'We ascended to his study, and he laid the *débris* before me. I could understand his regarding it as of small importance when I looked at it, for the metal was almost black, and the stones lustreless and dull. I rubbed one of them on my sleeve, however, and it glowed afterwards like a spark, in the dark hollow of my hand. The metal-work was in the form of a double-ring, but it had been bent and twisted out of its original shape.

' "You must bear in mind," said I, "that the Royal party made head* in England even after the death of the King, and that when they at last fled they probably left many of their most precious possessions buried behind them, with the intention of returning for them in more peaceful times."

' "My ancestor, Sir Ralph Musgrave, was a prominent Cavalier,* and the right-hand man of Charles II* in his wanderings," said my friend.

' "Ah, indeed!" I answered. "Well, now, I think that really should give us the last link that we wanted. I must congratulate you on coming into possession, though in rather a tragic manner, of a relic which is of great intrinsic value, but even of greater importance as an historical curiosity."

' "What is it, then?" he gasped in astonishment.

' "It is nothing less than the ancient crown of the Kings of England."

' "The crown!"

' "Precisely. Consider what the Ritual says. How does it run? 'Whose was it?' 'His who is gone.' That was after the execution of Charles. Then, 'Who shall have it?' 'He who will come.' That was Charles II, whose advent was already foreseen. There can, I think, be no doubt that this battered and shapeless diadem once encircled the brows of the Royal Stuarts."

' "And how came it in the pond?"

' "Ah, that is a question which will take some time to answer," and with that I sketched out the whole long chain of surmise and of proof which I had constructed. The twilight had closed in and the moon was shining brightly in the sky before my narrative was finished.

' "And how was it, then, that Charles did not get his crown when he returned?" asked Musgrave, pushing back the relic into its linen bag.

' "Ah, there you lay your finger upon the one point which we shall probably never be able to clear up. It is likely that the Musgrave who held the secret died in the interval, and by some oversight left this guide to his descendant without explaining the meaning of it. From that day to this it has been handed down from father to son, until at last it came within reach of a man who tore its secret out of it and lost his life in the venture."

'And that's the story of the Musgrave Ritual, Watson. They have the crown down at Hurlstone—though they had some legal bother, and a considerable sum to pay before they were allowed to retain it. I am sure that if you mentioned my name they would be happy to show it to you. Of the woman nothing was ever heard, and the probability is that she got away out of England, and carried herself, and the memory of her crime, to some land beyond the seas.'

THE GREEK INTERPRETER

DURING my long and intimate acquaintance with Mr Sherlock Holmes I had never heard him refer to his relations, and hardly ever to his own early life. This reticence upon his part had increased the somewhat inhuman effect which he produced upon me, until sometimes I found myself regarding him as an isolated phenomenon, a brain without a heart, as deficient in human sympathy as he was pre-eminent in intelligence. His aversion to women, and his disinclination to form new friendships, were both typical of his unemotional character, but not more so than his complete suppression of every reference to his own people. I had come to believe that he was an orphan with no relatives living, but one day, to my very great surprise, he began to talk to me about his brother.

It was after tea on a summer evening, and the conversation, which had roamed in a desultory, spasmodic fashion from golf clubs to the causes of the change in the obliquity of the ecliptic,* came round at last to the question of atavism* and hereditary aptitudes. The point under discussion was how far any singular gift in an individual was due to his ancestry, and how far to his own early training.

'In your own case,' said I, 'from all that you have told me it seems obvious that your faculty of observation and your peculiar facility for deduction are due to your own systematic training.'

'To some extent,' he answered thoughtfully. 'My ancestors were country squires, who appear to have led much the same life as is natural to their class. But, none the less, my turn that way is in my veins, and may have come with my grandmother, who was the sister of Vernet,* the French artist. Art in the blood is liable to take the strangest forms.'

'But how do you know that it is hereditary?'

'Because my brother Mycroft possesses it in a larger degree than I do.'

This was news to me, indeed. If there were another man with such singular powers in England, how was it that neither police nor public had heard of him? I put the question, with a hint that it was my companion's modesty which made him acknowledge his brother as his superior. Holmes laughed at my suggestion.

'My dear Watson,' said he, 'I cannot agree with those who rank modesty among the virtues. To the logician all things should be seen exactly as they are, and to under-estimate oneself is as much a departure from truth as to exaggerate one's own powers. When I say, therefore, that Mycroft has better powers of observation than I, you may take it that I am speaking the exact and literal truth.'

'Is he your junior?'

'Seven years my senior.'

'How comes it that he is unknown?'

'Oh, he is very well known in his own circle.'

'Where, then?'

'Well, in the Diogenes* Club, for example.'

I had never heard of the institution, and my face must have proclaimed as much, for Sherlock Holmes pulled out his watch.

'The Diogenes Club is the queerest club in London, and Mycroft, one of the queerest men. He's always there from a quarter to five till twenty to eight. It's six now, so if you care for a stroll this beautiful evening I shall be very happy to introduce you to two curiosities.'

Five minutes later we were in the street, walking towards Regent Circus.*

'You wonder,' said my companion, 'why it is that Mycroft does not use his powers for detective work. He is incapable of it.'

'But I thought you said—!'

'I said that he was my superior in observation and deduction. If the art of the detective began and ended in reasoning from an arm-chair, my brother would be the greatest criminal agent that ever lived. But he has no ambition and no energy. He will not even go out of his way to verify his own solutions, and would rather be considered wrong than take the trouble to prove himself right. Again and again I have taken a problem to him, and have received an explanation which has afterwards proved to be the correct one. And yet he was absolutely incapable of working out the practical points which must be gone into before a case could be laid before a judge or jury.'

'It is not his profession, then?'

'By no means. What is to me a means of livelihood is to him the merest hobby of a dilettante. He has an extraordinary faculty for figures, and audits the books in some of the Government departments. Mycroft lodges in Pall Mall, and he walks round the corner into Whitehall every morning and back every evening. From year's end to year's end he takes no other exercise, and is seen nowhere else, except only in the Diogenes Club, which is just opposite his rooms.'

'I cannot recall the name.'

'Very likely not. There are many men in London, you know, who, some from shyness, some from misanthropy, have no wish for the company of their fellows. Yet they are not averse to comfortable chairs and the latest periodicals. It is for the convenience of these that the Diogenes Club was started, and it now contains the most unsociable and unclubbable men in town.* No member is permitted to take the least notice of any other one. Save in the Strangers' Room,* no talking is, under any circumstances, permitted, and three offences, if brought to the notice of the committee, render the talker liable to expulsion. My brother was one of the founders, and I have myself found it a very soothing atmosphere.'

We had reached Pall Mall as we talked, and were walking down it from the St James's end. Sherlock Holmes stopped at a door some little distance from the Carlton,* and, cautioning me not to speak, he led the way into the hall. Through the glass panelling I caught a glimpse of a large and luxurious room in which a con-siderable number of men were sitting about and reading papers, each in his own little nook. Holmes showed me into a small chamber which looked out on to Pall Mall, and then, leaving me for a minute, he came back with a companion who I knew could only be his brother.

Mycroft Holmes was a much larger and stouter man than Sherlock. His body was absolutely corpulent, but his face, though massive, had preserved something of the sharpness of expression which was so remarkable in that of his brother. His eyes, which were of a peculiarly light watery grey, seemed to always retain that far-away, introspective look which I had only observed in Sherlock's when he was exerting his full powers.

'I am glad to meet you, sir,' said he, putting out a broad, fat hand, like the flipper of a seal. 'I hear of Sherlock everywhere since you became his chronicler. By the way, Sherlock, I expected to see you round last week to consult me over that Manor House case. I thought you might be a little out of your depth.'

'No, I solved it,' said my friend, smiling.

'It was Adams, of course?'

'Yes, it was Adams.'

'I was sure of it from the first.' The two sat down together in the bow-window of the club. 'To anyone who wishes to study mankind this is the spot,' said Mycroft. 'Look at the magnificent types! Look at these two men who are coming towards us, for example.'

'The billiard-marker* and the other?'

'Precisely. What do you make of the other?'

The two men had stopped opposite the window. Some chalk marks over the waistcoat pocket were the only signs of billiards which I could see in one of them. The other was a very small, dark fellow, with his hat pushed back and several packages under his arm.

'An old soldier, I perceive,' said Sherlock.

'And very recently discharged,' remarked the brother.

'Served in India, I see.'

'And a non-commissioned officer.'*

'Royal Artillery, I fancy,' said Sherlock.

'And a widower.'

'But with a child.'

'Children, my dear boy, children.'

'Come,' said I, laughing, 'this is a little too much.'

'Surely,' answered Holmes, 'it is not hard to say that a man with that bearing, expression of authority, and sun-baked skin is a soldier, is more than a private, and is not long from India.'

'That he has not left the service long is shown by his still wearing his "ammunition boots",* as they are called,' observed Mycroft.

'He has not the cavalry stride, yet he wore his hat on one side, as is shown by the lighter skin on that side of his brow. His weight is against his being a sapper.* He is in the artillery.'

'Then, of course, his complete mourning shows that he has lost someone very dear. The fact that he is doing his own shopping looks as though it were his wife. He has been buying things for children, you perceive. There is a rattle, which shows that one of them is very young. The wife probably died in child-bed. The fact that he has a picture-book under his arm shows that there is another child to be thought of.'

I began to understand what my friend meant when he said that his brother possessed even keener faculties than he did himself. He glanced across at me, and smiled. Mycroft took snuff from a tortoise-shell box and brushed away the wandering grains from his coat with a large, red silk handkerchief.

'By the way, Sherlock,' said he, 'I have had something quite after your own heart—a most singular problem—submitted to my judgment. I really had not the energy to follow it up, save in a very incomplete fashion, but it gave me a basis for some very pleasing speculations. If you would care to hear the facts—'

'My dear Mycroft, I should be delighted.'

The brother scribbled a note upon a leaf of his pocket-book, and, ringing the bell, he handed it to the waiter.

'I have asked Mr Melas to step across,' said he. 'He lodges on the floor above me, and I have some slight acquaintance with him, which led him to come to me in his perplexity. Mr Melas is a Greek by extraction, as I understand, and he is a remarkable linguist. He earns his living partly as interpreter in the law courts, and partly by acting as guide to any wealthy Orientals who may visit the Northumberland Avenue hotels. I think I will leave him to tell his own very remarkable experience in his own fashion.'

A few minutes later we were joined by a short, stout man, whose olive face and coal-black hair proclaimed his southern origin, though his speech was that of an educated Englishman. He shook hands eagerly with Sherlock Holmes, and his dark eyes sparkled with pleasure when he understood that the specialist was anxious to hear his story.

'I do not believe that the police credit me—on my word I do not,' said he, in a wailing voice. 'Just because they have never heard of it before, they think that such a thing cannot be. But I know that I shall never be easy in my mind until I know what has become of my poor man with the sticking-plaster upon his face.'

'I am all attention,' said Sherlock Holmes.

'This is Wednesday evening,' said Mr Melas; 'well, then, it was on Monday night—only two days ago, you understand—that all this happened. I am an interpreter, as, perhaps, my neighbour there has told you. I interpret all languages—or nearly all—but as I am a Greek by birth, and with a Grecian name, it is with that particular tongue that I am principally associated. For many years I have been the chief Greek interpreter in London, and my name is very well known in the hotels.

'It happens, not infrequently, that I am sent for at strange hours, by foreigners who get into difficulties, or by travellers who arrive late and wish my services. I was not surprised, therefore, on Monday night when a Mr Latimer, a very fashionably-dressed young man, came up to my rooms and asked me to accompany him in a cab, which was waiting at the door. A Greek friend had come to see him upon business, he said, and, as he could speak nothing but his own tongue, the services of an interpreter were indispensable. He gave me to understand that his house was some little distance off, in Kensington, and he seemed to be in a great hurry, bustling me rapidly into the cab when we had descended into the street.

'I say into the cab, but I soon became doubtful as to whether it was not a carriage in which I had found myself. It was certainly more roomy than the ordinary four-wheeled disgrace to London, and the fittings, though frayed, were of rich quality. Mr Latimer seated himself opposite to me, and we started off through Charing Cross and up the Shaftesbury Avenue. We had come out upon Oxford Street, and I had ventured some remark as to this being a roundabout way to Kensington, when my words were arrested by the extraordinary conduct of my companion.

'He began by drawing a most formidable-looking bludgeon loaded with lead from his pocket, and switched it backwards and forwards several times, as if to test its weight and strength. Then he placed it, without a word, upon the seat beside him. Having done this, he drew up the windows on each side, and I found to my astonishment that they were covered with paper so as to prevent my seeing through them.

'"I am sorry to cut off your view, Mr Melas," said he. "The fact is that I have no intention that you should see what the place is to which we are driving. It might possibly be inconvenient to me if you could find your way there again."

'As you can imagine, I was utterly taken aback by such an address. My companion was a powerful, broad-shouldered young fellow, and, apart from the weapon, I should not have had the slightest chance in a struggle with him.

'"This is very extraordinary conduct, Mr Latimer," I stammered. "You must be aware that what you are doing is quite illegal."

'"It is somewhat of a liberty, no doubt," said he, "but we'll make it up to you. But I must warn you, however, Mr Melas, that if at any time to-night you attempt to raise an alarm or do anything which is against my interests, you will find it a very serious thing. I beg you to remember that no one knows where you are, and that whether you are in this carriage or in my house, you are equally in my power."

'His words were quiet, but he had a rasping way of saying them which was very menacing. I sat in silence, wondering what on earth could be his reason for kidnapping me in this extraordinary fashion. Whatever it might be, it was perfectly clear that there was no possible use in my resisting, and that I could only wait to see what might befall.

'For nearly two hours we drove without my having the least clue as to where we were going. Sometimes the rattle of the stones told of a paved causeway, and at others our smooth, silent course suggested asphalt, but save this variation in sound there was nothing at all which could in the remotest way help me to form a guess as to where we were. The paper over each window was impenetrable to light, and a blue curtain was drawn across the glass-work in front. It was a quarter past seven when we left Pall Mall, and my watch showed me that it was ten minutes to nine when we at last came to a standstill. My companion let down the window and I caught a glimpse of a low, arched doorway with a lamp burning above it. As I was hurried from the carriage it swung open, and I found myself inside the house, with a vague impression of a lawn and trees on each side of me as I entered. Whether these were private grounds, however, or *bona-fide* country was more than I could possibly venture to say.

'There was a coloured gas-lamp inside, which was turned so low that I could see little save that the hall was of some size and hung with pictures. In the dim light I could make out that the person who had opened the door was a small, mean-looking, middle-aged man with rounded shoulders. As he turned towards us the glint of the light showed me that he was wearing glasses.

'"Is this Mr Melas, Harold?" said he.

'"Yes."

'"Well done! Well done! No ill-will, Mr Melas, I hope, but we could not get on without you. If you deal fair with us you'll not regret it; but if you try any tricks, God help you!"

'He spoke in a jerky, nervous fashion, and with some giggling laughs in between, but somehow he impressed me with fear more than the other.

'"What do you want with me?" I asked.

'"Only to ask a few questions of a Greek gentleman who is visiting us, and to let us have the answers. But say no more than you are told to say, or"—here came the nervous giggle again—"you had better never have been born."

'As he spoke he opened a door and showed the way into a room which appeared to be very richly furnished—but again the only light was afforded by a single lamp half turned down. The chamber was certainly large, and the way in which my feet sank into the carpet as I stepped across it told me of its richness. I caught glimpses of velvet chairs, a high, white marble mantelpiece, and what seemed to be a suit of Japanese armour at one side of it. There was a chair just under the lamp, and the elderly man motioned that I should sit in it. The younger had left us, but he suddenly returned through another door, leading with him a gentleman clad in some sort of loose dressing-gown, who moved slowly towards us. As he came into the circle of dim light which enabled me to see him more clearly, I was thrilled with horror at his appearance. He was deadly pale and terribly emaciated, with the protruding, brilliant eyes of a man whose spirit is greater than his strength. But what shocked me more than any signs of physical weakness was that his face was grotesquely criss-crossed with sticking-plaster, and that one large pad of it was fastened over his mouth.

' "Have you the slate, Harold?" cried the older man, as this strange being fell rather than sat down into a chair. "Are his hands loose? Now then, give him the pencil. You are to ask the questions, Mr Melas, and he will write the answers. Ask him first of all whether he is prepared to sign the papers."

'The man's eyes flashed fire.

' "Never," he wrote in Greek upon the slate.

' "On no conditions?" I asked at the bidding of our tyrant.

' "Only if I see her married in my presence by a Greek priest whom I know."

'The man giggled in his venomous way.

' "You know what awaits you, then?"

' "I care nothing for myself."

'These are samples of the questions and answers which made up our strange, half-spoken, half-written conversation. Again and again I had to ask him whether he would give in and sign the document. Again and again I had the same indignant reply. But soon a happy thought came to me. I took to adding on little sentences of my own to each question—innocent ones at first, to test whether either of our companions knew anything of the matter, and then, as I found that they showed no sign, I played a more dangerous game. Our conversation ran something like this:

' "You can do no good by this obstinacy. *Who are you?*"

' "I care not. *I am a stranger in London.*"

' "Your fate will be on your own head. *How long have you been here?*"

' "Let it be so. *Three weeks.*"

' "The property can never be yours. *What ails you?*"

' "It shall not go to villains. *They are starving me.*"

' "You shall go free if you sign. *What house is this?*"

' "I will never sign. *I do not know.*"

' "You are not doing her any service. *What is your name?*"

' "Let me hear her say so. *Kratides.*"

' "You shall see her if you sign. *Where are you from?*"

' "Then I shall never see her. *Athens.*"

'Another five minutes, Mr Holmes, and I should have wormed out the whole story under their very noses. My very next question might have cleared the matter up, but at that instant the door opened and a woman stepped into the room. I could not see her clearly enough to know more than that she was tall and graceful, with black hair, and clad in some sort of loose white gown.

' "Harold!" said she, speaking English with a broken accent, "I could not stay away longer. It is so lonely up there with only—oh, my God, it is Paul!"

'These last words were in Greek, and at the same instant the man, with a convulsive effort, tore the plaster from his lips, and screaming out "Sophy! Sophy!" rushed into the woman's arms. Their embrace was but for an instant, however, for the younger man seized the woman and pushed her out of the room, while the elder easily over-powered his emaciated victim, and dragged him away through the other door. For a moment I was left alone in the room, and I sprang to my feet with some vague idea that I might in some way get a clue to what this house was in which I found myself. Fortunately, however, I took no steps, for, looking up, I saw that the older man was standing in the doorway, with his eyes fixed upon me.

' "That will do, Mr Melas," said he. "You perceive that we have taken you into our confidence over some very private business. We should not have troubled you only that our friend who speaks Greek and who began these negotiations has been forced to return to the East. It was quite necessary for us to find someone to take his place, and we were fortunate in hearing of your powers."

'I bowed.

'"There are five sovereigns here," said he, walking up to me, "which will, I hope, be a sufficient fee. But remember," he added, tapping me lightly on the chest and giggling, "if you speak to a human soul about this—one human soul, mind—well, may God have mercy upon your soul!"

'I cannot tell you the loathing and horror with which this insignificant-looking man inspired me. I could see him better now as the lamp-light shone upon him. His features were peaky and sallow, and his little, pointed beard was thready and ill-nourished. He pushed his face forward as he spoke, and his lips and eyelids were continually twitching, like a man with St Vitus's Dance.* I could not help thinking that his strange, catchy little laugh was also a symptom of some nervous malady. The terror of his face lay in his eyes, however, steel grey, and glistening coldly, with a malignant, inexorable cruelty in their depths.

'"We shall know if you speak of this," said he. "We have our own means of information. Now, you will find the carriage waiting, and my friend will see you on your way."

'I was hurried through the hall, and into the vehicle, again obtaining that momentary glimpse of trees and a garden. Mr Latimer followed closely at my heels, and took his place opposite to me without a word. In silence we again drove for an interminable distance, with the windows raised, until at last, just after midnight, the carriage pulled up.

'"You will get down here, Mr Melas," said my companion. "I am sorry to leave you so far from your house, but there is no alternative. Any attempt upon your part to follow the carriage can only end in injury to yourself."

'He opened the door as he spoke, and I had hardly time to spring out when the coachman lashed the horse, and the carriage rattled away. I looked round me in astonishment. I was on some sort of a heathy common, mottled over with dark clumps of furze bushes. Far away stretched a line of houses, with a light here and there in the upper windows. On the other side I saw the red signal lamps of a railway.

'The carriage which had brought me was already out of sight. I stood gazing round and wondering where on earth I might be, when I saw someone coming towards me in the darkness. As he came up to me I made out that it was a railway porter.

'"Can you tell me what place this is?" I asked.

'"Wandsworth Common," said he.

' "Can I get a train into town?"

' "If you walk on a mile or so, to Clapham Junction," said he, "you'll just be in time for the last to Victoria."

'So that was the end of my adventure, Mr Holmes. I do not know where I was nor whom I spoke with, nor anything, save what I have told you. But I know that there is foul play going on, and I want to help that unhappy man if I can. I told the whole story to Mr Mycroft Holmes next morning, and, subsequently, to the police.'

We all sat in silence for some little time after listening to this extraordinary narrative. Then Sherlock looked across at his brother.

'Any steps?' he asked.

Mycroft picked up the *Daily News*, which was lying on a side table.

' "Anybody supplying any information as to the whereabouts of a Greek gentleman named Paul Kratides, from Athens, who is unable to speak English, will be rewarded. A similar reward paid to anyone giving information about a Greek lady whose first name is Sophy. X2473." That was in all the dailies. No answer.'

'How about the Greek Legation?'*

'I have inquired. They know nothing.'

'A wire to the head of the Athens police, then.'

'Sherlock has all the energy of the family,' said Mycroft, turning to me. 'Well, you take up the case by all means, and let me know if you do any good.'

'Certainly,' answered my friend, rising from his chair. 'I'll let you know, and Mr Melas also. In the meantime, Mr Melas, I should certainly be on my guard if I were you, for, of course, they must know through these advertisements that you have betrayed them.'

As we walked home together Holmes stopped at a telegraph office and sent off several wires.

'You see, Watson,' he remarked, 'our evening has been by no means wasted. Some of my most interesting cases have come to me in this way through Mycroft. The problem which we have just listened to, although it can admit of but one explanation, has still some distinguishing features.'

'You have hopes of solving it?'

'Well, knowing as much as we do, it will be singular indeed if we fail to discover the rest. You must yourself have formed some theory which will explain the facts to which we have listened.'

'In a vague way, yes.'

'What was your idea, then?'

'It seemed to me to be obvious that this Greek girl had been carried off by the young Englishman named Harold Latimer.'

'Carried off from where?'

'Athens, perhaps.'

Sherlock Holmes shook his head. 'This young man could not talk a word of Greek. The lady could talk English fairly well. Inference that she had been in England some little time, but he had not been in Greece.'

'Well, then, we will presume that she had come on a visit to England, and that this Harold had persuaded her to fly with him.'

'That is the more probable.'

'Then the brother—for that, I fancy, must be the relationship— comes over from Greece to interfere. He imprudently puts himself into the power of the young man and his older associate. They seize him and use violence towards him in order to make him sign some papers to make over the girl's fortune—of which he may be trustee— to them. This he refuses to do. In order to negotiate with him, they have to get an interpreter, and they pitch upon this Mr Melas, having used some other one before. The girl is not told of the arrival of her brother, and finds it out by the merest accident.'

'Excellent, Watson,' cried Holmes. 'I really fancy that you are not far from the truth. You see that we hold all the cards, and we have only to fear some sudden act of violence on their part. If they give us time we must have them.'

'But how can we find where this house lies?'

'Well, if our conjecture is correct, and the girl's name is, or was, Sophy Kratides, we should have no difficulty in tracing her. That must be our main hope, for the brother, of course, is a complete stranger. It is clear that some time has elapsed since this Harold established these relations with the girl—some weeks at any rate—since the brother in Greece has had time to hear of it, and come across. If they have been living in the same place during this time, it is probable that we shall have some answer to Mycroft's advertisement.'

We had reached our house in Baker Street whilst we had been talking. Holmes ascended the stairs first, and as he opened the door of our room he gave a start of surprise. Looking over his shoulder I was equally astonished. His brother Mycroft was sitting smoking in the arm-chair.

'Come in, Sherlock! Come in, sir,' said he blandly, smiling at our surprised faces. 'You don't expect such energy from me, do you, Sherlock? But somehow this case attracts me.'

'How did you get here?'

'I passed you in a hansom.'*

'There has been some new development?'

'I had an answer to my advertisement.'

'Ah!'

'Yes; it came within a few minutes of your leaving.'

'And to what effect?'

Mycroft Holmes took out a sheet of paper.

'Here it is,' said he, 'written with a J pen* on royal cream paper, by a middle-aged man with a weak constitution. "Sir," he says, "in answer to your advertisement of today's date, I beg to inform you that I know the young lady in question very well. If you should care to call upon me, I could give you some particulars as to her painful history. She is living at present at The Myrtles, Beckenham.— Yours faithfully, J. DAVENPORT."

'He writes from Lower Brixton,' said Mycroft Holmes. 'Do you not think that we might drive to him now, Sherlock, and learn these particulars?'

'My dear Mycroft, the brother's life is more valuable than the sister's story. I think we should call at Scotland Yard for Inspector Gregson, and go straight out to Beckenham. We know that a man is being done to death, and every hour may be vital.'

'Better pick up Mr Melas upon our way,' I suggested; 'we may need an interpreter.'

'Excellent!' said Sherlock Holmes. 'Send the boy for a four-wheeler,* and we shall be off at once.' He opened the table-drawer as he spoke, and I noticed that he slipped his revolver into his pocket. 'Yes,' said he, in answer to my glance, 'I should say from what we have heard that we are dealing with a particularly dangerous gang.'

It was almost dark before we found ourselves in Pall Mall, at the rooms of Mr Melas. A gentleman had just called for him, and he was gone.

'Can you tell me where?' asked Mycroft Holmes.

'I don't know, sir,' answered the woman who had opened the door. 'I only know that he drove away with the gentleman in a carriage.'

'Did the gentleman give a name?'

'No, sir.'

'He wasn't a tall, handsome, dark young man?'

'Oh, no, sir; he was a little gentleman, with glasses, thin in the face, but very pleasant in his ways, for he was laughing all the time that he was talking.'

'Come along!' cried Sherlock Holmes abruptly. 'This grows serious!' he observed, as we drove to Scotland Yard. 'These men have got hold of Melas again. He is a man of no physical courage, as they are well aware from their experience the other night. This villain was able to terrorize him the instant that he got into his presence. No doubt they want his professional services; but, having used him, they may be inclined to punish him for what they will regard as his treachery.'

Our hope was that by taking train we might get to Beckenham as soon as, or sooner than, the carriage. On reaching Scotland Yard, however, it was more than an hour before we could get Inspector Gregson and comply with the legal formalities which would enable us to enter the house. It was a quarter to ten before we reached London Bridge, and half-past before the four of us alighted on the Beckenham platform. A drive of half a mile brought us to The Myrtles—a large, dark house, standing back from the road in its own grounds. Here we dismissed our cab, and made our way up the drive together.

'The windows are all dark,' remarked the inspector. 'The house seems deserted.'

'Our birds are flown and the nest empty,' said Holmes.

'Why do you say so?'

'A carriage heavily loaded with luggage has passed out during the last hour.'

The inspector laughed. 'I saw the wheel-tracks in the light of the gate-lamp, but where does the luggage come in?'

'You may have observed the same wheel-tracks going the other way. But the outward-bound ones were very much deeper—so much so that we can say for a certainty that there was a very considerable weight on the carriage.'

'You get a trifle beyond me there,' said the inspector, shrugging his shoulders. 'It will not be an easy door to force. But we will try if we cannot make someone hear us.'

He hammered loudly at the knocker and pulled at the bell, but without any success. Holmes had slipped away, but he came back in a few minutes.

'I have a window open,' said he.

'It is a mercy that you are on the side of the force, and not against it, Mr Holmes,' remarked the inspector, as he noted the clever way in which my friend had forced back the catch. 'Well, I think that, under the circumstances, we may enter without waiting for an invitation.'

One after the other we made our way into a large apartment, which was evidently that in which Mr Melas had found himself. The inspector had lit his lantern, and by its light we could see the two doors, the curtain, the lamp and the suit of Japanese mail as he had described them. On the table stood two glasses, an empty brandy bottle, and the remains of a meal.

'What is that?' asked Holmes suddenly.

We all stood still and listened. A low, moaning sound was coming from somewhere above our heads. Holmes rushed to the door and out into the hall. The dismal noise came from upstairs. He dashed up, the inspector and I at his heels, while his brother, Mycroft, followed as quickly as his great bulk would permit.

Three doors faced us upon the second floor, and it was from the central of these that the sinister sounds were issuing, sinking sometimes into a dull mumble and rising again into a shrill whine. It was locked, but the key was on the outside. Holmes flung open the door and rushed in, but he was out again in an instant with his hand to his throat.

'It's charcoal!' he cried. 'Give it time. It will clear.'

Peering in, we could see that the only light in the room came from a dull, blue flame, which flickered from a small brass tripod in the centre. It threw a livid, unnatural circle upon the floor, while in the shadows beyond we saw the vague loom of two figures, which crouched against the wall. From the open door there reeked a horrible, poisonous exhalation, which set us gasping and coughing. Holmes rushed to the top of the stairs to draw in the fresh air, and then, dashing into the room, he threw up the window and hurled the brazen tripod out into the garden.

'We can enter in a minute,' he gasped, darting out again. 'Where is a candle? I doubt if we could strike a match in that atmosphere. Hold the light at the door and we shall get them out, Mycroft. Now!'

With a rush we got to the poisoned men and dragged them out on to the landing. Both of them were blue-lipped and insensible, with swollen, congested faces and protruding eyes. Indeed, so distorted were their features that, save for his black beard and stout figure, we might have failed to recognize in one of them the Greek interpreter who had parted from us only a few hours before at the Diogenes Club. His hands and feet were securely strapped together, and he bore over one eye the mark of a violent blow. The other, who was secured in a similar fashion, was a tall man in the last stage of emaciation, with several strips of sticking-plaster arranged in a grotesque pattern over his face. He had ceased to moan as we laid him down, and a glance showed me that for him, at least, our aid had come too late. Mr Melas, however, still lived, and in less than an hour, with the aid of ammonia and brandy, I had the satisfaction of seeing him open his eyes, and of knowing that my hand had drawn him back from the dark valley in which all paths meet.

It was a simple story which he had to tell, and one which did but confirm our own deductions. His visitor on entering his rooms had drawn a life preserver* from his sleeve, and had so impressed him with the fear of instant and inevitable death, that he had kidnapped him for the second time. Indeed, it was almost mesmeric the effect which this giggling ruffian had produced upon the unfortunate linguist, for he could not speak of him save with trembling hands and a blanched cheek. He had been taken swiftly to Beckenham, and had acted as interpreter in a second interview, even more dramatic than the first, in which the two Englishmen had menaced their prisoner with instant death if he did not comply with their demands. Finally, finding him proof against every threat, they had hurled him back into his prison, and after reproaching Melas with his treachery, which appeared from the newspaper advertisements, they had stunned him with a blow from a stick, and he remembered nothing more until he found us bending over him.

And this was the singular case of the Grecian Interpreter, the explanation of which is still involved in some mystery. We were able to find out, by communicating with the gentleman who had answered the advertisement, that the unfortunate young lady came of a wealthy Grecian family, and that she had been on a visit to some friends in England. While there she had met a young man named Harold Latimer, who had acquired an ascendancy over her and had eventually persuaded her to fly with him. Her friends, shocked at the event, had contented themselves with informing her brother at Athens, and had then washed their hands of the matter. The brother, on his arrival in England, had imprudently placed himself in the power of Latimer, and of his associate, whose name was Wilson Kemp— a man of the foulest antecedents. These two, finding that through his ignorance of the language he was helpless in their hands, had kept him a prisoner, and had endeavoured, by cruelty and starvation, to make him sign away his own and his sister's property. They had kept him in the house without the girl's knowledge, and the plaster over the face had been for the purpose of making recognition difficult in case she should ever catch a glimpse of him. Her feminine percep- tions, however, had instantly seen through the disguise when, on the occasion of the interpreter's first visit, she had seen him for the first time. The poor girl, however, was herself a prisoner, for there was no one about the house except the man who acted as coachman, and his wife, both of whom were tools of the conspirators. Finding that their secret was out and that their prisoner was not to be coerced, the two villains, with the girl, had fled away at a few hours' notice from the furnished house which they had hired, having first, as they thought, taken vengeance both upon the man who had defied and the one who had betrayed them.

Months afterwards a curious newspaper cutting reached us from Buda-Pesth. It told how two Englishmen who had been travelling with a woman had met with a tragic end. They had each been stabbed, it seems, and the Hungarian police were of opinion that they had quarrelled and had inflicted mortal injuries upon each other. Holmes, however, is, I fancy, of a different way of thinking, and he holds to this day that if one could find the Grecian girl one might learn how the wrongs of herself and her brother came to be avenged.

THE DANCING MEN

HOLMES had been seated for some hours in silence, with his long, thin back curved over a chemical vessel in which he was brewing a particularly malodorous product. His head was sunk upon his breast, and he looked from my point of view like a strange, lank bird, with dull grey plumage and a black top-knot.

'So, Watson,' said he suddenly, 'you do not propose to invest in South African securities?'*

I gave a start of astonishment. Accustomed as I was to Holmes's curious faculties, this sudden intrusion into my most intimate thoughts was utterly inexplicable.

'How on earth do you know that?' I asked.

He wheeled round upon his stool, with a steaming test-tube in his hand and a gleam of amusement in his deep-set eyes.

'Now, Watson, confess yourself utterly taken aback,' said he.

'I am.'

'I ought to make you sign a paper to that effect.'

'Why?'

'Because in five minutes you will say that it is all so absurdly simple.'

'I am sure that I shall say nothing of the kind.'

'You see, my dear Watson'—he propped his test-tube in the rack and began to lecture with the air of a professor addressing his class—'it is not really difficult to construct a series of inferences, each dependent upon its predecessor and each simple in itself. If, after doing so, one simply knock out all the central inferences and presents one's audience with the starting-point and the conclusion, one may produce a startling, though possibly a meretricious, effect. Now, it was not really difficult, by an inspection of the groove between your left forefinger and thumb, to feel sure that you did *not* propose to invest your small capital in the goldfields.'

'I see no connection.'

'Very likely not; but I can quickly show you a close connection. Here are the missing links of the very simple chain: 1. You had chalk between your left finger and thumb when you returned from the club last night. 2. You put chalk there when you play billiards to steady the cue. 3. You never play billiards except with Thurston. 4. You told me four weeks ago that Thurston had an option on some South African property which would expire in a month, and which he desired you to share with him. 5. Your cheque-book is locked in my drawer, and you have not asked for the key. 6. You do not propose to invest your money in this manner.'

'How absurdly simple!' I cried.

'Quite so!' said he, a little nettled. 'Every problem becomes very childish when once it is explained to you. Here is an unexplained one. See what you can make of that, friend Watson.' He tossed a sheet of paper upon the table, and turned once more to his chemical analysis.

I looked with amazement at the absurd hieroglyphics upon the paper.

'Why, Holmes, it is a child's drawing!' I cried.

'Oh, that's your idea!'

'What else should it be?'

'That is what Mr Hilton Cubitt,* of Ridling Thorpe Manor,* Norfolk, is very anxious to know. This little conundrum came by the first post, and he was to follow by the next train. There's a ring at the bell, Watson. I should not be very much surprised if this were he.'

A heavy step was heard upon the stairs, and an instant later there entered a tall, ruddy, clean-shaven gentleman, whose clear eyes and florid cheeks told of a life led far from the fogs of Baker Street. He seemed to bring a whiff of his strong, fresh, bracing, east-coast air with him as he entered. Having shaken hands with each of us, he was about to sit down, when his eye rested upon the paper with the curious markings, which I had just examined and left upon the table.

'Well, Mr Holmes, what do you make of these?' he cried. 'They told me that you were fond of queer mysteries, and I don't think you can find a queerer one than that. I sent the paper on ahead so that you might have time to study it before I came.'

'It is certainly rather a curious production,' said Holmes. 'At first sight it would appear to be some childish prank. It consists of a number of absurd little figures dancing across the paper upon which they are drawn. Why should you attribute any importance to so grotesque an object?'

'I never should, Mr Holmes. But my wife does. It is frightening her to death. She says nothing, but I can see terror in her eyes. That's why I want to sift the matter to the bottom.'

Holmes held up the paper so that the sunlight shone full upon it. It was a page torn from a note-book. The markings were done in pencil, and ran in this way:

Holmes examined it for some time, and then, folding it carefully up, he placed it in his pocket-book.

'This promises to be a most interesting and unusual case,' said he. 'You gave me a few particulars in your letter, Mr Hilton Cubitt, but I should be very much obliged if you would kindly go over it all again for the benefit of my friend, Dr Watson.'

'I'm not much of a story-teller,' said our visitor, nervously clasping and unclasping his great, strong hands. 'You'll just ask me anything that I don't make clear. I'll begin at the time of my marriage last year; but I want to say first of all that, though I'm not a rich man, my people have been at Ridling Thorpe for a matter of five centuries, and there is no better-known family in the county of Norfolk. Last year I came up to London for the Jubilee,* and I stopped at a boarding-house in Russell Square, because Parker, the vicar of our parish, was staying in it. There was an American young lady there—Patrick was the name—Elsie Patrick. In some way we became friends, until before my month was up I was as much in love as a man could be. We were quietly married at a registry office, and we returned to Norfolk a wedded couple. You'll think it very mad, Mr Holmes, that a man of a good old family should marry a wife in this fashion, knowing nothing of her past or of her people; but if you saw her and knew her it would help you to understand.

'She was very straight about it, was Elsie. I can't say that she did not give me every chance of getting out of it if I wished to do so. "I have had some very disagreeable associations in my life," said she; "I wish to forget all about them. I would rather never allude to the past, for it is very painful to me. If you take me, Hilton,* you will take a woman who has nothing that she need be personally ashamed of; but you will have to be content with my word for it, and to allow me to be silent as to all that passed up to the time when I became yours. If these conditions are too hard, then go back to Norfolk and leave me to the lonely life in which you found me." It was only the day before our wedding that she said those very words to me. I told her that I was content to take her on her own terms, and I have been as good as my word.

'Well, we have been married now for a year, and very happy we have been. But about a month ago, at the end of June, I saw for the first time signs of trouble. One day my wife received a letter from America. I saw the American stamp. She turned deadly white, read the letter, and threw it into the fire. She made no allusion to it afterwards and I made none, for a promise is a promise; but she has never known an easy hour from that moment. There is always a look of fear upon her face—a look as if she were waiting and expecting. She would do better to trust me. She would find that I was her best friend. But until she speaks I can say nothing. Mind you, she is a truthful woman, Mr Holmes, and whatever trouble there may have been in her past life, it has been no fault of hers. I am only a simple Norfolk squire, but there is not a man in England who ranks his family honour more highly than I do. She knows it well, and she knew it well before she married me. She would never bring any stain upon it—of that I am sure.

'Well, now I come to the queer part of my story. About a week ago—it was the Tuesday of last week—I found on one of the window-sills a number of absurd little dancing figures, like these upon the paper. They were scrawled with chalk. I thought that it was the stable-boy who had drawn them, but the lad swore he knew nothing about it. Anyhow, they had come there during the night. I had them washed out, and I only mentioned the matter to my wife afterwards. To my surprise she took it very seriously, and begged me if any more came to let her see them. None did come for a week, and then yesterday morning I found this paper lying on the sun-dial in the garden. I showed it to Elsie, and down she dropped in a dead faint. Since then she has looked like a woman in a dream, half dazed, and with terror always lurking in her eyes. It was then that I wrote and sent the paper to you, Mr Holmes. It was not a thing that I could take to the police, for they would have laughed at me, but you will tell me what to do. I am not a rich man; but if there is any danger threatening my little woman, I would spend my last copper to shield her.'

He was a fine creature, this man of the old English soil, simple, straight and gentle, with his great, earnest, blue eyes and broad, comely face. His love for his wife and his trust in her shone in his features. Holmes had listened to his story with the utmost attention, and now he sat for some time in silent thought.

'Don't you think, Mr Cubitt,' said he at last, 'that your best plan would be to make a direct appeal to your wife, and to ask her to share her secret with you?'

Hilton Cubitt shook his massive head.

'A promise is a promise, Mr Holmes. If Elsie wished to tell me, she would. If not, it is not for me to force her confidence. But I am justified in taking my own line—and I will.'

'Then I will help you with all my heart. In the first place, have you heard of any strangers being seen in your neighbourhood?'

'No.'

'I presume that it is a very quiet place. Any fresh face would cause comment?'

'In the immediate neighbourhood, yes. But we have several small watering-places not very far away. And the farmers take in lodgers.'

'These hieroglyphics have evidently a meaning. If it is a purely arbitrary one, it may be impossible for us to solve it. If, on the other hand, it is systematic, I have no doubt that we shall get to the bottom of it. But this particular sample is so short that I can do nothing, and the facts which you have brought me are so indefinite that we have no basis for an investigation. I would suggest that you return to Norfolk, that you keep a keen look-out, and that you take an exact copy of any fresh dancing men which may appear. It is a thousand pities that we have not a reproduction of those which were done in chalk upon the window-sill. Make a discreet inquiry, also, as to any strangers in the neighbourhood. When you have collected some fresh evidence, come to me again. That is the best advice which I can give you, Mr Hilton Cubitt. If there are any pressing fresh developments, I shall be always ready to run down and see you in your Norfolk home.'

The interview left Sherlock Holmes very thoughtful, and several times in the next few days I saw him take his slip of paper from his note-book and look long and earnestly at the curious figures inscribed upon it. He made no allusion to the affair, however, until one afternoon a fortnight or so later. I was going out, when he called me back.

'You had better stay here, Watson.'

'Why?'

'Because I had a wire from Hilton Cubitt this morning—you remember Hilton Cubitt, of the dancing men? He was to reach Liverpool Street at one-twenty. He may be here at any moment. I gather from his wire that there have been some new incidents of importance.'

We had not long to wait, for our Norfolk squire came straight from the station as fast as a hansom could bring him. He was looking worried and depressed, with tired eyes and a lined forehead.

'It's getting on my nerves, this business, Mr Holmes,' said he, as he sank, like a wearied man, into an arm-chair. 'It's bad enough to feel that you are surrounded by unseen, unknown folk who have some kind of design upon you; but when, in addition to that, you know that it is just killing your wife by inches, then it becomes as much as flesh and blood can endure. She's wearing away under it—just wearing away before my eyes.'

'Has she said anything yet?'

'No, Mr Holmes, she has not. And yet there have been times when the poor girl has wanted to speak, and yet could not quite bring herself to take the plunge. I have tried to help her; but I dare say I did it clumsily, and scared her off from it. She has spoken about my old family, and our reputation in the county, and our pride in our unsullied honour, and I always felt it was leading to the point; but somehow it turned off before we got there.'

'But you have found out something for yourself?'

'A good deal, Mr Holmes. I have several fresh dancing men pictures for you to examine, and, what is more important, I have seen the fellow.'

'What—the man who draws them?'

'Yes, I saw him at his work. But I will tell you everything in order. When I got back after my visit to you, the very first thing I saw next morning was a fresh crop of dancing men. They had been drawn in chalk upon the black wooden door of the tool-house, which stands beside the lawn in full view of the front windows. I took an exact copy, and here it is.' He unfolded a paper and laid it upon the table. Here is a copy of the hieroglyphics:

'Excellent!' said Holmes. 'Excellent! Pray continue.'

'When I had taken the copy I rubbed out the marks; but two mornings later a fresh inscription had appeared. I have a copy of it here':

Holmes rubbed his hands and chuckled with delight.

'Our material is rapidly accumulating,' said he.

'Three days later a message was left scrawled upon paper, and placed under a pebble upon the sun-dial. Here it is. The characters are, as you see, exactly the same as the last one. After that I determined to lie in wait; so I got out my revolver and I sat up in my study, which overlooks the lawn and garden. About two in the morning I was seated by the window, all being dark save for the moonlight outside, when I heard steps behind me, and there was my wife in her dressing-gown. She implored me to come to bed. I told her frankly that I wished to see who it was who played such absurd tricks upon us. She answered that it was some senseless practical joke, and that I should not take any notice of it.

'"If it really annoys you, Hilton, we might go and travel, you and I, and so avoid this nuisance."

'"What, be driven out of our own house by a practical joker?" said I. "Why, we should have the whole county laughing at us!"

'"Well, come to bed," said she, "and we can discuss it in the morning."

'Suddenly, as she spoke, I saw her white face grow whiter yet in the moonlight, and her hand tightened upon my shoulder. Something was moving in the shadow of the tool-house. I saw a dark, creeping figure which crawled round the corner and squatted in front of the door. Seizing my pistol I was rushing out, when my wife threw her arms round me and held me with convulsive strength. I tried to throw her off, but she clung to me most desperately. At last I got clear, but by the time I had opened the door and reached the house the creature was gone. He had left a trace of his presence, however, for there on the door was the very same arrangement of dancing men which had already twice appeared, and which I have copied on that paper. There was no other sign of the fellow anywhere, though I ran all over the grounds. And yet the amazing thing is that he must have been there

all the time, for when I examined the door again in the morning he
had scrawled some more of his pictures under the line which I had
already seen.'

'Have you that fresh drawing?'

'Yes; it is very short, but I made a copy of it, and here it is.'

Again he produced a paper. The new dance was in this form:

'Tell me,' said Holmes—and I could see by his eyes that he was
much excited— 'was this a mere addition to the first, or did it appear
to be entirely separate?'

'It was on a different panel of the door.'

'Excellent! This is far the most important of all for our purpose.
It fills me with hopes. Now, Mr Hilton Cubitt, please continue your
most interesting statement.'

'I have nothing more to say, Mr Holmes, except that I was angry
with my wife that night for having held me back when I might have
caught the skulking rascal. She said that she feared that I might come
to harm. For an instant it had crossed my mind that perhaps what she
really feared was that *he* might come to harm, for I could not doubt
that she knew who this man was and what he meant by these strange
signals. But there is a tone in my wife's voice, Mr Holmes, and a look
in her eyes which forbid doubt, and I am sure that it was indeed my
own safety that was in her mind. There's the whole case, and now
I want your advice as to what I ought to do. My own inclination is
to put half a dozen of my farm lads in the shrubbery, and when this
fellow comes again to give him such a hiding that he will leave us in
peace for the future.'

'I fear it is too deep a case for such simple remedies,' said Holmes.
'How long can you stop in London?'

'I must go back to-day. I would not leave my wife alone at night for
anything. She is very nervous and begged me to come back.'

'I dare say you are right. But if you could have stopped I might
possibly have been able to return with you in a day or two. Meanwhile,
you will leave me these papers, and I think that it is very likely that
I shall be able to pay you a visit shortly and to throw some light upon
your case.'

Sherlock Holmes preserved his calm professional manner until our visitor had left us, although it was easy for me, who knew him so well, to see that he was profoundly excited. The moment that Hilton Cubitt's broad back had disappeared through the door my comrade rushed to the table, laid out all the slips of paper containing dancing men in front of him, and threw himself into an intricate and elaborate calculation.

For two hours I watched him as he covered sheet after sheet of paper with figures and letters, so completely absorbed in his task that he had evidently forgotten my presence. Sometimes he was making progress, and whistled and sang at his work; sometimes he was puzzled and would sit for a long spell with a furrowed brow and a vacant eye. Finally he sprang from his chair with a cry of satisfaction, and walked up and down the room rubbing his hands together. Then he wrote a long telegram upon a cable form. 'If my answer to this is as I hope, you will have a very pretty case to add to your collection, Watson,' said he. 'I expect that we shall be able to go down to Norfolk to-morrow, and to take our friend some very definite news as to the secret of his annoyance.'

I confess that I was filled with curiosity, but I was aware that Holmes liked to make his disclosures at his own time and in his own way; so I waited until it should suit him to take me into his confidence.

But there was a delay in that answering telegram, and two days of impatience followed, during which Holmes pricked up his ears at every ring of the bell. On the evening of the second there came a letter from Hilton Cubitt. All was quiet with him, save that a long inscription had appeared that morning upon the pedestal of the sundial. He enclosed a copy of it, which is here reproduced:

Holmes bent over this grotesque frieze for some minutes and then suddenly sprang to his feet with an exclamation of surprise and dismay. His face was haggard with anxiety.

'We have let this affair go far enough,' said he. 'Is there a train to North Walsham to-night?'

I turned up the time-table. The last had just gone.

'Then we shall breakfast early and take the very first in the morning,' said Holmes. 'Our presence is most urgently needed. Ah, here is our expected cablegram.* One moment, Mrs Hudson—there may be an answer. No, that is quite as I expected. This message makes it even more essential that we should not lose an hour in letting Hilton Cubitt know how matters stand, for it is a singular and dangerous web in which our simple Norfolk squire is entangled.'

So, indeed, it proved, and as I come to the dark conclusion of a story which had seemed to me to be only childish and bizarre, I experience once again the dismay and horror with which I was filled. Would that I had some brighter ending to communicate to my readers; but these are the chronicles of facts, and I must follow to their dark crisis the strange chain of events which for some days made Ridling Thorpe Manor a household word through the length and breadth of England.

We had hardly alighted at North Walsham, and mentioned the name of our destination, when the station-master hurried towards us. 'I suppose that you are the detectives from London?' said he.

A look of annoyance passed over Holmes's face.

'What makes you think such a thing?'

'Because Inspector Martin from Norwich has just passed through. But maybe you are the surgeons. She's not dead—or wasn't by last accounts. You may be in time to save her yet—though it be for the gallows.'

Holmes's brow was dark with anxiety.

'We are going to Ridling Thorpe Manor,' said he, 'but we have heard nothing of what has passed there.'

'It's a terrible business,' said the station-master. 'They are shot, both Mr Hilton Cubitt and his wife. She shot him and then herself—so the servants say. He's dead, and her life is despaired of. Dear, dear! one of the oldest families in the county of Norfolk, and one of the most honoured.'

Without a word Holmes hurried to a carriage, and during the long, seven-miles drive he never opened his mouth. Seldom have I seen him so utterly despondent. He had been uneasy during all our journey from town, and I had observed that he had turned over the morning papers with anxious attention; but now this sudden realization of his worst fears left him in a blank melancholy. He leaned back in his seat, lost in gloomy speculation. Yet there was much around us to interest us, for we were passing through as singular a country-side as any in England, where a few scattered cottages represented the population of today, while on every hand enormous square-towered churches bristled up from the flat, green landscape and told of the glory and prosperity of old East Anglia.* At last the violet rim of the German Ocean* appeared over the green edge of the Norfolk coast, and the driver pointed with his whip to two old brick and timber gables which projected from a grove of trees. 'That's Ridling Thorpe Manor,' said he.

As we drove up to the porticoed front door I observed in front of it, beside the tennis lawn, the black tool-house and the pedestalled sun-dial with which we had such strange associations. A dapper little man, with a quick, alert manner and a waxed moustache, had just descended from a high dog-cart.* He introduced himself as Inspector Martin, of the Norfolk Constabulary, and he was considerably astonished when he heard the name of my companion.

'Why, Mr Holmes, the crime was only committed at three this morning! How could you hear of it in London and get to the spot as soon as I?'

'I anticipated it. I came in the hope of preventing it.'

'Then you must have important evidence of which we are ignorant, for they were said to be a most united couple.'

'I have only the evidence of the dancing men,' said Holmes. 'I will explain the matter to you later. Meanwhile, since it is too late to prevent this tragedy, I am very anxious that I should use the knowledge which I possess in order to ensure that justice be done. Will you associate me in your investigation, or will you prefer that I should act independently?'

'I should be proud to feel that we were acting together, Mr Holmes,' said the inspector earnestly.

'In that case I should be glad to hear the evidence and to examine the premises without an instant of unnecessary delay.'

Inspector Martin had the good sense to allow my friend to do things in his own fashion, and contented himself with carefully noting the results. The local surgeon, an old, white-haired man, had just come down from Mrs Hilton Cubitt's room, and he reported that her injuries were serious, but not necessarily fatal. The bullet had passed through the front of her brain, and it would probably be some time before she could regain consciousness. On the question of whether she had been shot or had shot herself he would not venture to express any decided opinion. Certainly the bullet had been discharged at very close quarters. There was only the one pistol found in the room, two barrels of which had been emptied. Mr Hilton Cubitt had been shot through the heart. It was equally conceivable that he had shot her and then himself, or that she had been the criminal, for the revolver lay upon the floor midway between them.

'Has he been moved?' asked Holmes.

'We have moved nothing except the lady. We could not leave her lying wounded upon the floor.'

'How long have you been here, doctor?'

'Since four o'clock.'

'Anyone else?'

'Yes, the constable here.'

'And you have touched nothing?'

'Nothing.'

'You have acted with great discretion. Who sent for you?'

'The housemaid, Saunders.'

'Was it she who gave the alarm?'

'She and Mrs King, the cook.'

'Where are they now?'

'In the kitchen, I believe.'

'Then I think we had better hear their story at once.'

The old hall, oak-panelled and high-windowed, had been turned into a court of investigation. Holmes sat in a great, old-fashioned chair, his inexorable eyes gleaming out of his haggard face. I could read in them a set purpose to devote his life to this quest until the client whom he had failed to save should at last be avenged. The trim Inspector Martin, the old grey-headed country doctor, myself and a stolid village policeman made up the rest of that strange company.

The two women told their story clearly enough. They had been aroused from their sleep by the sound of an explosion, which had been followed a minute later by a second one. They slept in adjoining rooms, and Mrs King had rushed in to Saunders. Together they had descended the stairs. The door of the study was open and a candle was burning upon the table. Their master lay upon his face in the centre of the room. He was quite dead. Near the window his wife was crouching, her head leaning against the wall. She was horribly wounded, and the side of her face was red with blood. She breathed heavily, but was incapable of saying anything. The passage, as well as the room, was full of smoke and the smell of powder. The window was certainly shut and fastened upon the inside. Both women were positive upon the point. They had at once sent for the doctor and for the constable. Then, with the aid of the groom and the stable-boy, they had conveyed their injured mistress to her room. Both she and her husband had occupied the bed. She was clad in her dress—he in his dressing-gown, over his night-clothes. Nothing had been moved in the study. So far as they knew, there had never been any quarrel between husband and wife. They had always looked upon them as a very united couple.

These were the main points of the servants' evidence. In answer to Inspector Martin they were clear that every door was fastened upon the inside and that no one could have escaped from the house. In answer to Holmes, they both remembered that they were conscious of the smell of powder from the moment that they ran out of their rooms upon the top floor. 'I commend that fact very carefully to your attention,' said Holmes to his professional colleague. 'And now I think that we are in a position to undertake a thorough examination of the room.'

The study proved to be a small chamber, lined on three sides with books, and with a writing-table facing an ordinary window, which looked out upon the garden. Our first attention was given to the body of the unfortunate squire, whose huge frame lay stretched across the room. His disordered dress showed that he had been hastily aroused from sleep. The bullet had been fired at him from the front, and had remained in his body after penetrating the heart. His death had certainly been instantaneous and painless. There was no powder-marking either upon his dressing-gown or on his hands. According to the country surgeon, the lady had stains upon her face, but none upon her hand.

'The absence of the latter means nothing, though its presence may mean everything,' said Holmes. 'Unless the powder from a badly fitting cartridge happens to spurt backwards, one may fire many shots without leaving a sign. I would suggest that Mr Cubitt's body may now be removed. I suppose, doctor, you have not recovered the bullet which wounded the lady?'

'A serious operation will be necessary before that can be done. But there are still four cartridges in the revolver. Two have been fired and two wounds inflicted, so that each bullet can be accounted for.'

'So it would seem,' said Holmes. 'Perhaps you can account also for the bullet which has so obviously struck the edge of the window?'

He had turned suddenly, and his long, thin finger was pointing to a hole which had been drilled right through the lower window-sash about an inch above the bottom.

'By George!' cried the inspector. 'How ever did you see that?'

'Because I looked for it.'

'Wonderful!' said the country doctor. 'You are certainly right, sir. Then a third shot has been fired, and therefore a third person must have been present. But who could that have been, and how could he have got away?'

'That is the problem which we are now about to solve,' said Sherlock Holmes. 'You remember, Inspector Martin, when the servants said that on leaving their room they were at once conscious of a smell of powder, I remarked that the point was an extremely important one?'

'Yes, sir; but I confess I did not quite follow you.'

'It suggested that at the time of the firing the window as well as the door of the room had been open. Otherwise the fumes of powder could not have been blown so rapidly through the house. A draught in the room was necessary for that. Both door and window were only open for a short time, however.'

'How do you prove that?'

'Because the candle has not guttered.'

'Capital!' cried the inspector. 'Capital!'

'Feeling sure that the window had been open at the time of the tragedy, I conceived that there might have been a third person in the affair, who stood outside this opening and fired through it. Any shot directed at this person might hit the sash. I looked, and there, sure enough, was the bullet mark!'

'But how came the window to be shut and fastened?'

'The woman's first instinct would be to shut and fasten the window. But, hullo! what is this?'

It was a lady's hand-bag which stood upon the study table— a trim little hand-bag of crocodile-skin and silver. Holmes opened it and turned the contents out. There were twenty fifty-pound notes of the Bank of England, held together by an India-rubber band— nothing else.

'This must be preserved, for it will figure in the trial,' said Holmes, as he handed the bag with its contents to the inspector. 'It is now necessary that we should try to throw some light upon this third bullet, which has clearly, from the splintering of the wood, been fired from inside the room. I should like to see Mrs King, the cook, again . . . You said, Mrs King, that you were awakened by a *loud* explosion. When you said that, did you mean that it seemed to you to be louder than the second one?'

'Well, sir, it wakened me from my sleep, and so it is hard to judge. But it did seem very loud.'

'You don't think that it might have been two shots fired almost at the same instant?'

'I am sure I couldn't say, sir.'

'I believe that it was undoubtedly so. I rather think, Inspector Martin, that we have now exhausted all that this room can teach us. If you will kindly step round with me we shall see what fresh evidence the garden has to offer.'

A flower-bed extended up to the study window, and we all broke into an exclamation as we approached it. The flowers were trampled down, and the soft soil was imprinted all over with footmarks. Large, masculine feet they were, with peculiarly long, sharp toes. Holmes hunted about among the grass and leaves like a retriever after a wounded bird. Then, with a cry of satisfaction, he bent forward and picked up a little brazen cylinder.

'I thought so,' said he; 'the revolver had an ejector, and here is the third cartridge. I really think, Inspector Martin, that our case is almost complete.'

The country inspector's face had shown his intense amazement at the rapid and masterful progress of Holmes's investigations. At first he had shown some disposition to assert his own position; but now he was overcome with admiration, and ready to follow without question wherever Holmes led.

'Whom do you suspect?' he asked.

'I'll go into that later. There are several points in this problem which I have not been able to explain to you yet. Now that I have got so far I had best proceed on my own lines, and then clear the whole matter up once and for all.'

'Just as you wish, Mr Holmes, so long as we get our man.'

'I have no desire to make mysteries, but it is impossible at the moment of action to enter into long and complex explanations. I have the threads of this affair all in my hand. Even if this lady should never recover consciousness we can still reconstruct the events of last night and ensure that justice be done. First of all I wish to know whether there is any inn in this neighbourhood known as "Elrige's?" '

The servants were cross-questioned, but none of them had heard of such a place. The stable-boy threw a light upon the matter by remembering that a farmer of that name lived some miles off in the direction of East Ruston.

'Is it a lonely farm?'

'Very lonely, sir.'

'Perhaps they have not heard yet of all that happened here during the night?'

'Maybe not, sir.'

Holmes thought for a little, and then a curious smile played over his face.

'Saddle a horse, my lad,' said he. 'I shall wish you to take a note to Elrige's Farm.'

He took from his pocket the various slips of the dancing men. With these in front of him he worked for some time at the study-table. Finally he handed a note to the boy, with directions to put it into the hands of the person to whom it was addressed, and especially to answer no questions of any sort which might be put to him. I saw the outside of the note, addressed in straggling, irregular characters, very unlike Holmes's usual precise hand. It was consigned to Mr Abe Slaney, Elrige's Farm, East Ruston, Norfolk.

'I think, Inspector,' Holmes remarked, 'that you would do well to telegraph for an escort, as, if my calculations prove to be correct, you may have a particularly dangerous prisoner to convey to the county gaol. The boy who takes this note could no doubt forward your telegram. If there is an afternoon train to town, Watson, I think we should do well to take it, as I have a chemical analysis of some interest to finish, and this investigation draws rapidly to a close.'

When the youth had been dispatched with the note, Sherlock Holmes gave his instructions to the servants. If any visitor were to call asking for Mrs Hilton Cubitt no information should be given as to her condition, but he was to be shown at once into the drawing-room. He impressed these points upon them with the utmost earnestness. Finally he led the way into the drawing-room, with the remark that the business was now out of our hands, and that we must while away the time as best we might until we could see what was in store for us.

The doctor had departed to his patients, and only the inspector and myself remained.

'I think I can help you to pass an hour in an interesting and profitable manner,' said Holmes, drawing his chair up to the table and spreading out in front of him the various papers upon which were recorded the antics of the dancing men. 'As to you, friend Watson, I owe you every atonement for having allowed your natural curiosity to remain so long unsatisfied. To you, inspector, the whole incident may appeal as a remarkable professional study. I must tell you first of all the interesting circumstances connected with the previous consultations which Mr Hilton Cubitt has had with me in Baker Street.' He then shortly recapitulated the facts which have already been recorded.

'I have here in front of me these singular productions, at which one might smile had they not proved themselves to be the forerunners of so terrible a tragedy. I am fairly familiar with all forms of secret writings, and am myself the author of a trifling monograph upon the subject, in which I analyse one hundred and sixty separate ciphers; but I confess that this is entirely new to me. The object of those who invented the system has apparently been to conceal that these characters convey a message, and to give the idea that they are the mere random sketches of children.

'Having once recognized, however, that the symbols stood for letters, and having applied the rules which guide us in all forms of secret writings, the solution was easy enough. The first message submitted to me was so short that it was impossible for me to do more than say with some confidence that the symbol X stood for E. As you are aware, E is the most common letter in the English alphabet and it predominates to so marked an extent that even in a short sentence one would expect to find it most often. Out of fifteen symbols in the first message four were the same, so it was reasonable to set this down as E. It is true that in some cases the figure was bearing a flag, and in some cases not, but it was probable from the way in which the flags were distributed that they were used to break the sentence up into words. I accepted this as an hypothesis, and noted that E was represented by

'But now came the real difficulty of the inquiry. The order of the English letters after E is by no means well marked, and any

preponderance which may be shown in an average of a printed sheet may be reversed in a single short sentence. Speaking roughly, T, A, O, I, N, S, H, R, D, and L are the numerical order in which letters occur;* but T, A, O, and I are very nearly abreast of each other, and it would be an endless task to try each combination until a meaning was arrived at. I, therefore, waited for fresh material. In my second interview with Mr Hilton Cubitt he was able to give me two other short sentences and one message, which appeared—since there was no flag—to be a single word. Here are the symbols:

Now, in the single word I have already got the two E's coming second and fourth in a word of five letters. It might be "sever", or "lever", or "never". There can be no question that the latter as a reply to an appeal is far the most probable, and the circumstances pointed to its being a reply written by the lady. Accepting it as correct we are now able to say that the symbols

stand respectively for N, V, and R.

'Even now I was in considerable difficulty, but a happy thought put me in possession of several other letters. It occurred to me that if these appeals came, as I expected, from someone who had been intimate with the lady in her early life, a combination which contained two E's with three letters between might very well stand for the name "ELSIE". On examination I found that such a combination formed the termination of the message which was three times repeated. It was certainly some appeal to "Elsie". In this way I had got my L, S, and I. But what appeal could it be? There were only four letters in the word which preceded "Elsie", and it ended in E. Surely the word must be "COME". I tried all other four letters ending in E, but could find none to fit the case. So now I was in possession of C, O, and M, and I was in a position to attack the first message once more, dividing it into words and putting dots for each symbol which was still unknown. So treated it worked out in this fashion:

.M .ERE ..E SL.NE.

Now, the first letter can only be A, which is a most useful discovery, since it occurs no fewer than three times in this short sentence, and the H is also apparent in the second word. Now it becomes:

AM HERE A.E SLANE.

Or, filling in the obvious vacancies in the name:

AM HERE ABE SLANEY

I had so many letters now that I could proceed with considerable confidence to the second message, which worked out in this fashion:

A. ELRI.ES

Here I could only make sense by putting T and G for the missing letters, and supposing that the name was that of some house or inn at which the writer was staying.'

Inspector Martin and I had listened with the utmost interest to the full and clear account of how my friend had produced results which had led to so complete a command over our difficulties.

'What did you do then, sir?' asked the inspector.

'I had every reason to suppose that this Abe Slaney was an American, since Abe is an American contraction, and since a letter from America had been the starting-point of all the trouble. I had also every cause to think that there was some criminal secret in the matter. The lady's allusions to her past and her refusal to take her husband into her confidence both pointed in that direction. I therefore cabled to my friend, Wilson Hargreave, of the New York Police Bureau, who has more than once made use of my knowledge of London crime. I asked him whether the name of Abe Slaney was known to him. Here is his reply: "The most dangerous crook in Chicago." On the very evening upon which I had his answer Hilton Cubitt sent me the last message from Slaney. Working with known letters it took this form:

ELSIE .RE.ARE TO MEET THY GO.

The addition of a P and a D completed a message which showed me that the rascal was proceeding from persuasion to threats, and my knowledge of the crooks of Chicago prepared me to find that he might very rapidly put his words into action. I at once came to Norfolk with my friend and colleague, Dr Watson, but, unhappily, only in time to find that the worst had already occurred.'

'It is a privilege to be associated with you in the handling of a case,' said the inspector warmly. 'You will excuse me, however, if I speak frankly to you. You are only answerable to yourself, but I have to answer to my superiors. If this Abe Slaney, living at Elrige's, is indeed the murderer, and if he has made his escape while I am seated here, I should certainly get into serious trouble.'

'You need not be uneasy. He will not try to escape.'

'How do you know?'

'To fly would be a confession of guilt.'

'Then let us go to arrest him.'

'I expect him here every instant.'

'But why should he come?'

'Because I have written and asked him.'

'But this is incredible, Mr Holmes! Why should he come because you have asked him? Would not such a request rather rouse his suspicions and cause him to fly?'

'I think I have known how to frame the letter,' said Sherlock Holmes. 'In fact, if I am not very much mistaken, here is the gentleman himself coming up the drive.'

A man was striding up the path which led to the door. He was a tall, handsome, swarthy fellow, clad in a suit of grey flannel, with a Panama hat, a bristling black beard and a great, aggressive, hooked nose, and flourishing a cane as he walked. He swaggered up the path as if the place belonged to him, and we heard his loud, confident peal at the bell.

'I think, gentlemen,' said Holmes quietly, 'that we had best take up our position behind the door. Every precaution is necessary when dealing with such a fellow. You will need your handcuffs, Inspector. You can leave the talking to me.'

We waited in silence for a minute—one of those minutes which one can never forget. Then the door opened, and the man stepped in. In an instant Holmes clapped a pistol to his head, and Martin slipped the handcuffs over his wrists. It was all done so swiftly and deftly that the fellow was helpless before he knew that he was attacked. He glared from one to the other of us with a pair of blazing black eyes. Then he burst into a bitter laugh.

'Well, gentlemen, you have the drop on me this time. I seem to have knocked up against something hard. But I came here in answer to a letter from Mrs Hilton Cubitt. Don't tell me that she is in this? Don't tell me that she helped to set a trap for me?'

'Mrs Hilton Cubitt was seriously injured, and is at death's door.'

The man gave a hoarse cry of grief which rang through the house.

'You're crazy!' he cried fiercely. 'It was he that was hurt, not she. Who would have hurt little Elsie? I may have threatened her, God forgive me, but I would not have touched a hair of her pretty head. Take it back—you! Say that she is not hurt!'

'She was found badly wounded by the side of her dead husband.'

He sank with a deep groan on to the settee, and buried his face in his manacled hands. For five minutes he was silent. Then he raised his face once more, and spoke with the cold composure of despair.

'I have nothing to hide from you, gentlemen,' said he. 'If I shot the man he had his shot at me, and there's no murder in that. But if you think I could have hurt that woman, then you don't know either me or her. I tell you there was never a man in this world loved a woman more than I loved her. I had a right to her. She was pledged to me years ago. Who was this Englishman that he should come between us? I tell you that I had the first right to her, and that I was only claiming my own.'

'She broke away from your influence when she found the man that you are,' said Holmes sternly. 'She fled from America to avoid you, and she married an honourable gentleman in England. You dogged her and followed her, and made her life a misery to her in order to induce her to abandon the husband whom she loved and respected in order to fly with you, whom she feared and hated. You have ended by bringing about the death of a noble man and driving his wife to suicide. That is your record in this business, Mr Abe Slaney, and you will answer for it to the law.'

'If Elsie dies I care nothing what becomes of me,' said the American. He opened one of his hands and looked at a note crumpled up in his palm. 'See here, mister,' he cried, with a gleam of suspicion in his eyes, 'you're not trying to scare me over this, are you? If the lady is hurt as bad as you say, who was it that wrote this note?' He tossed it forward on to the table.

'I wrote it to bring you here.'

'You wrote it? There was no one on earth outside the Joint* who knew the secret of the dancing men. How came you to write it?'

'What one man can invent another can discover,' said Holmes. 'There is a cab coming to convey you to Norwich, Mr Slaney. But, meanwhile, you have time to make some small reparation for the injury you have wrought. Are you aware that Mrs Hilton Cubitt has herself lain under grave suspicion of the murder of her husband, and that it was only my presence here and the knowledge which I happened to possess which has saved her from the accusation? The least that you owe her is to make it clear to the whole world that she was in no way, directly or indirectly, responsible for his tragic end.'

'I ask nothing better,' said the American. 'I guess the very best case I can make for myself is the absolute naked truth.'

'It is my duty to warn you that it will be used against you,' cried the inspector, with the magnificent fair-play of the British criminal law.

Slaney shrugged his shoulders.

'I'll chance that,' said he. 'First of all, I want you gentlemen to understand that I have known this lady since she was a child. There were seven of us in a gang in Chicago, and Elsie's father was the boss of the Joint. He was a clever man, was old Patrick. It was he who invented that writing, which would pass as a child's scrawl unless you just happened to have the key to it. Well, Elsie learned some of our ways; but she couldn't stand the business, and she had a bit of honest money of her own, so she gave us all the slip and got away to London. She had been engaged to me, and she would have married me, I believe, if I had taken over another profession; but she would have nothing to do with anything on the cross. It was only after her marriage to this Englishman that I was able to find out where she was. I wrote to her, but got no answer. After that I came over, and, as letters were of no use, I put my messages where she could read them.

'Well, I have been here a month now. I lived in that farm, where I had a room down below, and could get in and out every night, and no one the wiser. I tried all I could to coax Elsie away. I knew that she read the messages, for once she wrote an answer under one of them. Then my temper got the better of me, and I began to threaten her. She sent me a letter then, imploring me to go away, and saying that it would break her heart if any scandal should come upon her husband. She said that she would come down when her husband was asleep at three in the morning, and speak with me through the end window, if I would go away afterwards and leave her in peace. She came down and brought money with her, trying to bribe me to go. This made me mad, and I caught her arm and tried to pull her through the window. At that moment in rushed the husband with his revolver in his hand. Elsie had sunk down upon the floor, and we were face to face. I was heeled also, and I held up my gun to scare him off and let me get away. He fired and missed me. I pulled off almost at the same instant, and down he dropped. I made away across the garden, and as I went I heard the window shut behind me. That's God truth, gentlemen, every word of it, and I heard no more about it until that lad came riding up with a note which made me walk in here, like a jay, and give myself into your hands.'

A cab had driven up whilst the American had been talking. Two uniformed policemen sat inside. Inspector Martin rose and touched his prisoner on the shoulder.

'It is time for us to go.'

'Can I see her first?'

'No, she is not conscious. Mr Sherlock Holmes, I only hope that if ever again I have an important case I shall have the good fortune to have you by my side.'

We stood at the window and watched the cab drive away. As I turned back my eye caught the pellet of paper which the prisoner had tossed upon the table. It was the note with which Holmes had decoyed him.

'See if you can read it, Watson,' said he, with a smile.

It contained no word, but this little line of dancing men:

'If you use the code which I have explained,' said Holmes, 'you will find that it simply means "Come here at once." I was convinced that it was an invitation which he would not refuse, since he could never imagine that it could come from anyone but the lady. And so, my dear Watson, we have ended by turning the dancing men to good when they have so often been the agents of evil, and I think that I have fulfilled my promise of giving you something unusual for your note-book. Three-forty is our train, and I fancy we should be back in Baker Street for dinner.'

*

Only one word of epilogue. The American, Abe Slaney, was condemned to death at the winter assizes* at Norwich; but his penalty was changed to penal servitude in consideration of mitigating circumstances, and the certainty that Hilton Cubitt had fired the first shot. Of Mrs Hilton Cubitt I only know that I have heard she recovered entirely, and that she still remains a widow, devoting her whole life to the care of the poor and to the administration of her husband's estate.

THE SIX NAPOLEONS

It was no very unusual thing for Mr Lestrade, of Scotland Yard, to look in upon us of an evening, and his visits were welcome to Sherlock Holmes, for they enabled him to keep in touch with all that was going on at the police headquarters.* In return for the news which Lestrade would bring, Holmes was always ready to listen with attention to the details of any case upon which the detective was engaged, and was able occasionally, without any active interference, to give some hint or suggestion drawn from his own vast knowledge and experience.

On this particular evening Lestrade had spoken of the weather and the newspapers. Then he had fallen silent, puffing thoughtfully at his cigar. Holmes looked keenly at him.

'Anything remarkable on hand?' he asked.

'Oh, no, Mr Holmes, nothing very particular.'

'Then tell me all about it.'

Lestrade laughed.

'Well, Mr Holmes, there is no use denying that there *is* something on my mind. And yet it is such an absurd business that I hesitated to bother you about it. On the other hand, although it is trivial, it is undoubtedly queer, and I know that you have a taste for all that is out of the common. But in my opinion it comes more in Dr Watson's line than ours.'

'Disease?' said I.

'Madness, anyhow. And a queer madness too! You wouldn't think there was anyone living at this time of day who had such a hatred of Napoleon the First* that he would break any image of him that he could see.'

Holmes sank back in his chair.

'That's no business of mine,' said he.

'Exactly. That's what I said. But then, when the man commits burglary in order to break images which are not his own, that brings it away from the doctor and on to the policeman.'

Holmes sat up again.

'Burglary! This is more interesting. Let me hear the details.'

Lestrade took out his official note-book and refreshed his memory from its pages.

'The first case reported was four days ago,' said he. 'It was at the shop of Morse Hudson, who has a place for the sale of pictures and statues in the Kennington Road. The assistant had left the front shop for an instant, when he heard a crash, and, hurrying in found a plaster bust of Napoleon, which stood with several other works of art upon the counter, lying shivered into fragments. He rushed out into the road, but, although several passers-by declared that they had noticed a man run out of the shop, he could neither see anyone nor could he find any means of identifying the rascal. It seemed to be one of those senseless acts of hooliganism which occur from time to time, and it was reported to the constable on the beat as such. The plaster cast was not worth more than a few shillings, and the whole affair appeared to be too childish for any particular investigation.

'The second case, however, was more serious and also more singular. It occurred only last night.

'In Kennington Road, and within a few hundred yards of Morse Hudson's shop, there lives a well-known medical practitioner, named Dr Barnicot, who has one of the largest practices upon the south side of the Thames. His residence and principal consulting-room is at Kennington Road, but he has a branch surgery and dispensary at Lower Brixton Road,* two miles away. This Dr Barnicot is an enthu-siastic admirer of Napoleon, and his house is full of books, pictures, and relics of the French Emperor. Some little time ago he purchased from Morse Hudson two duplicate plaster casts of the famous head of Napoleon by the French sculptor Devine.* One of these he placed in his hall in the house at Kennington Road, and the other on the mantelpiece of the surgery at Lower Brixton. Well, when Dr Barnicot came down this morning he was astonished to find that his house had been burgled during the night, but that nothing had been taken save the plaster head from the hall. It had been carried out, and had been dashed savagely against the garden wall, under which its splintered fragments were discovered.'

Holmes rubbed his hands.

'This is certainly very novel,' said he.

'I thought it would please you. But I have not got to the end yet. Dr Barnicot was due at his surgery at twelve o'clock, and you can imagine his amazement when, on arriving there, he found that the window had been opened in the night, and that the broken pieces of his second bust were strewn all over the room. It had been smashed to atoms where it stood. In neither case were there any signs which could give us a clue as to the criminal or lunatic who had done the mischief. Now, Mr Holmes, you have got the facts.'

'They are singular, not to say grotesque,' said Holmes. 'May I ask whether the two busts smashed in Dr Barnicot's rooms were the exact duplicates of the one which was destroyed in Morse Hudson's shop?'

'They were taken from the same mould.'

'Such a fact must tell against the theory that the man who breaks them is influenced by any general hatred of Napoleon. Considering how many hundreds of statues of the great Emperor must exist in London, it is too much to suppose such a coincidence as that a promiscuous iconoclast should chance to begin upon three specimens of the same bust.'

'Well, I thought as you do,' said Lestrade. 'On the other hand, this Morse Hudson is the purveyor of busts in that part of London, and these three were the only ones which had been in his shop for years. So although, as you say, there are many hundreds of statues in London, it is very probable that these three were the only ones in that district. Therefore a local fanatic would begin with them. What do you think, Dr Watson?'

'There are no limits to the possibilities of monomania,' I answered. 'There is the condition which the modern French psychologists have called the "*idée fixe*",* which may be trifling in character, and accompanied by complete sanity in every other way. A man who had read deeply about Napoleon, or who had possibly received some hereditary family injury through the great war, might conceivably form such an "*idée fixe*", and under its influence be capable of any fantastic outrage.'

'That won't do, my dear Watson,' said Holmes, shaking his head; 'for no amount of "*idée fixe*" would enable your interesting monomaniac to find out where these busts were situated.'

'Well, how you do *you* explain it?'

'I don't attempt to do so. I would only observe that there is a certain method in the gentleman's eccentric proceedings. For example, in Dr Barnicot's hall, where a sound might arouse the family, the bust was taken outside before being broken, whereas in the surgery, where there was less danger of an alarm, it was smashed where it stood. The affair seems absurdly trifling, and yet I dare call nothing trivial when

I reflect that some of my most classic cases have had the least promising commencement. You will remember, Watson, how the dreadful business of the Abernetty family was first brought to my notice by the depth which the parsley had sunk into the butter upon a hot day. I can't afford, therefore, to smile at your three broken busts, Lestrade, and I shall be very much obliged to you if you will let me hear of any fresh developments of so singular a chain of events.'

The development for which my friend had asked came in a quicker and an infinitely more tragic form than he could have imagined. I was still dressing in my bedroom next morning, when there was a tap at the door, and Holmes entered, a telegram in his hand. He read it aloud:

Come instantly, 131, Pitt Street, Kensington.* LESTRADE.

'What is it, then?' I asked.

'Don't know—may be anything. But I suspect it is the sequel of the story of the statues. In that case our friend the image-breaker has begun operations in another quarter of London. There's coffee on the table, Watson, and I have a cab at the door.'

In half an hour we had reached Pitt Street, a quiet little backwater just beside one of the briskest currents of London life. No. 131 was one of a row, all flat-chested, respectable, and most unromantic dwellings. As we drove up we found the railings in front of the house lined by a curious crowd. Holmes whistled.

'By George! it's attempted murder at the least. Nothing less will hold the London message boy. There's a deed of violence indicated in that fellow's round shoulders and outstretched neck. What's this, Watson? The top step swilled down and the other ones dry. Footsteps enough, anyhow! Well, well, there's Lestrade at the front window, and we shall soon know all about it.'

The official received us with a very grave face and showed us into a sitting-room, where an exceedingly unkempt and agitated elderly man, clad in a flannel dressing-gown, was pacing up and down. He was introduced to us as the owner of the house—Mr Horace Harker, of the Central Press Syndicate.*

'It's the Napoleon bust business again,' said Lestrade. 'You seemed interested last night, Mr Holmes, so I thought perhaps you would be glad to be present now that the affair has taken a very much graver turn.'

'What has it turned to, then?'

'To murder. Mr Harker, will you tell these gentlemen exactly what has occurred?'

The man in the dressing-gown turned upon us with a most melancholy face.

'It's an extraordinary thing,' said he, 'that all my life I have been collecting other people's news, and now that a real piece of news has come my own way I am so confused and bothered that I can't put two words together. If I had come in here as a journalist I should have interviewed myself and had two columns in every evening paper. As it is, I am giving away valuable copy by telling my story over and over to a string of different people, and I can make no use of it myself. However, I've heard your name, Mr Sherlock Holmes, and if you'll only explain this queer business I shall be paid for my trouble in telling you the story.'

Holmes sat down and listened.

'It all seems to centre round that bust of Napoleon which I bought for this very room about four months ago. I picked it up cheap from Harding Brothers, two doors from the High Street Station. A great deal of my journalistic work is done at night, and I often write until the early morning. So it was to-day. I was sitting in my den, which is at the back of the top of the house, about three o'clock, when I was convinced that I heard some sounds downstairs. I listened, but they were not repeated, and I concluded that they came from outside. Then suddenly, about five minutes later, there came a most horrible yell—the most dreadful sound, Mr Holmes, that ever I heard. It will ring in my ears as long as I live. I sat frozen with horror for a minute or two. Then I seized the poker and went downstairs. When I entered this room I found the window wide open, and I at once observed that the bust was gone from the mantelpiece. Why any burglar should take such a thing passes my understanding, for it was only a plaster cast, and of no real value whatever.

'You can see for yourself that anyone going out through that open window could reach the front doorstep by taking a long stride. This was clearly what the burglar had done, so I went round and opened the door. Stepping out into the dark I nearly fell over a dead man who was lying there. I ran back for a light, and there was the poor devil,* a great gash in his throat and the whole place swimming in blood. He lay on his back, his knees drawn up, and his mouth horribly open.

I shall see him in my dreams. I had just time to blow on my police-whistle, and then I must have fainted, for I knew nothing more until I found the policeman standing over me in the hall.'

'Well, who was the murdered man?' asked Holmes.

'There's nothing to show who he was,' said Lestrade. 'You shall see the body at the mortuary, but we have made nothing of it up to now. He is a tall man, sunburnt, very powerful, not more than thirty. He is poorly dressed, and yet does not appear to be a labourer. A horn-handled clasp-knife was lying in a pool of blood beside him. Whether it was the weapon which did the deed, or whether it belonged to the dead man, I do not know. There was no name on his clothing, and nothing in his pockets save an apple, some string, a shilling map of London, and a photograph. Here it is.'

It was evidently taken by a snap-shot from a small camera. It represented an alert, sharp-featured simian man with thick eyebrows, and a very peculiar projection of the lower part of the face like the muzzle of a baboon.

'And what became of the bust?' asked Holmes, after a careful study of this picture.

'We had news of it just before you came. It has been found in the front garden of an empty house in Campden House Road.* It was broken into fragments. I am going round now to see it. Will you come?'

'Certainly. I must just take one look round.' He examined the carpet and the window. 'The fellow had either very long legs or was a most active man,' said he. 'With an area beneath, it was no mean feat to reach that window-ledge and open that window. Getting back was comparatively simple. Are you coming with us to see the remains of your bust, Mr Harker?'

The disconsolate journalist had seated himself at a writing-table.

'I must try and make something of it,' said he, 'though I have no doubt that the first editions of the evening papers are out already with full details. It's like my luck! You remember when the stand fell at Doncaster?* Well, I was the only journalist in the stand, and my journal the only one that had no account of it, for I was too shaken to write it. And now I'll be too late with a murder done on my own doorstep.'

As we left the room we heard his pen travelling shrilly over the foolscap.

The spot where the fragments of the bust had been found was only a few hundred yards away. For the first time our eyes rested upon this presentment of the great Emperor, which seemed to raise such frantic and destructive hatred in the mind of the unknown. It lay scattered in splintered shards upon the grass. Holmes picked up several of them and examined them carefully. I was convinced from his intent face and purposeful manner that at last he was upon a clue.

'Well?' asked Lestrade.

Holmes shrugged his shoulders.

'We have a long way to go yet,' said he. 'And yet—and yet—well, we have some suggestive facts to act upon. The possession of this trifling bust was worth more in the eyes of this strange criminal than a human life. That is one point. Then there is the singular fact that he did not break it in the house, or immediately outside the house, if to break it was his sole object.'

'He was rattled and hustled by meeting this other fellow. He hardly knew what he was doing.'

'Well, that's likely enough. But I wish to call your attention very particularly to the position of this house in the garden of which the bust was destroyed.'

Lestrade looked about him.

'It was an empty house, and so he knew that he would not be disturbed in the garden.'

'Yes, but there is another empty house farther up the street which he must have passed before he came to this one. Why did he not break it there, since it is evident that every yard that he carried it increased the risk of someone meeting him?'

'I give it up,' said Lestrade.

Holmes pointed to the street-lamp above our heads.

'He could see what he was doing here, and he could not there. That was the reason.'

'By Jove! that's true,' said the detective. 'Now that I come to think of it, Dr Barnicot's bust was broken not far from his red lamp.* Well, Mr Holmes, what are we to do with that fact?'

'To remember it—to docket it.* We may come on something later which will bear upon it. What steps do you propose to take now, Lestrade?'

'The most practical way of getting at it, in my opinion, is to identify the dead man. There should be no difficulty about that. When we have found who he is and who his associates are, we should have a good start in learning what he was doing in Pitt Street last night, and who it was who met him and killed him on the doorstep of Mr Horace Harker. Don't you think so?'

'No doubt; and yet it is not quite the way in which I should approach the case.'

'What would you do then?'

'Oh, you must not let me influence you in any way. I suggest that you go on your line and I on mine. We can compare notes afterwards, and each will supplement the other.'

'Very good,' said Lestrade.

'If you are going back to Pitt Street you might see Mr Horace Harker. Tell him from me that I have quite made up my mind, and that it is certain that a dangerous homicidal lunatic with Napoleonic delusions was in his house last night. It will be useful for his article.'

Lestrade stared.

'You don't seriously believe that?'

Holmes smiled.

'Don't I? Well, perhaps I don't. But I am sure that it will interest Mr Horace Harker and the subscribers of the Central Press Syndicate. Now, Watson, I think that we shall find that we have a long and rather complex day's work before us. I should be glad, Lestrade, if you could make it convenient to meet us at Baker Street at six o'clock this evening. Until then I should like to keep this photograph found in the dead man's pocket. It is possible that I may have to ask your company and assistance upon a small expedition which will have to be undertaken to-night, if my chain of reasoning should prove to be correct. Until then, good-bye, and good luck!'

Sherlock Holmes and I walked together to the High Street, where he stopped at the shop of Harding Brothers, whence the bust had been purchased. A young assistant informed us that Mr Harding would be absent until after noon, and that he was himself a newcomer, who could give us no information. Holmes's face showed his disappointment and annoyance.

'Well, well, we can't expect to have it all our own way, Watson,' he said at last. 'We must come back in the afternoon, if Mr Harding will not be here until then. I am, as you have no doubt surmised, endeavouring to trace these busts to their source, in order to find if there is not something peculiar which may account for their remarkable fate.

Let us make for Mr Morse Hudson, of the Kennington Road, and see if he can throw any light upon the problem.'

A drive of an hour brought us to the picture-dealer's establishment. He was a small, stout man with a red face and a peppery manner.

'Yes, sir. On my very counter, sir,' said he. 'What we pay rates and taxes for I don't know, when any ruffian can come in and break one's goods. Yes, sir, it was I who sold Dr Barnicot his two statues. Disgraceful, sir! A Nihilist plot,* that's what I make it. No one but an Anarchist would go about breaking statues. Red republicans,* that's what I call 'em. Who did I get the statues from? I don't see what that has to do with it. Well, if you really want to know, I got them from Gelder & Co., in Church Street, Stepney. They are a well-known house in the trade, and have been this twenty years. How many had I? Three—two and one are three—two of Dr Barnicot's and one smashed in broad daylight on my own counter. Do I know that photograph? No, I don't. Yes, I do though. Why, it's Beppo!* He was a kind of Italian piece-work man, who made himself useful in the shop. He could carve a bit, and gild a frame, and do odd jobs. The fellow left me last week, and I've heard nothing of him since. No, I don't know where he came from nor where he went to. I had nothing against him while he was here. He was gone two days before the bust was smashed.'

'Well, that's all we could reasonably expect to get from Morse Hudson,' said Holmes, as we emerged from the shop. 'We have this Beppo as a common factor, both in Kennington and in Kensington, so that is worth a ten-mile drive. Now, Watson, let us make for Gelder & Co., of Stepney, the source and origin of busts. I shall be surprised if we don't get some help down there.'

In rapid succession we passed through the fringe of fashionable London, hotel London, theatrical London, literary London, commercial London, and, finally, maritime London,* till we came to a riverside city of a hundred thousand souls, where the tenement houses swelter and reek with the outcasts of Europe. Here, in a broad thoroughfare, once the abode of wealthy city merchants we found the sculpture works for which we searched. Outside was a considerable yard full of monumental masonry. Inside was a large room in which fifty workers were carving or moulding. The manager, a big blond German, received us civilly, and gave a clear answer to all Holmes's questions. A reference to his books showed that hundreds of casts had been taken from a marble copy of Devine's head of Napoleon, but that the three which had been sent to Morse Hudson a year or so before had been half of a batch of six, the other three being sent to Harding Brothers, of Kensington. There was no reason why those six should be different to any of the other casts. He could suggest no possible cause why anyone should wish to destroy them—in fact, he laughed at the idea. Their wholesale price was six shillings, but the retailer would get twelve or more. The cast was taken in two moulds from each side of the face, and then these two profiles of plaster of Paris were joined together to make the complete bust. The work was usually done by Italians in the room we were in. When finished the busts were put on a table in the passage to dry, and afterwards stored. That was all he could tell us.

But the production of the photograph had a remarkable effect upon the manager. His face flushed with anger, and his brows knotted over his blue Teutonic eyes.

'Ah, the rascal!' he cried. 'Yes, indeed, I know him very well. This has always been a respectable establishment, and the only time that we have ever had the police in it was over this very fellow. It was more than a year ago now. He knifed another Italian in the street, and then he came to the works with the police on his heels, and he was taken here. Beppo was his name—his second name I never knew. Serve me right for engaging a man with such a face. But he was a good workman—one of the best.'

'What did he get?'

'The man lived, and he got off with a year. I have no doubt he is out now; but he has not dared to show his nose here. We have a cousin of his here, and I dare say he could tell you where he is.'

'No, no,' cried Holmes, 'not a word to the cousin—not a word, I beg you. The matter is very important, and the farther I go with it the more important it seems to grow. When you referred in your ledger to the sale of those casts I observed that the date was 3rd June of last year. Could you give me the date when Beppo was arrested?'

'I could tell you roughly by the pay-list,' the manager answered. 'Yes,' he continued, after some turning over of pages, 'he was paid last on May 20th.'

'Thank you,' said Holmes. 'I don't think that I need intrude upon your time and patience any more.' With a last word of caution that he should say nothing as to our researches we turned our faces westward once more.

The afternoon was far advanced before we were able to snatch a hasty luncheon at a restaurant. A news-bill at the entrance announced 'Kensington Outrage. Murder by a Madman', and the contents of the paper showed that Mr Horace Harker had got his account into print after all. Two columns were occupied with a highly sensational and flowery rendering of the whole incident. Holmes propped it against the cruet stand* and read it while he ate. Once or twice he chuckled.

'This is all right, Watson,' said he. 'Listen to this: "It is satisfactory to know that there can be no difference of opinion upon this case, since Mr Lestrade, one of the most experienced members of the official force, and Mr Sherlock Holmes, the well-known consulting expert, have each come to the conclusion that the grotesque series of incidents, which have ended in so tragic a fashion, arise from lunacy rather than from deliberate crime. No explanation save mental aberration can cover the facts." The Press, Watson, is a most valuable institution, if you only know how to use it. And now, if you have quite finished, we will hark back to Kensington, and see what the manager of Harding Brothers has to say to the matter.'

The founder of that great emporium proved to be a brisk, crisp little person, very dapper and quick, with a clear head and a ready tongue.

'Yes, sir, I have already read the account in the evening papers. Mr Horace Harker is a customer of ours. We supplied him with the bust some months ago. We ordered three busts of that sort from Gelder & Co., of Stepney. They are all sold now. To whom? Oh, I dare say by consulting our sales book we could very easily tell you. Yes, we have the entries here. One to Mr Harker, you see, and one to Mr Josiah Brown, of Laburnum Lodge, Laburnum Vale, Chiswick, and one to Mr Sandeford, of Lower Grove Road, Reading. No, I have never seen this face which you show me in the photograph. You would hardly forget it—would you, sir?—for I've seldom seen an uglier.* Have we any Italians on the staff? Yes, sir, we have several among our workpeople and cleaners. I dare say they might get a peep at that sales book if they wanted to. There is no particular reason for keeping a watch upon that book. Well, well, it's a very strange business, and I hope that you'll let me know if anything comes of your inquiries.'

Holmes had taken several notes during Mr Harding's evidence, and I could see that he was thoroughly satisfied by the turn which affairs were taking. He made no remark, however, save that, unless we hurried, we should be late for our appointment with Lestrade. Sure enough, when we reached Baker Street the detective was already there, and we found him pacing up and down in a fever of impatience. His look of importance showed that his day's work had not been in vain.

'Well?' he asked. 'What luck, Mr Holmes?'

'We have had a very busy day, and not entirely a wasted one,' my friend explained. 'We have seen both the retailers and also the wholesale manufacturers. I can trace each of the busts now from the beginning.'

'The busts!' cried Lestrade. 'Well, well, you have your own methods, Mr Sherlock Holmes, and it is not for me to say a word against them, but I think I have done a better day's work than you. I have identified the dead man.'

'You don't say so?'

'And found a cause for the crime.'

'Splendid!'

'We have an inspector who makes a speciality of Saffron Hill and the Italian quarter.* Well, this dead man had some Catholic emblem round his neck,* and that, along with his colour, made me think he was from the South. Inspector Hill knew him the moment he caught sight of him. His name is Pietro Venucci, from Naples,* and he is one of the greatest cut-throats in London. He is connected with the Mafia,* which, as you know, is a secret political society, enforcing its decrees by murder. Now you see how the affair begins to clear up. The other fellow is probably an Italian also, and a member of the Mafia. He has broken the rules in some fashion. Pietro is set upon his track. Probably the photograph we found in his pocket is the man himself, so that he may not knife the wrong person. He dogs the fellow, he sees him enter a house, he waits outside for him, and in the scuffle receives his own death-wound. How is that, Mr Sherlock Holmes?'

Holmes clapped his hands approvingly.

'Excellent, Lestrade, excellent!' he cried. 'But I didn't quite follow your explanation of the destruction of the busts.'

'The busts! You never can get those busts out of your head. After all, that is nothing; petty larceny, six months at the most. It is the murder that we are really investigating, and I tell you that I am gathering all the threads into my hands.'

'And the next stage?'

'Is a very simple one. I shall go down with Hill to the Italian quarter, find the man whose photograph we have got, and arrest him on the charge of murder. Will you come with us?'

'I think not. I fancy we can attain our end in a simpler way. I can't say for certain, because it all depends—well, it all depends upon a factor which is completely outside our control. But I have great hopes—in fact, the betting is exactly two to one—that if you will come with us tonight I shall be able to help you to lay him by the heels.'

'In the Italian quarter?'

'No; I fancy Chiswick is an address which is more likely to find him. If you will come with me to Chiswick tonight, Lestrade, I'll promise to go to the Italian quarter with you to-morrow, and no harm will be done by the delay. And now I think that a few hours' sleep would do us all good, for I do not propose to leave before eleven o'clock, and it is unlikely that we shall be back before morning. You'll dine with us, Lestrade, and then you are welcome to the sofa until it is time for us to start. In the meantime, Watson, I should be glad if you would ring for an express messenger,* for I have a letter to send, and it is important that it should go at once.'

Holmes spent the evening in rummaging among the files of the old daily papers with which one of our lumber-rooms* was packed. When at last he descended it was with triumph in his eyes, but he said nothing to either of us as to the result of his researches. For my own part, I had followed step by step the methods by which he had traced the various windings of this complex case, and, though I could not yet perceive the goal which we would reach, I understood clearly that Holmes expected this grotesque criminal to make an attempt upon the two remaining busts, one of which, I remembered, was at Chiswick. No doubt the object of our journey was to catch him in the very act, and I could not but admire the cunning with which my friend had inserted the wrong clue in the evening paper so as to give the fellow the idea that he could continue his scheme with impunity. I was not surprised when Holmes suggested that I should take my revolver with me. He had himself picked up the loaded hunting-crop* which was his favourite weapon.

A four-wheeler* was at the door at eleven, and in it we drove to a spot at the other side of Hammersmith Bridge.* Here the cabman was directed to wait. A short walk brought us to a secluded road fringed with pleasant houses, each standing in its own grounds. In the light of a street lamp we read 'Laburnum Villa' upon the gate-post of one of them. The occupants had evidently retired to rest, for all was dark save for a fanlight over the hall door, which shed a single blurred circle on to the garden path. The wooden fence which separated the grounds from the road threw a dense black shadow upon the inner side, and here it was that we crouched.

'I fear that you'll have a long time to wait,' Holmes whispered. 'We may thank our stars that it is not raining. I don't think we can even venture to smoke to pass the time. However, it's a two to one chance that we get something to pay us for our trouble.'

It proved, however, that our vigil was not to be so long as Holmes had led us to fear, and it ended in a very sudden and singular fashion. In an instant, without the least sound to warn us of his coming, the garden gate swung open, and a lithe, dark figure, as swift and active as an ape, rushed up the garden path. We saw it whisk past the light thrown from over the door and disappear against the black shadow of the house. There was a long pause, during which we held our breath, and then a very gentle creaking sound came to our ears. The window was being opened. The noise ceased, and again there was a long silence. The fellow was making his way into the house. We saw the sudden flash of a dark lantern inside the room. What he sought was evidently not there, for again we saw the flash through another blind, and then through another.

'Let us get to the open window. We will nab him as he climbs out,' Lestrade whispered.

But before we could move the man had emerged again. As he came out into the glimmering patch of light we saw that he carried something white under his arm. He looked stealthily all round him. The silence of the deserted street reassured him. Turning his back upon us, he laid down his burden, and the next instant there was the sound of a sharp tap, followed by a clatter and rattle. The man was so intent upon what he was doing that he never heard our steps as we stole across the grass plot. With the bound of a tiger Holmes was on his back, and an instant later Lestrade and I had him by either wrist, and the handcuffs had been fastened. As we turned him over I saw his hideous, sallow face, with writhing, furious features glaring up at us, and I knew that it was indeed the man of the photograph whom we had secured.

But it was not our prisoner to whom Holmes was giving his attention. Squatted on the doorstep, he was engaged in most carefully examining that which the man had brought from the house. It was a bust of Napoleon like the one which we had seen that morning, and it had been broken into similar fragments. Carefully Holmes held each separate shard to the light, but in no way did it differ from any other shattered piece of plaster. He had just completed his examination, when the hall lights flew up, the door opened and the owner of the house, a jovial, rotund figure in shirt and trousers, presented himself.

'Mr Josiah Brown, I suppose?' said Holmes.

'Yes, sir; and you no doubt are Mr Sherlock Holmes? I had the note which you sent by the express messenger, and I did exactly what you told me. We locked every door in the inside and awaited developments. Well, I'm very glad to see that you have got the rascal. I hope, gentlemen, that you will come in and have some refreshment.'

However, Lestrade was anxious to get his man into safe quarters, so within a few minutes our cab had been summoned and we were all four upon our way to London. Not a word would our captive say; but he glared at us from the shadow of his matted hair, and once, when my hand seemed within his reach, he snapped at it like a hungry wolf. We stayed long enough at the police-station to learn that a search of his clothing revealed nothing save shillings and a long sheath knife, the handle of which bore copious traces of recent blood.

'That's all right,' said Lestrade, as we parted. 'Hill knows all these gentry, and he will give a name to him. You'll find that my theory of the Mafia will work out all right. But I'm sure I am exceedingly obliged to you, Mr Holmes, for the workmanlike way in which you laid hands upon him. I don't quite understand it all yet.'

'I fear it is rather too late an hour for explanations,' said Holmes. 'Besides, there are one or two details which are not finished off, and it is one of those cases which are worth working out to the very end. If you will come round once more to my rooms at six o'clock to-morrow I think I shall be able to show you that even now you have not grasped the entire meaning of this business, which presents some features which make it absolutely original in the history of crime. If ever I permit you to chronicle any more of my little problems, Watson, I foresee that you will enliven your pages by an account of the singular adventure of the Napoleonic busts.'

When we met again next evening, Lestrade was furnished with much information concerning our prisoner. His name, it appeared, was

Beppo, second name unknown. He was a well-known ne'er-do-well among the Italian colony. He had once been a skilful sculptor and had earned an honest living, but he had taken to evil courses, and had twice already been in gaol—once for a petty theft and once, as we had already heard, for stabbing a fellow-countryman. He could talk English perfectly well. His reasons for destroying the busts were still unknown, and he refused to answer any questions upon the subject; but the police had discovered that these same busts might very well have been made by his own hands, since he was engaged in this class of work at the establishment of Gelder & Co. To all this information, much of which we already knew, Holmes listened with polite attention; but I, who knew him so well, could clearly see that his thoughts were elsewhere, and I detected a mixture of mingled uneasiness and expectation beneath that mask which he was wont to assume. At last he started in his chair and his eyes brightened. There had been a ring at the bell. A minute later we heard steps upon the stairs, and an elderly, red-faced man with grizzled side-whiskers was ushered in. In his right hand he carried an old-fashioned carpet-bag, which he placed upon the table.

'Is Mr Sherlock Holmes here?'

My friend bowed and smiled. 'Mr Sandeford, of Reading, I suppose?' said he.

'Yes, sir. I fear that I am a little late; but the trains were awkward. You wrote to me about a bust that is in my possession.'

'Exactly.'

'I have your letter here. You said, "I desire to possess a copy of Devine's Napoleon and am prepared to pay you ten pounds for the one which is in your possession." Is that right?'

'Certainly.'

'I was very much surprised at your letter, for I could not imagine how you knew that I owned such a thing.'

'Of course you must have been surprised, but the explanation is very simple. Mr Harding, of Harding Brothers, said that they had sold you their last copy, and he gave me your address.'

'Oh, that was it, was it? Did he tell you what I paid for it?'

'No, he did not.'

'Well, I am an honest man, though not a very rich one. I only gave fifteen shillings for the bust, and I think you ought to know that before I take ten pounds from you.'

'I am sure the scruple does you honour, Mr Sandeford. But I have named that price, so I intend to stick to it.'

'Well, it is very handsome of you, Mr Holmes. I brought the bust up with me, as you asked me to do. Here it is!' He opened his bag, and at last we saw placed upon our table a complete specimen of that bust which we had already seen more than once in fragments.

Holmes took a paper from his pocket and laid a ten-pound note upon the table.

'You will kindly sign that paper, Mr Sandeford, in the presence of these witnesses. It is simply to say that you transfer every possible right that you ever had in the bust to me. I am a methodical man, you see, and you never know what turn events might take afterwards. Thank you, Mr Sandeford; here is your money, and I wish you a very good evening.'

When our visitor had disappeared Sherlock Holmes's movements were such as to rivet our attention. He began by taking a clean white cloth from a drawer and laying it over the table. Then he placed his newly acquired bust in the centre of the cloth. Finally he picked up his hunting-crop and struck Napoleon a sharp blow on the top of the head. The figure broke into fragments, and Holmes bent eagerly over the shattered remains. Next instant, with a loud shout of triumph, he held up one splinter, in which a round, dark object was fixed like a plum in a pudding.

'Gentlemen,' he cried, 'let me introduce you to the famous black pearl of the Borgias.'*

Lestrade and I sat silent for a moment, and then, with a spontaneous impulse, we both broke out clapping as at the well-wrought crisis of a play. A flush of colour sprang to Holmes's pale cheeks, and he bowed to us like the master dramatist who receives the homage of his audience. It was at such moments that for an instant he ceased to be a reasoning machine and betrayed his human love for admiration and applause. The same singularly proud and reserved nature which turned away with disdain from popular notoriety was capable of being moved to its depth by spontaneous wonder and praise from a friend.

'Yes, gentlemen,' said he, 'it is the most famous pearl now existing in the world, and it has been my good fortune, by a connected chain of inductive reasoning, to trace it from the Prince of Colonna's bedroom at the Dacre Hotel, where it was lost, to the interior of this, the last of the six busts of Napoleon which were manufactured by Gelder

& Co., of Stepney. You will remember, Lestrade, the sensation caused by the disappearance of this valuable jewel, and the vain efforts of the London police to recover it. I was myself consulted upon the case; but I was unable to throw any light upon it. Suspicion fell upon the maid of the Princess, who was an Italian, and it was proved that she had a brother in London, but we failed to trace any connection between them. The maid's name was Lucretia Venucci, and there is no doubt in my mind that this Pietro who was murdered two nights ago was the brother. I have been looking up the dates in the old files of the paper, and I find that the disappearance of the pearl was exactly two days before the arrest of Beppo for some crime of violence—an event which took place in the factory of Gelder & Co., at the very moment when these busts were being made. Now you clearly see the sequence of events, though you see them, of course, in the inverse order to the way in which they presented themselves to me. Beppo had the pearl in his possession. He may have stolen it from Pietro, he may have been Pietro's confederate, he may have been the go-between of Pietro and his sister. It is of no consequence to us which is the correct solution.

'The main fact is that he *had* the pearl, and at that moment, when it was on his person, he was pursued by the police. He made for the factory in which he worked, and he knew that he had only a few minutes in which to conceal this enormously valuable prize, which would otherwise be found on him when he was searched. Six plaster casts of Napoleon were drying in the passage. One of them was still soft. In an instant Beppo, a skilful workman, made a small hole in the wet plaster, dropped in the pearl, and with a few touches covered over the aperture once more. It was an admirable hiding-place. No one could possibly find it. But Beppo was condemned to a year's imprisonment, and in the meanwhile his six busts were scattered over London. He could not tell which contained his treasure. Only by breaking them could he see. Even shaking would tell him nothing for as the plaster was wet it was probable that the pearl would adhere to it—as, in fact, it has done. Beppo did not despair, and he conducted his search with considerable ingenuity and perseverance. Through a cousin who works with Gelder he found out the retail firms who had bought the busts. He managed to find employment with Morse Hudson, and in that way tracked down three of them. The pearl was not there. Then with the help of some Italian employee, he succeeded in finding out where the other three busts had gone. The first was at Harker's. There he was dogged by his confederate, who held Beppo responsible for the loss of the pearl, and he stabbed him in the scuffle which followed.'

'If he was his confederate, why should he carry his photograph?' I asked.

'As a means of tracing him if he wished to inquire about him from any third person. That was the obvious reason. Well, after the murder I calculated that Beppo would probably hurry rather than delay his movements. He would fear that the police would read his secret, and so hastened on before they should get ahead of him. Of course, I could not say that he had not found the pearl in Harker's bust. I had not even concluded for certain that it was the pearl; but it was evident to me that he was looking for something, since he carried the bust past the other houses in order to break it in the garden which had a lamp overlooking it. Since Harker's bust was one in three, the chances were exactly as I told you—two to one against the pearl being inside it. There remained two busts, and it was obvious that he would go for the London one first. I warned the inmates of the house, so as to avoid a second tragedy, and we went down, with the happiest results. By that time, of course, I knew for certain that it was the Borgia pearl that we were after. The name of the murdered man linked the one event with the other. There only remained a single bust—the Reading one—and the pearl must be there. I bought it in your presence from the owner—and there it lies.'

We sat in silence for a moment.

'Well,' said Lestrade, 'I've seen you handle a good many cases, Mr Holmes, but I don't know that I ever knew a more workmanlike one than that. We're not jealous of you at Scotland Yard. No, sir, we are damned proud of you,* and if you come down tomorrow there's not a man, from the oldest inspector to the youngest constable, who wouldn't be glad to shake you by the hand.'

'Thank you!' said Holmes. 'Thank you!' and as he turned away it seemed to me that he was more nearly moved by the softer human emotions than I had ever seen him. A moment later he was the cold and practical thinker once more. 'Put the pearl in the safe, Watson,' said he, 'and get out the papers of the Conk-Singleton forgery case. Goodbye, Lestrade. If any little problem comes your way I shall be happy, if I can, to give you a hint or two as to its solution.'

HIS LAST BOW

AN EPILOGUE OF SHERLOCK HOLMES*

IT was nine o'clock at night upon the second of August—the most terrible August in the history of the world.* One might have thought already that God's curse hung heavy over a degenerate earth, for there was an awesome hush and a feeling of vague expectancy in the sultry and stagnant air. The sun had long set, but one blood-red gash, like an open wound, lay low in the distant west. Above, the stars were shining brightly; and below, the lights of the shipping glimmered in the bay. The two famous Germans stood beside the stone parapet of the garden walk, with the long, low, heavily-gabled house behind them, and they looked down upon the broad sweep of the beach at the foot of the great chalk cliff on which Von Bork, like some wandering eagle, had perched himself four years before. They stood with their heads close together, talking in low, confidential tones. From below, the two glowing ends of their cigars might have been the smouldering eyes of some malignant fiend looking down in the darkness.

A remarkable man this Von Bork—a man who could hardly be matched among all the devoted agents of the Kaiser.* It was his talents which had first recommended him for the English mission, the most important mission of all, but since he had taken it over those talents had become more and more manifest to the half-dozen people in the world who were really in touch with the truth. One of these was his present companion, Baron Von Herling, the Chief Secretary of the legation,* whose huge 100-horse-power Benz car* was blocking the country lane as it waited to carry its owner back to London.

'Things are moving very fast now and quite in accordance with the time-table. So far as I can judge the trend of events, you will probably be back in Berlin within the week,' the secretary was saying. 'When you get there, my dear Von Bork, I think you will be surprised at the warm welcome you will receive. I happen to know what is thought in the All-Highest* quarters of your work in this country.' He was a huge man, the secretary, deep, broad, and tall, with a slow, heavy fashion of speech which had been his main asset in his political career.

Von Bork laughed in a deprecating way.

'They are not very hard to deceive, these Englanders,' he remarked. 'A more docile, simple folk could not be imagined.'

'I don't know about that,' said the other, thoughtfully. 'They have strange, unexpected limits and one must learn to allow for them. It is that surface simplicity of theirs which makes a trap for the stranger. One's first impression is that they are entirely soft. Then you come suddenly upon something very hard, and you know that you have reached the limit, and must adapt yourself to the fact. They have, for example, their insular conventions which simply *must* be observed.'

'Meaning "good form" and "playing the game" and that sort of thing?' Von Bork sighed as one who had suffered much.

'Meaning British prejudice and convention, in all its queer manifestations. As an example I may quote one of my own worst blunders— I can afford to talk of my blunders, for you know my work well enough to be aware of my successes. It was on my first arrival. I was invited to a week-end gathering at the country-house of a Cabinet Minister. The conversation was amazingly indiscreet.'

Von Bork nodded. 'I've been there,' said he, dryly.

'Exactly. Well, I naturally sent a *résumé* of the information to Berlin. Unfortunately, our good Chancellor is a little heavy-handed in these matters, and he transmitted a remark which showed that he was aware of what had been said. This, of course, took the trail straight up to me. You've no idea the harm that it did me. There was nothing soft about our British hosts on that occasion, I can assure you. I was two years living it down. Now you, with this sporting pose of yours—'

'No, no, don't call it a pose. A pose is an artificial thing. This is quite natural. I am a born sportsman. I enjoy it.'

'Well, that makes it the more effective. You yacht against them, you hunt with them, you play polo, you match them in every game. Your four-in-hand* takes the prize at Olympia*—I have even heard that you go to the length of boxing with the young officers. What is the result? Nobody takes you seriously. You are a "good old sport", "quite a decent fellow for a German", a hard-drinking, night-club, knock-about-town, devil-may-care young fellow. And all the time this quiet country-house of yours is the centre of half the mischief in England, and the sporting squire—the most astute secret-service man in Europe. Genius, my dear Von Bork—genius!'

'You flatter me, Baron. But certainly I may claim that my four years in this country have not been unproductive. I've never shown you my little store. Would you mind stepping in for a moment?'

The door of the study opened straight on to the terrace. Von Bork pushed it back, and, leading the way, he clicked the switch of the electric light. He then closed the door behind the bulky form which followed him, and carefully adjusted the heavy curtain over the latticed window. Only when all these precautions had been taken and tested did he turn his sun-burned, aquiline face to his guest.

'Some of my papers have gone,' said he. 'When my wife and the household left yesterday for Flushing* they took the less important with them. I must, of course, claim the protection of the Embassy for the others.'

'Everything has been most carefully arranged. Your name has already been filed as one of the personal suite. There will be no difficulties for you or your baggage. Of course, it is just possible that we may not have to go. England may leave France to her fate. We are sure that there is no binding treaty between them.'

'And Belgium?' He stood listening intently for the answer.

'Yes, and Belgium, too.'

Von Bork shook his head. 'I don't see how that could be. There is a definite treaty there. It would be the end of her—and what an end! She could never recover from such a humiliation.'

'She would at least have peace for the moment.'

'But her honour?'

'Tut, my dear sir, we live in a utilitarian age. Honour is a mediaeval conception. Besides, England is not ready. It is an inconceivable thing, but even our special war-tax of fifty millions, which one would think made our purpose as clear as if we had advertised it on the front page of *The Times*, has not roused these people from their slumbers. Here and there one hears a question. It is my business to find an answer. Here and there also there is irritation. It is my business to soothe it. But I can assure you that so far as the essentials go—the storage of munitions, the preparation for submarine attack, the arrangements for making high explosives—nothing is prepared. How then can England come in, especially when we have stirred her up such a devil's brew of Irish civil war,* window-breaking furies,* and God knows what to keep her thoughts at home?'

'She must think of her future.'

'Ah, that is another matter. I fancy that in the future we have our own very definite plans about England, and that your information will be very vital to us. It is to-day or to-morrow with Mr John Bull.* If he prefers to-day we are perfectly ready. If it is to-morrow we shall be more ready still. I should think they would be wiser to fight with allies than without them, but that is their own affair. This week is their week of destiny. But let us get away from speculation and back to *real-politik*. You were speaking of your papers.'

He sat in the armchair with the light shining upon his broad, bald head, while he puffed sedately at his cigar and watched the movements of his companion.

The large oak-panelled, book-lined room had a curtain hung in the further corner. When this was drawn it disclosed a large brass-bound safe. Von Bork detached a small key from his watch-chain, and after some considerable manipulation of the lock he swung open the heavy door.

'Look!' said he, standing clear, with a wave of his hand.

The light shone vividly into the opened safe, and the secretary of the Embassy gazed with an absorbed interest at the rows of stuffed pigeon-holes with which it was furnished. Each pigeon-hole had its label, and his eyes, as he glanced along them, read a long series of such titles as 'Fords', 'Harbour-Defences', 'Aeroplanes', 'Ireland', 'Egypt',* 'Portsmouth Forts',* 'The Channel',* 'Rosyth',* and a score of others. Each compartment was bristling with papers and plans.

'Colossal!' said the secretary. Putting down his cigar he softly clapped his fat hands.

'And all in four years, Baron. Not such a bad show for the hard-drinking, hard-riding country squire. But the gem of my collection is coming and there is the setting all ready for it.' He pointed to a space over which 'Naval Signals' was printed.

'But you have a good *dossier* there already?'

'Out of date and waste paper. The Admiralty in some way got the alarm and every code has been changed. It was a blow, Baron—the worst set-back in my whole campaign. But thanks to my cheque-book and the good Altamont, all will be well to-night.'

The Baron looked at his watch, and gave a guttural exclamation of disappointment.

'Well, I really can wait no longer. You can imagine that things are moving at present in Carlton House Terrace* and that we have all to be at our posts. I had hoped to be able to bring news of your great *coup*. Did Altamont name no hour?'

Von Bork pushed over a telegram.

'Will come without fail to-night and bring new sparking-plugs.* ALTAMONT.'

'Sparking-plugs, eh?'

'You see, he poses as a motor expert and I keep a full garage. In our code everything likely to come up is named after some spare part. If he talks of a radiator it is a battleship, of an oil-pump a cruiser, and so on. Sparking-plugs are naval signals.'

'From Portsmouth at midday,' said the secretary, examining the superscription. 'By the way, what do you give him?'

'Five hundred pounds for this particular job. Of course, he has a salary as well.'

'The greedy rogue. They are useful, these traitors, but I grudge them their blood-money.'

'I grudge Altamont nothing. He is a wonderful worker. If I pay him well, at least he delivers the goods, to use his own phrase. Besides, he is not a traitor. I assure you that our most Pan-Germanic Junker* is a sucking dove in his feelings towards England as compared with a real bitter Irish-American.'*

'Oh, an Irish-American?'

'If you heard him talk you would not doubt it. Sometimes I assure you I can hardly understand him. He seems to have declared war on the King's English as well as on the English King. Must you really go? He may be here any moment.'

'No; I'm sorry, but I have already over-stayed my time. We shall expect you early to-morrow, and when you get that signal-book through the little door on the Duke of York's steps* you can put a triumphant *Finis* to your record in England. What! Tokay!* He indicated a heavily-sealed, dust-covered bottle which stood with two high glasses upon a salver.

'May I offer you a glass before your journey?'

'No, thanks. But it looks like revelry.'

'Altamont has a nice taste in wines, and he took a fancy to my Tokay. He is a touchy fellow and needs humouring in small things. He is absolutely vital to my plans, and I have to study him, I assure you.' They had strolled out on to the terrace again, and along it to the farther end, where, at a touch from the Baron's chauffeur, the

great car shivered and chuckled. 'Those are the lights of Harwich,*
I suppose,' said the secretary, pulling on his dust coat. 'How still and
peaceful it all seems! There may be other lights within the week, and
the English coast a less tranquil place! The heavens, too, may not be
quite so peaceful, if all that the good Zeppelin* promises us comes
true. By the way, who is that?'

Only one window showed a light behind them. In it there stood
a lamp, and beside it, seated at a table, was a dear old ruddy-faced
woman in a country cap. She was bending over her knitting and stopping occasionally to stroke a large black cat upon a stool beside her.

'That is Martha,* the only servant I have left.'

The secretary chuckled.

'She might almost personify Britannia,' said he, 'with her complete
self-absorption and general air of comfortable somnolence. Well, *au
revoir*, Von Bork!'* With a final wave of his hand he sprang into the
car, and a moment later the two golden cones from the headlights shot
forward through the darkness. The secretary lay back in the cushions
of the luxurious limousine, with his thoughts full of the impending
European tragedy, and hardly observing that as his car swung round
the village street it nearly passed over a little Ford* coming in the
opposite direction.

Von Bork walked slowly back to the study when the last gleams
of the motor lamps had faded into the distance. As he passed he
observed that his old housekeeper had put out her lamp and retired.
It was a new experience to him, the silence and darkness of his widespread house, for his family and household had been a large one. It
was a relief to him, however, to think that they were all in safety, and
that, but for that one old woman who lingered in the kitchen, he had
the whole place to himself. There was a good deal of tidying up to
do inside his study and he set himself to do it until his keen, handsome face was flushed with the heat of the burning papers. A leather
valise stood beside his table, and into this he began to pack very neatly
and systematically the precious contents of his safe. He had hardly
got started with the work, however, when his quick ears caught the
sound of a distant car. Instantly he gave an exclamation of satisfaction, strapped up the valise, shut the safe, locked it, and hurried out
on to the terrace. He was just in time to see the lights of a small car
come to a halt at the gate. A passenger sprang out of it and advanced
swiftly towards him, while the chauffeur, a heavily-built, elderly man,

with a grey moustache, settled down like one who resigns himself to a long vigil.

'Well?' asked Von Bork eagerly, running forward to meet his visitor.

For answer the man waved a small brown-paper parcel triumphantly above his head.

'You can give me the glad hand* tonight, mister,' he cried. 'I'm bringin' home the bacon at last.'

'The signals?'

'Same as I said in my cable.* Every last one of them, semaphore, lamp-code, Marconi*—a copy, mind you, not the original. The sucker that sold it would have handed over the book itself. That was too dangerous. But it's the real goods, and you can lay to that.' He slapped the German upon the shoulder with a rough familiarity from which the other winced.

'Come in,' he said. 'I'm all alone in the house. I was only waiting for this. Of course, a copy is better than the original. If an original were missing they would change the whole thing. You think it's all safe about this copy?'

The Irish-American had entered the study and stretched his long limbs from the arm-chair. He was a tall, gaunt man of sixty, with clear-cut features and a small goatee beard which gave him a general resemblance to the caricatures of Uncle Sam. A half-smoked sodden cigar hung from the corner of his mouth, and as he sat down he struck a match and relit it. 'Makin' ready for a move?' he remarked, as he looked round him. 'Say, mister,' he added, as his eyes fell upon the safe from which the curtain was now removed, 'you don't tell me you keep your papers in that?'

'Why not?'

'Gosh, in a wide-open contraption like that! And they reckon you to be some spy. Why, a Yankee crook would be into that with a can-opener.* If I'd known that any letter of mine was goin' to lie loose in a thing like that I'd have been a mutt to write to you at all.'

'It would puzzle any of your crooks to force that safe,' Von Bork answered. 'You won't cut that metal with any tool.'

'But the lock?'

'No; it's a double combination lock. You know what that is?'

'Search me,' said the American.

'Well, you need a word as well as a set of figures before you can get the lock to work.' He rose and showed a double radiating disc round the keyhole. 'This outer one is for the letters, the inner one for the figures.'

'Well, well, that's fine.'

'So it's not quite as simple as you thought. It was four years ago that I had it made, and what do you think I chose for the word and figures?'

'It's beyond me.'

'Well, I chose "August" for the word, and "1914" for the figures, and here we are.'

The American's face showed his surprise and admiration.

'My, but that was smart! You had it down to a fine thing.'

'Yes; a few of us even then could have guessed the date. Here it is, and I'm shutting down to-morrow morning.'

'Well, I guess you'll have to fix me up too. I'm not stayin' in this goldarned country all on my lonesome. In a week or less, from what I see, John Bull will be on his hind legs and fair rampin'. I'd rather watch him from over the water.'

'But you're an American citizen?'*

'Well, so was Jack James an American citizen, but he's doin' time in Portland* all the same. It cuts no ice with a British copper to tell him you're an American citizen. "It's British law and order over here," says he. By the way, mister, talking of Jack James, it seems to me you don't do much to cover your men.'

'What do you mean?' Von Bork asked, sharply.

'Well, you are their employer, ain't you? It's up to you to see that they don't fall down. But they do fall down and when did you ever pick them up? There's James—'

'It was James's own fault. You know that yourself. He was too self-willed for the job.'

'James was a bonehead—I give you that. Then there was Hollis.'

'The man was mad.'

'Well, he went a bit woozy towards the end. It's enough to make a man bughouse* when he has to play a part from mornin' to night with a hundred guys all ready to set the coppers wise to him. But now there is Steiner—'

Von Bork started violently, and his ruddy face turned a shade paler.

'What about Steiner?'

'Well, they've pulled him, that's all. They raided his store last night, and he and his papers are all in Portsmouth Jail. You'll go off and he, poor devil, will have to stand the racket, and lucky if he gets clear with his life. That's why I want to get over the salt water as soon as you do.'

Von Bork was a strong, self-contained man, but it was easy to see that the news had shaken him.

'How could they have got on to Steiner?' he muttered. 'That's the worst blow yet.'

'Well, you nearly had a darned sight worse one, for I believe they are not far off me.'

'You don't mean that!'

'Sure thing. My landlady down Fratton* way had some inquiries, and when I heard of it I guessed it was time for me to hustle. But what I want to know, mister, is how the coppers know these things? Steiner is the fifth man you've lost since I signed on with you, and I know the name of the sixth if I don't get a move on. How do you explain it, and ain't you ashamed to see your men go down like this?'

Von Bork flushed crimson.

'How dare you speak in such a way!'

'If I didn't dare things, mister, I wouldn't be in your service. But I'll tell you straight what is in my mind. I've heard that with you German politicians, when an agent has done his work you are not very sorry to see him put away where he can't talk too much.'

Von Bork sprang to his feet.

'Do you dare to suggest that I have given away my own agents!'

'I don't stand for that, mister, but there's a stool pigeon* or a cross* somewhere, and it's up to you to find out where it is. Anyhow, I am taking no more chances. It's me for little Holland, and the sooner the better.'

Von Bork had mastered his anger.

'We have been allies too long to quarrel now at the very hour of victory,' he said. 'You've done splendid work and taken big risks and I can't forget it. By all means go to Holland, and you can get a boat from Rotterdam to New York. No other line will be safe a week from now when Von Tirpitz* gets to work. But let us settle up, Altamont. I'll take that book and pack it with the rest.'

The American held the small parcel in his hand, but made no motion to give it up.

'What about the dough?' he asked.

'The what?'

'The boodle. The reward. The five hundred pounds. The gunner turned durned nasty at the last, and I had to square him with an extra hundred dollars or it would have been nitsky* for you and me. "Nothin' doin'!" says he, and he meant it too, but the last hundred did it. It's cost me two hundred pounds from first to last, so it isn't likely I'd give it up without gettin' my wad.'

Von Bork smiled with some bitterness. 'You don't seem to have a very high opinion of my honour,' said he; 'you want the money before you give up the book.'

'Well, mister, it is a business proposition.'

'All right. Have your way.' He sat down at the table and scribbled a cheque, which he tore from the book, but he refrained from handing it to his companion. 'After all, since we are to be on such terms, Mr Altamont,' said he, 'I don't see why I should trust you any more than you trust me. Do you understand?' he added, looking back over his shoulder at the American. 'There's the cheque upon the table. I claim the right to examine that parcel before you pick the money up.'

The American passed it over without a word. Von Bork undid a winding of string and two wrappers of paper. Then he sat gazing for a moment in silent amazement at a small blue book which lay before him. Across the cover was printed in golden letters *Practical Handbook of Bee Culture*. Only for one instant did the master-spy glare at this strangely-irrelevant inscription. The next he was gripped at the back of his neck by a grasp of iron, and a chloroformed sponge was held in front of his writhing face.

'Another glass, Watson?' said Mr Sherlock Holmes, as he extended the dusty bottle of Imperial Tokay.* 'We must drink to this joyous reunion.'

The thickset chauffeur, who had seated himself by the table, pushed forward his glass with some eagerness.

'It is a good wine, Holmes,' he said, when he had drunk heartily to the sentiment.

'A remarkable wine, Watson. Our noisy* friend upon the sofa has assured me that it is from Franz Joseph's special cellar at the Schoenbrunn Palace.* Might I trouble you to open the window, for chloroform vapour does not help the palate.'

The safe was ajar, and Holmes who was now standing in front of it was removing *dossier* after *dossier*, swiftly examining each, and then packing it neatly in Von Bork's valise. The German lay upon the sofa sleeping stertorously, with a strap round his upper arms and another round his legs.

'We need not hurry ourselves, Watson. We are safe from interruption. Would you mind touching the bell? There is no one in the house except old Martha, who has played her part to admiration. I got her the situation here when first I took the matter up. Ah, Martha, you will be glad to hear that all is well.'

The pleasant old lady had appeared in the doorway. She curtseyed with a smile to Mr Holmes, but glanced with some apprehension at the figure upon the sofa.

'It is all right, Martha. He has not been hurt at all.'

'I am glad of that, Mr Holmes. According to his lights he has been a kind master. He wanted me to go with his wife to Germany yesterday, but that would hardly have suited your plans, would it, sir?'

'No, indeed, Martha. So long as you were here I was easy in my mind. We waited some time for your signal to-night.'

'It was the secretary, sir; the stout gentleman from London.'

'I know. His car passed ours. But for your excellent driving, Watson, we should have been the very type of Europe under the Prussian Juggernaut. What more, Martha?'

'I thought he would never go. I knew that it would not suit your plans, sir, to find him here.'

'No, indeed. Well, it only meant that we waited half an hour or so on the hill until I saw your lamp go out and knew that the coast was clear. You can report to me to-morrow in London, Martha, at Claridge's Hotel.'*

'Very good, sir.'

'I suppose you have everything ready to leave?'

'Yes, sir. He posted seven letters to-day. I have the addresses, as usual. He received nine; I have these also.'

'Very good, Martha. I will look into them tomorrow. Good-night. These papers,' he continued, as the old lady vanished, 'are not of very great importance for, of course, the information which they represent has been sent off long ago to the German Government. These are the originals which could not safely be got out of the country.'

'Then they are of no use?'

'I should not go so far as to say that, Watson. They will at least show our people what is known and what is not. I may say that a good many of these papers have come to him through me, and I need not add are thoroughly untrustworthy. It would brighten my declining years to see a German cruiser navigating the Solent* according to the mine-field plans which I have furnished. But you, Watson'—he stopped his work and took his old friend by the shoulders—'I've hardly seen you in the light yet. How have the years used you?* You look the same blithe boy as ever.'

'I feel twenty years younger, Holmes. I have seldom felt so happy as when I got your wire asking me to meet you at Harwich with the car. But you, Holmes—you have changed very little—save for that horrible goatee.'

'These are the sacrifices one makes for one's country, Watson,' said Holmes, pulling at his little tuft. 'To-morrow it will be but a dreadful memory. With my hair cut and a few other superficial changes I shall no doubt reappear at Claridge's to-morrow as I was before this American stunt*—I beg your pardon, Watson; my well of English seems to be permanently defiled—before this American job came my way.'

'But you had retired, Holmes. We heard of you as living the life of a hermit among your bees and your books in a small farm upon the South Downs.'

'Exactly, Watson. Here is the fruit of my leisured ease, the *magnum opus** of my latter years!' He picked up the volume from the table and read out the whole title, '*Practical Handbook of Bee Culture, with some Observations upon the Segregation of the Queen. Alone I did it.* Behold the fruit of pensive nights and laborious days, when I watched the little working gangs as once I watched the criminal world of London.'

'But how did you get to work again?'

'Ah! I have often marvelled at it myself. The Foreign Minister* alone I could have withstood, but when the Premier* also deigned to visit my humble roof—! The fact is, Watson, that this gentleman upon the sofa was a bit too good for our people. He was in a class by himself. Things were going wrong, and no one could understand why they were going wrong. Agents were suspected or even caught, but there was evidence of some strong and secret central force. It was absolutely necessary to expose it. Strong pressure was brought upon me to look into the matter. It has cost me two years, Watson, but they have not been devoid of excitement. When I say that I started my pilgrimage at Chicago,* graduated in an Irish secret society at

Buffalo,* gave serious trouble to the constabulary* at Skibbereen* and so eventually caught the eye of a subordinate agent of Von Bork, who recommended me as a likely man, you will realize that the matter was complex. Since then I have been honoured by his confidence, which has not prevented most of his plans going subtly wrong and five of his best agents being in prison. I watched them, Watson, and I picked them as they ripened. Well, sir, I hope that you are none the worse?'

The last remark was addressed to Von Bork himself, who, after much gasping and blinking, had lain quietly listening to Holmes's statement. He broke out now into a furious stream of German invective, his face convulsed with passion. Holmes continued his swift investigation of documents, his long, nervous fingers opening and folding the papers while his prisoner cursed and swore.

'Though unmusical, German is the most expressive of all languages,' he observed, when Von Bork had stopped from pure exhaustion. 'Hullo! Hullo!' he added, as he looked hard at the corner of a tracing before putting it in the box. 'This should put another bird in the cage. I had no idea that the paymaster was such a rascal, though I have long had an eye upon him. Dear me, Mister Von Bork, you have a great deal to answer for.'

The prisoner had raised himself with some difficulty upon the sofa and was staring with a strange mixture of amazement and hatred at his captor.

'I shall get level with you, Altamont,' he said, speaking with slow deliberation. 'If it takes me all my life I shall get level with you!'

'The old sweet song,'* said Holmes. 'How often have I heard it in days gone by! It was a favourite ditty of the late lamented Professor Moriarty. Colonel Sebastian Moran has also been known to warble it. And yet I live and keep bees upon the South Downs.'

'Curse you, you double traitor!' cried the German, straining against his bonds and glaring murder from his furious eyes.

'No, no, it is not so bad as that,' said Holmes, smiling. 'As my speech surely shows you, Mr Altamont of Chicago had no existence in fact. He was a concoction, a myth, an isolated strand from my bundle of personalities. I used him and he is gone.'

'Then who are you?'

'It is really immaterial who I am, but since the matter seems to interest you, Mr Von Bork, I may say that this is not my first acquaintance with the members of your family. I have done a good deal of business in Germany in the past, and my name is probably familiar to you.'

'I would wish to know it,' said the Prussian grimly.

'It was I who brought about the separation between Irene Adler and the late King of Bohemia when your cousin Heinrich was the Imperial Envoy.* It was I also who saved from murder, by the Nihilist Klopman, Count Von und Zu Grafenstein, who was your mother's elder brother. It was I—'

Von Bork sat up in amazement.

'There is only one man—' he cried.

'Exactly,' said Holmes.

Von Bork groaned and sank back on the sofa. 'And most of that information came through you!' he cried. 'What is it worth? What have I done? It is my ruin for ever!'

'It is certainly a little untrustworthy,' said Holmes. 'It will require some checking and you have little time to check it. Your admiral* may find the new guns rather larger than he expects, and the cruisers perhaps a trifle faster.'

Von Bork clutched at his own throat in despair.

'There are a good many other points of detail which will, no doubt, come to light in good time. But you have one quality which is very rare in a German, Mr Von Bork: you are a sportsman, and you will bear me no ill will when you realize that you, who have outwitted so many other people, have at last been outwitted yourself. After all, you have done your best for your country and I have done my best for mine, and what could be more natural? Besides,' he added, not unkindly, as he laid his hand upon the shoulder of the prostrate man, 'it is better than to fall before some more ignoble foe. These papers are now ready, Watson. If you will help me with our prisoner, I think that we may get started for London at once.'

It was no easy task to move Von Bork, for he was a strong and a desperate man. Finally, holding either arm, the two friends walked him very slowly down the garden path, which he had trod with such proud confidence when he received the congratulations of the famous diplomatist only a few hours before. After a short final struggle he was hoisted, still bound hand and foot, into the spare seat of the little car. His precious valise was wedged in beside him.

'I trust that you are as comfortable as circumstances permit,' said

Holmes, when the final arrangements were made. 'Should I be guilty of a liberty if I lit a cigar and placed it between your lips?'

But all amenities were wasted upon the angry German.

'I suppose you realize, Mr Sherlock Holmes,' said he, 'that if your Government bears you out in this treatment it becomes an act of war?'

'What about your Government and all this treatment?' said Holmes, tapping the valise.

'You are a private individual. You have no warrant for my arrest. The whole proceeding is absolutely illegal and outrageous.'

'Absolutely,' said Holmes.

'Kidnapping a German subject.'

'And stealing his private papers.'

'Well, you realize your position, you and your accomplice here. If I were to shout for help as we pass through the village—'

'My dear sir, if you did anything so foolish you would probably enlarge the too-limited titles of our village inns by giving us "The Dangling Prussian" as a sign-post. The Englishman is a patient creature, but at present his temper is a little inflamed and it would be as well not to try him too far. No, Mr Von Bork, you will go with us in a quiet, sensible fashion to Scotland Yard, whence you can send for your friend Baron Von Herling and see if even now you may not fill that place which he has reserved for you in the Ambassadorial suite. As to you, Watson, you are joining up with your old service, as I understand, so London won't be out of your way. Stand with me here upon the terrace, for it may be the last quiet talk that we shall ever have.'

The two friends chatted in intimate converse for a few minutes, recalling once again the days of the past whilst their prisoner vainly wriggled to undo the bonds that held him. As they turned to the car Holmes pointed back to the moonlit sea and shook a thoughtful head.

'There's an east wind coming, Watson.'

'I think not, Holmes. It is very warm.'

'Good old Watson! You are the one fixed point in a changing age. There's an east wind coming all the same, such a wind as never blew on England yet. It will be cold and bitter, Watson, and a good many of us may wither before its blast. But it's God's own wind none the less, and a cleaner, better, stronger land will lie in the sunshine when the storm has cleared. Start her up, Watson, for it's time that we were on our way. I have a cheque for five hundred pounds which should be cashed early, for the drawer is quite capable of stopping it, if he can.'

EXPLANATORY NOTES

THE SIGN OF THE FOUR

First published in *Lippincott's Magazine* of Philadelphia in February 1890 under the title *The Sign of the Four*. ACD's diary notes on completing the MS also refer to it by this title, though a page in the MS in ACD's handwriting calls it 'The Sign of Four'. ACD himself used both titles. The first British edition, published by Spencer Blackett in October 1890, used the shorter title, but since the formula 'the Sign of the Four' is used throughout the story itself this version of the title is retained in the present edition.

3 *Beaune*: wine (red and white) produced in the area around Beaune, in the region of Burgundy, France.

black-letter volume: books printed in the German or Gothic type used by early printers.

the Afghan campaign: the Second Anglo-Afghan War (1878–80) in which Watson was wounded (see *A Study in Scarlet*).

4 *"A Study in Scarlet"*: a novel, the first Holmes narrative, published in 1887.

5 *the fifth proposition of Euclid*: Euclid (*c*.300 BC) was a Greek mathematician, famous for his *Elements* of geometry. The fifth proposition of Book I states that if two sides of a triangle are equal in length, then the angles opposite these sides are equal, and if the two sides are extended below the base of the triangle, the angles thus formed are also equal to one another.

Jezail bullet: a Jezail was a large heavy rifle used by the Afghans.

magnifiques, coup-de-maîtres, and tours-de-force: (French) 'magnificent', 'master-strokes' (properly *coups-de-maître*), 'great feats'.

6 *lunkah*: a strong, thin Indian cigar open at both ends.

Trichinopoly: a cigar of dark tobacco manufactured near Trichinopoly in southern India.

bird's-eye: a style of cut tobacco.

lithotypes: prints from an etched stone surface.

11 *Langham Hotel*: the Langham Hotel in Portland Place. It was at a dinner at the Langham with Oscar Wilde and ACD on 30 August 1889 that Marshall Stoddart commissioned *The Sign of the Four* and *The Picture of Dorian Gray*.

Andaman Islands: chain of 204 islands in the eastern Bay of Bengal. During the great Indian Mutiny in 1857, the British opened a convict settlement on the islands, housing around 700 inmates, largely political prisoners. Prisoners were forced to perform heavy labour in chains and shackles, and there was an enormous mortality rate. By 1901, the penal colony housed almost twelve thousand convicts. It was closed upon Indian independence in 1947.

12 *Lyceum Theatre*: a theatre on the Strand associated with, among others, the celebrated actor-manager Sir Henry Irving (1878–1902), and Irish actor and writer Bram Stoker (1847–1912), author of *Dracula*.

14 *Winwood Reade's Martyrdom of Man*: a history of the world by Winwood Reade (1838–75), notorious for its atheistic point of view.

15 *back files of The Times*: Samuel Palmer published a quarterly index to *The Times*.

four-wheeler: a closed carriage with the driver seated at the front.

17 *hansoms*: a hansom was a two-wheeled covered carriage. It had room for two passengers inside with the driver on the outside. Named after its designer, Joseph Hansom (1803–83), the hansom was ubiquitous in the London of the 1880s.

street arab: a street urchin.

18 *the Surrey side*: the common way to refer to the side of London south of the Thames, then the mostly poorer side of the capital.

Sahib: a term of respect in various Indian languages, originally from Arabic and Turkish. It was in common use in British India for Indians to address British superiors. The correct female form is *sahiba*, but in British India the preferred term when addressing British women was *memsahib*, a conflation of the English 'ma'am' and *sahib*.

khitmutgar: Hindi for butler or manservant.

19 *of the first water*: used of diamonds to mean of the highest clarity, colour, etc.

hookah: tobacco pipe in which smoke is inhaled through a bowl of perfumed water.

20 *Chianti*: wine produced in the Chianti area of central Tuscany.

Tokay: a heavy sweet white wine produced in the area around the Hungarian town of Tokay (Tokaj in Hungarian), in the foothills of the Carpathian Mountains.

21 *Corot*: Jean-Baptiste Camille Corot (1796–1875), French landscape and figure painter.

Salvator Rosa: an Italian painter (1615–73) of the Neapolitan School, whose 'romantic' landscapes were much admired in eighteenth-century England.

Bouguereau: Adolphe William Bouguereau (1825–1905), French painter of mythological and religious subjects.

modern French school: recent French painting.

Pondicherry Lodge: Pondicherry is a town on the east coast of India.

23 *chaplet*: here, a small coronet.

   quinine: a substance extracted from the bark of the cinchona tree, employed as a cure for malaria. It was in common use in tropical areas of the British Empire, and is one of the principal ingredients of tonic water. It was first introduced to Europeans in the seventeenth century by a Jesuit apothecary who witnessed its use by the Quechua people in Peru.

   Agra: capital of the Agra district of India (and until 1648 capital of India). Famous for the Taj Mahal mausoleum and the Agra Fort.

24 *Venetian carafe*: presumably made of coloured glass.

25 *"Le mauvais goût mène au crime"*: (French) 'bad taste leads to crime', a phrase immortalized by the novelist Stendhal (1783–1842).

26 *befrogged*: fastened or ornamented with 'frogs', i.e. buttons covered with silk or other material which pass through loops on the opposite side.

   Astrakhan: fine lambswool, originally from Middle Eastern sheep, named after the Russian city of Astrakhan on the Caspian Sea.

   lappets: ear-flaps.

   valetudinarian: someone suffering from frequent sickness or pain, or who has a weak constitution, and whose chief concern becomes their own ill health.

27 *nostrums*: questionable remedies, often with secret properties or ingredients, highly praised but of dubious effectiveness. From Latin *nostrum remedium*, literally 'our cure', meaning a patented medicine.

   strychnine: a substance obtained from the dried seeds of an Indian tree. Even a small dose causes convulsions and death.

28 *benefit*: benefit fights for boxers who had fallen on hard times were common in the contemporary boxing fraternity.

   joined the fancy: (slang) became a prizefighter.

30 *Ballarat*: some of the richest gold mines were discovered in the area near the city of Ballarat in Victoria, Australia.

32 *carboys*: large, rigid containers for liquids, especially corrosive ones, from Persian *qarabah*, from Arabic *qarraba*, 'big jug'.

   lath: a narrow strip of wood often used as groundwork for plaster.

33 *snibbed*: fastened.

34 *Senegambia*: a region of West Africa, between the Senegal and Gambia rivers. Originally conquered by the Portuguese, at the time it comprised French Senegambia (modern Senegal), British Senegal (modern Gambia and the islands of Los), and a variety of independent kingdoms.

36 *creosote*: a distillation from wood tar, used for treating wood. It was also used in Victorian medicine.

36 *a sum in the rule of three*: shorthand for a form of cross-multiplication, often learned by rote.

rigor mortis: stiffening of the body after death, due to the contraction of muscles.

37 *"risus sardonicus"*: 'sardonic smile', an apparently grinning expression caused by the spasm of the facial muscles, one of the symptoms of tetanus.

39 *Il n'y a pas des sots si incommodes que ceux qui ont de l'esprit!*: (French) 'There are no fools so troublesome as those who have some wit'. Properly *Il n'y a point de sots si incommodes que ceux qui ont de l'esprit*, number 451 of the *Maximes* of La Rochefoucauld (1613–80).

40 *mare's-nest*: an illusory but much-vaunted discovery.

Toby: for Victorian readers the name would have instantly brought to mind the trained live dog introduced into Punch and Judy shows in the first half of the nineteenth century.

"Wir sind gewohnt . . . verstehen": (German) 'We are used to seeing that people despise what they do not understand'. From part 1 of *Faust* by J. W. Goethe (1749–1832).

41 *half-pay surgeon*: a surgeon drawing his army pension.

42 *stair-rods*: brass rods on steps to keep the carpeting in place.

vagabone: vagabond.

wiper: viper. The cockney accent pronounced 'v' as 'w', as frequently seen in the works of Dickens, though by the 1880s this feature may already have disappeared.

hook it: (slang) 'get lost', 'go away'.

43 *slowworm*: a harmless, legless lizard.

guyed at: mocked, jeered.

lurcher: a breed of hunting dog.

44 *bull's-eye*: a lantern with a focusing lens.

Blondin: Charles Blondin was the alias used by Jean-François Gravelet (1824–97), who crossed the Niagara Falls on a tightrope in 1855.

45 *pocket*: here perhaps with the original meaning of a small bag.

Martini bullet: a bullet from a Martini-Henry rifle, a common weapon in the British infantry from 1871 until the 1890s.

48 *tendo Achillis*: or Achilles' tendon, the tendon of the heel, so called because it was the only vulnerable part of the body of Achilles, the greatest Greek warrior of the Trojan War.

49 *Jean Paul*: a popular mode of referring to Johann Paul Friedrich Richter (1763–1825), a German philosopher and humorist.

Carlyle: Thomas Carlyle (1795–1881), Scottish historian and atheist, author of two essays on Richter.

51 *punts*: a flat-bottomed boat with a square-cut bow developed on the River Thames.

skiffs: a small boat.

coke: carbonized coal, used as fuel for furnaces.

53 *wherry*: a light, shallow rowing boat.

sheets: the space at the bow or stern of the boat.

54 *wharfingers*: wharf-owners.

Millbank Penitentiary: a prison on the north bank of the Thames (now the site of Tate Britain), built from Jeremy Bentham's designs for the panopticon, a kind of prison where the sense of constant and total surveillance would be ultimately internalized by each prisoner. Millbank was more sanitary than other prisons, but it had an extremely harsh regime. Prisoners were required to remain in permanent, total silence, and wore special caps to prevent any eye contact with other inmates. They worked at making shoes and mailbags. The prison was torn down between 1890 and 1903.

56 *Three bob and a tanner*: three shillings ('bob') and sixpence (a 'tanner').

57 *Port Blair*: chief settlement of the Andaman Islands, first occupied in 1789 and refounded in 1856.

Rutland Island: the southernmost of the five largest Andaman Islands, collectively known as 'the great Andaman'.

58 *Digger Indians of America*: a vague term, no longer in use, used for a variety of related groups of North American Paiute Indians, from their practice of digging for roots.

Terra del Fuegians: properly 'Fuegians' or 'Tierra del Fuegians', the indigenous inhabitants of Tierra del Fuego at the southern tip of South America.

These massacres are invariably concluded by a cannibal feast: erroneous but popular view of the inhabitants of the islands, perhaps first originating in ninth-century Arab accounts of India and China.

60 *cooling medicine*: preparation believed to lower the temperature of the blood.

61 *retorts*: a glassware device used for distillation.

pea-jacket: an outer coat of coarse, heavy wool, usually navy in colour and double-breasted, originally worn by sailors. From Dutch or West Frisian *pij*, the name of the material used.

63 *outré*: (French) outlandish or bizarre. A word perhaps borrowed from Poe's Dupin.

bandanna: spotted handkerchief.

66 *police-boat*: the Thames Police, founded in 1839, patrolled the river with a fleet of rowing boats and a small number of steam launches.

67 *miracle plays*: medieval dramas about the lives and miracles of the saints.

Stradivarius violins: ones built by Antonio Stradivari of Cremona (1644–1737).

the Buddhism of Ceylon: Theravada Buddhism is the predominant religion practised by the Sinhala-speaking majority on the island of Ceylon (now Sri Lanka), while the Tamil-speaking population of the island is mostly Hindu. There was an ethnographic debate in the 1880s concerning the origins of the small Tamil-speaking Muslim minority in Ceylon.

bon vivant: (French) one who lives well, who enjoys good living.

bumper: a full measure, usually for a toast. Perhaps from French *Bon-père*, traditional monastic toast.

68 *To the Tower*: i.e. the Tower of London.

clipper: a fast sailing ship of the nineteenth century, here a fast ship.

One of our greatest statesmen . . . rest: this aphorism is usually attributed to William Gladstone (1809–98), four times British prime minister.

69 *the Downs*: sheltered anchorage in the English Channel, between the Thames Estuary and the Straits of Dover. It was a common holding spot for ships.

70 *lighters*: flat-bottomed barge-like boats used to transport cargo from ship to shore.

night-glasses: binoculars with large lenses for seeing better in the dark.

71 *a priori*: presumptive. (Latin) 'from the earlier'.

72 *Newfoundland dog*: large black hunting dog with a bushy coat.

coursed: pursued.

73 *ulster*: long loose overcoat. So called because first manufactured in Belfast.

75 *I can swing over the job*: i.e. be hanged for it.

lagged: slang for 'arrested'.

76 *digging drains at Dartmoor*: a common expression for serving time at the infamous prison at Princetown in Dartmoor Forest. It was built in the early nineteenth century for French prisoners of war.

the Brazils: then a popular usage for what we now call Brazil.

78 *Benares metal-work*: Benares was the former name of the Indian city Varanasi on the Ganges, the most holy city of the Hindu religion, renowned for its fine gold filigree.

hasp: fastening or catch.

79 *tenner*: ten pounds.

81 *ague*: fever, or, archaically, malaria.

the Queen's shilling: 'to take the Queen's shilling' means to join the British Army. A shilling used to be given on enlistment.

3rd Buffs: the 3rd East Kent Regiment of Foot, one of the oldest regiments in the British Army.

82 *indigo-planter*: indigo is a blue dye extracted from an Indian plant.

coolies: day-labourers, from the Tamil *kuli*.

great mutiny: the Indian Mutiny of 1857–8, a massive but ultimately unsuccessful revolt against British rule, which began with the rebellion of 35,000 'sepoys', the term used for Indian soldiers in the service of the British East India Company. It was contained by July 1858, but changed the way British India was governed. After the war, the British East India Company was dissolved and India was thenceforth governed by direct rule from Britain for the next ninety years, the period known as the Raj.

North-west Provinces: a political division of British India.

83 *whisky-pegs*: slang for 'highballs', whisky or brandy with soda.

cheroots: cigars with both ends clipped.

nullah: Hindi for ravine or valley.

Sepoys: see note to p. 82.

3rd Bengal Fusiliers: more probably the 3rd Bengal Infantry which took the British side during the mutiny.

Shahgunge: a suburb of Agra.

84 *Lucknow*: an Indian city besieged during the mutiny.

Cawnpore: Kanpur, a city on the Ganges, the site of a massacre of European women and children in 1857.

85 *Punjaubees*: Punjabis. Sikhs are predominantly from the Punjab.

Chilian Wallah: the British won the Punjab in a battle at Chilian Wallah in 1849.

bang: or *bhang*, a narcotic drink made from leaves of Indian hemp.

firelock: a muzzle-loading rifle.

86 *Feringhee*: Indian term for Europeans.

rajah: Indian prince ruling a territory.

87 *the Company's Raj*: i.e. the authority of the British East India Company.

moidores: from Portuguese *moeda d'ouro*, 'gold coin'. A Portuguese coin which came into use in Engand in the eighteenth century. The word persisted as a name for the sum of 27 shillings, the coin's approximate value.

89 *Rajpootana*: or Rajputana, a vast region of north-west India, consisting of some twenty states.

91 *of the first water*: see note to p. 19.

"the Great Mogul": an enormous gem said to have been discovered by an Indian slave in 1701 and lost.

Wilson: Brigadier General Archdale Wilson (1803–74), commander of the Bengal artillery when the mutiny broke out, captured in Delhi on 20 September 1857.

91 *Sir Colin*: Sir Colin Campbell relieved Lucknow on 17 November 1857.

 Colonel Greathed: later Sir Edward Harris Greathead (1812–81) who entered Agra on 10 October 1857.

 Pandies: nickname for the mutineers, after Mangal Pandey, one of its early instigators, executed for mutiny.

92 *sergeant of guides*: the Corps of Guides was an elite Indian regiment raised in 1846.

 jack-in-office: a self-important petty official.

 Blair Island: see note to p. 57.

93 *send in my papers*: 'resign my commission'.

94 *facer*: slang for a blow to the face; here in the figurative sense of a blow to fortunes.

96 *Mahomet Singh, Abdullah Khan, and Dost Akbar*: of all the names given, only 'Singh' is a plausibly Sikh name.

 chokey: police station, from Hindi *chauki*.

97 *Pathan*: Indian term for Afghan.

 Jiddah: more usually 'Jeddah', a city in modern-day Saudi Arabia, important as the principal gateway for pilgrims on their way to Mecca.

100 *Schade dass die Natur . . . Schelmen der Stoff*: (German) 'Nature, alas, made only one being out of you although there was material for a good man and a rogue.' From *Xenian* (1796), a collection by Goethe and Schiller.

A SCANDAL IN BOHEMIA

First published in the *Strand* in July 1891, and in the New York *Strand* in October 1891. Syndicated in a number of American newspapers in the autumn of 1891, occasionally under different titles (e.g. 'A Woman's Wit', 'The King's Sweetheart'). Collected in *The Adventures of Sherlock Holmes* (1892).

102 *Trincomalee*: on the coast of Ceylon (Sri Lanka), and acquired by the British as a naval base in 1795.

103 *civil practice*: Watson has returned to regular medical practice in London having been invalided from the Army Medical Corps.

 spirit case: a stand for decanters which was lockable. Also known as a 'tantalus' because the servants could see but not open the decanters. (In Greek mythology, Tantalus (in Greek *Tantalos*) was punished by having to stand in a pool of water under a low-lying fruit tree. Tormented by hunger and thirst, the fruit and the water were always just out of his reach.)

 gasogene: an early form of soda siphon.

 to go into harness: i.e. back to work.

104 *slavey*: a maidservant given the most menial tasks.

iodoform: an iodine compound used as an antiseptic.

nitrate of silver: a caustic compound, also used as an antiseptic.

last post: by 1900 there were between six and twelve daily postal deliveries to a household in London. One could expect a letter within London to reach its recipient two to four hours after posting.

105 *Continental Gazetteer*: a geographical dictionary of Europe.

Egria . . . Carlsbad: Egria, presumably from 'Agria', the Latin name for Eger, then a German-speaking town in Bohemia, now the Czech town of Cheb; Carlsbad, Karlsbad (Czech: Karlovy Vary), a town with a famous spa, now in the Czech Republic.

the death of Wallenstein: Albrecht Wenzel Eusebius von Wallenstein (1583–1634) was a Bohemian military leader during the Thirty Years War who was assassinated at Eger.

106 *brougham*: a light, four-wheeled, covered carriage, with seats for two or more people inside, pulled by one or two horses.

Boswell: James Boswell (1740–95), biographer and travelling companion of Samuel Johnson.

astrakhan: see note to p. 26.

beryl: a precious stone.

vizard mask: a mask concealing the eyes (related to 'visor').

108 *La Scala*: Teatro alla Scala, the great opera house of Milan.

110 *Langham*: see note to p. 11.

a cabinet: a cabinet photograph, the style adopted for photographic portraiture from 1870, usually a thin photo mounted on card, measuring 4¼ inches by 6½ inches.

111 *the two crimes which I have elsewhere recorded*: in *A Study in Scarlet* and *The Sign of the Four*.

groom: someone employed to feed and care for horses.

112 *Chubb lock*: a patent lock made by Chubb & Sons, advertised in 1887 to be pick-proof.

ostlers: stablemen, especially at an inn (from 'hostel').

half-and-half: a drink of half ale and half porter or some other bitter beer.

shag tobacco: finely cut loose tobacco (so fine that it looks like 'shag', or matted wool), usually of inferior quality.

Inner Temple: one of the Inns of Court, the professional associations for barristers and judges in London.

113 *hansom cab*: see note to p. 17.

landau: a four-wheeled, two-seated carriage. It had a divided top so that it could be open, closed, or half-closed.

113 *twenty-five minutes to twelve*: English law used to require marriages to be solemnized before noon, though it was actually extended to 3 p.m. in May 1886.

115 *Mrs Turner*: presumably should read 'Mrs Hudson', since the same slip was corrected in the MS of another story ('The Empty House').

smoke rocket: a smoke-emitting device used by plumbers to identify leaks.

cap: a percussion cap.

116 *Mr John Hare*: famous Victorian character actor (1844–1921).

scissors-grinder: knife-grinder.

118 *ulster*: see note to p. 73.

A CASE OF IDENTITY

Published in the *Strand* in September 1891 and the New York *Strand*, September–October 1891. Collected in *The Adventures of Sherlock Holmes* (1892).

124 *outré*: see note to p. 63.

stale and unprofitable: from *Hamlet*, I.ii, 'How weary, stale, flat, and unprofitable | Seem to me all the uses of this world!'

125 *brilliant*: a diamond or other gem cut to show off its brilliance.

Duchess-of-Devonshire fashion: after a portrait by Thomas Gainsborough of Georgina Spencer, 5th Duchess of Devonshire (1757–1806), a novelist and reformer as well as renowned beauty and leader of fashion.

135 *bisulphate of baryta*: barium hydrogen sulphate, first prepared in 1843 by J. J. Berzelius. It is a chemical curiosity of no practical use.

THE RED-HEADED LEAGUE

Published in the *Strand* in August 1891 and the New York *Strand* in September 1891, syndicated in a variety of American newspapers between 8 August and 6 December 1891. Collected in *The Adventures of Sherlock Holmes* (1892).

140 *the very simple problem presented by Miss Mary Sutherland*: i.e. 'A Case of Identity' (pp. 124–39 in this volume), although due to a confusion over the order of the stories it did not appear in the *Strand* until September, a month *after* the publication of 'The Red-Headed League'.

141 *an average commonplace British tradesman, obese, pompous, and slow*: as a tradesman, Jabez Wilson is a member of the petite bourgeoisie or lower middle classes, a category which saw a huge expansion in nineteenth-century Britain, often at pains to distinguish themselves from the proletariat.

shepherd's check trousers: woollen cloth trousers in black-and-white check.

Albert chain: a watch chain of heavy links, named after Prince Albert, husband of Queen Victoria.

Freemason: a member of the ancient society of the Masons, a secret fraternity who meet in private 'lodges' to conduct quasi-religious rituals and whose members pledge to support one another.

142 *the strict rules of your order*: Freemasons were sworn to keep secret the various signs, words, and rites revealed to them.

arc and compass breastpin: correctly 'square and compass', the emblems of the Masons' original craft of stonemasonry.

"Omne ignotum pro magnifico": (Latin) 'everything unknown is taken to be marvellous', an epigram by Tacitus from his *Life of Agricola*, composed around AD 98.

143 *at scratch*: from the beginning, with no advance preparation; 'scratch' means the starting point of a race.

the Morning Chronicle: a real newspaper but one which had in fact closed in 1862.

pawnbroker's business: the pawnbroker paid an important economic role in the lives of Victorians from a wide variety of social classes, struggling with the economic vicissitudes and social ambitions that characterized life in the era. People with an immediate need for cash could leave possessions as security with the pawnbroker in exchange for a loan (of a fraction of a value of the item). Items not 'redeemed' for the amount of the loan within twelve months were sold.

the City: the site of London's financial centre.

144 *crib*: a situation or a job.

145 *a coster's orange barrow*: a coster was a fruit-seller who usually sold fruit from a barrow.

146 *cobbler's wax*: used by shoemakers to make thread more supple.

147 *four pounds a week*: one of the definitions of the middle class at the time was a minimum income of £300 per annum. Hugh Boone in 'The Man with the Twisted Lip' earned £2 a week as a reporter.

billet: job.

press: an upright cupboard.

148 *foolscap paper*: a paper size used in Europe and the British Commonwealth.

planked down: a slang term meaning to pay down money. From 'boards' as a cant word for shillings.

149 THE RED-HEADED LEAGUE IS DISSOLVED. OCT. *9*, *1890*: as many scholars have pointed out, the dates, days, and periods of time given in this story are hopelessly contradictory and confused.

151 *Sarasate*: Pablo Martín Melitón de Sarasate y Navascués (1844–1908), a Spanish Romantic violinist and composer.

152 *We travelled by the Underground as far as Aldersgate*: the only instance of Holmes and Watson on the London Underground, which opened in 1863 and was fully part of the fabric of London life by this time. Aldersgate was the name for what is now the Barbican station.

Three gilt balls: the sign of a pawnbroker's shop.

153 *black-letter editions*: see note to p. 3.

154 *hansoms*: see note to p. 17.

155 *pea-jacket*: see note to p. 61.

hunting-crop: a short whip without a lash but with a leather loop. 'Heavy' here means that it is a 'loaded' hunting-crop, i.e. weighted with lead or iron.

the Sholto murder and the Agra treasure: the reference is to the events of *The Sign of the Four*.

rubber: his game of whist. 'Rubber' is a unit of scoring in whist.

smasher: thieves' slang for one who passes counterfeit money.

crack a crib: thieves' slang meaning to break into a building.

157 *napoleons*: French gold coins.

dark lantern: a lantern that could be darkened when lit without extinguishing the flame by means of a sliding screen.

partie carrée: (French) 'square match', i.e. a party of four.

159 *Jump*: i.e. 'run for it'.

swing for it: hang for it. Presumably John Clay is offering to take the punishment while his accomplice escapes.

skirts: the lower part of a frock coat.

derbies: slang for handcuffs.

161 *"L'homme c'est rien—l'œuvre c'est tout"*: correctly '*L'homme n'est rien—l'œuvre tout*' (French): 'The man is nothing, the work, everything.'

THE MAN WITH THE TWISTED LIP

Published in the *Strand* in December 1891 and the New York *Strand* in January 1892. It appeared in the *Philadelphia Inquirer* in December 1891 as 'The Strange Tale of a Beggar'. Collected in *The Adventures of Sherlock Holmes* (1892).

162 *opium*: the cultivation and trade of the ancient narcotic opium, obtained by the processing of poppy-seed pods, was actively promoted by the British East India Company. By the late nineteenth century when this story takes place, the British government was (unsuccessfully) trying to limit the use of the drug.

De Quincey's description of his dreams and sensations: i.e. *Confessions of an English Opium-Eater*, first published in 1821, by Thomas De Quincey (1785–1859).

laudanum: a tincture of opium in alcohol, a common pain reliever in Victorian Britain.

James: an error. Watson's name is, in fact, John.

163 *opium den*: an establishment where opium was sold and smoked. In the West, they were usually owned and operated by the Chinese. The dens supplied patrons with opium as well as the equipment—pipes, lamps, etc.—necessary for its consumption.

hansom: see note to p. 17.

slop shop: a shop selling cheap, ready-made clothes and bedding. The name comes from an old meaning of 'slop' as a loose covering garment for workmen.

gin shop: a liquor or wine store.

164 *a small brazier of burning charcoal*: opium smokers would lie back and hold the long opium pipes over lamps that would heat and vaporize the drug.

165 *skirt*: the lower part of a frock coat.

opium pipe: an opium pipe consisted of a long stem and metal bowl.

166 *Lascar*: or Lashkar, Laskar. An Anglo-Persian word which originally meant a non-combatant but came to refer to non-white, especially Indian, shipboard personnel who supplemented the crews of European ships in the East.

dog-cart: a light, open, two-wheeled carriage drawn by a single horse, with two transverse seats back to back. It was an extremely common means of transport in the late nineteenth century.

167 *wrack*: 'rack' clouds, i.e. a mass of cloud driven before the wind in the upper air.

Cannon Street: terminus of the South Eastern Railway.

168 *a box of bricks*: i.e. a box of wooden blocks for a child to build with.

169 *a small deal box*: deal is an inexpensive wood derived from pines.

170 *wax vestas*: short wax matches, named from Vesta, the Roman goddess of the hearth.

Threadneedle Street: best known for being the site of the Bank of England.

173 *mousseline-de-soie*: French, 'muslin of silk', a thin silk fabric similar to muslin.

an old campaigner: i.e. a war veteran.

174 *galvanized*: stimulated by means of a so-called galvanic current, a means of electricity (from Luigi Galvani, who first described the phenomenon in 1792).

175 *a flyleaf of a book*: the blank page between the endpapers of a book and the first page proper.

175 *octavo size*: a printer's term for the size of page obtained by folding a printer's sheet into eight leaves, making sixteen pages. 'Folio size' is two leaves and 'quarto' four.

177 *a sort of Eastern divan*: or 'diwan', a Turkish/Persian word; a bench or sofa covered with cushions.

shag tobacco: see note to p. 112.

brier pipe: more usually 'briar'. A pipe made of briar wood.

Gladstone bag: a small leather travelling bag or portmanteau, opening out flat, named after William Gladstone (1809–98), prime minister of England.

178 *the Surrey side*: see note to p. 18.

Bow Street: i.e. Bow Street Police Station.

frogged jacket: see note ('befrogged') to p. 26.

181 *greenroom*: a backstage room to accommodate actors before and after performances, or during the show when they are not onstage.

backed a bill: served as a guarantor or surety.

dollars: slang for a crown, or five-shilling piece.

THE BLUE CARBUNCLE

First published in the *Strand*, January 1892, and in the New York *Strand* in February 1892. It was also syndicated to several American newspapers in January 1892. Its title in the *Philadelphia Enquirer* was 'The Christmas Goose that Swallowed a Diamond'. Collected in *The Adventures of Sherlock Holmes* (1892).

184 *four million human beings . . . a few square miles*: the 1891 census put the population of London at 4,231,431.

185 *commissionaire*: a member of the Corps of Commissionaires, founded to give employment to war veterans. Members wore a uniform and worked as porters, messengers, gatekeepers, attendants, and similar jobs.

billycock: a low-crowned felt hat, also known as a 'bowler', named for William Coke for whom it was reputedly first designed in 1850.

187 *lime-cream*: a popular lime-scented hair cream.

It is a question of cubic capacity . . . something in it: a principle of the Victorian science of phrenology, based on measurements of the skull. Phrenologists believed that intelligence, temperament, self-esteem, and a host of other characteristics were dictated by the physical size of the brain, observable through the shape of different parts of the skull. It was part of a general Victorian scientific fascination with the idea of heredity.

188 *crop*: pouch in the gullet of a bird that may be used for storage or digestion.

189 *carbuncle*: from Latin *carbunculus*, a little coal. The jeweller's name for a garnet when cut *en cabochon*, i.e. shaped and polished but not faceted,

usually with a domed top and flat bottom. Garnets come in shades of red,
white, yellow, green, brown, purple, and black, but never blue.

referred to the Assizes: the assizes, which existed until 1974, were travelling
courts which tried serious offences in the provinces at periodic intervals.
A criminal case in London would not have been heard by an assize court,
but in the Courts of Justice or Central Criminal Court.

upper-attendant: the head attendant or duty manager in the front or upper
part of the hotel (rather than 'below stairs').

190 *morocco casket*: a casket covered in morocco leather, a tanned leather made
from goatskin.

Inspector Bradstreet, B Division: the Metropolitan Police District was
divided into twenty-two (nowadays sixty-three) divisions. In 1887, when
the story is set, 'B' division covered Knightsbridge, Chelsea, and Fulham,
so the events occurred outside the Inspector's designated area.

191 *the Globe . . . Echo*: in 1887, there were six principal evening papers. The
Star, although listed here, was not founded until the following year.

the Amoy River in Southern China: Amoy (Xiamen) is a city and port on the
island of the same name, facing Taiwan. The River Jiu-lung flows through the
city, and there is no 'Amoy River'. No garnet has ever been found in China.

a vitriol-throwing: throwing sulphuric acid at the face as an act of revenge.

this forty-grain weight: gems were more usually weighed in carats, the precise weight of which varied from country to country. An English carat is
3.163 troy grains, so the Blue Carbuncle weighs 12.62 carats.

crystallized charcoal: in fact only diamonds are pure crystallized carbon.
A garnet contains no carbon.

192 *Scotch bonnet*: also known as a tam-o'-shanter, a woollen brimless cap with
a pompom in the centre.

193 *disjecta membra*: (Latin) 'dismembered limbs'. A phrase first found in
Horace's *Satires* (i.4): *Invenias disjecti membra poetae*—'You will still find
the limbs of the dismembered poet' (i.e. a great poet's talent can be dis-
cerned even from a short quotation or poor translation).

near the Museum: i.e. the British Museum on Great Russell Street, a few
blocks from where the goose was found.

194 *Covent Garden*: Covent Garden Market, though in reality it was only
a fruit, vegetable, and flower market.

seven years' penal servitude: penal servitude, introduced in 1853 originally
as a substitution for transportation, was a term of imprisonment that
usually included excruciating forced labour. Some of the labour had economic use—such as net-making and oakum picking—while some of it was
purely punitive.

a horsey-looking man: i.e. who looked like someone involved in horse racing
or the horse trade (rather than resembling a horse).

195 *so warm over such a trifle*: 'warm' in the now obsolete sense of 'angry', 'hostile', 'excited'.

196 *the "Pink 'Un"*: the popular nickname for the *Sporting Times* (1865–1931), a weekly printed on pink paper.

197 *the King of Proosia*: i.e. the King of Prussia, used here to mean a remote and powerful personage.

   a four-wheeler: see note to p. 15.

198 *the basket chair*: a basket-work or wicker chair.

200 *Pentonville*: Pentonville prison on the Caledonian Road, opened in 1842. It had a notoriously harsh disciplinary regime which served as a model for other prisons in England and Europe.

THE SPECKLED BAND

First published in the *Strand* in February 1892, in the New York *Strand* in March 1892, and syndicated in various American newspapers between February and November 1892. Collected in *The Adventures of Sherlock Holmes* (1892).

204 *dog-cart*: see note to p. 166.

206 *the Regency*: the last nine years of the reign of George III, 1811–20, when the monarch's insanity rendered him unfit to rule and his son, the future George IV, acted as regent.

   Calcutta: then the capital of British India, and one of the great Victorian colonial cities.

   Bengal Artillery: the Bengal Artillery of the East India Company, merged with the Royal Artillery after the Indian Mutiny of 1857.

207 *gipsies*: or 'gypsies', also called by their own term, 'Romani'. A distinct ethnic group in Europe who migrated from northern India, beginning perhaps in the fourteenth century. In Victorian England they represented unconventionality, otherness, freedom, and criminality.

   correspondent: here an agent in one country who transacts business on behalf of someone in another.

   half-pay Major of Marines: an officer on reduced pay while not on active service.

209 *county coroner*: county coroners, chosen for life, were charged with inquiring into unnatural deaths upon inspection of the corpse.

213 *high gaiters*: leather or cloth coverings for the upper legs (as distinct from regular gaiters, or 'spats', which cover the ankles), worn by country landowners and farmers.

   hunting-crop: see note to p. 155.

   bile-shot eyes: used in a figurative sense, with 'bile' indicating anger.

   jack-in-office: see note to p. 92.

214 *Doctors' Commons*: a society for doctors of civil law, with a library where wills were stored. Here an anachronism as wills had been transferred to Somerset House in 1867.

the fall in agricultural prices: there was an agricultural depression between 1877 and 1879. Moreover, the introduction of compulsory education for children in 1880 increased labour costs.

Each daughter can claim an income of £250: for an idea of the meaning of this sum, see note to p. 147.

Eley's No. 2: Eley actually manufactured ammunition, not weaponry. ACD presumably intended a Webley No. 2.

217 *white-counterpaned*: a counterpane is a bedspread.

Wilton carpet: a woven wool carpet with loops cut open into a thick pile. Named after the Wiltshire town where it is made.

218 *camp bed*: a folding or collapsible bed.

219 *hasp*: see note to p. 78.

221 *Palmer and Pritchard*: Dr William Palmer (1824–56) and Dr Edward William Pritchard (1825–65), two notorious nineteenth-century English poisoners, both of whom were members of the Royal College of Surgeons.

223 *dark lantern*: see note to p. 157.

224 *swamp adder*: a fictional snake. It most resembles an Indian cobra.

Violence does . . . digs for another: an allusion to Ecclesiastes 1:2: 'He that diggeth a pit shall fall into it; and whoso breaketh an hedge, a serpent shall bite him.'

THE MUSGRAVE RITUAL

Published in the *Strand* in May 1893 and in *Harper's Weekly* (New York) on 13 May 1893. Collected in *The Memoirs of Sherlock Holmes* (1893).

227 *rough-and-tumble work in Afghanistan*: we know from *A Study in Scarlet* that Watson was an assistant surgeon with the 5th Northumberland Fusiliers and the Berkshires during the Second Afghan War of 1878–80. He was wounded and returned to London where he met Holmes.

hair-trigger: a firearm with a sensitive second trigger.

Boxer cartridges: a generic name for any centre-fire cartridge, a form of ammunition perfected by Colonel Boxer in 1867.

a patriotic V. R.: the initials stand for 'Victoria Regina', Latin for 'Queen Victoria'. Perhaps in honour of her Golden Jubilee in 1887.

228 *commonplace book*: a scrapbook used to compile useful facts, recipes, poems, etc.

230 *his branch was a cadet one*: i.e. a younger branch of the family.

230 *mullioned windows*: windows divided by vertical shafts.

member for the district: i.e. a Member of Parliament for western Sussex, likely one of the sparsely populated 'rotten boroughs' disproportionately represented in the House of Commons until the Reform Act of 1884 equalized electoral arrangements between towns and rural areas.

231 *I preserve*: raise and protect game and fish for private hunting.

pheasant months: October to January, when the shooting of pheasant is legal in Britain.

Don Juan: aristocratic libertine of European literature, the subject of such works as Tirso de Molina's *El burlador de Sevilla* (?1630), Molière's *Don Juan* (1665), Mozart's *Don Giovanni* (1787), or Byron's *Don Juan* (1819–24).

233 *blazonings and charges*: the details of the family coat of arms.

235 *mere*: a lake or pond.

236 *Whose was it? . . .* : T. S. Eliot used some of the wording of the Musgrave Ritual in his play *Murder in the Cathedral* (1935) about Thomas à Becket.

238 *dog-cart*: see note to p. 166.

240 *billets*: small pieces of wood cut from logs.

242 *Charles I*: Charles I (1600–49) was King of England, Scotland, and Ireland from 1625 to 1649, when he was beheaded, following disputes between King and Parliament which had led to civil war.

243 *made head*: i.e. resisted or advanced in spite of.

Cavalier: a supporter of the Royalist party during the English Civil War, as opposed to the Parliamentarian Roundheads.

Charles II: Charles II (1630–85) held the throne for a short time after the execution of his father, Charles I. He fled England in 1651 after defeat by Oliver Cromwell, and lived in exile on the Continent. He was restored to the throne in 1660.

THE GREEK INTERPRETER

First published in the *Strand* in September 1893 and in *Harper's Weekly* (New York) on 16 September 1893. Collected in *The Memoirs of Sherlock Holmes* (1893).

245 *the obliquity of the ecliptic*: the inclination of the Earth's equator to the apparent path of the sun. Due to planetary perturbations, this angle has been diminishing for the past four thousand years.

atavism: the recurrence of an ancestral characteristic in descendants, especially after a long interval. It was also a term used by the Italian criminologist and physician Cesare Lombroso (1835–1909) whose ideas about the hereditary nature of criminality were influential in Victorian Britain.

Vernet: Émile Jean Horace Vernet (1789–1863), a French painter of military works.

246 *Diogenes*: Diogenes is a Greek name shared by a number of historical figures. The best known and most likely to be referred to in the name of the fictional club is Diogenes of Sinope (b. 412 or 404 BC, d. 323 BC), a Greek philosopher and one of the founders of Cynic philosophy.

Regent Circus: either Piccadilly Circus or Oxford Circus. When John Nash (1752–1835) was planning these two 'piazzas' he called them 'the first Regent Circus' and 'the second Regent Circus', but they quickly became known as Piccadilly Circus and Oxford Circus. The use of this archaic name indicates how unfamiliar London still was to ACD in 1893.

247 *the most unsociable and unclubbable men in town*: a great number of men-only clubs sprouted in London over the course of the second half of the nineteenth century, for men, bachelors, and married men alike, to socialize, network, and relax in an atmosphere of social exclusivity.

the Strangers' Room: when a member brought a guest to his club, they were usually restricted to a 'Strangers' dining room and denied access to the rest of the building.

the Carlton: the Carlton Club, the premier Conservative political club in England, founded in 1832.

248 *billiard-marker*: an employee of a billiard parlour, assisting players and keeping the score. Billiards was a fashionable upper-class pastime at the time.

non-commissioned officer: often abbreviated to NCO, an officer promoted from within the ranks.

"ammunition boots": official army boots issued to non-commissioned personnel.

sapper: a soldier who performs military engineering duties, such as the building of fortifications and fieldworks.

254 *St Vitus's Dance*: a neurological disorder now known as chorea or Sydenham's chorea, characterized by involuntary twitching and movements.

255 *the Greek Legation*: a legation was a diplomatic representative office lower than an embassy. The distinction between embassy and legation was removed after the Second World War.

257 *hansom*: see note to p. 17.

J pen: a broad-pointed pen. The letter 'J' may be a nib size.

four-wheeler: see note to p. 15.

260 *life preserver*: a kind of short club with a weighted head used as a weapon.

THE DANCING MEN

First published in the UK in the *Strand* in December 1903, and in the US in *Collier's Weekly* on 5 December 1903. Collected in *The Return of Sherlock Holmes* (1905).

262 *South African securities*: i.e. shares in South African property. Shares in the extensive gold fields discovered in the Transvaal in 1886.

263 *Cubitt*: Cubitt is indeed an old Norfolk name.

Ridling Thorpe Manor: the first mention was misprinted in the *Strand* as 'Riding Thorpe Manor', but all subsequent references are to 'Ridling Thorpe'. All American editions have 'Riding Thorpe Manor' throughout.

264 *the Jubilee*: Queen Victoria's Diamond Jubilee, marking her sixtieth year on the throne, was celebrated on 21 June 1897. It was also a tribute to the British Empire, then in its heyday, covering more than a fifth of the globe.

If you take me, Hilton: erroneously printed as 'If you take me, John' in *Collier's Weekly*.

271 *cablegram*: usually shortened to 'cable', i.e. a telegram.

272 *the glory and prosperity of old East Anglia*: East Anglia, consisting largely of the modern counties of Norfolk and Suffolk, was an Anglo-Saxon kingdom from the 6th to the 9th century.

the German Ocean: an alternative name for the North Sea until the First World War.

dog-cart: see note to p. 166.

279 *the numerical order in which letters occur*: ACD borrows this method of deciphering cryptograms from Edgar Allan Poe's story 'The Gold Bug'.

282 *no one on earth outside the Joint*: a saloon or other meeting place for an underground or criminal gang (and thus referring by extension the gang itself, as in the 'Lodge' in Freemasonry).

285 *the winter assizes*: see note to p. 189.

THE SIX NAPOLEONS

Published in the *Strand* in May 1904 and in *Collier's Weekly* on 30 April 1904. Collected in *The Return of Sherlock Holmes* (1905).

286 *police headquarters*: i.e. New Scotland Yard, the headquarters of the Metropolitan Police.

Napoleon the First: Napoleon Bonaparte (1769–1821), the emperor, as distinct from his son, Napoleon II (1811–32), the King of Rome, or his nephew, Napoleon III (1808–73).

287 *Lower Brixton Road*: there is no 'Lower Brixton Road', but Brixton road runs south from Kennington to Brixton Rise. The area is sometimes described as 'Lower Brixton'.

the French sculptor Devine: perhaps from Paul de Vigne (1843–1901), Belgian sculptor who lived in Paris until 1882.

288 *French psychologists have called the "idée fixe"*: (French) 'fixed idea'.

Though not a clinical term, it was first used by psychologists in the 1830s and had gained popular currency by the end of the century.

289 *Pitt Street, Kensington*: a short road running parallel to Kensington High Street.

the Central Press Syndicate: an invented name, a fictional version of the Central News Agency which gathered and sold news to subscribing newspapers. Jack the Ripper sent two notes to the Central News Agency in 1888.

290 *poor devil*: thus in the MS, but softened to 'poor fellow' in the *Strand* and subsequent texts.

291 *Campden House Road*: originally 'Camden Road' in the MS, amended to 'Camden House Road' and then changed to 'Campden House Road' in the *Strand* and book editions. Camden Road is in north London, running between Camden and Seven Sisters, whereas Campden House Road (now Hornton Street) was in Kensington, west London.

Doncaster: Doncaster is renowned since the early eighteenth century for horse racing, notably the St Leger Stakes.

292 *his red lamp*: 'You ask about the red lamp,' says the postscript to the preface of ACD's *Round the Red Lamp* (1894): 'It is the usual sign of the general practitioner in England.'

to docket it: i.e. to file it. A term used by the police of the period who kept a separate 'docket' for each case.

294 *A Nihilist plot*: the Nihilist movement was a nineteenth-century Russian political group which rejected all forms of authority. Following the assassination of Tsar Alexander II in 1881, they were known in Europe for espousing the use of violence to bring about political change.

Red republicans: radical leaders of the 1848 Revolution in France were known as Red Republicans, after the red caps they wore. There was a London socialist newspaper in 1850 called the *Red Republican*.

Beppo: diminutive form of 'Giuseppe'.

fashionable London . . . maritime London: this sequence is of areas which are all north of the river and would not be on the route from Kennington to Stepney. It has been pointed out that the directions would make more sense if the journey was from Kensington rather than Kennington.

296 *cruet stand*: a small stand of metal, ceramic, or glass which holds containers for condiments, e.g. salt and pepper shakers, bottles of vinegar or oil.

for I've seldom seen an uglier: originally 'for he looks like the missing link'.

297 *Saffron Hill and the Italian quarter*: in the late nineteenth century there were two centres of Italian immigrants in London. The older of the two was in Holborn and known as 'Saffron Hill'; according to the Italian consul in 1895 its typical inhabitants included 'plaster-bust sellers'. The newer area was in Soho, inhabited by a somewhat higher social class of Italian immigrants.

297 *some Catholic emblem round his neck*: likely a small medallion showing the Blessed Virgin or a saint.

Pietro Venucci, from Naples: the MS replaces 'Florence' with 'Naples'.

the Mafia: a Sicilian secret criminal society. Since the characters are from Naples, they would more properly have belonged to the Camorra.

298 *express messenger*: a special messenger who would convey a letter the entire distance, or from the local sorting office, at a prepaid or partly prepaid rate of threepence per mile. The Express Delivery Service was established by the Post Office in 1891. The Post Office introduced free postal delivery to all households in England in 1897.

lumber-rooms: storage rooms, usually at the top of a house.

the loaded hunting-crop: see note to p. 155.

four-wheeler: see note to p. 15.

a spot at the other side of Hammersmith Bridge: since Chiswick is on the same side of the river as Hammersmith, they must have crossed Hammersmith Bridge, driven as far as Barnes, and then returned across the river to Chiswick.

302 *the famous black pearl of the Borgias*: originally from Spain, the Borgias became a powerful political and religious family in fifteenth-century Italy, with a reputation for scheming and ruthlessness.

304 *damned proud of you*: in the MS, 'damned' was changed at a late stage to 'very'.

HIS LAST BOW

First published in the *Strand*, September 1917, and in *Collier's Weekly* on 22 September 1917. Collected in *His Last Bow* (October 1917). The text here is, with minor exceptions, that of the *Strand*, which differs more from the book version than any other Holmes story. While it would be natural to assume the book text, being the later edition, as the standard text, it contains too many obviously inferior discrepancies, such as repetitions and inaccuracies. Moreover it inexplicably changes much of Altamont's American slang, which is such a feature of the story, back to British English.

305 AN EPILOGUE OF SHERLOCK HOLMES: this is the only point where the book text has been given preference over the *Strand* text, where the subtitle was 'The War Service of Sherlock Holmes'.

the most terrible August in the history of the world: i.e. August 1914. Austria-Hungary, with Germany's backing, had declared war on Serbia in late July, starting a chain reaction which had brought Russia, Germany, France, and the British Empire into the war within the month.

the Kaiser: William II, Friedrich Wilhelm Victor Albert von Hohenzollern (1859–1941), king of Prussia and emperor of Germany (and a grandson of Queen Victoria).

the legation: i.e. embassy.

Benz car: 1886 Benz Patent Motorwagen designed by Karl Benz (later of Mercedes-Benz), regarded as the first automobile.

All-Highest: a term used of the Kaiser, employed mockingly here by ACD.

306 *four-in-hand*: a vehicle drawn by four horses.

Olympia: the Olympia amphitheatre in Kensington, opened in 1886, capable of seating 10,000.

307 *Flushing*: the English name for the Dutch seaport of Vlissingen, of great strategic importance.

Irish civil war: Roger Casement procured but failed to deliver arms for the so-called Easter Rising of 1916. The rebellion was quashed but the execution of its leaders by the British led to the cause gaining widespread popular support in Ireland. In 1914, the Germans had sold arms to militias on both sides of the Irish conflict.

window-breaking furies: militant suffragettes. Between 1910 and 1914 the Women's Social and Political Union engaged in window-breaking and, occasionally, arson.

308 *Mr John Bull*: 'John Bull' is a term for English public opinion.

'Egypt': the Germans considered fomenting revolt in the British colonies of Egypt, India, and South Africa in the event of hostilities.

'Portsmouth Forts': Portsmouth was England's chief naval station.

'The Channel': i.e. the English Channel.

'Rosyth': a town and important naval base in Scotland. It was a ship-repair station during the First World War.

Carlton House Terrace: the German Embassy was at 9 Carlton House Terrace in London.

309 *sparking-plugs*: motor accessories discharging an electric spark to ignite the engine.

Pan-Germanic Junker: *Junker* means 'country squire' in German. The landed gentry in Prussia and eastern Germany were politically conservative. Bismarck was a *Junker*.

Irish-American: Irish immigrants and their descendants in the US contributed a great deal of funds to the Fenian cause. Altamont is a name more typical of the Anglo-Irish Protestant Ascendancy, and somewhat improbable as the name of an Irish-American Catholic Fenian.

the Duke of York's steps: the steps to the bronze statue of Frederick Augustus, Duke of York (1763–1827), the second son of George III, on Waterloo Place. The steps adjoined the German embassy on Carlton House Terrace.

Tokay: see note to p. 20. Tokay was a fashionable wine in the London of the period, but here it is also associated with the Austro-Hungarian Empire.

310 *Harwich*: a seaport in Essex, then a submarine and destroyer base.

Zeppelin: Count Ferdinand von Zeppelin (1838–1917), a German military officer who built the first dirigible airship in 1900, named after him. The Zeppelin was a sort of controllable balloon, capable of long-range flights. The Germans used it for bombing raids on London during the First World War, though its capabilities were overestimated by both sides.

Martha: self-evidently not Mrs Hudson. Martha is a biblical name synonymous with servant.

au revoir, Von Bork: a dig by ACD at the Francophilic affectations of Frederick the Great and the German imperial upper classes.

Ford: Henry Ford (1863–1947) had opened up an English factory in 1912 for his mass-produced and inexpensive Model T.

311 *glad hand*: a deliberately ostentatious Americanism, here meaning 'to thank'.

cable: since they are both in England, he means a telegram, but the idea is presumably that the American is used to thinking of communicating with Europeans via cable.

semaphore, lamp-code, Marconi: flag-signalling, lightflash-signalling, wireless telegraphy. Guglielmo Marconi (1874–1937) was a pioneer of radio technology.

can-opener: in 1917, still clearly an Americanism (as opposed to 'tin-opener').

312 *you're an American citizen*: the imprisonment of US citizens (often Irish-born) by the British government was a source of tension at times between the two countries.

Portland: the Isle of Portland, a peninsula in Dorset, was the location of a naval base and a large prison. The Irish patriot and Fenian leader Michael Davitt was imprisoned at Portland, which he made famous as the location of his *Leaves from a Prison Diary* (1884).

bughouse: candidate for a lunatic asylum, the implication being that he was seeing 'bugs', i.e. in the advanced stages of delirium tremens or drug addiction.

313 *Fratton*: a district of Portsmouth.

a stool pigeon: a person set up as a decoy.

a cross: treachery.

Von Tirpitz: Admiral Alfred von Tirpitz (1849–1930) was responsible for building up the German navy in the years leading up to the First World War, and, as naval commander from August 1914 to March 1916, he advocated the unrestricted use of submarine warfare.

314 *nitsky*: 'nothing', a playful calque from a Yiddish parody of Russian *nyet* ('no') and the common Russian suffix *-sky*.

Imperial Tokay: Imperial Tokay came from one particular vineyard and is no longer made. See note to p. 20.

noisy: the implication is that the chloroform made him talk, shout, snore, or similar.

Schoenbrunn Palace: Schönbrunn Palace was the summer residence of the Austrian royal family in Vienna.

315 *Claridge's Hotel*: a high-end establishment acquired by Claridge in 1808, located in Brook Street.

316 *the Solent*: the arm of water between the Isle of Wight and the mainland.

How have the years used you?: if we follow the chronology of the stories, the previous recorded meeting between Holmes and Watson took place in 1903 ('The Creeping Man'), eleven years prior to this.

stunt: an obvious Americanism in 1917.

magnum opus: Latin, 'great work'.

Alone I did it: Holmes is quoting the warrior Gaius Martius Coriolanus in Act V scene vi of Shakespeare's *Coriolanus*. In the play, Coriolanus is killed immediately after uttering this line.

Foreign Minister: Grey had been Foreign Secretary since December 1905.

Premier: Herbert Henry Asquith (1852–1928) was prime minister from 1908 to 1916.

Chicago: Chicago was one of the powerhouses of Irish-American nationalist politics and plotting. It had been the centre of the 'Triangle', an ultra faction of the Fenian secret society, Clann na Gael (more properly 'Clann na nGael', meaning 'Family of the Gaels') in the 1880s.

317 *Buffalo*: a city on the shore of Lake Erie in New York State, traditionally a clearing house and rendezvous point between east and west in Irish-American nationalist politics. This is a direct allusion to the activities of two Buffalo Clann na Gael leaders, John A. Murphy (who was sent to Ireland to distribute relief funds after the Easter Rising) and John T. Ryan (who attempted to forge an Irish-German alliance in the United States).

the constabulary: i.e. the Royal Irish Constabulary, the major police force in British-ruled Ireland from the early nineteenth century until independence in 1922. It was a mostly Catholic force but had a tense relationship with the rural poor, and their barracks were frequent objects of attack by the Fenians.

Skibbereen: a small town in County Cork, Ireland. Skibbereen had suffered appallingly during the Great Famine (1845–50) and became a hotbed of early Fenianism.

'The old sweet song': presumably a reference to the popular Victorian parlour song, 'Love's Old Sweet Song' (published 1884), by Irish composer James Lynam Molloy and lyricist G. Clifton Bingham. Its first line is 'Once in the dear dead days beyond recall'.

318 *Irene Adler . . . the Imperial Envoy*: a reference to 'A Scandal in Bohemia', though in the story it is Adler who separates herself from the King of Bohemia, fleeing with her new husband once she realizes that Holmes is on the case.

Your admiral: i.e. Admiral von Tirpitz. See note to p. 313.

The
Oxford
World's
Classics
Website

www.worldsclassics.co.uk

- Browse the full range of Oxford World's Classics online
- Sign up for our monthly e-alert to receive information on new titles
- Read extracts from the Introductions
- Listen to our editors and translators talk about the world's greatest literature with our Oxford World's Classics audio guides
- Join the conversation, follow us on Twitter at OWC_Oxford
- Teachers and lecturers can order inspection copies quickly and simply via our website

www.worldsclassics.co.uk

American Literature

British and Irish Literature

Children's Literature

Classics and Ancient Literature

Colonial Literature

Eastern Literature

European Literature

Gothic Literature

History

Medieval Literature

Oxford English Drama

Philosophy

Poetry

Politics

Religion

The Oxford Shakespeare

A complete list of Oxford World's Classics, including Authors in Context, Oxford English Drama, and the Oxford Shakespeare, is available in the UK from the Marketing Services Department, Oxford University Press, Great Clarendon Street, Oxford OX2 6DP, or visit the website at www.oup.com/uk/worldsclassics.

In the USA, visit www.oup.com/us/owc for a complete title list.

Oxford World's Classics are available from all good bookshops. In case of difficulty, customers in the UK should contact Oxford University Press Bookshop, 116 High Street, Oxford OX1 4BR.

Late Victorian Gothic Tales

JANE AUSTEN
Emma
Mansfield Park
Persuasion
Pride and Prejudice
Selected Letters
Sense and Sensibility

MRS BEETON
Book of Household Management

MARY ELIZABETH BRADDON
Lady Audley's Secret

ANNE BRONTË
The Tenant of Wildfell Hall

CHARLOTTE BRONTË
Jane Eyre
Shirley
Villette

EMILY BRONTË
Wuthering Heights

ROBERT BROWNING
The Major Works

JOHN CLARE
The Major Works

SAMUEL TAYLOR COLERIDGE
The Major Works

WILKIE COLLINS
The Moonstone
No Name
The Woman in White

CHARLES DARWIN
The Origin of Species

THOMAS DE QUINCEY
The Confessions of an English
    Opium-Eater
On Murder

CHARLES DICKENS
The Adventures of Oliver Twist
Barnaby Rudge
Bleak House
David Copperfield
Great Expectations
Nicholas Nickleby
The Old Curiosity Shop
Our Mutual Friend
The Pickwick Papers

TROLLOPE IN OXFORD WORLD'S CLASSICS

A SELECTION OF   **OXFORD WORLD'S CLASSICS**

HANS CHRISTIAN ANDERSEN	**Fairy Tales**
J. M. BARRIE	**Peter Pan in Kensington Gardens** and **Peter and Wendy**
L. FRANK BAUM	**The Wonderful Wizard of Oz**
FRANCES HODGSON BURNETT	**The Secret Garden**
LEWIS CARROLL	**Alice's Adventures in Wonderland** and **Through the Looking-Glass**
CARLO COLLODI	**The Adventures of Pinocchio**
KENNETH GRAHAME	**The Wind in the Willows**
ANTHONY HOPE	**The Prisoner of Zenda**
THOMAS HUGHES	**Tom Brown's Schooldays**

ANTON CHEKHOV

About Love and Other Stories
Early Stories
Five Plays
The Princess and Other Stories
The Russian Master and Other Stories
The Steppe and Other Stories
Twelve Plays
Ward Number Six and Other Stories

FYODOR DOSTOEVSKY

Crime and Punishment
Devils
A Gentle Creature and Other Stories
The Idiot
The Karamazov Brothers
Memoirs from the House of the Dead
Notes from the Underground and
    The Gambler

NIKOLAI GOGOL

Dead Souls
Plays and Petersburg Tales

ALEXANDER PUSHKIN

Eugene Onegin
The Queen of Spades and Other Stories

LEO TOLSTOY

Anna Karenina
The Kreutzer Sonata and Other Stories
The Raid and Other Stories
Resurrection
War and Peace

IVAN TURGENEV

Fathers and Sons
First Love and Other Stories
A Month in the Country

	Six French Poets of the Nineteenth Century
HONORÉ DE BALZAC	Cousin Bette Eugénie Grandet Père Goriot
CHARLES BAUDELAIRE	The Flowers of Evil The Prose Poems and Fanfarlo
BENJAMIN CONSTANT	Adolphe
DENIS DIDEROT	Jacques the Fatalist The Nun
ALEXANDRE DUMAS (PÈRE)	The Black Tulip The Count of Monte Cristo Louise de la Vallière The Man in the Iron Mask La Reine Margot The Three Musketeers Twenty Years After The Vicomte de Bragelonne
ALEXANDRE DUMAS (FILS)	La Dame aux Camélias
GUSTAVE FLAUBERT	Madame Bovary A Sentimental Education Three Tales
VICTOR HUGO	The Essential Victor Hugo Notre-Dame de Paris
J.-K. HUYSMANS	Against Nature
PIERRE CHODERLOS DE LACLOS	Les Liaisons dangereuses
MME DE LAFAYETTE	The Princesse de Clèves
GUILLAUME DU LORRIS and JEAN DE MEUN	The Romance of the Rose

ÉMILE ZOLA	**L'Assommoir**
	The Attack on the Mill
	La Bête humaine
	La Débâcle
	Germinal
	The Kill
	The Ladies' Paradise
	The Masterpiece
	Nana
	Pot Luck
	Thérèse Raquin

THOMAS AQUINAS	Selected Philosophical Writings
FRANCIS BACON	The Essays
WALTER BAGEHOT	The English Constitution
GEORGE BERKELEY	Principles of Human Knowledge and Three Dialogues
EDMUND BURKE	A Philosophical Enquiry into the Origin of Our Ideas of the Sublime and Beautiful Reflections on the Revolution in France
CONFUCIUS	The Analects
DESCARTES	A Discourse on the Method
ÉMILE DURKHEIM	The Elementary Forms of Religious Life
FRIEDRICH ENGELS	The Condition of the Working Class in England
JAMES GEORGE FRAZER	The Golden Bough
SIGMUND FREUD	The Interpretation of Dreams
THOMAS HOBBES	Human Nature and De Corpore Politico Leviathan
DAVID HUME	Selected Essays
NICCOLÒ MACHIAVELLI	The Prince
THOMAS MALTHUS	An Essay on the Principle of Population
KARL MARX	Capital The Communist Manifesto
J. S. MILL	On Liberty and Other Essays Principles of Political Economy and Chapters on Socialism
FRIEDRICH NIETZSCHE	Beyond Good and Evil The Birth of Tragedy On the Genealogy of Morals Thus Spoke Zarathustra Twilight of the Idols

JOHN BUCHAN	**Huntingtower** **The Thirty-Nine Steps**
JOSEPH CONRAD	**Heart of Darkness and Other Tales** **Lord Jim** **Nostromo** **The Secret Agent** **Under Western Eyes**
FORD MADOX FORD	**The Good Soldier**
JOHN GALSWORTHY	**The Forsyte Saga**
JAMES JOYCE	**A Portrait of the Artist as a Young Man** **Dubliners** **Occasional, Critical, and Political Writing** **Ulysses**
RUDYARD KIPLING	**The Jungle Books** **Just So Stories** **Kim** **War Stories and Poems**
D. H. LAWRENCE	**The Rainbow** **Sons and Lovers** **The Widowing of Mrs Holroyd and Other Plays** **Women in Love**
ROBERT TRESSELL	**The Ragged Trousered Philanthropists**
KATHERINE MANSFIELD	**Selected Stories**
VIRGINIA WOOLF	**Flush** **The Mark on the Wall and Other Short Fiction** **Mrs Dalloway** **Orlando: A Biography** **A Room of One's Own and Three Guineas** **To the Lighthouse**
W. B. YEATS	**The Major Works**